W9-AZJ-717

Praise for *Wherever Grace Is Needed*

"Bass draws her characters, particularly the adolescents, very well."
—*Publishers Weekly*

"Bass introduces wonderfully needy characters who discover their untapped strength. The teens and their relationships are particularly well developed. Kristin Hannah fans and readers attracted to Lisa Genova's novels will appreciate this novel. Definitely buy for readers who demand character growth and relationships in their fiction."
—*Library Journal*

"Readers of all ages can enjoy this thoughtful story of two families overcoming tremendous challenges. Beautifully exploring the complexity of sorrow, loss, healing, and forgiveness, *Wherever Grace Is Needed* provides insight into the significance of home and belonging."
—*Voya*

"Bass's characters are created as likable, genuine, imperfect, and complicated people with whom the reader will find it easy to share empathetic feelings. A terrific vacation read."
—*Courier of Montgomery County*

Praise for *Miss You Most of All*

"The world Elizabeth Bass has created is full of life, humor, heartache, and hope. You'll be happy to enter it and sad to leave."
—Lorna Landvik

"Bass's sparkling debut will inspire laughs and tears. . . . With bountiful grace and a real feeling for her characters, Bass creates a three-hanky delight."
—*Publishers Weekly*

"A funny, poignant, and deeply satisfying novel. What I loved about it most of all was the authentic portrait of a family with all its imperfect and humble acts of love—those things that truly make our lives worthwhile."
—Nancy Thayer

"Incredibly funny, genuinely heartbreaking, and strangely comforting, *Miss You Most of All* is completely wonderful."
—Beth Harbison

"A deliciously great book for those who love real books that depict real life, with all the mess, tears, joy, and laughter that living on this planet— or in this case the Sassy Spinster Farm—involves."
—Cathy Lamb

"Utterly warmhearted, *Miss You Most of All* is a special experience from start to finish."
—Holly Chamberlin

Books by Elizabeth Bass

MISS YOU MOST OF ALL

WHEREVER GRACE IS NEEDED

THE WAY BACK TO HAPPINESS

LIFE IS SWEET

Published by Kensington Publishing Corporation

Life Is Sweet

Elizabeth Bass

KENSINGTON BOOKS
www.kensingtonbooks.com

KENSINGTON BOOKS are published by

Kensington Publishing Corp.
119 West 40th Street
New York, NY 10018

Copyright © 2014 by Elizabeth Bass

All rights reserved. No part of this book may be reproduced in any form
or by any means without the prior written consent of the Publisher, ex-
cepting brief quotes used in reviews.

All Kensington titles, imprints, and distributed lines are available at
special quantity discounts for bulk purchases for sales promotion, pre-
miums, fund-raising, educational, or institutional use.

Special book excerpts or customized printings can also be created to fit
specific needs. For details, write or phone the office of the Kensington
Special Sales Manager: Attn. Special Sales Department. Kensington
Publishing Corp., 119 West 40th Street, New York, NY 10018. Phone:
1-800-221-2647.

Kensington and the K logo Reg. U.S. Pat. & TM Off.

eISBN-13: 978-0-7582-8145-6
eISBN-10: 0-7582-8145-5
First Kensington Electronic Edition: October 2014

ISBN-13: 978-0-7582-8144-9
ISBN-10: 0-7582-8144-7
First Kensington Trade Paperback Printing: October 2014

10 9 8 7 6 5 4 3 2 1

Printed in the United States of America

Chapter 1

A goggle-eyed face peered through the window of the Strawberry Cake Shop. It had been a while, but Becca recognized the
type right away—a female in her mid-twenties, anxious, emotionally forlorn. A Tina fan. The woman was pressed against the
plate glass, binocularing her hands in order to get a better view
inside. If she'd had little suckers on her feet, she probably would
have taken up residence there, like a gecko.

I do not need this today. As subtly as possible, Becca performed a
three-quarter turn to face away from the gawker and continued
with what she was doing, which was icing a cake.

Pam, her oldest friend in Leesburg and a helper at the shop,
had a harder time ignoring the person outside. Unacquainted
with the reality of goldfish-bowl living, she edged toward the
door.

"We don't open for another ten minutes," Becca said before
Pam could flip the Closed sign to Open.

Pam halted, tense from the pressure vibes the gawker was
sending. "But there's a customer."

"That's not a customer, that's a . . ." She almost said *parasite,* which would have been mean. Accurate, but mean. Pam already faulted Becca for having a cold, shriveled heart because she'd bailed on her marriage after six months. No need to hand her more character critique ammo. ". . . a nostalgia pilgrim."

"How are you going to sell this stuff if you turn away people at the door?" Pam nodded to the display case of cakes, cupcakes, and brownies that they had worked all morning getting ready. It was almost full, and would be packed as soon as Becca finished icing the latest batch.

"I never turn away anyone during business hours," Becca said. "And I don't have trouble selling."

"Right. So tell me again why we both have freezers full of day-olds?"

Becca didn't let the dig bother her. "We're turning a profit."

Finally. It had taken her a long time to be able to claim that. Eighteen nervous months of outgoing payments being higher than incoming cash. The shop's setup costs had been more than she'd estimated, mostly because the building—a defunct hardware store downtown—had required unforeseen repairs and alterations. A burst pipe during month two had nearly scuttled the entire enterprise. Lately she'd been letting a few things go—carrying pans upstairs to her apartment's dishwasher instead of getting the shop's fixed, for instance. She also could have used a handyman to fix all the wobbling tables and sticking doors around the place. But for the present, she was pleased with the turnover of the baked goods themselves.

Besides, the leftovers were usually a by-product of experimentation, not lack of customers. The orange cream cupcakes had not been a success. Neither had rum raisin—which was insane, because they were the best cupcakes ever. When Becca stuck to the classics and a few of the time-tested varieties, the store sometimes sold out before closing time.

"You're not exactly Sara Lee yet," Pam said. "You can't take customers for granted." She shot nervous glances at the human gecko at the window as she filled the cream and milk thermoses.

Becca kept her focus on the thick glob of buttercream she was gently ploughing over the golden surface of a lemon cake. "That's not a customer," she muttered.

"How do you know?"

She arched a brow at Pam. "Believe me, I can tell. At most, she'll buy a token cupcake."

"One cupcake is a sale."

True. And usually anyone wanting to buy anything gave her a thrill. But if the tax on her psyche cost more than the sale of a two-dollar cupcake, it wasn't worth it. She hadn't moved two thousand miles to a small city and opened a cake store to exploit her once-upon-a-time fame. In fact, she'd run this far for the express purpose of reinventing herself. She just wanted to bake, own a business, and be somewhat normal. Was that too much to ask?

Apparently so.

Gecko Girl rapped on the door and pointed at her watch. In reply, Becca lifted a sorry-Charlie glance and nodded at the large wall clock that showed the time to be six minutes till eleven. Gecko Girl responded with an exaggerated frowny face. Becca pretended not to see it and went back to her icing.

Pam looked as if she might have a nervous breakdown. "*Five minutes*. What's the harm in being a little flexible?"

Becca relented with a laugh. "Okay. Knock yourself out."

But even as she gave the go-ahead, she braced herself.

Wiping her hands on her apron, Pam hurried to the door. She flipped the sign, and then turned the dead bolt to open the door.

The early bird nearly flattened Pam in her race across the room. For a second, it looked as though the person might attempt to bound over the counter like a high hurdle, but at the last minute physics got the best of her and she ended up draped over the glass display case, gaping at Becca.

"It's really you! I can't believe it! I'm so so so excited!"

Becca tried to smile. "Can I help you?"

The woman's face lit up so that her eyes were practically shooting sparks of adoration. She was a breathless Roman candle of fangirldom. "God, yes! I'm dying to know what it was like to work with Jake Flannery. I always thought he was *so cute*. My first crush. Of course, I was only seven or eight at the time, but I bet he was really cute in person. You were probably in love with him, too, right? Although, I guess you couldn't *really* be in love with him, since he was your dad and all."

"He wasn't, actually." Becca aimed for patience and understanding, but wasn't sure she managed either. "He was an actor playing my dad."

"Yeah, right—plus, he was a ghost!" The woman blinked, and then laughed nervously. "I bet you still call Jake sometimes just to say 'Good night, Daddy.' That was always my favorite part of the show. Poor ghosty guy had to wander around his house where his family couldn't see him anymore, and he'd try to help them with their problems—like you having to deal with that bitchy kid at school, the one played by Abby Wooten. Then you'd say 'Good night, Daddy,' to him at the end, and then the studio audience would go *awwww*."

Could the woman handle learning that those *awwwws* were prerecorded? Or would her head simply explode? Becca decided not to find out.

"I haven't talked to Jake since we got cancelled," she said. "Seventeen years ago."

Seventeen years. How could people care about something that happened to fictional people in a box in their living room so long ago?

The woman's face collapsed in a frown. "Oh God, that's *so sad*. But you were in love with him, right? I mean, how could you not be?" Before Becca could answer, excitement overwhelmed the woman again and she shouted toward the ceiling, "I can't believe I'm standing here having a conversation with Rebecca Hudson! You were, like, my first best friend."

It never took long, that leap from strained amusement and (*admit it, Becca*) flattery to being creeped out. "And you're my first customer of the day," she said, gently steering the woman back to the land of sanity. "What can I get for you?"

The woman gasped as if Becca had just asked her on a girls-day-out date. "Oh! Okay, first, can I get a picture of us together?"

Becca tried hard to keep her lips set in a smile as she gestured at her Strawberry Cake Shop apron. She was covered in flour and powdered sugar, and her hair was pulled back in a net. She could just imagine the captions if a photo of herself looking like this hit the Internet. *Former Child Star Now Kitchen Worker.* A few years earlier, she'd been photographed going into a strip mall where there was a family planning clinic. LITTLE TINA TERMINATES BABY!, a tabloid headline had screamed over a grainy photo, even though Becca had been headed for the nail salon next door.

"I'm not in my picture-taking clothes this morning," she told the woman. "I'm in cupcake-selling clothes. Would you like to buy something?"

The woman had to unhook herself from the case she was plastered against to see inside the glass. She blinked at the neat rows of cupcakes and cakes as if they were a complete surprise to her. As though she hadn't realized she was in a bakery at all. "Pretty! You make these? This is what Tina does all grown up?"

Becca's jaw clenched, and she couldn't help shooting a dagger gaze at Pam, who stood apart, bemused by it all.

Belatedly, their visitor peered around the shop the way most people did when they first walked in. The only objects decorating the brick walls were horsey things, old black-and-white pictures and stuff she'd found at garage sales. A jockey's silks under glass. Ads for ancient vet remedies. Crops and hats and spurs.

"Where's *Me Minus You?*"

On cable, in reruns. Becca bit back the temptation to lapse into snark. "The television stuff's not really my thing anymore."

The woman swung back to her, gaping in horror, as if Becca had just bad-mouthed apple pie and motherhood. "But it's who you are."

A volcanic mass of irritation started belching steam in Becca's gut. "The lemon cupcakes are the freshest," she said through a tight smile.

The woman's eyes turned red and bulgy. She actually appeared to be on the verge of tears. "I drove all the way from Delaware to see you. Why else would I have come so far? This is just like an ordinary bakery."

Becca bagged a lemon cupcake and thrust it across the counter. "Here—on the house."

For a moment, the woman seemed so petulant and disappointed that Becca thought she would refuse the offering. Which, frankly, would have given her some hope for the woman's mental health. Anger might have been a first step down the long road to recovery from old sitcom overidentification. But then her gaze met Becca's again, and that spark of the crazy reignited. "Could you autograph it?"

Fine. Becca snatched the bag back and grabbed a ballpoint from the cup next to the cash register. Clicking it, she asked, "Your name is . . . ?"

"Megan—but could you add something personal? And could you put a lot of x's and o's before your signature?"

When she was done, the lip of the bag read:
Megan,
Your best friend, Tina, thinks you should get a life already.
xoxo,
Rebecca Hudson

The woman grabbed it back from her and read the words greedily. Her smile dissolved. She said nothing at first, and Becca worried she would cry. Instead, her face went red, and she flashed her outrage through bloodshot eyes. " *'Get a life'?* Is that supposed to be a joke?"

"Not exactly."

"You're telling *me* to get a life? And who the hell are *you?*" Megan asked, the bag crinkling in her hands. "Some washed-up has-been working in a bakery. You don't know the first thing about me!"

Would the word *irony* mean anything to this woman? Becca took a deep breath, already regretting the stupid autograph. Impulse control had never been her strong suit. "I'm sorry. The fact is, you don't know me, either."

"I do so," the woman shot back. "I've been a fan since I was this high." Her hand disappeared beneath the cash register. "I always thought you were a nice person, but you're obviously just a bitch—just like your guest appearance on *Malibu High School*! No wonder they killed off your character." She marched to the door but turned back, her gaze dark with warning. She raised a fist, which was still clutching the white bag with a strawberry stamped on it. "Don't think the whole world won't hear what kind of person you really are. I have a blog!"

She slammed the door behind her.

Pam crossed her arms. "Great PR job there, boss."

Becca lifted her shoulders. "I tried."

"*That* was trying?"

"Believe it or not." Props to the woman for sticking the knife in and twisting it with her last snarky reference to *Malibu High School*, which had been a traumatic experience. Becca had played a horrible character, and the show had starred her nemesis from *Me Minus You*, Abby Wooten. During the run of the earlier show, Abby and Becca had been pals, although by the time of the cancellation, their friendship had cooled. After Becca got written off *Malibu High School*, Abby had dropped her like a hot potato. Becca's career never recovered, and neither had her faith in Hollywood friendships.

"Megan was nuts," she said in her own defense now.

"Well, yes. She did seem a little deranged."

A little! But a little or a lot, what did it matter? Fandom was insane. How much did it take for a brain to flip the switch from harmless fan to Mark David Chapman? Becca didn't want to find out. "It's weird. Just when I assume I've finally been forgotten for something I did when I was twelve, some Tina-crazy person pops up."

"Oh look." Pam peered out the window. "Your secret admirer's back."

Oh God. Becca was ready to duck behind something solid and dial 911, assuming Pam was talking about crazy Megan—but that didn't add up. The woman probably never wanted to see her again. Ducking didn't make sense, either. Becca might be a million not-very-good things, but she'd never been a coward.

She came around the counter to investigate from Pam's angle. Her secret admirer was sitting on the bench on the sidewalk in front of the shop. She'd seen the older man before—he was hard to miss. His shambling appearance would have been more at home in a Depression-era photograph than modern-day, gentrified Leesburg. He definitely didn't look like a *Me Minus You* fanatic . . . which might be the only thing he had going for him, actually.

"He never comes in, even when we have free samples." Becca peered at the skinny old guy, curious. "You think he's on a diet? Diabetic?"

"Just a crazy old coot, is what I'm guessing," Pam said.

Most likely he wasn't a day over fifty-five, but his frayed appearance made him seem older. As always, a well-worn pork-pie hat was perched on his head, which probably accounted for Pam's having called him crazy. Pam was old-time mainline Virginia all the way; she would battle quirkiness to her dying breath, even as it sprang up around her like dandelions.

"I wonder what he wants," Becca said.

"Wants?" Pam snorted. "He wants what all these vagrants flooding our city want—a free ride."

Becca tried not to laugh. Leesburg, Virginia, was hardly a pit of urban decay flooded with vagrants. But evidently inside Pam's head there existed an alternate universe in which Leesburg's few placid, historic streets teemed with homeless people, panhandlers, and hookers.

Having only a moment ago acknowledged her own good fortune, Becca experienced a swell of sympathy for this down-on-his-luck guy. "I can't give him a free ride, but I wonder if he'd settle for a free cupcake." She circled back to the other side of the counter, took a coconut cupcake from the display case, dropped it in a paper sack, and grabbed two napkins.

"Oh no." Pam trailed her to the front door. "Don't feed him. That will just make the problem worse."

"There is no problem. He's just a man sitting on a bench, who looks like he could use some cheering up."

She stepped out of her shop onto the brick sidewalk and stopped in front of the bench, which was shaded by her shop's awning. The stranger lurched to his feet, his curious, anxious gaze traveling from Becca to Pam hovering behind her.

"I thought you might enjoy this." Becca held out the bag with the Strawberry Cake Shop stamped on it.

Wary eyes lingered on Becca, but her smile persuaded the man to take the sack and peek at the contents. "Damn," he said approvingly in a low, resonant voice. "Looks good enough to eat."

"That's the idea," she said.

He glanced down at her again. His height was probably close to six feet, although his lankiness and slouch made it hard to judge. He had kind, sad eyes. She also noted something that looked like oil stains on the legs of his pants.

"Thank you, thank you very much." His voice had a leisurely timbre to it, yet not a trace of a Southern drawl. Like her, he was probably not a native, but he certainly didn't look like the typical yuppie settlers who populated Loudoun County, most of whom were DC commuters. "I hope you didn't think I was sitting here hoping to freeload."

"No, but I've seen you out here before."

"I just like this spot." He pointed to the early-nineteenth-century buildings surrounding them. "Nice town."

"The natives are friendly, too, once they get used to you." Becca tossed a glance back at Pam, whose brows arched skeptically, as if she was still waiting for the man to produce a butcher knife and hack them both to pieces in broad daylight.

"My name's Walt," the man said.

"Nice to meet you, Walt. I'm Becca."

"Becca, is it?" he repeated, as if surprised. "Becca . . . ?"

"Becca Hudson."

The man's smile faded a shade, but he nodded. "Thank you for the treat, Becca. I'm sure I'll enjoy it."

"You're welcome."

Without another word, Walt turned and walked away, his pace brisk. Becca felt a pang, as if she'd chased him off.

"He had shifty eyes," Pam declared when he'd turned the corner onto Market Street. "I hope he wasn't casing the joint. He might come back later and rob us."

Pam's community watch paranoia made Becca laugh. She'd thought his eyes looked more sad than shifty. And his expression when she'd first approached him stayed with her—as if he'd been afraid of something. "You think everyone looks shifty who hasn't lived here for fifty years. I thought he was downright civilized." Albeit in a hurry to get away from them after a few minutes.

All at once, Pam drew back, her lips breaking into a smile at something over Becca's shoulder. Or, more likely, someone. Becca turned as her ex-husband approached. Cal always cadged free coffee when he was in town. This morning was starting to feel like a *Mister Rogers' Neighborhood* parade of regulars and special visitors.

"Why, look who's already up and about at"—Pam checked her watch—"eleven thirty!"

He smiled. "You're wasted selling cupcakes, Pam. You should hire yourself out to the city. They could install you up on city hall like a clock on a bell tower. Then you could just shout the time at people."

"Most people in this town have figured out how to set an alarm clock by their seventh birthday," Pam said.

He scratched his unshaven cheek and turned his attention to Becca. If the man hadn't inherited a horse farm, he would have shown great promise as a hobo. He could have been hanging out with Walt. "Got any coffee?"

"Help yourself," Becca said. He always did.

"See?" Pam followed them into the cake shop. "You feed these guys and they start flocking around, expecting handouts. Like pigeons."

Cal made himself at home, scooting around to the back to retrieve the Ravens mug he kept by the sink and then back out to the coffee station. The Strawberry Cake Shop's rectangular room was split into two: the front half was for customers, with a few marble-topped tables for stopping . . . but not for staying forever. Becca had opted not to put in comfy furniture, to discourage one-cup lounge lizards from planting themselves in the shop all day. Behind the long oak display counter, a remnant from the hardware store, all the innards of the kitchen stood in plain view—stainless-steel appliances, mixers, a sink loaded with mixing bowls and pans, and the island where all the icing and finishing work were done. Only the storage room off the side, which contained another utility sink and shelves loaded with all of Becca's supplies, was hidden from the front of the shop.

A mishmash of things Becca loved embellished the front half of the shop. Framed vintage photographs and posters hung on the exposed brick walls alongside horse stuff—odds and ends including photos of horses, including her own horse, Harvey. From the high, pressed-tin ceiling above hung three 1920s light fixtures with heavy white cut-glass shades that made changing light bulbs a death-defying act.

While Pam inspected a picture of herself soaring over a fence in full hunting regalia on her gelding, Crackers, Becca returned to icing duty. Wafer-thin sugared lemon slices she'd prepared in her apartment the night before stood at the ready to be used as garnish.

"You look like something puked up by a barn cat," Becca said to Cal.

He smiled. "Poker night. Didn't get to bed until four."

"Four o'clock?" Pam straightened her shoulders. "*I* was up at seven to meet Floyd at the barn. He never showed up, by the way. Honestly, Cal, Butternut Knoll needs a new farrier. Floyd's a no-show half the time . . . although that's probably a blessing, because I suspect that's the half when he's drunk."

"I can guarantee you he was drunk this morning," Cal said.

Pam's face fell and then reddened. "He was with *you?* You were out boozing with Floyd hours before he was supposed to be at the farm shoeing Crackers?"

"How was I supposed to know?"

"Because it's *your* business, you dumb cluck!" Pam exclaimed. She and Cal had been friends forever—really forever, since preschool—despite their inability to sit together in a room for five minutes without arguing. They'd even argued during a trip the three of them had taken to Vegas, which had spontaneously turned into Cal and Becca's wedding weekend. In retrospect, she wished they'd argued *that* ill-fated decision over a little more. Or had foregone the last martini that had preceded their making it.

Surprisingly, that brief wedding ceremony was probably the one time Cal and Pam were in a room together and managed to refrain from sniping at each other. Becca's memory of the blessed event was fuzzy, but she couldn't actually recall Pam saying anything before the officiant had pronounced them man and wife. Then she'd gathered Becca and Cal to her for a group hug, burst into tears, and passed out in the Chapel of Hope.

"I'm going to have to reschedule," Pam complained now.

Cal smiled. "Well, you can be sure he'll show up next time. After last night, he needs the money."

"Terrific." Pam shook her head. "I'll see if I can get Floyd out to the barn this afternoon. You will be there, won't you?"

"Of course, I'm on my way back out to the Knoll right now. Just had to loop through town to pick up some stuff." As Pam went to the storeroom to retrieve her phone from her purse and make the call, Cal emptied his leftover coffee into the sink and grabbed a ginger-pepper brownie off a cooling rack.

"How's business?" he asked.

"We're one pilfered brownie away from destitution," Becca deadpanned.

He gobbled it down. Reddish stubble on his unshaven jaw,

bed head that would give way to helmet head later in the afternoon, a fleece over worn-out jeans—looking at him, she felt the mix of affection and irritation she imagined she might have felt for a brother, if she'd ever had one. When she'd first met him, his rumpled, laid-back ways made him so different from the guys she was used to. As a recent refugee from LA, she'd found his lack of ambition refreshing, even sexy. He was an earthy guy who wanted nothing more than to manage the horse farm that had been left to him, where his family had lived for over a hundred years. Her past celebrity was a novelty to him, and maybe it made him notice her at first, but he didn't treat her any differently because of it.

She'd fallen in love with Butternut Knoll, and the friends she'd made riding there. She'd been intoxicated by her new life, by the idea of belonging to this town, these people. Just having such a tight circle of friends was a wonder to her. She had lost her mother and had felt so all alone in the world. Orphaned. Discovering and being embraced by these Leesburg friends was like having a big family for the first time in her life. Cal had been part of that, and along with romanticizing her new life, she'd romanticized him.

Until she'd flown home from Vegas and realized to her shame that she'd just married someone she liked a whole lot, but didn't really love.

"Peevish Pam working out as a helper?" he asked between bites.

Pam was a real estate agent by trade, but the Realtor she'd worked for had folded during the last economic slump. Pam now worked part-time for Becca and picked up real estate commissions on a freelance basis.

"It's been great. I can actually catch my breath during the day." The first year Becca had tried to go it alone, which had been stressful. "And she's trying to get me to improve my people skills."

He almost choked on his brownie. "*People* skills? Is that what they call bullying these days?"

"She doesn't treat everyone the way she treats you."

"That makes me feel special." He lingered another moment as if there was something he wanted to say. Their encounters always seemed to end this way now. Awkwardly. Because, a year on from their divorce, there was nothing left to say. They'd made a mistake, and righted it, and now it was a lucky thing they remained friends.

"Well . . . I guess I'd better go and see what else I can screw up today," he said. "Sounds like I've already made a head start and I didn't even know it."

He gazed at her. She looked away.

"Are you coming out to the stables today?" he asked.

"I'll be by after work, around seven."

When he was gone, she wondered if she should have given him some personal encouragement, told him that he wasn't as hopeless as he pretended to be. She still felt a residual protective impulse. And, pathetic as it sounded, her ex-husband was the closest thing she had to family now, real or televised.

But if she thought about *that* too long she would do desperate things . . . which was sort of why she'd ended up marrying Cal in the first place.

Chapter 2

"Hurry, Matthew, I'm *starving*."

Olivia's pencil-like, ten-year-old frame long-jumped down the sidewalk ahead of him. She was the most energetic starving person on the planet.

"How can you be hungry?" Matthew asked. "I packed your noontime smorgasbord myself."

She turned, jutting her lower jaw out so that her lower teeth protruded like a little monster. A food monster. "That was hours ago. And I gave the cookie away."

"Why?"

"Because Grover wanted it. He never gets cookies."

Matthew had to think twice to remember that Grover was a real child, not a Muppet or an imaginary friend. Kids these days and their weird names. Back when he was in elementary school, half his friends had been named Jason. Life had been simpler then.

"Why are you smiling?" Olivia asked him.

"No reason."

"And why are you moving sooooo slow?" She took his hand and tugged him down the sidewalk, nearly knocking them into a woman maneuvering a baby carriage out the door of the card shop.

Matthew murmured an apology and, too late, darted to hold the door for the harried mom, with whom he felt a newfound kinship. Before, he'd often wondered why Nicole wore a hunted look some evenings, but now he knew. Dealing with your own messy work-life problems was exhausting enough without another little person's schedule and headaches to squeeze in, too. To Matthew, Olivia had always seemed like an easy-care kid. But that was before she'd been left in his sole care for longer than, say, a trip to the hairdresser's.

A month. He pushed the thought out of his mind when Olivia dropped his hand and skipped the last ten feet to the door of the bakery, ending with an impatient hop. "This is *the best* place!"

She'd been rattling on about it all week—every day after school she'd begged to go to the Strawberry Cake Shop. According to Olivia, other kids got to go all the time, but apparently Nicole wasn't as keen on the place. As Matthew opened the door and found himself stepping into a warm world where the smells of butter and baking chocolate wrapped around him like a comforting, aromatic blanket, he could see why Nicole wouldn't be a fan. He couldn't imagine any of the desserts behind the glass case passing her lips. She wasn't big on sweets.

If the mouthwatering smell had left him in doubt whether the creations behind the case were good, the line inside would have convinced him. The clientele today was heavy on perfectly made-up moms and girls in ballet clothes, all of whom seemed to know exactly what they wanted. Cupcakes flew off the shelves. There were also double cupcakes—more like mini cakes—and full-sized cakes that were available either as whole cakes or by the slice. Iced brownies cut into wedges sat under a cake cover, and next to the cash register were two glass jars—one filled with peanut butter cookies, one with chocolate chip.

Aside from the food offerings, he saw at once what attracted Olivia to this place, and kept Nicole away. There were horses everywhere—pictures of horses, figurines, a bridle hanging on the wall. (*Is that sanitary?* he wondered.) Olivia was wild about horses, but after a year of begging she hadn't succeeded in wheedling Nicole to shell out for riding lessons.

"See that?" Olivia pointed at a picture of a horse, a white one, with a woman standing next to him in one of those ridiculous black helmets. "That's Harvey."

"Help you?" the woman behind the counter asked Matthew, goosing his attention forward.

Before he could decide what he wanted, much less speak, Olivia piped up for both of them. "A small green cake, please."

Matthew had no idea what she was talking about until the woman reached under the counter and carefully picked up a small green-iced cake by the doily it was sitting on. "What is that?"

"Green cake," Olivia said, as if that made any sense.

"Yeah, but—"

The woman working the counter interrupted him. "It's strawberry cake. White cake layered with strawberries and cream, thin layer of marzipan, and then icing." She plopped it in a small box and tied it with string before he had even absorbed what she said. Her no-nonsense, slightly husky voice distracted him. Also, he had a difficult time processing the words because he was so busy looking at her. His gaze felt riveted by her face.

"It's really good," Olivia assured him. "I have it whenever I come in with friends."

"Anything else?" the woman asked.

He shook his head.

"That's eight dollars and twenty-eight cents."

Matthew dug into his jeans pocket, hoping he had enough. He'd been thinking a dollar for a cookie, maybe. Or a cupcake— he looked longingly at them sitting next to their cheery $2.25 price markers.

He fished out a five and several ones and forked them over. Olivia grabbed the box off the counter while Matthew waited for the change. "I see Monica outside!" she said, and darted toward the door.

He had only a vague memory of who Monica was.

"She's a sweet kid," the cake lady said to him, handing him a fistful of coins.

At first he thought she was reassuring him about Monica, then realized she meant Olivia. "Oh yeah." *Why is my brain not working?* "Thanks—she's great."

"Olivia introduced herself the first time she came in here. She's nuts about horses, just like I was."

"Her mom isn't nuts about them," he said.

"Mine wasn't, either." She laughed, nodding around the room. "Maybe she was right. I was one of the horse-mad kids who actually retained the mental illness into adulthood."

It was then that he made the connection between this woman and the woman in the picture Olivia had pointed out to him—in the picture the helmet covered her short reddish-brown hair and threw a shadow over brilliant blue eyes, and the ridiculous chin strap disguised the delicate shape of her face.

Delicate probably wouldn't have been the first word he'd use to describe her, though. She was slender and long-limbed, although she didn't have Nicole's conscientiously thin look. Of course, when you lived in a buttercream icing world, it probably wasn't easy to keep up the Kate Moss standard.

But the structure of the bones in her face was delicate. And the smile was the same as he saw in the picture, he realized now, feeling his own lips tilt up in response. There was still something else about her . . . almost as if he knew her from somewhere.

He could feel his forehead puckering as his eyes narrowed in thought. "Haven't we . . . ?"

Before he could vocalize something that sounded like the world's oldest pickup line, she directed her attention to someone behind him who elbowed forward.

"Can I have a chocolate chip cookie?" the kid asked.

Backing up a step, Matthew gave way, feeling dazed. "I'd better find Olivia," he announced unnecessarily.

The woman sent him a perfunctory nod. "Thanks for stopping by."

The shop was too warm. Maybe it was the smell of the place—all that sweet, buttery scent. The very air seemed to clog his arteries, cutting off oxygen to his brain. How else could he explain his desire to stand there, waiting to hear that voice again. Honey with a hint of gravel.

He turned and headed for the door. He needed to get out of there, to breathe fresh air again.

Outside, Gayle Minter, Monica's mother, touched his arm. "How long is Nicole going to be working on the West Coast?"

"Three more weeks."

"I'll bet you miss her."

He nodded, although he couldn't help glancing back through the glass at the cake lady. What was the matter with him?

Monica's mom was still talking to him. When he looked back at her, he could see her lips moving, but he hadn't heard a word she'd said.

"I'm sorry?" he interrupted, having missed her words completely.

"I said, Olivia could stay the night. It would give you a little time to catch your breath."

Yes, that's what he needed. Time to catch his breath. "That would be terrific," he said. "We just need to go home and grab her things."

Gayle Minter's brow wrinkled. "We were talking about this weekend."

"Oh. Right." Heat crept up his neck. "Well—even better. Although hopefully Nicole will be back for a weekend visit."

He sought Olivia's gaze and pleaded silently for them to go before he made an even bigger idiot of himself. He could have sworn Monica's mother was eyeing him judgmentally, no doubt because she questioned his capabilities as stand-in dad. He was starting to have doubts himself.

Meanwhile, he could just imagine all the e-mail piling up in his inbox, since he was supposed to be working from home. Or, more specifically, from Nicole's home. His boss was being extremely patient this month.

"Bye, Monica—see you tomorrow. Don't forget to wear blue!" The two girls laughed at some private joke before Olivia skipped over to Matthew.

"What were you talking about with Mrs. Minter?" Olivia asked as they headed home.

"She wants you to come over for a sleepover this weekend."

"Oh." She started taking extra-long steps, a goofy walk she wouldn't be caught dead doing in public in a year or two. "I bet she's worried we aren't going to invite Monica to my birthday party. She's a new girl at our school, and she didn't get invited to Missy Dolan's. Missy thinks Monica's a snob."

Matthew was a novice when it came to the politics of birthday parties, and adolescent girl friendships. Olivia seemed to have a new best friend every week. "Are you going to invite her?"

"Of course! Monica rides. She has her own horse and everything. I can't even get Mom to let me take lessons."

Matthew hitched his throat, wanting to stay far from this topic. He wasn't Olivia's father, so he wasn't in a position to override Nicole's wishes. When the subject had first come up, he hadn't seen that it was all that big a deal. Lots of kids rode horses, he'd told Nicole, and they had the money.

"Money?" Nicole's voice had looped up in irritation. "Did having money help Christopher Reeve?"

"That was just a fluke. A really unfortunate, rare accident."

"It happens more often than you'd think," Nicole had said. "And he was jumping—which of course is what Olivia dreams of doing."

"Right—dreams. She's a long way from doing anything very risky. You can't keep her in a bubble forever, you know."

Wrong thing to say. Nicole's face had reddened right up to her hairline. "You know nothing. I send Olivia out into the world every day, and then go to work and hear stories about kidnappings, school shootings, drunk crossing guards. I have to worry about *everything*—about what she eats, about her schoolwork, about whether she's the one-in-a-million kid who'll have a bad reaction to a vaccine. Whether or not to put her on top of a fifteen-hundred-pound animal and watch her flying over fences? That's an easy call for me."

"But—"

"You're not her father," Nicole had said, finishing the discussion.

It was how a lot of their discussions about Olivia ended. No matter how much he cared about Olivia, he couldn't even claim stepfather status. Nicole's ex-husband—the guy who maybe could have influenced her on this issue, if he'd stuck around—had left her for another woman, moved to Boston, and started a new family when Olivia was five. Nearly six years later, Nicole was still in no hurry to marry again. She didn't even want to move in together, so Matthew lived a split existence, shuttling between Nicole's place and the town house he'd rented here to be closer to her but never actually stayed in much because he spent most of his free time at Nicole's.

"If I got a horse, I'd want him to look just like Harvey," Olivia was saying.

"Harvey?" The name always made him think of giant rabbits.

"Harvey is the name of Becca's horse. You know—the white horse in the picture in the cake shop? I showed him to you."

"Oh right." With startling sharpness, the woman behind the counter came back to him. The short hair, the lightly freckled skin, the dry voice. He couldn't shake that weird connection he'd felt when he talked to her, as if he already knew her.

"Harvey's a thoroughbred," Olivia continued, her tone expert. "A true white thoroughbred."

They turned onto their street and walked the rest of the way home with Olivia chattering about horses, Monica, and what her mother could possibly have against all things equine.

Matthew continued along, only half-listening.

Becca. The name suited her.

Chapter 3

"I don't see why you have to work like a dog around here," Erin said. "It's not like you own the place anymore."

Becca maneuvered a wheelbarrow around a gopher hole. She'd never considered herself an owner of Butternut Knoll Stables, even though she'd lived here the six months of her marriage to Cal. The whole time it had felt as if she had been playing at being a wife. At first, in full denial mode, she'd attempted to compensate for what she felt in her heart had been a mistake. She'd ironed Cal's clothes until they were cardboard stiff, baked fresh bread on weekends, and made new curtains for the farmhouse. She would become super-wife.

But the harder she tried, the more they argued. When such a loose thread had knit them together, it only took a few tugs for the unraveling to begin.

"I didn't marry you for your housekeeping skills," he'd told her when she complained that he hadn't noticed all the little improvements she was making.

"Why *did* you marry me?"

"Didn't you hear the man? 'To love and to cherish,' " he said.

She was too embarrassed to admit she didn't remember exactly what the justice of the peace had said that night. She vowed never to overindulge again. She even attempted to reform Cal, until she realized that her nagging just made them both miserable. And then she'd discovered a series of flirtatious texts Cal had been sending to female clients, and she realized he'd probably just been playing at being a husband. Deciding to leave had been surprisingly easy. It was the only honest thing to do.

There's something the matter with me. She needed to look before she leapt, and then had to leap back out again.

She grunted, trying to make it seem as if the wheelbarrow pushing caused it. The exertion was real; the new compost pile was farther from the barn. "Think of it this way. If I didn't do this, Cal would have to hire more people. And then he'd raise boarding prices."

Her friend minced around a more fragrant obstacle and took a swig of Diet Coke. "Still, you should have let Marv handle your divorce. He's done a good job for everybody I know, including Bob." Bob was Erin's husband, who gave Becca the creeps. "Your lawyer let you walk away from a gold mine."

Becca laughed and gestured toward the ancient barn, and then to the farmhouse, which needed painting. "You call this a gold mine?" The setup was beautiful, but not wildly profitable. After expenses, the money Cal made from Butternut Knoll probably wouldn't even cover Erin's yearly shoe bill. "There's more money in cupcakes."

"I suspect Cal isn't the most careful with the books," Erin said.

She suspected right. From what Becca had witnessed during their short marriage, "the books" usually just ended up being receipts tossed haphazardly into a drawer in Cal's kitchen. Which was another reason Becca had wanted no part of the farm in the divorce, in addition to the fact that she didn't feel she deserved it.

"It's enough of a headache worrying about my own business," Becca said. "When I'm here, I just enjoy riding and getting in some physical work."

Erin shook her head. "With all you do here, it's like you've got two jobs."

"It's all stuff I enjoy." She thought of her mom, coming back from the end of a day working in a busy office, catching a snatch of a show she'd recorded, and then sometimes heading out for a second shift of retail or telemarketing... She'd even cleaned rooms in a hotel once. *That* had been hard work. "My life is a picnic."

Erin studied Becca as she dumped the wheelbarrow onto the pile. Then she cracked up. "Only you would say that as you're hauling around horse shit."

Becca laughed. When she had moved to Leesburg without knowing anyone, she worried about making friends. But she'd met Erin and Pam at Butternut Knoll soon after her arrival, and they'd invited her to join the book club they attended. Within a month or two, the three of them had started skipping book club, preferring to hang out together rather than with a bunch of people straining to come up with things to say about *Ulysses*, which none of them had finished, much less parsed. They'd dubbed their own get-togethers "Not-Book-Club."

When they returned to the barn, Erin headed for her car. "I'll drop by the shop tomorrow and check on you and Pam, okay? I feel so out of the loop now that you two are coworkers. It sounds like such fun."

"For work, it is."

Erin's life didn't involve nine-to-five. Her grandfather had been a Wall Street tycoon, and had married three times. When he'd died, his fortune had been distributed among his many progeny, but what had managed to trickle down to Erin enabled her to live a life without worries. She'd quit her hated office job and never bothered to find another one. This was about the same time she'd married Bob the Despicable. It all seemed very unfulfilling to Becca, especially since Erin didn't have her much-wished-for kids yet. Lately Erin didn't seem as happy with her charmed life, either.

Becca deposited the wheelbarrow in the barn and then strolled to the fence. Harvey's milky white coat made him stand out in the dusk light. Seeing her, he trotted over, tossing his white mane in expectation of the customary farewell treat. She dug a carrot out of her pocket and clasped it in her closed fist. Harvey halted in front of her and extended his neck over the fence, attempting to nuzzle the treat from her hand. She opened her palm for him, getting that blast of hot breath and horse slobber as he took the carrot from her. He chomped contentedly and she gave him a final pat for the evening, lingering to rub her knuckles on that soft nose before turning and strolling to her car.

At the shop today she had told that customer she was horse-mad, and it was true. Sometimes when she was with Harvey, she wondered if this was the way people felt when they looked at their homes, or even their children. She'd craved a horse since she was tiny. While some girls her age had mooned over boy bands, she'd been into *Black Beauty* and *Misty of Chincoteague*. Getting a horse—a real thoroughbred—had been the miracle of her life . . . even if she hadn't understood the real cost of that miracle at the time. She understood it now, and appreciated it more than ever. Life and cynicism might harden her exterior to a brittle rocky crust, but the gooey center of her would always be that little kid gasping at the sight of a horse of her very own.

Driving home, she felt spooked. Thoughts of the past had been creeping up on her all day—ever since the Tina fan had turned up. And now it seemed almost as if there were a ghost following her. The ghost of her mother. Becca actually flicked her gaze toward the rearview mirror a few times, expecting to see Ronnie Hudson there in the backseat, watching her, humming her favorite tune, "Till There Was You." Her mom had hummed it all the time, so that Becca had been familiar with the melody long before she'd heard The Beatles sing the lyrics, or had seen Shirley Jones in *The Music Man*.

What would her mother think of her now? Becca honestly didn't know, but she suspected she'd be glad she was in business for herself. And she would have approved of baking. Becca's love of cake had come directly from her mom. Not fancy ones—Ronnie

Hudson hadn't had time for baking from scratch, and probably preferred boxed layer cakes anyway. As long as there was cake, Ronnie had said, you had a little happiness on a plate.

For all her mom's hard work and sacrifice, they had never gotten into specifics of what Becca's future should be. Her mother had never nagged her about finding a man or becoming a big star. Nothing like that. "When you're older, you'll have an incredible life," she'd occasionally told Becca when she'd whined about not getting whatever instant gratification she hankered after at the moment. As if she'd *needed* anything. "Don't be so impatient."

An incredible life. Her mother made it sound as if someday Becca would have a Jimmy Stewart movie moment and suddenly find herself surrounded by angels and do-gooders. But her mother had been a hardworking optimist, a practical romantic who loved to sing sappy love songs to herself while she worked till she dropped.

Becca hadn't inherited the optimist gene. So far the most incredible thing about her life seemed to be how steep a nosedive it had taken since her teens. But even after Becca had dropped out of acting and then, later, dropped out of college halfway to her business degree to try to sidestep her way back into the entertainment industry, Ronnie hadn't uttered a word of criticism, or reproach, or even too much disappointment. Ditto when she became a culinary school dropout. "It all adds up eventually," she'd said.

After Becca had reached her majority and got her sitcom money and her own place, Ronnie never said Becca hadn't visited enough—she hadn't—or invited her over enough, even though her mom loved her condo. She remembered exactly how her mother had looked sitting on the white couch—a peacock in Becca's tasteful, too-grown-up-too-fast monochrome world. Even though Ronnie had loved visiting, she'd never overstayed her welcome. She hadn't had time. Until nearly the end, she'd kept busy working. And then she was gone, leaving behind so little, aside from the aching emptiness in Becca's heart, and so many regrets.

Some days, like today, it was as if her mother was right there trying to tell her to pay attention to something.

Becca shivered. *It's just my imagination.* All day she'd felt uneasy, as if something momentous had happened and she'd missed it. But it had just been a normal day.

She glanced down at her gas gauge needle touching the red. Okay, that was one thing she'd definitely missed. Outside town, she pulled into a gas station. She usually filled up at the place around the corner from her apartment, but she didn't want to risk having to walk partway home if she ran out of gas. It was already dark.

The outer pumps were all full, so she slid into the one closest to the door, hopped out, and began to pump her gas. Her thoughts continued to sift through the non-events of the day until someone burst out the gas station door, waving his arms at her as if she were about to blow the place up.

"You can't do that!" The guy wore a blue vest with a name tag that read *Steve—Manager*. He looked like a teenager.

"Can't do what?"

"Pump your own gas. This is Full Service."

Was he kidding? He'd nearly given her a heart attack. "Should I hand the reins over to you, then?" she asked.

His eyes bulged. Evidently she'd just committed another service station faux pas. "I'm the manager. I don't pump gas. I shouldn't even be out here now. We have another guy . . ." He put his hands on his bony hips and turned in a circle, scanning the premises. He finally caught sight of his coworker dozing on the grass not far from the air pump. Steve loped over to the guy and nudged him with the toe of his sneaker.

The man bolted up and Steve started yelling at him.

Good help really is hard to find, Becca thought. Thank heavens she had Pam.

The gas station guys came back toward her—the formerly sleeping employee followed by Steve, who was barking at him like a drill sergeant berating a lax recruit. The slacker lifted his doleful gaze to meet Becca's. She sucked in her breath as recognition hit.

"Ma'am, I'm sorry, but—"

Whatever Steve was saying, she didn't hear it. Under the lights of the station, there was no denying the other man's distinctive features—the slightly stooped posture, the sad eyes, the hat. It was the old guy from this morning. Walt.

As he recognized her, too, his face twisted in discomfort. "Oh." He shuffled. "Hi."

Steve caught up to them. "Never mind, Walt—I said you were fired."

"Fired!" Becca couldn't believe it. "That's idiotic. I pumped my own gas—so what? I didn't even know this place was full service." Who knew full service existed anymore?

"You're going to be charged for full service," Steve warned her.

"Fine. I can live with that."

"Good." He turned to the old man. "You're still fired, Walt."

"Are you crazy?" Becca asked. Walt started to mumble that it wasn't necessary for her to defend him, but she was too angry at the little pipsqueak to stop now. She didn't want to be responsible for a man's being fired—especially not by some pimply, service station Napoleon. "I'm going to write a letter to the owners of this place to let them know how unreasonable you're being."

Steve sneered at her. "Write my boss and tell him I fired an employee for sleeping instead of doing the work he's paid to do? I'd appreciate it, ma'am. Might even make Employee of the Month."

Twit. Becca squared her shoulders. "No one I know will ever buy gas here again. I'll tell everyone. I'll post signs. I'll"—she cast about for a dire warning—"I'll start a Twitter campaign!"

"Never mind, Rebecca." Walt shrugged off his employee vest. "I'm done here."

She removed the nozzle from her tank and slammed it back in its slot at the pump. "You can count that as one good thing that's happened to you today." She glared at Steve while waiting for the machine to spit out her receipt.

"Your check will be mailed to you," Steve told Walt.

A shadow of worry passed across Walt's face, but he nodded curtly. "Okay."

The manager turned and strolled back into the station, making a show of shaking his head in disgust.

Jackass.

Becca took a deep breath. "I'm so sorry, Walt."

"It's my own damn fault," he said.

"But—"

"Don't worry about it. You aren't responsible."

"I wasn't paying attention," she said. "To which pump I was at, I mean. I always go to self-service places. And it's just so trivial!"

"It's happened before," Walt confessed. "I . . . I haven't been getting enough sleep at night."

He looked sheepish, as if part of him longed to scurry away. Yet he kept his eyes on her—a direct, searching gaze that seemed reluctant to let go.

She shifted uncomfortably. She wished he wouldn't look at her quite so intently. Maybe he'd seen *Me Minus You* at some point. Or maybe he was just a weirdo. "Anyway, I hope you can find something better than this."

"Me too." He didn't look very optimistic, though. He ambled away, a discouraged Eeyore of a man.

Becca sagged back into her car. As she was pulling out, her headlights beamed straight onto Walt walking along the shoulder of the road.

He didn't have a car?

Alongside him, she tapped the brakes and lowered the passenger window. "Can I give you a lift?"

He hesitated. Maybe she should have, too. Offering a stranger a ride on a dark night wasn't the smartest move, but she'd feel stupid taking back the offer now. And she had lost the guy his job. The least she could do was not let him walk home.

Walt got in, and as he was buckling the seat belt, she pulled out her cell phone and speed-dialed the first number that came up, which was Pam's. "Hi, it's me. I'm going to be a little late meeting you."

"Becca?" Pam sounded understandably confused. "I'm at home, and—wait, what are you talking about?"

"Remember that guy from this morning, the one in front of the store? I'm giving him a lift home."

"You're *what?*"

"It's a long story, but I'm taking him to somewhere on . . ." She turned to Walt. "Where is it?"

"The Marquis apartments on Ferber Road," Walt said.

Becca tried not to frown.

"Oh God—did I hear that right?" Pam moaned into the phone. "You're driving some old vagrant out to Ferber Road? Are you insane?"

"Exactly," Becca answered in a measured tone. "I should be getting back to you in about, let's say, ten minutes?"

"One second past ten minutes, I'm calling the police."

"Perfect," Becca said. "Cheerio!"

After she shoved the phone back into her pocket, she caught Walt watching her. "You shouldn't be doing this," he said.

"Doing what?"

"Giving rides to strangers."

She attempted a laugh. "Probably not."

"It's no joke. Maybe you don't know the crazy criminal types that are out there."

"But you're an expert on them, I guess."

"After eight-plus years in the penitentiary? Yeah, I'd call myself an expert."

Oh great.

"I'm trying to do you a favor here," she reminded him.

Her answer only seemed to agitate him. *Terrific.* An agitated ex-con.

"Didn't you hear me?" he asked. "I said I'd done time."

"Yes, I got that." How much longer until Pam called the police?

"Pull over to the side of the road and let me out," he said. "I don't want to trouble you more than I have."

"We're almost there." Also, the last thing she wanted to do at the moment was stop the car on a dark road.

She hooked a right turn onto Ferber. The Marquis wasn't far. It was an old motel that had been turned into a sort of flophouse for the poorest of the poor and migrant workers. A few years ago, Pam had spearheaded an effort to have the city condemn the building and buy the land, claiming it harbored a bad element. Becca had thought the whole thing was a tempest in a teapot stirred up by hysterical home owners.

Now, as she approached, she caught a glimpse of teenagers hunched against a wall, sizing up her vehicle. Overhead, on the second-story passage, a young boy and a toddler in a diaper leaned through the balcony railing, watching the teens.

Walt was watching the young men, too. "Let me out here," he said when she was still a hundred feet or so away.

Eight-plus years in prison. He knew best.

She stopped.

"Thanks for the ride," he said.

She would never understand what came over her, but in the next moment something sounding very much like her own voice blurted out, "If you need work to tide you over, you can help out at the cake shop."

That impulse control problem. She really needed to get a handle on it.

"That's kind of you," Walt answered. "But baking's not my thing."

She should have been relieved that he was turning her down. She'd offered, he'd refused. End of story. No one could say she hadn't tried to make amends. Instead, she argued, "You don't have to bake. You could help me out doing odd jobs, or making deliveries. Not permanently, but—well, I know how it is when money's tight."

"I'd never have thought that," he said.

"Yeah, well." She nodded toward the two kids. "There but for the grace of God and a hardworking mom." A sitcom nest egg hadn't hurt, either.

A long silence stretched.

"I'm serious," she said. "My mom worked like a mule. I used to almost resent it, but now I understand. Life is hard when you're on your own."

Walt sat with his head drooping. "Listen, Rebecca—"

"Becca," she corrected.

"Becca." He took a breath. "I told you I was in jail, but I didn't tell you everything. I didn't say what for, or—"

She cut him off. "I don't need to know everything." Some sordid story. "Did you assault anybody?"

He shook his head. "Not exactly."

This guy wasn't exactly his own best press agent.

"Did you ever hurt a child?" she asked.

"No." His lips clamped firmly shut.

"The bakery opens to customers at eleven. I'm usually there by nine."

He hesitated, almost seeming to agonize over whether to reject her offer, but finally reached for the door. "I'll see you at nine, then."

As she drove away, the triumphant rush of do-gooder euphoria was followed fast by a chaser of dread. Eight years in prison. What did it mean to "not exactly" assault someone?

What have I done?

Maybe the first sign of being over the hill was when you liked the music in the grocery store more than what played on the radio in your own car. But who wouldn't be relieved to hear Rod Stewart singing granny songs after being stuck in the Justin Bieber mobile?

Matthew dug in his pocket for the list he'd scribbled. "We need bread—something wheaty."

"But not crunchy," Olivia specified. "That stuff you bought last time was like cardboard. Even Grover wouldn't eat it."

"Okay. First, though—"

Olivia cut him off. "I'm gonna go look at shampoo, okay?"

Shampoo wasn't on the list. Not that he cared, but he wondered what else was missing. "I didn't know you needed any."

"I didn't say I was going to *buy* shampoo. I just want to look at it."

"You're going to look at shampoo," he repeated in an honest effort to understand.

She bobbed on her heels. "Yeah."

"Okay, but—"

As soon as the word *okay* left his mouth, she bolted.

He jerked a cart free from the pile at the front of the store and made his way toward the produce. He grabbed the easy stuff first—bananas, apples, grapes. If Nicole were here, she would be lingering over kiwis and pinching mangos for ripeness, but even though he vowed to do a better job than he had been preparing food from scratch, that level of shopping was beyond him. He did linger in front of a two-dollar pineapple, wondering how much effort it would take to reduce it to edible chunks, before he wheeled on toward the dairy section.

A man with a toddler in his cart advanced on him from the opposite direction, hailing him with a smile. "Matthew!"

Recognition hit Matthew, followed by panic. *Name, name.* He swallowed. *Jim? Jack? Jeff?*

"Dave," the guy said.

"Dave," Matthew blurted, as if the name had been on the tip of his tongue. Dave was one of Nicole's work people, a face he saw at Christmas parties and never thought about again for the following twelve months. He hadn't even known Dave and his wife—what's-her-name—lived in Leesburg, but they must. Doubtful there would be any other reason he would be wandering around a grocery store at nine at night with a toddler. The kid's lips had an orange halo from the open bag of chips in the basket. She looked up at Matthew, bored and sleepy as she stuffed another Cheeto in and smacked on it.

"I guess you're getting pretty lonely right about now what with Nicole out on the West Coast," Dave said.

"Oh, surviving."

"Great opportunity for her, though. I could see why she was raring to go."

"Yeah."

"Nicole's brilliant," Dave said. "I mean, she has to be brilliant to have been chosen to go out there with Bob and his team."

"Right." He remembered Bob better because he was Nicole's boss. His was the name that came up most often when she griped about work.

As the kid in the basket stuffed another Cheeto in her mouth, Dave leaned on the cart and dropped his voice to a concerned murmur. "I ran into Erin the other day."

"Who?"

"Bob's wife. *That* was awkward."

"Why?"

Dave's brows darted up like question marks. "Haven't you heard? Bob cheats on her like crazy."

Matthew tried to remember. Maybe Nicole *had* said something about Bob flirting with coworkers. And now they were off together on the other side of the country for a monthlong business trip.

Dave shook his head in disbelief. "The guy could double for the mayor of Munchkin City and he lays more pipe than anybody I know. Why did Erin marry him? She's actually kind of hot—plus, I've heard she's loaded. I'll never understand women."

Matthew mumbled in agreement and started to edge away.

Dave sighed. "I gotta get some wipes before I leave the store so I can clean up Miss Cheez Doodle." He tapped the toddler's head. "Otherwise Gina'll kill me. I'm doing the shopping to give her downtime—but all the goodwill points I earned coming here will evaporate if she has to mop up the kid when I get home." He grinned bigger. "See you around."

"Sure thing."

Matthew stood in a daze next to the yogurt. Maybe he would call Nicole when he got home, just to see how she was doing.

Rousing himself again, he speed-shopped through the rest of the list, but he remained distracted. Off-list items slipped in, and his vow about preparing meals from scratch went out the window when he came to the frozen pizzas.

He tracked down Olivia at the magazines. She clutched the latest editions of *Horse and Rider, Seventeen,* and *People,* and evidently expected an argument. "If you don't want to pay for these you can take them out of my allowance."

"It's okay. Toss them in."

"Really?" Her expression was equal parts joy and suspicion. "Mom hates it when I buy magazines, especially horse ones."

"She probably thinks it's a waste of money because you don't have a horse."

"Yet." Olivia grinned. "But when I do, I'll know absolutely everything."

In the checkout line, he spaced out again. *Bob.* He had only a vague memory of the guy. Did he look like the mayor of Munchkin City? Bald—check. Mustache—check. But he wasn't *that* short.

"Becca!" Olivia shouted.

At the same time Matthew glanced up, the woman in front of them pivoted, her pensive expression breaking into a smile when she saw Olivia. "Hey there."

"I'm getting *Horse and Rider,*" Olivia told Becca. "My favorite magazine."

"I'm buying Frosted Flakes," Becca answered. "My favorite worry food."

For the first time, Olivia looked into their own cart and sighed in despair. "You got lemon yogurt. Ick."

"Go grab something you like better," Matthew said.

She darted off.

He turned back to Becca with a smile, intending to make

chitchat, but her preoccupied expression took him in another direction. "Something wrong?" he asked.

"Have you ever had a gut feeling about someone . . . ?"

Yes—you.

She shrugged. "I worry I'm trusting someone *way* too much. But trust is supposed to be a good thing, right?"

"Not if it's a stranger."

"But that's just it. This person *is* a stranger, and yet I don't feel the usual distance I sense from people before I get to know them."

Her words made him wonder. He had felt a weird connection to this woman from the start. Was this Feel Odd Connections to Strangers Day? Or was it her? Maybe it was like the six degrees of separation theory—except the whole world intersected through the cake lady.

He tried to rein in his ridiculous thoughts. He'd never been an illogical person. "You've never met this person before?"

"Not before today."

"It's a guy?" His stab of disappointment surprised him. *Why should it matter to me?*

"Not a boyfriend," she said. "Or even boyfriend material. Just a man."

Relief flooded him at her words, followed by a pinch of absurdity for feeling anything but neutral over the fact that this woman was saying that some man he didn't even know wasn't boyfriend material. It had nothing to do with him. *She* had nothing to do with him. *Get a grip.*

He fell back on reassuring conventionalities. "Sometimes you gotta go with your gut."

A smile spread across her face. "I barely know you—actually, I don't know you at all—and here I am asking you who I can trust. That's probably proof that my instincts are off-kilter."

"My name's Matthew."

"Becca." She tilted her head. "And you're Olivia's . . . ?"

He thought for a moment. "Significant-other-dad? Olivia's

mom is out of town on a job, so here I am. Buying forbidden horse magazines and the wrong kind of yogurt. Guardian fail all over the place."

"I bet you're doing great."

Her groceries glided forward, and Matthew started unloading his basket. "I probably should have used the self-checkout," she said, noticing the meagerness of her pile next to his. "But half the time that takes me longer than waiting in line."

He watched her interact with the cashier, admiring the easy way she had of talking to people. She wasn't overly friendly or effusive, just straightforward. *So there's a man in her life, but not a boyfriend. What did that mean?* Maybe there was a boyfriend she hadn't mentioned. Not that it was any of his business. His mind was obviously searching for a distraction from his own worries, which at this point only amounted to a vague uneasiness about Bob.

When she was done paying, Becca grabbed her grocery sack and smiled at him. "Have a good evening."

"You too." He turned to the cashier but was aware of Becca's progress toward the exit. His reluctance to see her go grew with each step. When she was nearly to the door, he called her name.

She spun back.

"As long as I'm practicing my dad skills," he said, "I should probably add that it never hurts to remember the old stranger-danger lesson. Trust but verify, as the man said."

Becca let the answer soak in, then nodded. "Right. Of course."

She turned to go, and he blurted out, "It tasted great, by the way."

She swung around. "What?"

"The strawberry cake. I had a slice after dinner. It was amazing."

"Thanks." Finally, she was able to make it out the door.

He turned back to the cashier, whose unblinking eyes and pinched lips disintegrated his smile. Clearly, she considered him a pathetic grocery store lothario.

"Does that woman look familiar to you?" he asked.

"Uh-huh."

Thank God. It wasn't just him.

"She comes in here twice a week," the woman explained over the *beep* of the grocery scanner.

Olivia skidded up behind him in time to stuff an armload of yogurt and two bags of chips onto the counter before the cashier had finished.

Matthew eyed the stuff critically, especially the chips. "Those weren't on the list."

She lifted her chin. "Neither was frozen pizza."

"Yeah, but—" He stopped, not in the mood to argue the comparative nutritional values of pizza and chips.

Olivia looked around. "Where's Becca?"

"She just left."

"Dang! I wanted to ask her about my birthday party. We should have it at the horse barn where she keeps Harvey."

"You want to have a party in a barn?"

"Not *in* the barn," Olivia said, rolling her eyes. "With the horses."

"I doubt Nicole will go for that."

"Not even if I plan it all out so she doesn't have to?" She tugged on Matthew's sleeve. "And not even if you nag her for me?"

"Oh no," he said, in his most emphatic, leave-me-out-of-this tone.

"Please, Matthew? She listens to you."

"Not when it comes to horses." Or anything to do with Olivia, actually.

"Well, shoot. Anyway, I can still ask Becca about it when I see her tomorrow."

"When will you see her tomorrow?"

"When you buy me a cupcake after school."

Even as he shook his head, a part of him was already relenting. That cake had tasted awfully good.

* * *

After he got home and Olivia retreated to her room—ostensibly to finish her homework, but probably to read her magazines—he called Nicole, who picked up on the second ring.

"Hey there!" Her voice was a little too loud, and the sounds of a bar or busy restaurant floated in the background. Wasn't it late to be out barhopping on a work night?

"What are you calling about?" she asked. "Is something wrong?"

"No, I just wondered what you were up to." He hitched his throat. "Wondered how you were, I mean."

"Right now, I'm tired and grumpy and having dinner with some of the gang. What's up?"

"Nothing in particular." His grip on the phone tensed. "I ran into Dave at the grocery store tonight. He hinted that Bob had cheated on his wife."

Nicole laughed. "I believe that falls under the category of old news."

"Really? I hadn't heard."

"Why would you? You barely know the guy. For that matter, you barely know Dave."

True. He frowned. "*Is* Bob cheating on her?"

Nicole let out a huff of exasperation and lowered her voice. "Look—it's sort of awkward to talk about here, and I can't believe we're wasting minutes gossiping anyway. Give me a buzz later, okay? Maybe before bedtime."

"It's already ten thirty here."

"Oh hell. I keep forgetting the time difference."

So did he. "It's okay."

"I meant to call you tonight or tomorrow anyway," she said. "I'm not going to be able to make it back this weekend. We're hoping to get something done on Friday if the weather's better, so it won't make sense to fly back for what would probably be just a day and a half."

He bit back a sigh. Nicole didn't need to hear his disappointment. Back when she'd been assigned to the wave project, she'd warned that she might have to spend a few weekends in Oregon.

"Call me this weekend," she said. "We'll have more time to talk on Saturday. And we really do need to talk."

"Really?" Alarm spiked in his chest.

"Give O hugs for me!" she chimed, and rang off.

For a few minutes, he perched on the edge of Nicole's queen-sized bed with its fluffy rose comforter and extravagant mountain of pillows, combing through every word of their short conversation, trying to weigh the meaning of each pause and inflection. What did she mean, they had a lot to talk about? And why exactly was it hard to talk about Bob?

Before calling, he'd convinced himself that his uneasiness about Nicole was just the normal product of distance and the paranoia that Dave guy had seeded in his brain. Also, there was that weirdness with the cake lady, Becca. He hadn't been tempted by another woman in years. And he wasn't really tempted now. He was just . . .

Attracted to her. That was it. Men checked women out. Women checked men out. It wasn't cheating—it was life.

But it wasn't *his* life. For two years he'd been dedicated to Nicole. He'd moved to be close to Nicole. He'd asked Nicole to marry him.

And she'd said no.

At the time, they discussed her refusal and agreed that it was not the right time. Nicole was too fresh from her divorce, he had no idea what dedication and patience being a parent took, and neither of them were so strapped for funds that they couldn't afford to keep their own places. They were in a privileged position of being able to live the best of both worlds—committed, but independent. In love, but not tethered.

Now he wondered if that wasn't exactly what he was missing in his life. A tether.

Chapter 4

Becca bolted up in the dark out of an unsound sleep and glanced at the glowing block letters of her alarm clock. *1:52 A.M.* Had she woken from a nightmare? She tried to think back, but the only thing she could call up from her tormented attempt at shut-eye was a blond kid with bad skin and a Napoleon complex.

Trust but verify, Matthew had said. Good advice. She just hadn't known how to verify. Now she remembered that there was one person who could tell her more about Walt.

Steve.

She climbed out of bed and shrugged a hoodie over her pajamas. Maybe she was crazy. Maybe it would all be a big waste of time. She couldn't even be sure Steve would still be at the station when she got there, but she had to at least try to talk to him. At nine in the morning, an old ex-con she'd promised a job was going to show up at the bakery door. Knowing whether he'd been an ax murderer in a previous life would be useful information to have.

I must have been insane. This was probably how a lot of well-meaning women ended up as swindle victims. Or in the morgue with toe tags.

Ten minutes later she stepped through the doors of the deserted gas station and food mart, prepared to eat crow. Relief filled her when she noted the blond figure slumped behind the register, eyelids heavy, reading a magazine. Steve looked up and recognized her. His lips flattened to the point of invisibility.

"I was just doing my job," he said.

"I know. I came to apologize."

He eyed her doubtfully. "At two A.M.?"

She strolled over to the counter. "You see, I have my own Walt headache now. I promised him a job."

The guy did everything short of smacking his forehead. Strangely, she almost liked him in that moment. At least, she felt a sense of camaraderie between them. "Why?" he asked.

"Guilt," she confessed.

"Oh man. He was only here for a week and a half, but he was pretty useless. I hope you've got some other workers to pick up the slack."

"Well . . ." She hadn't worked up the nerve to break the news about her new hire to Pam, who would be absolutely thrilled to have an ex-con as a coworker. "See, I don't have a lot of experience with personnel, like you must have."

He sat up straighter.

"I'm not a big outfit like this. . . ." She tried to assume a look of awe as she gestured around the brightly lit room with its shelves of snack food, refrigerated cases, and displays of lighters, car air fresheners, and beef jerky. "You must all do some serious background and reference checking before you hire someone. . . ."

He grunted in surprise. "You came to *me* to give a reference for Walt?"

"Not a recommendation. Just to know . . . a little."

Steve gnawed on his chapped lower lip. "I'm not sure I can say anything. The station could get sued."

"I doubt that. In any case, this is just an informal talk. I mean,

Walt hasn't really *applied* for a job or anything. I just need to know, in a casual way—you know, person to person?—whether I should be afraid for my life."

He chewed this over for a few seconds more, then came out with it in a rush. "He was a jailbird, but that was a while back, and he finished his parole."

"He told me that himself. He didn't say why, though. . . ."

"I talked to some guy in California, and he told me he's an old druggie. Like, heavy-duty junkie, maybe. Then he knocked over a liquor store and got sent up for that. Armed robbery."

"Oh God."

"I think it was a really long time ago. Like, way back in the nineties. The officer said he'd been clean since then."

"Oh. That's good, I guess." Dandy.

"Yeah, so now he's basically just a washed-up old loser. Can't imagine him working up the energy to rob anybody these days."

She nodded. She was having a hard time squaring the soft-spoken Walt with the words *junkie* and *armed robbery*. "Well, thanks for giving me the info. That's what I needed to know."

"You still going to give him a job?"

"I don't see why not."

"You will, in a couple of days." After a moment, he hunched his shoulders in a shrug. "Then again, he might not even show up for work at all."

"That would solve my problem then, wouldn't it?"

Half of her hoped that Steve's prediction would come true and Walt wouldn't even show up, yet the other half was rooting for the old guy to pull himself back together. So she wasn't entirely disappointed to see him standing by the bakery door when she came downstairs to open up.

"Morning," he said.

She remembered he didn't have a car. "How did you get here?"

"I walked a ways and caught a bus."

Given Leesburg's limited transportation system, there was no telling when he'd left Ferber Road in order to arrive here on time. She still didn't know what she was going to do with him now that she had him.

Inside, she flipped on the light. Usually this was her favorite part of the day—arriving, getting things set up, and beginning a day's work in solitude. Now she tottered around with self-conscious movements, as if she inadvertently found herself on-stage before a live audience. "First thing, I usually make coffee," she said, narrating her own actions for lack of anything else to say. "For myself. Want a cup?"

Walt looked as if he could use a jump-start. His face appeared sallow and puffy, as though he'd just rolled out of bed. He scratched his forearm in a way she'd noticed before. She couldn't tell if he had itchy skin or if it was a nervous tic.

"Thank you, but I don't drink a lot," he said. "And only decaf now."

"I have a pot for decaf, too," she said.

He hurried over. "Then let me make it. You just get on with your business."

This is *my business*, she thought resentfully. But she stepped back, letting him take charge of the coffee as she went around flipping things on—more lights, the computer she kept at the shop, the ovens. "If you need any help . . ."

"I think I've got it," he said. "I've worked in kitchens some."

"Have you?" She imagined the prison mess hall from *The Shaw-shank Redemption*, which was the most intimate experience she'd had with life behind bars.

"Coffee shop back in California." He caught her eye. "That's where I come from."

"Oh?" She did a pretty good job pretending she hadn't known that. At least, she knew that was where he had lived while he was in jail. She had to remind herself that there was probably more to the guy than the fact that he'd done time. "Me too," she said. "Lived there most of my life, in fact."

"Why'd you leave?"

Telling the man her life story wasn't really what she'd planned—

especially the first hour they were stuck together. But she didn't have a lot of other small talk to offer. "I just wanted a change, and a place that would be good for Harvey, my horse." She nodded at the photograph of herself and Harvey. "Actually, when I decided to move from LA, I tossed a dart at a map to decide where."

The map had been attached to a demographic chart at the film distribution company where she'd ended up in a snoozer of a job, with areas of the country color-coded to reflect people's age, disposable income, and movie-going habits. The moment the dart had landed in northern Virginia, it had felt as if the state was calling her. And once she'd hopped on the Internet and viewed the place, with its green hills dotted with horses and its charming small towns, she hadn't been able to resist the lure. She could start over here—live simply and do things she loved, among people who didn't view a normal, unpublicized life as a come-down. It was her second chance at life.

"Maybe it was rash, but I just wanted something different. I needed to retrench."

Walt nodded. "I understand that feeling."

"Why did you leave California?" she asked.

He turned away and started loading the second coffeemaker. "Just looking for something."

That sounded ominous. Maybe it would be best if they tried to avoid chitchat. She retreated to the back of the kitchen and began planning. She preheated the two ovens, which usually stayed on most of the day. She liked to start the day baking the small things that were best fresh—cookies, brownies, cupcakes. The larger cakes she baked later in the day, because cakes usually tasted better after sitting overnight anyway.

She turned to the storage room, but then stopped herself. The room had no windows, just a back door that stayed bolted. Going in there, she would be out of sight of the street. Cornered. Vulnerable.

Oh hell. *If you're that nervous about the old guy, you should tell him to go right now.*

She took a deep breath. "Walt?"

He snapped to attention. "If you want, I can get the floors all washed and shiny for your customers," he offered. "The front window could use cleaning, too. And then . . . didn't you say something about deliveries?"

He hurried past her, into the storage room. Some homing instinct must have told him where she kept the cleaning supplies, because he went right to the broom. "Okay?"

Looking into those hound-dog eyes, she couldn't bring herself to tell him to go. She answered with a nod that was more obedient than enthusiastic. "Okay."

The phone rang and she scrambled for it, hoping it was Pam or Erin. It just so happened that Pam had a showing and wouldn't be in until the afternoon, so all morning Becca would be on her own with the ex-jailbird.

With Walt. She had to stop thinking of him as a jailbird.

Looking at the little display on her phone, she didn't recognize the number, although the area code was Los Angeles. Which was weird, because this was the shop's phone. Also, it would be early in Los Angeles. "Strawberry Cake Shop," she answered.

"Oh—hello!" The woman's voice jangled a nerve. Not that her actual voice sounded familiar, but the tone did. The speaker exclaimed in that show-business eagerness of someone who was "on." It was the phone enthusiasm of actors, agents, and desperate entertainment journalists, the kind of bubbly effusiveness that she could imagine flatlining the instant one party hung up. "I'm trying to reach Rebecca Hudson?"

"Speaking."

"Really? Rebecca Hudson from *Me Minus You?*"

This was odd. Weeks went by now, occasionally even months, without that show cropping up. Seventeen years was a long time, and even in the age of YouTube, video-on-demand, and DVD boxed sets of everything, people had short memories. Most days she was able to convince herself that her attempt to ride off into the sunset had been successful. But this was the second day in a row that someone had sought her out because of the show.

She hesitated before admitting, "Yes, that's me."

"Oh, terrific! Rebecca, my name is Renee Jablonsky. I'm the casting director for the reality show *Celebrities in Peril!* And as it happens, we're putting together a super-special child star edition."

"I hope you mean former child star." Presumably putting actual children in peril wasn't considered entertainment. Yet.

"Correct. And would you believe, Rebecca, that during our round-table session, yours was one of the first names that came up? So many of us here grew up with *Me Minus You* and are such big fans of your work!"

"Thank you. But my work now is making cakes."

"I know—that's so adorable and small towny. It could almost be a TV show! And what great publicity it would be for your little bakery to have you back in the limelight."

Becca was gripping the phone so hard, for a moment she wondered which would crack first—the phone's plastic shell or the bones in her hand. "I'm sorry. It's hard to describe how much I'm not interested in doing a reality show. Especially not one with the word *peril* in the title."

The woman chuckled. "It's actually not dangerous. It's managed risk."

"Uh-huh."

"That business with the shark last season was just extremely bad luck. And Mackenzie totally survived it."

"I don't—"

"The doctors were even able to save her leg—all but one little chunk."

Oh Lord. "I'm sorry, I have a business to run here. And it's not show business."

The woman's skeptical grunt conveyed her firm belief that only fools turned down opportunities to be on television. "Here's the deal, Rebecca. We pay a flat fee for each week that you stay on the show, and it's not really a huge time commitment, because each edition of the show is limited to a six-week run."

"I'm still not interested," Becca said. "In fact, the only thing I'm curious about is how you found the number for my store."

A few too many coincidences had cropped up in the past day. She glanced over at Walt, sweeping between tables at the front of the shop. First, he had been camped outside her store. He was from California. Last night, she'd offered him a job, and now this woman from California was pestering her. Walt certainly didn't look like a television production company spy. . . .

Renee demolished the conspiracy theory. "We Googled you."

An article about her had appeared in the local paper back when she'd opened the bakery, but it hadn't been picked up nationally. Becca was pretty sure the Strawberry Cake Shop wasn't among the top listings on a search of her name.

She brought up the web browser on the shop's little netbook now.

"Some kook wrote a blog about visiting your store," the woman said.

Becca typed her name into the web browser and did a search. Sure enough, the first story that came up was *"My Morning with the Bakery Bitch"* at a blog called Megan's Musings. She skimmed a few lines. "I did not toss a cupcake at her," she grumbled into the phone. "I would never do that. I have respect for cupcakes."

Renee chuckled over the line. "Yeah, well, I got a kick out of it. We like feisty! And when I saw it and realized I could get in touch with you, it just felt lucky, because we'd been trying to hunt you down ever since a couple of *Saved by the Bell* kids fell through."

Hunting her down sounded apt. "I wouldn't think you'd have trouble drumming up talent for your show." She used the word *talent* in its Hollywood sense, meaning warm bodies on a set, not Webster's definition of a person with artistic aptitude. There was no shortage of kids who had strutted before a camera at some time or another, either under their own steam or at the behest of an ambitious stage parent.

"We have lots of candidates, but it's early days yet, and frankly, we're hoping to find someone who can add a little sass to the lineup."

"I'm not sassy, or bitchy," Becca said. "Or if I am, it's just something I do as a non-professional now, for free."

"Well, why give it away?" Renee asked. "Sell it, honey!"

Even as a joke, the insinuation that she should just pimp herself out for financial gain made it all that much easier for her to bring the conversation to an abrupt end. "Thanks for calling, but as I said, I'm not interested. At all. In fact, I'm very busy right now and need to go."

As she clicked the End Call button, she could still hear the tinny voice of Renee Jablonsky bleating at her through the device's tiny speaker.

She blew out a breath.

Walt angled a glance her way. "Something wrong?"

"Oh no. Just a nuisance call."

"You get lots of those?"

"Not really, no." She frowned. "Why would I?"

"I don't know." He shrugged. "Unless it's on account of you were on television."

She felt astonished, and suspicious again. Just whom had she invited into her life? "When did you find that out?" she asked him.

"I knew from looking at you. There are televisions everywhere, even in jails."

"And yet you let me think that you were just a harmless guy sitting on a bench in front of the store. Pam worried you were a bum, but it turns out you're something even worse—a stalker."

"No, I'm not." He eyed her clutching the phone, ready to call 911. "I don't care that you were on TV. But it's a fact, isn't it?"

"Yes, it's a fact. And you didn't mention it."

"I didn't think you would have wanted me to."

"Is this some kind of shakedown? Because let me assure you, the expression 'blood from a turnip' would not be out of place in any kind of extortion scheme involving my finances at the moment."

"I don't want anything. *You* talked to me yesterday, and offered me a ride home," he reminded her. "*You* told me to come in today."

True. Still, a part of her brain wondered if this man had mastered some kind of circumstantial jiujitsu that allowed him to be in the right place at the right time to play on her sympathy and get her to invite him into her life. Which she never should have done. She saw that now. It was madness. She should have given him a twenty-dollar bill to assuage her guilt and then left him alone.

"Look, I know I asked you to come work here, but maybe it would be best if we—"

"Set some ground rules?" he asked, cutting her off. "Fine by me. I won't mention television again. Heck, I don't even like TV."

"That wasn't really what I—"

"And if you want, I'll tell you all about what I did, because you got a right to know."

She thought about this. If he tried to candy-coat his crimes, she would know right off that he was not only a criminal, but an unreformed weasel. "What did you do?"

"Armed robbery. Well, actually, I had a drug possession before that. Then, I got caught robbing a liquor store with a buddy. But I can't even say that it was all his idea and I just drove the car or something like that. I planned it. I got us the guns we used. I was cranked up on coke, which doesn't excuse anything. But just so you know."

Okay, maybe passing the buck wasn't his style. The man still had serious problems. He made her uneasy. Probably had something to do with the words *armed, robbery,* and *cranked up on coke.*

"I'm clean now, though," he assured her. "Have been for over a decade. And I finished my parole."

"Look—"

"I'll just stay a week or two. You don't have to pay me, even. If I could just work one week, and then you could provide me with some kind of reference, that would be a big help."

"You can't work for nothing. That's crazy."

He laughed. "Believe me, I've done it before."

"The Strawberry Cake Shop isn't a lockup."

"But you're just doing this for charitable reasons. I get that, and I appreciate it."

"Look, I might have to pay you minimum wage, but you're not going to be a slave here." Looking into his sad eyes, she felt a surge of anger at herself for being such an idiot as to fear this man. This was how the poor got poorer. How people slid from bad luck to disaster. Because people like her were too uptight, too removed from their own humanity to give them an opportunity. "In fact, forget that—you're an employee here, and you'll start off at the same salary that my other employee started at. It won't make you rich, but . . ."

But maybe it would give him a fighting chance.

"Well, all right. Whatever you say. But it's just for a week." He went back to sweeping. "Or two."

Becca nodded, then froze.

Wait. What had just happened? A minute earlier, she'd intended to tell him to go. Somehow he'd not only succeeded in hanging on, he'd also brought her around to insisting on paying him above minimum wage for the privilege of being on pins and needles for the next week. Or two.

How had he managed that?

Chapter 5

Olivia's current scheme was to combine her love of horses with her upcoming birthday party. "Mom can't say no if it's for my birthday, can she?" She glanced at Matthew but didn't wait for an answer, probably fearing what it would be. "And then, once she sees how fun it is, and how it's not a big deal, she'll let me ride all the time."

"What if some of the people who you might want to have at your birthday party don't like horses?" Matthew asked her.

Her brow puckered. "Why would I want to be friends with someone who doesn't like horses?"

"Because if you limit yourself to people who only like the exact same things you like, you're going to end up with no friends."

"Lots of people like horses."

"Some people are afraid of them."

"Only people like Mom," she scoffed.

"Okay—case in point. Wouldn't you want to be friends with your mom?"

"You mean, if she wasn't my mother?"

"Right."

Olivia's face contorted in thought. "You mean if she was just another kid in middle school?"

"Yes."

"Same grade as me?"

Great. He'd intended this to be one of those slam-dunk questions. "The point is, it's hard enough to find people in the world you want to be friends with without setting up arbitrary boundaries."

"How can it be hard to find people to be friends with?" Olivia asked. "That's crazy. I'm surrounded by a whole school full of people. And then there are, like, hundreds of schools like mine in this country—maybe even thousands—and then hundreds of countries. Right? There are *so many* people in the world, it's mind-boggling. And Mom said I could only invite twelve."

"Yes, I know, but . . ." He'd completely lost the thread of his argument. Conversations with Olivia often ended with him trying to chase down some face-saving pat phrase, and he frantically sought one now. "You don't want to measure people with too rigid a yardstick."

"I'm not measuring anybody," she argued. "I'm just trying to make up a guest list."

He was relieved to approach the cake shop and end the conversation. Twenty feet from the door, however, Olivia stopped dead in her tracks. In front of the shop, a man was sleeping on a bench, his hat pulled over his eyes. A few feet away, a couple of boys leaning against a tree were spitting sunflower seeds at the sleeping man. Olivia's hands flexed into fists, and before Matthew knew what was happening, she exploded into a run. She hit the biggest boy full tilt. "Quit it!" she yelled, nearly knocking him over. The bag of seeds went flying.

The older boy's return shove sent her sprawling to the pavement.

"Hey!" Matthew sped forward.

But Olivia was quicker. Before Matthew reached the melee, she rebounded from the sidewalk and leapt on the boy's back like a pro wrestler. "Leave him alone!" she yelled.

The boy tried to shake her off. "Leave *me* alone, freak!"

Matthew jumped into the fray and pulled Olivia off. She was still bristling with anger. "You're disgusting! I'm going to tell Ms. Andrews what you did!"

"We weren't doing anything." They looked Matthew up and down, obviously trying to size up whether he was an adult who could actually wield any authority. "We were just feeding seeds to the birds."

"Liar!" Olivia yelled.

Matthew glanced over at the man, who was waking now. When he sat up, sunflower seeds cascaded down his clothing. The guy brushed them off with a confused frown.

Why had the man been sleeping on a bench in the middle of Leesburg?

"Come on, Olivia." Belatedly, Matthew added to the boys, "You two should be ashamed of yourselves." Their faces were set in expressions of resentment. Matthew tugged Olivia away from them.

"They shouldn't be able to get away with that," she said, outraged.

"Well . . . the man was asleep. There was no harm done."

"No harm done?" Olivia yelled. "They were *spitting* on him."

"Spitting seeds," he agreed. "I saw."

"It was so mean—and disgusting!" She flashed one last angry stare back. "I'm never sharing my lunch with him again."

"Wait." Matthew spun back, but the two boys were sprinting down the street. "That was Grover?" *That little punk?*

"Grover and his big brother, Justin," Olivia said. "I hate boys."

He shook his head. It was like Hell's Kitchen in Leesburg all of a sudden. He glared at the man on the bench. Weren't there laws against vagrancy? At that moment, another woman passed by the bench, giving wide berth to the man, and Matthew felt a pang as he opened the door for Olivia. Seeing someone treating the man like a pariah made him embarrassed for his own uncharitable thoughts.

As they stood in line, he commented, "It was good of you to stand up for someone less fortunate."

"Do you think that man's homeless?" Olivia asked.

"I don't know." Matthew peered over the people in front of them, catching just a glimpse of the top of Becca's head. She stood at a butcher-block island in the back of the store, chopping something. Another woman with blond hair swirled into a bun was helping customers.

"If he's homeless," Olivia said, "he might be hungry."

"Or he might just be a guy who fell asleep."

She twisted her lips in skepticism. "That bench doesn't look very comfortable. I don't think I could fall asleep there."

It was finally their turn in line. Matthew was prepared just to grab some stuff and leave, but when they reached the counter, Becca noticed them and came forward, smiling. "I thought I spotted you two."

"Olivia insisted we come," he said. "She wanted to—"

"Can I have two carrot cupcakes, please?" Olivia said, interrupting.

"Of course." Becca bagged up the cupcakes and handed them over.

"I'll be right back, Matthew." As soon as the sack touched Olivia's hand, she dashed for the door.

He watched her go, then turned back to Becca. What now? "Well, she *did* want to talk to you. But apparently something's come up."

Becca laughed lightly and leaned against the end of the counter. "Ten-year-olds aren't known for long attention spans."

"When Olivia wants something, her attention can stay fastened on that one thing as if it had been bolted to her brain. I don't know why . . ." He glanced at the closed door, as if it would offer him some clues about the vagaries of Olivia's behavior.

"Well, at any rate, I'm glad I have the chance to thank you." His expression must have reflected his cluelessness, because Becca added, "For your wise counseling last night."

He had to think for a moment to remember. *Stranger danger,* or something like that. "Did it do you any good?"

"Sort of. I took your advice—trust but verify—but then ignored the findings."

He frowned. "Look, if you're in some kind of trouble . . ." He was about to tell her that she should go to the police, or consult a lawyer, but she waved away his second attempt to give advice.

"Nah, I think it will all work out."

The woman behind the counter with her released a skeptical grunt, which was the first time Matthew realized anyone was listening to them.

Becca smiled again, more tightly. "But thanks for the offer—and for the late-night help. If you're ever out of work, you could find a second career as an agony aunt."

"Have Platitudes, Will Travel." He laughed. "Something tells me I'm better off as a government policy analyst."

"Is that what you do?"

"I'm afraid so. Not exactly Palladin."

The woman behind the counter tapped Becca's shoulder and nodded toward the front window. "What's going on out there?"

Matthew turned. While he'd been talking with Becca, a drama had been unfolding in front of the store. A police cruiser idled at the curb, its lights flashing, and a group had gathered.

Olivia. He hurried for the door. He should have been paying attention, not chatting with the cake lady. As he stepped out of the shop, the scene in progress stunned him. The crowd was bigger than he'd expected. In the center of it all were two uniformed officers, the guy who'd been sleeping on the bench, and Olivia.

Olivia, to his dismay, was standing at a rigid forward-leaning angle, like an attack dog preparing to charge. At a cop.

"He was *not!*" she shouted at one of the uniformed men.

Oh Lord. Matthew muscled forward through the crowd.

Olivia rolled her eyes in relief when she saw him. "Matthew, tell them that he wasn't bothering me."

He tensed. Someone had been bothering her? "Who?"

"Walt," she said in exasperation, and then pointed to the man on the bench.

Matthew's brain tried to catch up. How had Olivia managed to strike up a first-name acquaintance with a street person? She'd only left the shop a few minutes ago.

The cop explained. "Sir, we received a phone tip that this man was bothering people. When we drove up, we found him with this young lady . . ."

The man named Walt blinked in confusion. "I just fell asleep. I didn't mean to harm anybody. Especially not the girl."

"He didn't hurt me," Olivia said. "That's idiotic!"

"Olivia . . ." Matthew said, smiling nervously at the policemen.

"Well, it is," she insisted. "*I* bugged *him*. First, I woke him up when the boys were spitting seeds at him, and then I wanted to give him a cupcake."

Was that why she had peeled out of the cake shop? So she could give away her spare cupcake?

The second cop looked at Walt. "Sir, we have regulations about sleeping in public spaces here. Vagrancy laws. If you don't have a place to stay . . ."

"I didn't mean to fall asleep," Walt said. "I just dozed off, is all."

Someone jostled past Matthew. Becca.

"He's not a vagrant," she told the policeman. "Walt works for me. I'm sure he didn't mean to break the law."

"No, I didn't." Walt's answer, spoken to Becca, seemed as much to reassure her as the two cops.

"It was Grover and Justin Sams who called you," Olivia said. "I'd bet anything on it. They were spitting seeds at Walt while he was asleep, and I chased them off. *They're* the ones you should arrest. They live over on Loudoun Street. I don't know the number, but I can show you the house."

Olivia was fired up and ready to go, but one of the cops stopped her. "We're not arresting anyone. We received a complaint, so we had to check it out. We're just glad no one was hurt."

Walt looked apologetic. "I'm sorry, officers. It won't happen again."

"That's fine." With a nod of agreement, the cop and his partner circled back to their cruiser.

The crowd started to break up.

"Walt, come on in," Becca said. "I'll get you some coffee."

"Just a sip of decaf would hit the spot," he said. "If it's no trouble."

Matthew was eager to hustle Olivia away from there. "Stupid Grover," she muttered.

"Yes, Grover is stupid, but you shouldn't talk to the police like that."

"How? I was just telling them the truth, and they were being so slow and stupid."

"I think *methodical* and *thorough* are the right words in this context," he told her.

"Okay, but all those people were standing around looking at Walt like he was a criminal. I had to say something. You were the one who told me it was good to stand up for people."

"Yeah, but . . ." They'd gone a few steps when he remembered that he still owed Becca for the cupcakes. He turned back around and flagged her down as she was going inside. "Wait—I forgot to pay you."

She stopped in the door as if she intended to block him bodily from approaching the cash register. "Those cupcakes are on the house, with my thanks."

"Thanks?" he asked.

"For standing up for Walt." She smiled at Olivia. "But bringing that man cupcakes was like bringing coals to Newcastle. I might not be able to pay people much, but people who work for me get all the cupcakes they want."

Olivia's eyes bugged. "Wow. Can I work for you?"

Becca laughed. "Maybe in a few years."

"I thought maybe Walt was hungry," Olivia explained. "He looked homeless."

"Olivia—" Matthew warned.

Before he could finish the rebuke, Becca interrupted him. "Forget it. I hope if I'm ever in trouble, someone like Olivia will be on my side."

Olivia tugged on Matthew's jacket. "Can we stay? I wanted to ask her about the stables."

Matthew hesitated. "I need to get back, O."

Becca stepped down and walked right up to Olivia. "Tell you what. If you ever want to try riding, I'll take you out with Harvey."

Oh great, Matthew thought, just as Olivia exploded with joy.

"Seriously?" Olivia asked.

Becca must have caught his less-than-thrilled expression, because she added the caveat, "If your mom will let you."

Olivia stopped hopping with elation and came back down to earth with a thud. "Oh."

"I really appreciate what you did today," Becca told her again. "Thank you."

Olivia shrugged. "I'm sorry I blurted out the bit about Grover and his brother spitting on Walt. I didn't mean to tell him that part. I hope he's not upset."

"He'll be okay. He's survived worse, I think."

Her attempt to make Olivia feel better caused Matthew to smile in gratitude. He mouthed a thank-you at Becca and pulled Olivia away, back toward home.

"It would be so awesome if I could learn to ride," she said, obviously unable to suppress the dream. "And on Harvey!"

"I know, but . . ."

"Mom'll never let me," she finished for him. "Why does she have to be against the one thing I really want?"

"She's looking out for you. She doesn't want you to get hurt."

Olivia rolled her eyes. "I wouldn't get hurt. Doesn't she know what this means to me? It's all I ever talk about."

"But you've probably wanted other things and then forgotten about them once you had them." He was thinking about her Xbox, which she seemed freakishly indifferent to.

She crossed her arms as she marched alongside him. "When I

grow up, I'm going to get a horse, and maybe I'll go to the Olympics and get a gold medal. And then Mom'll see that she was wrong."

He would have smiled, but her solemn expression sobered him. It would be easy to shrug off her words as the dreams of a ten-year-old. But if ten-year-olds didn't dream big—and occasionally realize those dreams—where would the world be?

"I wish you could talk to her," she said.

"I do, too," he said. "But she's your mom, and I'm . . ."

Olivia's head bobbed in a sage nod. "I know—she'll never listen to you. You're just the babysitter."

After closing, Becca rushed upstairs to get ready for Not-Book-Club night. Her apartment, which for untold years had been used as warehouse space above the hardware store, remained half-finished—a testament to her weak financial planning skills. The only part she had renovated was the kitchen, because she'd had to install it from scratch and fixing it up had cost more than she expected. So now one side of the cavernous loft held a gourmet kitchen with granite counters, custom cabinets, the biggest refrigerator she could afford, and an island surrounded by almost-comfortable bar stools. The rest of the place was rough exposed brick and unfinished Sheetrock, peeling ceiling and window paint, pitted flooring and baseboards missing in action.

For a while, she'd tried to use partitions to divide the open room into homey stations—a living room station, a study area, her bedroom. But after Erin had dubbed her décor "call center cozy," she'd scrapped most of the partitions. Now there remained just one decorative screen blocking off her bed and old wardrobe from the kitchen. Although sometimes she wondered why she bothered. Except on Not-Book-Club nights, she was the only person up here.

Still, she thanked heaven for the screen now as she tossed unfolded laundry, shoes, and cat toys behind it. Then she did a quick sweep of the wide pine plank floors.

Soon after she moved to Leesburg, she'd bought the building

with the intention of opening the bakery on the ground floor and renting out the upstairs. By the time of her wedding, the loft still remained unrenovated and unrented. In hindsight, she suspected there was a subconscious reason she'd set the rent so high that she'd had no takers. Even before the wedding, when she'd de-bated the wisdom of marrying Cal so quickly and moving out to Butternut Knoll, the thought *if it doesn't work out there's always the warehouse* had flitted through her mind on more than one occa-sion. The memory made her cringe in shame. Jumping into a marriage with one eye on the groom and one eye on an escape hatch/refuge had been wrong. Just wrong. She'd been old enough to know better, but foolish enough to plunge ahead anyway.

The marriage, of course, was a huge misstep, which she'd real-ized almost before the ink was dry on the license. The only thing she could say in her defense was that she'd tried to right the wrong as soon as possible, moving into the warehouse before their six-month anniversary had rolled around.

She performed a swift tidying up of the kitchen, and went over her one rug with the vacuum, which never failed to send the cats scurrying under the bed. Seeing as how they had both been rescued from much rougher lives as barn cats, Willie and Cash should have been fearless. Willie, a scrappy gray tabby, was three-legged, and her black cat, Cash, was missing an eye. Both were old-to-ancient. Cal had been contemplating putting them down before a fox finished them off, the fate of one of their con-temporaries, so Becca had stepped in and brought them to the loft. Except for their terror of the vacuum, they had made the transition from near-feral barn cats to pampered feline domestic royalty surprisingly well. To spare their feelings, she ran the vile machine as rarely as possible. Also, she hated to vacuum.

Pam was the first to arrive. She eyed the ubiquitous cupcakes Becca had arranged on a platter and sighed. "I brought a salad as-sortment."

"I thought you were going to make lasagna."

"I was." She nodded toward the cupcakes. "But lately I've been eating so many of those little bastards, I have to go light to compensate. Ever since I started working at the shop, my diet consists of equal parts butter, sugar, and celery."

"I know that feeling. In the beginning, about eighty percent of my daily intake of calories was cupcakes." Now that her recipes needed less "testing" and her days weren't quite so frantic, she'd achieved a better nutritional equilibrium.

"And yet you're still thin," Pam said in disgust. "Must be your Hollywood genes."

That was rich. In Hollywood, during her worst gawky adolescent phase, she'd been hanging out offstage during a long day of filming when she'd overheard the director tell someone to "get the little heifer onto the set, pronto." She'd laughed to herself and peered through a crack in the wall to see who would be dragged onstage. Abby Wooten had been really snarky to her lately, so she'd secretly hoped it was her.

Becca was still peeking when the assistant director had tugged on her sleeve.

"You're needed, kiddo," he'd said.

She could still remember flailing through the next scene, heat shooting through her body in waves. She'd only had two lines of dialogue, but her flubs had caused six retakes. Just moving her arms and legs had required effort—with every movement of her awkward body, she could feel the director's cold eye on her. Even her mouth and lungs couldn't seem to coordinate that day. She wondered how many others on the set had caught the "little heifer" comment. When she looked over and saw Abby's smirk, she had her answer. Everybody had heard it.

Usually she was able to laugh at herself, but not that afternoon. She had been too worried that she'd open her mouth and a ruminant bray would come out.

"They want waifs," her agent had said sharply, months later when she was out of work. "Waifs are in. Or gamins. Maybe when you get a growth spurt and you lose that daddy-long-legs thing, you'll be a gamin."

The growth spurt had come, but gamin or not, casting directors no longer cared. By that time, Becca's name had become synonymous with cancelled sitcoms and shelved pilots. She'd lost her momentum. The only other part of any significance came when she was almost fifteen, when she'd gotten the mean girl guest part in _Malibu High School_. Abby was a regular cast member on the show, playing the queen bee mean girl at MHS. After a few episodes, the producers suddenly decided that they had one meanie too many, and sent Becca's character over a cliff in a convertible. The fiery crash had also finished off her career, and any semblance of friendship with Abby.

During her late teens and early twenties, she'd told herself that she didn't care, that she could fit in somewhere else. She found a job with a production company when she'd dropped out of college, but working behind the scenes had never felt right, either.

So, no, she didn't carry the Hollywood gene, whatever that was. She just bore the scars. But that was hard to explain without provoking a cry-me-a-river reaction. Most people didn't get the concept of being washed up at the age of fifteen, or couldn't guess what it felt like to become a has-been before you'd ever had a chance to consciously decide to be anything.

To divert the conversation onto a more pleasant topic, she snapped open Pam's Tupperware lids and hunted down serving spoons. "The stuff you brought looks yummy."

Pam sighed, and Becca sensed it wasn't about the food. "What are you going to do about Walt?" Pam asked her.

"Why should I have to do anything about him? He's fine."

"No, he's not. He's a hobo with a criminal record."

She'd felt compelled to warn Pam about Walt's jail time, since she would probably be in the store alone with him from time to time. "He's not a hobo," she said. "He has a place to live."

Mentioning the Marquis didn't help her case any. The whole town knew what Pam thought of that seedy place. "He passed out on the sidewalk," Pam said.

"He just nodded off. It could've happened to anybody."

"On a bench?" Pam shot her a disbelieving stare. "Who does that?"

Hobos, Becca thought.

"Also, have you noticed his skin? It's so flaky you can see it coming off of him in drifts. It's disgusting."

"Okay, so he's a little crusty." Becca uncorked a bottle of wine. "Have some sympathy. He's old, poor, and he lives in a noisy apartment complex."

"He's not that old. He's still young enough to be a serial killer," Pam said. "Anyway, lots of people are old, and they don't sleep on the job."

Becca poured out two glasses. "I'm not going to fire him for falling asleep on a break." She wasn't Steve. "That's what breaks are for."

Pam drummed her nails on the granite. "You'll feel different about your protégé when you discover he's taken all the money from the register and hotfooted it out of town."

"That's not going to happen."

"Wanna bet?"

Becca thought for a moment before she decided to call Pam's bluff. By the time Erin knocked at the door, twenty dollars was riding on the chance that Walt would rob her blind.

"Great," Becca said as she went to answer the door. "If I lose, I'll be broke. I'll have to borrow the twenty dollars from you to pay off the debt."

Pam laughed. "You're right. Either way, I'm out twenty dollars."

Erin crossed the threshold, nonplussed by their laughter. "What's so funny?"

"We were placing bets on whether Becca's new employee will rip her off."

"The hobo?" Erin asked.

Becca sighed. Maybe she was fighting a losing battle. But she wasn't ready to give up on Walt yet. She told him she'd keep him on for a couple of weeks, and that was what she intended to do.

Erin put her clutch purse down on the counter, handed Becca a baguette and another bottle of wine, and perched on a bar stool next to Pam.

"I heard you have a boyfriend," Erin said to Becca. "Some dreamy single dad who likes cupcakes."

Becca had to think for a moment before she realized that Erin was talking about what's-his-name. Matthew. She shot a playfully accusatory look at Pam.

"The guy with the kid is cute," Pam said, "you have to admit that."

"He's also married," Becca added. "Or as good as. The kid is his girlfriend's daughter. The girl's come into the store lots of times—she loves to yak at me about horses—but I don't think I've ever seen her mother."

Pam took a moment to absorb this new information. "What a jerk. He flirts with you every time he comes in."

"No, he doesn't. He's never tried to pass himself off as available. We've just talked a few times—idle chitchat." Becca frowned. "Except the one time I met him by chance at the grocery store. I was worried about what to do about Walt, and Matthew gave me some advice."

"Is he who I have to thank for having a serial killer as a coworker?" Pam asked.

"Walt is not a serial killer. And Matthew warned me against blindly taking Walt's word—so there."

"So I have him to thank for giving you advice that you chose to ignore," Pam grumbled. "I wish you'd asked me instead."

"I knew what you'd say." Becca tried to veer the conversation off the subject of Walt. "The point is, Matthew's as good as married, he has an adorable kid, and I'm not a home wrecker. So that's that."

Pam looked vaguely disappointed. "It's so strange that you haven't dated anybody since your divorce. Poor Cal would probably have felt better if you *had* met someone. I think he's still confused about why you would run away and move into this squat. He's in a rut."

Becca and Cal had never analyzed their bust-up in depth. It had been obvious that their marriage had been a mistake brought on by infatuation intersecting with an alcohol-fueled weekend in Vegas, so a full rundown of its failure had never seemed necessary to Becca. Pam usually seemed more curious about the state of their post-divorce relationship than Becca was. "Cal was always in a rut," she told Pam. "The rut of permanent adolescence."

Erin, who had been uncharacteristically silent up to now, gazed around the apartment almost affectionately. Which was odd, since Erin had fussy decorative taste and usually complained about the cat fur and the echo. Now she looked as if she'd never been there before. "This place. I love it. It's so minimalist."

"That's a generous way to describe it," Pam said.

"I'm serious," Erin said. "It's such a refuge. I wish I had something like this."

The word *refuge* put Becca's trouble antennae on high alert. She couldn't help remembering her own thoughts about the warehouse during her marriage. Was Erin in some kind of distress? Erin's colonial house was the pride of her life. The place she wanted to raise a family, when she and Bob finally started one.

Pam flashed a quick, raised-brow glance at Becca before focusing on Erin again. "You have a refuge. It's called your house."

Erin shrugged. "Yeah, but . . ."

Becca poured Erin a glass of wine. "Is something wrong?"

Erin took a long time weighing the question before answering. "Probably not."

"*Probably* not?" Pam repeated.

"It's Bob." Erin bit her lip. "I think he's having an affair."

The statement sucked air out of the room.

"There's this woman at work," Erin said in a rush. "You know—the old story. A few months ago, I found an Ann Taylor jacket in the backseat of his car. Bland business attire, not anything I'd wear. He told me that a colleague must have left it there one day after they'd gone out to lunch."

"Sounds reasonable," Becca said.

Erin nodded. "That's what I thought at the time. No big deal, right? But then, a week later, I walked into Bob's study without knocking, and the minute he saw me, he slammed his computer shut—like he was terrified I would see what he was doing. He saw me and then *thunk!* MacBook closed."

"Hmph." Pam tapped her fingers, thinking. "Maybe he was looking at porn."

Erin dismissed the possibility with a wave. "Oh, Bob knows I don't care about his porn thing."

Miraculously, Becca and Pam avoided gawping at each other. *Bob has a porn thing?*

"Sure he doesn't have a secret life as a spy?" Becca asked, grasping for any other explanation for his secrecy, and also to lighten the grim mood. After all . . . a jacket, an incident with the computer . . . these didn't necessarily add up to infidelity.

"That actually crossed my mind," Erin said. "But I don't think he'd be good at it. He can't even hide what he's up to when he's all the way across the country."

"I forgot." Bob was supposed to be gone for most of the month. "But maybe it's good that he's away right now," Becca said.

"If he's not in the office, he's not around Ann Taylor," Pam pointed out.

"That's what I hoped," Erin said. "But things have been weird since he left. He never calls me."

"You haven't talked to him since he left?" Pam asked.

"I have, but I call him. Every time."

Becca let out a breath. This was sounding less like a sordid, other-woman scenario and more like a typical long-distance relationship problem.

"Wouldn't you expect your husband to call you?" Erin glanced over her wineglass at both of them.

"Don't ask me," Pam said. "Everything I know about marriage, I've learned from *Cosmo* and TV. So, basically, all couples are doomed . . . unless you memorize infinite lists of ten things to keep your man happy in the sack."

Becca shot her a look. *Way to put her fears at rest, Pam.*

Erin seemed too absorbed in her own thoughts to notice. "This morning I called Bob, and Ann Taylor answered his phone. 'This is Nicole,' she said. Very brusque and businessy. I thought I had the wrong number. I said, 'I'm trying to reach Bob.' There was a long silence, and then the woman said, 'Oh—this is so weird. I must have picked up his phone by mistake.'"

Erin watched them for their reactions. Becca tried to keep her expression neutral, but Pam let out a groan. "Wonder how *that* happened!"

"It might be the truth." Becca felt skeptical, but she didn't want to throw fuel on Erin's smoldering suspicions. "She obviously was at work, right? She answered the phone in a businesslike way, you said."

"But when would the phones have gotten switched?" Erin asked. "How? Except maybe if they'd both left their phones out—say, on a table in a hotel room—and picked up the wrong ones in the morning when they were rushing out the door."

Becca frowned. "There could be other ways . . ."

"Plus, it's Nicole." Erin took another slug of wine. Becca made a mental note to stop after one bottle was consumed. "Bob talks about Nicole all the time—about how brilliant she is. They both went to MIT, a detail that's come up about a hundred times. Natch. He loves to remind me that I'm a college dropout, and make cracks about how I don't have a profession."

Becca hated Bob, but she tried not to allow her feelings against Despicable He to run amok. "But maybe it's not"—*an affair* sounded so soap opera–ish, and Erin's thoughts seemed to be melodramatic enough already—"serious. Maybe he just thinks she's smart and an asset to his team."

"Of course she's an asset," Erin said, finishing off her glass of wine as if she were swallowing down the last sip of bitterness. "She's brilliant and beautiful. Probably talented in all sorts of ways."

"So? You're beautiful, too," Becca said. "And smart."

Erin buried her head in her hands. "I wasn't smart enough not to marry some guy who was going to run off with the first coworker who smiled at him. I wasn't smart enough to try to make something of my life so I wouldn't feel so lost now."

"Enough with the self-loathing," Pam said. "*You're* not the problem—it's what Bob's up to that's causing trouble. We need to do a house search for serious evidence. Do you know his passwords?"

Becca shook her head. "No, no. You can't go snooping like that."

Pam blinked at her. "How would you do it?"

"I wouldn't snoop at all. It's not right. How would you feel if someone dug through all your files and stuff? If Bob hasn't done anything and then he finds out that Erin's been spying on him, she's going to come off as a paranoid nut wife."

"Well, if you're going to be all ethical . . ." Pam took a sip of wine and turned back to Erin. "Is Nicole married?"

Erin shrugged. "I can't remember."

"We should find that out, at least," Pam said.

Becca shook her head. "The other woman—and we don't even know if she is that, in the lurid sense—doesn't matter. Neither does her marital status. The person who matters to Erin is Bob, because he *is* married."

Erin bit her lip, considering. "No, I don't think that matters so much. At least, not to him."

Becca planted her hands on her hips. "Why wouldn't it matter that Bob swore a vow to love you till death do you part?"

"Because he made that exact same vow to someone before me." Erin smiled miserably. "And then I came along."

Chapter 6

Nicole arrived home late the next Friday night for a weekend visit and proceeded to collapse. She slept in Saturday morning while Matthew and Olivia worked like elves in the kitchen, trying not to make too much noise. Olivia insisted that her mother's homecoming, however temporary, called for waffles. Matthew was pretty sure the waffles would be a self-serving gesture. He cut up a fruit salad.

When Nicole stumbled into the kitchen and saw them, she smiled. "You don't know how good it is not to be heading down to a crappy breakfast buffet."

Olivia left her waffle station long enough to give her mom a hug. "I'd love to live in a hotel. Like Eloise."

"Eloise wasn't at a Best Western," Nicole said. Matthew handed her a cup of coffee and she took a seat at the breakfast table. "What's been going on around here?"

Olivia breathlessly cataloged the events of the past weeks, culminating in the story about giving a cupcake to the man she thought was homeless—"Only he wasn't, he just looked it"—and standing up to Leesburg's finest on his behalf. "And now the cake lady says I can ride Harvey any time I want. Harvey's her horse."

The silence that followed bristled with Nicole's we-are-not-pleased vibes.

"I've got an idea for my birthday," Olivia said. "I could have a horse party."

"It's a little late for that, isn't it? I mean, that's a lot to arrange." Nicole flicked a glance at Matthew. "For one thing, we'd need to come up with twelve horses in two weeks."

"I bet Becca could help," Olivia said.

Nicole blinked. "Becca?"

"The cake lady," Matthew and Olivia explained in unison.

"Oh right." Nicole stared thoughtfully at her empty plate. "Well . . . I'll think about it."

Olivia looked as if she might drop the batter ladle. "You will?"

Matthew was stunned, too.

Nicole smiled as if their surprise was coming out of left field. "Let me have a few cups of coffee before I commit to anything, but I don't see why the idea should be off the table."

Maybe because it went against every opinion she'd ever stated on the subject? Matthew wondered what had happened to make her consider changing her mind.

Showing incredible restraint, Olivia didn't beg or wheedle. Probably she knew better than to push her luck. "Are you going to be back for Career Day at school?" she asked, already moving on to the next thing.

"When is it?" Nicole asked.

"The Wednesday after my birthday."

"Oh. I should be," Nicole said. "I think we'll finish up somewhere around then."

That *somewhere* didn't escape Matthew.

"Can I sign you up to talk? I could get my class contribution over with for the year."

"Your what?" Matthew asked.

"Everybody has to either bring a show-and-tell, or give a talk about vacation or a favorite book or something, or bring someone to Fall Career Day or Spring Career Day."

Matthew laughed. "So a kid can either bring his pet turtle or his mother and they both count for the same?"

"Turtles are really interesting," Olivia said. "More interesting than some people's parents, for sure. I wish I could have one."

Nicole lifted her hands. "Please. No reptiles. I'll be glad to show up myself and do a short presentation." She spooned some fruit salad onto her plate. "And on the off chance that I can't make it, Matthew could substitute for me. He might be as entertaining as a turtle."

Olivia's brow crinkled. "Matthew?"

He took a deep breath. "Don't worry, Olivia. My talk about writing economic impact studies always knocks 'em cold."

He was a little confused as to why he might have to substitute for Nicole, though. If she was going to be back for the birthday party, surely the Career Day afterward wasn't in question. And why had she opened the door to a birthday party at a stable? When he and Nicole were clearing up the breakfast things, he took advantage of Olivia's not being within earshot to ask.

"I thought you were dead-set against horses," he reminded her.

Nicole sighed. "I really don't know about Olivia. Why couldn't she be like every other kid in the world and want a cat or dog?"

"I'm sure she wouldn't turn one down if you wanted to give her one."

"Well, I don't, particularly. At least horses don't shed all over the house."

"It's not that crazy a wish. Lots of kids want to learn to ride, especially around here. Raising a girl in horse country and telling them they can't ride is a little like raising a kid by the ocean and telling them they shouldn't swim."

"I guess you're right," Nicole said. "I was hoping the mania would fade, but it obviously won't."

Was she actually relenting?

Nicole rinsed a cup in the sink and handed it to him to transfer to the dishwasher. "It's not just that I'm tired of rehashing the horse argument for the umpty-millionth time. The way things are going out in Oregon, maybe the timing isn't that bad to give Olivia a treat. Absentee mom guilt is wearing me down."

He frowned. "Did something go wrong with the test?"

Her groan said it all, but she added, "It's a train wreck. There's no way I'll be finished out there in a week, or even probably two weeks. In fact, by the time Olivia's birthday rolls around, I might be stuck in Hawaii."

His brain scrambled to keep up. First, she'd never mentioned the possibility of the test site moving to Hawaii. Second, who in their right mind would ever feel *stuck* in Hawaii? "You're going to Hawaii? When?"

"Next week," she said.

"You and Bob?"

"Of course. He's the lead engineer."

"I know . . . but both of you need to go? And why Hawaii?"

"Some of the equipment isn't functioning well. It's a little hard to explain to a layman, but we need to investigate how the hydrofoils respond under different wave velocity conditions, and confer about partnering with a company that has another project underway in Hawaii."

"Couldn't you just Skype?" he blurted out.

"Sure," she shot back. "I could just call in while everybody else is on site doing all the work."

"I'm sorry," he said. "Dumb suggestion."

"Look, if taking care of Olivia's too much for you, I guess I could send her to my mom's for a few weeks. I just hated to take her out of school in the middle of the semester. But if it's too much trouble . . ."

"No," he said quickly, ashamed to have sounded reluctant, or impatient. "I'm happy to stay here a few more weeks. As long as it takes. I'm sort of getting the single dad routine down, actually."

She shook her head. "I'll call Mom."

"Honestly, Nicole—it's no problem."

"Is your boss hassling you about not being in your office all the time?"

"No, of course not," he said. "On paper, at least, the Feds are supposed to encourage telecommuting and flextime."

"You don't have to work from home so much. I could get Olivia back in at the Y after school."

"She says she hates it there, and I don't like the idea of being so far away in case something comes up with her during the day. It's no problem."

Nicole nodded. "Lucky thing your job's low-pressure enough that it doesn't matter so much."

He frowned at her dismissive tone—it was almost the same one Olivia had used when she'd called him the babysitter. Okay, he wasn't doing innovative research that had the potential to save the planet, but still . . .

"So why all the concern about my going to Hawaii?" she asked.

Did she really need it spelled out? "I miss you."

She grasped his hand. "Aw—that's a sweet thing to say." Letting go, she added, "Believe me, I'll be back as soon as I can. But in the meantime, do you think you could manage a birthday party with twelve eleven-year-olds?"

He gulped. "You mean, arrange the party?"

"Yeah. And you might need to oversee it, if I can't get back in time. In fact, maybe you should just plan on that."

"Okay, but—"

"You're good at research stuff. Or maybe . . . maybe you could talk to the cake lady? You seem to have an in there, and she's got that horse Olivia's always talking about. She might be able to steer us toward a whatchacallit."

"Stable?" Olivia was going to be ecstatic.

"Do you think she could give you some guidance?" Nicole asked.

"Probably."

"Good. Ask her." She let out a sigh. "At least if Olivia is going to get involved with horsey types, it will be with celebrity-caliber people and not just the typical local yokels."

He drew back in confusion. "Celebrity?"

Nicole laughed. "Don't tell me you didn't know that the cake lady is our local celeb."

Becca? "The woman who owns the Strawberry Cake Shop?"

"You've lived in Leesburg six months and you haven't heard this? They even wrote her up in the paper once. She used to be on some sitcom. *Me Minus You.* It was such a dumb show—I never missed an episode when I was ten. Didn't you recognize her? Rebecca Hudson."

Rebecca Hudson. It was one of those second-tier celebrity names that got burned into your brain without your knowing quite how. But suddenly, it all made sense. "I thought I had met her before or something," he said. "It was driving me crazy."

"Talk to her and see what she says. Or just comb the Internet. If you hook up with anyplace where a party's doable on such short notice, go for it. We can spring it on Olivia."

"Don't you want to let her know what's going on now?"

"Oh God, no. If we told her what we were up to, we'd never hear the end of it. I was hoping to rest this weekend, not be dragged around to horse barns."

"I'll see what I can do."

"I certainly don't expect you to stick around here all week-end," she told him. "This is your chance to rest, too. You probably haven't been in your place much these past few weeks."

"I haven't missed it." Nicole's house had begun to seem more like home than his empty town house.

But he caught her drift. Nicole had been living in hotels and surrounded by work and coworkers. She probably craved some quiet alone time with Olivia.

On the way back to his place, he thought about Becca. Rebecca Hudson. He hadn't really watched *Me Minus You* unless someone else in his family just happened to be looking at it. He had vague memories of sitting through it with his sisters. But that evidently had been enough to make her seem familiar to him. It wasn't some kind of special connection between himself and Becca, then. It was just the same connection everyone between the ages of twenty and forty probably felt toward her. Nothing special at all.

When he stopped the car, he looked around him in confusion. He'd thought he was driving to his place. Instead, he was parked right in front of the Strawberry Cake Shop.

He'd intended to wait till later in the afternoon to talk to her, but since he was here . . .

It was still early, and there weren't any people around. In fact, they weren't even quite open yet. When Matthew peered through the door, the older guy, Walt, appeared, broom in hand, unlocked the door, and beckoned him in.

"We got a visitor," he called out to Becca.

She hurried over, wearing a Strawberry Cake Shop bib apron over a long-sleeved T-shirt and jeans.

"She doesn't like early birds," her doorkeeper said, "but we'll make an exception for you or Olivia."

While Walt went back to sweeping, Matthew quickly explained his party dilemma to Becca. As he spoke, it occurred to him how little he knew about arranging a tween birthday party, horses, and hosting parties in general. As he wound up by telling her that this all needed to happen two weeks from today, he was already gearing up for her to say that there was no way. Her lips were pursed into a frown.

"Maybe I shouldn't be bugging you about this?" he asked in conclusion. "I just thought since you have a horse, you might know of a stable with the facilities for something like this. . . ."

"Oh, I know just the place," she assured him. "I can probably get you a good rate, too. The barn where I keep Harvey would be perfect, and I have an in with the owner."

"Great." So why did she look so doubtful?

"It's the timing that could be a problem," she said, reading his mind. "I'll have to check with the owner to see if the stable is available that day, and if he can get everything set up. You'll need to get parents to sign releases. . . ."

"You mean, legal papers?"

"Riding isn't necessarily dangerous, but horses are animals, and unpredictable. Accidents happen. Parents have to know that, and be able to accept it."

"Okay. That makes sense." He thought of Nicole. She would probably be the person who would have the hardest time signing a release.

"Also, the parents have to be advised to dress the kids in appropriate clothes. They don't have to show up in paddock boots and jodhpurs, but party dresses won't work, either."

"Olivia's not really a party dress kind of girl," he said.

She nodded.

"Excuse me." Walt shuffled forward. "I shouldn't be eavesdropping, but I was. I'd like to pay for Olivia's birthday cake. You can take it out of my pay, Rebecca."

"Becca," she corrected him automatically.

"Becca," he said. "Please."

She shook her head. "I'll provide the cake."

Matthew stepped in before they got into a useless argument. "I'm happy to buy the cake myself. It's not a problem."

"The cake is on the house," she insisted. "I'll call Cal about scheduling the party."

"Cal?"

"The stable owner. He's also my ex-husband."

This new information sprinted through his mind. *So she was married . . . no, divorced . . . but evidently still had a relationship with the guy.* He'd just watched *His Girl Friday* with Olivia. Now "exhusband" called to mind Cary Grant.

Not that it mattered.

"That's great," he said. Then, seeing the confused pinch of her brows, he added quickly, "Great for me, that you know someone."

"If there's a conflict, I'll let you know. Also, if the weekend you need is free, I should probably take you over to Butternut Knoll to check the place out. Would sometime Monday be okay? The shop's closed then, so it would work best for me."

"Monday would be good." He couldn't believe that this was actually falling into place so easily.

"That way you can see what you're getting yourself into."

"A tween birthday party? I'm not sure I can know what I'm in for until I'm in the center of it."

She smiled. "And then it will be too late to turn back."

"I can't turn back now anyway. What would the alternative be? I don't think having the usual movie night and slumber party will work."

"Why not?"

"A single guy overseeing a dozen eleven-year-olds? That wouldn't go over very well. Most of the moms around here seem to see me as an oddity as it is."

"That's crazy. Believe me, you're doing as good a job as most parents. And certainly better than a lot of dads." She reached for a business card and began to write on the back, pressing down with such vehemence that he half-expected the pen's point to cut right through the card stock.

For some reason, he felt the need to reassure her. "I was just guessing. Most of the moms have been great. Very helpful, actually."

She offered him the card. "Here. You can usually reach me here, but just in case a question crops up when we're closed, I wrote down my home phone and my e-mail."

"Thanks," he said, taking it. "So you'll let me know what you hear from Ca—?" He almost said Cary.

"Cal," she said. "Yeah, I'll give you a buzz. Which would be easier if I knew your number, right?"

He fumbled to give her one of his cards.

She glanced at it and tossed it next to the register. "I'll call you as soon as I have news."

He bought a cupcake as a snack for later and left the shop feeling buoyed—because he'd taken the first step toward having Olivia's party in hand. It had nothing to do with having Becca's number in his pocket.

That was just business.

When she called to confirm that Butternut Knoll was available for a party on Olivia's birthday, Becca had offered Matthew a ride out to the stables on Monday. He wasn't about to refuse. Though he had lived in Leesburg for half a year, he hadn't explored the area enough to familiarize himself with the more pastoral byroads off the well-beaten path of the freeway in and out of DC. Beyond that stretched an unknown patchwork of quaint towns, McMansion subdivisions, farms, and Civil War memorials. If he tried to find the stables on his own, he'd probably end up lost on a battle-field.

Also, this gave him more time to talk to Becca.

On a whim, he Googled her and found lots of pictures of an adorable little kid he recognized now both from memory and from his new acquaintance with the grown-up Becca. Also, the search resulted in the occasional "Whatever Happened To?" headline, a photo of a slightly crushed cupcake, and Macaulay Culkin pictures. At first he wondered if there had been some kind of connection between Becca and Macaulay Culkin, who was looking a little cadaverous these days, but a quick experiment convinced him that an Internet search of any child star's name resulted in photos of Macaulay Culkin. He seemed to be the Google poster child for former child actors.

The only recent hit he received was a blogger who seemed to have been a fan of Becca's but who now had a lot to say on the subject of "arrogant has-beens" who thought they owed their loyal public nothing. The crushed cupcake photo was on this woman's blog, Megan's Musings. According to the post, the orig-inal was residing in her freezer until she could decide whether there was any value in keeping it. The signature on the bag, she reported with glee, was nearly worthless.

The thought of some weirdo out there stalking a nearly forgotten child star from the nineties made him shake his head. Who cared?

Of course, there he was, looking up whatever he could find on her. Guiltily, he killed the screen, feeling as if he'd just been caught peeping through an actual window.

The next afternoon, he met Becca in front of the cupcake store exactly at one o'clock. She was waiting on the bench, her purse slung over her shoulder, ready to go, and stood as he walked up. "We can take my car," she said.

He looked around, expecting to see a sporty convertible or a European import, and was amused when she unlocked the doors of an old Subaru hatchback. The interior was a weird combination of farmy smells and vanilla.

"What?" she asked, catching him smile as they buckled up.

"I guess I was expecting a Jag, or something more . . ."

"More Hollywood?"

He caught an undertone of disappointment in the question. "I guess."

Her mouth set in a tense line, which at first he chalked up to the need to focus on traffic and getting them out of town. Not that traffic in Leesburg was what anyone would call hectic.

He shifted. "People probably make all sorts of stupid assumptions, I guess."

She shot a raised-brow look at him. "Were you a *Me Minus You* fan?"

"God, no," he said, before he realized how that probably sounded to her. "I mean, I'm sure it was a good show. I'm not a TV critic. It just wasn't my thing."

"Mine, either, actually," she said.

"You didn't watch your own show?"

"That would have been weird. Besides, it conflicted with *Star Trek*. No DVRs back then."

"You're a Trekkie?" He sat up straighter. "Me too."

She cut another glance at him. "What would you say if I told you that I sat one table away from Captain Picard at my first awards banquet?"

"Seriously?"

"I even have his autograph on a napkin somewhere."

"You mean it's not hanging on your mantel?"

She laughed. "First, I don't have a mantel, and second, I actually had a huge geeky crush on Data, so maybe I didn't prize Patrick Stewart's autograph like I should have. In fact, I spilled my Shirley Temple on the napkin."

"It's still pretty damn cool."

She focused on the road again, and remained quiet until they turned onto a rutted asphalt road with no lane markers. Her tone became more businesslike. "The horse-friendly acreage in the area is really shrinking, but this is all pasture open to riding." With a tilt of her head, she indicated the fields out their windows. "On the day of the party, Cal will probably ride the kids around the ring for a little bit, just to make sure they can all stay upright on a horse. Then we can take them on a very gentle trail ride."

"We?"

"I was going to help Cal out." She caught what must have been a furrowed-brow expression. "Don't worry—*you* won't have to get up on horseback. I'd bring a book, though. Waiting for the trail riders to get back could be boring."

He hadn't actually been thinking about the party. Instead, he'd been wondering again about Becca's relationship with her ex. "You two still hang out?"

She hung a right onto a dirt road, and the Subaru trundled through an open gate. "I keep my horse here—he's used to it, and I get a former spouse discount. Plus, Cal's an old pal of my best friend, Pam, so . . . yeah. He's around sort of a lot. But there's no big reunion in the works, if that's what you mean."

As if you have any right to ask, her sidewise glance silently added.

"I didn't mean to pry." It seemed odd to be apologizing for an innocuous small-talk remark when last night he'd been doing Internet searches and staring at childhood photos of her.

"I just don't want you to worry that Cal and I will be playing out some kind of romantic comedy while we're supposed to be watching the kids," she said. "He's a great riding instructor. I've watched him. There's nothing about teaching kids to ride that he doesn't know. Also, part of his brain is permanently stuck in twelve-year-old land, so he's usually a big hit with the bubblegum set."

"I wasn't really worried."

But maybe he should have been, he realized when they rattled up the dirt road to a cavernous old barn. Someone was just walking out with a saddled, snorting beast that struck him as imposingly huge. The animal was much bigger than the ponies Matthew remembered riding at Camp Kayahuga when he was a kid. Damn. It began to sink in why Nicole was so freaked out. "Just slipping off that horse while it was standing still could do some serious damage," he observed.

Becca pulled back a little and sent him a puzzled look. "Why would anyone fall off a horse that wasn't moving?"

It was the kind of sensible, are-you-kidding question he could imagine Olivia asking him. Although Olivia would probably voice it at a much higher volume.

Becca waved him forward. "Come on. I want to introduce you to the love of my life."

I thought it was all over between you two. The thought died when Becca climbed onto the first rail of a wood paddock fence, put her fingers in her mouth, and released an eardrum-piercing whistle.

Several clusters of horses were grazing in the pasture, and a few looked up at the sudden sound, but only one large white horse trotted over. Matthew recognized it as the horse from the pictures in the Strawberry Cake Shop. When the animal bowed his long neck over the fence for a pat, Becca pressed herself against him, then drew back and nuzzled his nose, finally dipping her hand into her pocket and producing some carrots for him on her outstretched palm.

While the horse munched noisily, Becca looked over at Matthew. "This is Harvey."

Olivia's dream horse. He seemed especially huge. "How old is he?"

"Twenty-one—almost an old man. But he still has some spring left in him. Someone gave him to me when we were both ridiculously young. We've been through a lot together."

"So you brought him with you from California?"

"Of course. I could never part with Harvey." She nuzzled his neck. "Through thick and thin. Right, buddy?"

The horse snorted in agreement.

Becca looked over at Matthew again and laughed. "Okay, now that I have you thoroughly creeped out by the horse-human bond, let's go find Cal."

It didn't take long. A rusty-haired guy lumbered over, obliterating any remaining thoughts of Cary Grant. The man had the weathered look of a guy who spent most of his days outdoors, and his mud-stained jeans would never pass for a dapper wardrobe. Still, he possessed a nice, reassuring smile and a firm handshake, and didn't waste any time before giving Matthew a tour to check out the facilities and meet quite a few of the prospective equine party participants. All of them seemed smaller and more sedate in their stalls than the horses outside. Cal ended by showing him the area in the yard—non-horse accessible—where they would set up a tent with a table for cake, punch, and presents. He then presented Matthew with permission slips and accident waivers for the parents to sign off on.

The waivers gave him pause—he didn't like to think about any of the girls having a birthday party incident—but he could see the sense of it, especially from the viewpoint of Butternut Knoll. And Becca had already told him that the parents would need to be warned of risks.

"I'm impressed," he commented on the way home.

Becca swung toward him. "Really? Cal impressed you?"

"The whole thing did. When you work in front of a computer all the time, you can't help feeling wistful about who's making a good living doing something that allows him being out and moving around all day."

" 'Making a good living' is a relative term."

"But you know how it is. Seeing someone who's escaped the

nine-to-five trap is like being a zoo animal watching one of the others hop the fence and make a break for freedom."

She smiled. "Zoo escapes always end badly for someone. Usually the escapee."

"Maybe you've never been chained to a desk."

"Oh yes, I have. Only for a few years, but I get what you're saying. Being outdoors all day seems idyllic, at least if you don't have to wear a hard hat and an orange vest."

But she'd walked away from it all—from living out here, and from her marriage. What had happened? He had to remind himself that it was none of his business, and train his thoughts back on something that was. "I think it will be a great party," he said. "I just have to report back to Nicole and then convince the other parents to come."

Becca mashed down on the brake.

One second they were talking, the next his heart was in his throat, as if they were about to crash. Her sudden stop tossed them both forward against their shoulder belts. Grabbing the armrest, Matthew scanned the road for some pothole or critter he hadn't seen.

After a moment's hesitation, Becca sped up again. "Sorry," she said. "I thought I saw something."

They drove in silence for the moment. Matthew stayed focused on the road.

"Nicole . . . that's Olivia's mother?" Becca asked after a bit. "Your girlfriend?"

"Yes." *Girlfriend* always seemed so high-schoolish. Then again, *partner* sounded like they ran a law firm. Also, they just didn't seem to be together enough to be real partners. Especially lately. After Saturday morning, they hadn't hung out at all over the weekend, and they'd barely talked when he'd driven her to the airport early this morning.

"You said Nicole's away on business. Is she some kind of corporate high flyer?"

"She's an energy research engineer."

From Becca's reaction, you would have thought he had announced that she was a drug dealer or something. She swallowed. "And she's out on the West Coast?"

"Right. But it sounds as if the project's moving to Hawaii."

"Hawaii? Really? People get to go on business trips there?"

"Could be why she's not in a hurry to wind things up," he said, joking. "Or maybe it's just me."

"I'm sorry, I shouldn't have pried." Becca pressed against the seat back. "I bet it's hard for her to be away from Olivia." Hastily, she added, "And you."

"I know we miss her," he said. "I hope she misses both of us." Although, as he voiced the words, he felt even less certain that Nicole thought of him much at all while she was away.

"I hope so, too," Becca said.

Matthew was too busy scanning the road for fleet-footed critters to be puzzled by her response.

Chapter 7

When Pam came into work the next morning, Becca felt skittish. After learning during their drive back to town that Matthew was the significant other of the notorious Nicole, she had contemplated calling Pam right away. But she hadn't. Gossiping about Erin didn't feel right, especially now when she realized that Matthew was caught up in the situation, too. On the other hand, it didn't feel right *not* to talk to her about it.

"Where's Walt?" Pam asked, looking around.

"I haven't seen him yet today." Something wasn't right about that guy. "Do you think he moonlights?"

"Moonlights as what? An armed burglar?"

Becca rolled her eyes. Unfortunately, Walt was a worry. He was an okay worker the first thing in the morning, but he tended to fade after an hour. She spent a lot of his shift trying to get him to eat something and bringing him beverages he never drank.

"Erin told me she was going to drop by today," Pam said.

Oh God. Erin. Becca tried to push her uneasiness for her friend out of her mind. She preferred worrying about Walt.

"So how did Cal take meeting Matthew?" Pam asked. "When I was talking to him Sunday night, he was freaked out over meeting his rival."

Becca turned back to the bowl of cookie dough she was scooping onto baking sheets. "He was fine, and I don't know what you're talking about. I divorced Cal. That's history. Matthew is not his rival. I hope you told him that. There's nothing going on with either of them."

Before, she thought the teasing about Matthew was humorous. Now it seemed more dangerous. Becca would admit she had a little crush on him. Although it wasn't a crush, exactly. Matthew was just one of those guys whom she looked at wistfully sometimes and thought *all the good ones are taken.* And he was taken by the woman who was evidently at the center of Erin's marital mess.

"Pam, Matthew has a girlfriend. You know that." With vehemence, she dropped a melon baller of dough onto the cookie sheet. "Also, his girlfriend has a daughter whom he looks on as practically his own."

Heartbreak potential all around.

She slapped the spatula harder against the dough than was called for. These poor cookies were going to end up snickerdoodle wafers. Well, too bad. She picked up the pan, took it to the oven, and heaved it onto a rack with more force than usual.

Pam scurried after her and gently shut the oven door. "What's the matter?"

"Nothing. Why?"

"You never abuse dough. Or kitchen equipment. Plus, you've been distracted ever since I got here." Even though they were alone, Pam lowered her voice. "He didn't make a pass at you yesterday, did he?"

Becca drew back. "Who? Matthew?"

"Cal," Pam replied, then did a double-take. "Did Matthew try something?"

"Of course not. Neither of them did, or would. Cal . . . well, that's impossible. And Matthew—"

"I know, he's practically married. And we all know that married guys never misbehave. You do sort of like him, though, don't you?"

It was almost as if she was rooting for an inappropriate entanglement. Why? "Not the way you're thinking."

"Okay, but it's clear that *something* happened out there," Pam insisted.

Becca grabbed her friend's arm. Quite possibly, she was about to make a colossal error. No one would call Pam the world's most discreet woman. In fact, she was practically the WikiLeaks of Leesburg. But Becca didn't know who else to turn to, and she was about to burst.

"Pam, Matthew's girlfriend's name is Nicole."

Pam blinked. "Do you think she's Ann Taylor?"

"Matthew's Nicole works as an energy research engineer, just like Bob. And for the past month she's been on a business trip on the West Coast."

As each new revelation sank in, Pam sucked in her breath a little more. Finally, when she was puffed up like a full tire, she expelled her air and asked, "What should we do?"

Becca took it as a good sign that she hadn't bounded across the room for her cell phone yet. "I don't know."

"Did you ask him about Bob?"

She shot Pam a look. "How was I going to work that question into casual conversation? 'Oh, is your absent girlfriend working with a serial wife betrayer named Bob?' What kind of person would do that?"

"My kind," Pam said.

"We were already driving back from the barn when all this came up. There wasn't much time. And I was so stunned. When he mentioned Nicole, I nearly drove us into a ditch."

Pam mulled over their quandary for a moment. "We've got to tell Erin."

"Tell her what? What do we know now that adds anything except color commentary? She's already aware that there's a woman named Nicole working with Bob."

"You're right. And she knows that Bob is a cheater. She knew that from the beginning."

Becca shook her head. Why Bob? Erin never had trouble meeting men. They practically flocked to her. "Why did she marry him?"

"Because she was in her late twenties, and the late twenties are the Bermuda Triangle of dating. Everybody thinks it's the sweet spot, the perfect time to tie the knot, but that's exactly wrong. Women in their late twenties are just panicked about turning thirty, and plus they convince themselves that they've started hearing that old biological clock *tick-tick-tick*ing away. High school and college sweethearts have young love propelling them to the altar. Women over thirty . . . well, they're lucky to find anyone. But marriages between people in their late twenties? Nothing but hormones and fear. Makes for disastrous decisions."

Like a lot of Pam's theories, it sounded reasonable if you didn't think about it too hard. Or at all. Becca nibbled her lower lip. "Maybe it's Matthew who should be warned."

"He might already know. Could be why he's mooning over you."

"He's not mooning."

"I've seen the way that man looks at you. Like he's smitten."

"It's just a residual TV effect," Becca assured her with a dismissive wave. "People have a hard time looking away. I'm pop culture roadkill."

"Poor guy. Taking care of that little girl, and all the while the mother is cheating on him." Pam tapped her fingers. "We could drop him an anonymous note."

"That would be awful. Can you imagine receiving a note like that?"

"Wouldn't you want to know?"

It was such a *Dear Abby* conundrum. "An anonymous note isn't knowing," Becca said. "It's just knowing that someone else thinks he or she knows. And what if we're wrong?"

"How could we be? There aren't any variables left."

Becca took a moment to think. "Matthew did say that Nicole had been transferred to Hawaii."

Pam straightened. "Bob's not in Hawaii."

"See? We could have it all wrong."

The bell rang, and Erin breezed in. She greeted them with a bright smile that Becca couldn't remember seeing for weeks. She had the straightest, whitest dental presentation in Leesburg. *Maybe we really do have it all wrong about Nicole*, Becca thought. As Erin approached, swinging a shopping bag, she looked positively joyous.

Maybe even a little manic.

Instinctively, Becca and Pam stepped away from each other, chuckling nervously. They provided a tableau vivant of the term *guilty secret*, which did not escape Erin's notice.

"What's going on?" she asked. "You two look like you're plotting world domination."

"We were just talking about..." Mid-sentence, Pam's gaze became deer-in-the-headlights vacant. She swung toward Becca for rescue.

"About my drive out to the barn with Matthew," Becca finished for her.

"The hottie who's *practically* married?" Erin asked. "So what happened?"

"Nothing!" Pam blurted, her spill-all impulse apparently evaporating.

"Nothing," Becca echoed. "He's hosting a birthday party at Butternut Knoll. Which reminds me . . . I might need to borrow Lulu for an afternoon the Saturday after next, if we're a horse short."

"No problem," Erin assured her. "It's weird that the guy is having to arrange all this, isn't it? Where is this practically-a-wife of his? We're sure she actually exists, right?"

"Oh, she exists," Pam muttered.

Becca glowered at Pam and struggled to segue to a different topic. Her gaze alit on Erin's shopping bag. "Did you buy something?"

"Wait till you see!" Erin practically cackled as she produced a scrap of black nylon. "Bathing suit. I've decided to surprise Bob."

"Is he coming back?"

"No—he's in Hawaii."

Only the most rigid discipline kept Becca from looking at Pam. Her neck muscles practically groaned with the effort it took to keep smiling at Erin's new bathing suit and not pivot toward her other friend.

"Hawaii!" Pam exclaimed, too brightly.

"Can you believe it?" Erin asked. "He called me last night from Honolulu—no warning that he was being moved there at all."

Becca and Pam continued to gape at her until Becca felt Pam goose her with an elbow. The only thing she could think to say was to repeat, "Hawaii!"

Erin nodded. "And after I hung up with Bob, I thought, *What better time to go pay him a visit?* I'm not doing anything here except wondering if my marriage is falling apart. Why should I let that happen if I can do something about it?" Mad optimism burst out of her like sunbeams. "My plane leaves tomorrow morning." She appealed to Pam. "You wouldn't mind giving me a ride to Dulles, would you? Even if it's insanely early?"

"No, of course not," Pam said. "But you're really just going to jet off like that? What about . . ."

"Ann Taylor?" A hint of a dark cloud threatened all that sunniness, but Erin shrugged it off. "I've been thinking about that ever since I talked to you guys that night at Not-Book-Club. I could be all wrong about her. Maybe I'm just overreacting."

"But if you're not?" Becca blurted out.

Erin laughed. "Well, okay. Maybe he's having a hot fling with Nicole, the sky-high-IQ coworker. Should I just cool my heels here and let her steal my husband?"

Becca grappled with the question. To her, Bob's having an affair seemed more like a welcome emergency exit than a conjugal roadblock. But Erin obviously didn't see it that way.

Pam also remained silent. It was easy to dislike Bob and think

Erin would be better off without him. It wasn't as easy to tell her so.

"Besides," Erin continued, "it's a trip to Hawaii, right?" She lifted up the scrap of silky nylon and netting. "Emilio Pucci. If nothing else, I'll be able to work on my tan."

The conversation lagged after that, and finally Erin announced that she had a ton of packing to do, and that she needed to meet her trainer, Mike, who'd said he could squeeze her in for a last workout before her vacation. After extracting a promise from Pam to pick her up the next morning at five, she breezed out.

Becca sank against one of the counters as Pam rushed over to help a newly arrived customer. Her whole body was tense from the effort of not betraying what she knew about Nicole. But why hadn't she?

She felt torn, and guilty. After the customer paid, she turned to Pam.

"I think we've just failed a friendship test," Becca told her.

Pam lifted her arms in frustration. "I know! I didn't know what to say. So I said nothing. And now I've got to drive her to the airport."

"What kind of friends are we? We're letting her jet off directly into Hurricane Nicole."

"But it's like you said," Pam said. "What could we really have told her?' "

"That there really is a Nicole, and that she's in Hawaii right now with Bob?"

"But she knows that. Well, not that Nicole's in Hawaii, but she knows the woman exists and is a threat. She even said she's going there to save her marriage. There's nothing we could add. It's not as if Matthew told you that his practically-a-wife was a cheating whore."

When Pam was arguing for discretion, the world was out of whack.

"I still worry. We're letting her run off to Hawaii armed with nothing but an Emilio Pucci bathing suit."

"Who knows? Maybe Emilio Pucci can save a marriage."

"Maybe." When it came to rescuing troubled marriages, Becca tended to be skeptical. It seemed to her that by the time people realized there was a problem, the troubles were like the asteroid heading toward the doomed planet. Not a lot to be done but run screaming down the street.

Which probably explained why she had ducked out of her marriage at the first sign of trouble. Preemptive marital asteroid evasion.

But what about Matthew? Disaster was heading right toward him, and as far as she knew, the poor man had no idea.

After receiving Nicole's go-ahead in an e-mail, Matthew told Olivia about the plans for the party and handed her the invitations to fill in. No lottery jackpot winner had ever responded with such unbridled elation. "Seriously?" she asked, after the first wave of shrieking and Tigger-hopping around the kitchen had subsided.

Matthew's hearing might never be the same, but Olivia's joy was worth a burst eardrum or two. The kid was happiness on legs.

"Mom actually agreed to this?"

"She actually did."

Olivia spun around and then stopped again even more abruptly, gasping. "Does this mean that she's going to buy me my own horse?"

"One thing at a time."

Even this little disappointment didn't dampen her spirits entirely. She evidently viewed a riding party as a parental gateway to full-on equine capitulation. "I bet by next year she'll let me have one."

"For the party, Becca said you could ride what's-his-name."

Olivia went perfectly still. "Harvey?"

He nodded. "I've even talked to Harvey. He's looking forward to meeting you."

Her gaze flicked upward in annoyance, letting him know he'd overstepped that fuzzy boundary between teasing and treating her like a child. But her thoughts were whirring faster than his, already distracting her with a new, pressing problem. "What am I going to wear?"

"Becca said jeans and sturdy shoes," he said. "It's written in the information from the stable containing the permission slip I'm going to include with the invitations."

"I can't wear my regular clothes to ride Harvey." Her tone indicated that his suggestion was offensive not just to her but to the horse, as well. He'd never seen her worry about clothes before, but until now she'd never had a date with a thoroughbred. Some girls dreamed of a prince on a charger. Olivia just dreamed of the charger.

"I doubt Harvey will mind."

"*I'll* mind. And there will be pictures and stuff, and Monica will have jodhpurs and boots and everything. I wish I had *something* that looked like riding clothes." She paced in front of him, strategizing. "Do you think I'd be more likely to get something else from Mom if I called, or e-mailed?"

Nicole had already sounded a little cranky about the party's price tag. He couldn't deny that renting a stable for an afternoon was a whole lot more expensive than pizzas and a slumber party.

"I'll buy you some riding clothes," he said.

Olivia sucked in a breath. "Really?"

"I'll ask Becca the name of a . . . a place that sells stuff like that."

"A tack store." Olivia's happiness level soared right back up to thirty on a scale of one-to-ten. "Thank you, Matthew!" She gave him a brief, boa-constrictor squeeze. "You're a better dad than my dad."

Realistically, it was faint praise—her dad hadn't been much of a dad at all—but in the moment, it seemed by far the nicest compliment anyone had ever paid him. It made him want to buy her a lifetime supply of dressage jackets and riding boots.

"I have to call everybody!"

He stopped her before she could run out. "First, you've got to fill out the invitations and stuff the envelopes."

Her shoulders sank. "Oh. Okay." Realism didn't bring her down for long, however. "Maybe it will be even better if I don't tell anybody ahead of time anyway. Then they'll open the invitations and be *so shocked*. It'll be awesome!"

He doubted her friends would think it was as awesome as Olivia did, but what did he know? His mind was already mulling over the next problem. Shopping.

Not his forte.

"I can't wait to tell Monica I'm riding Harvey on my birthday," she said. "Just last week she brought in her horse's pedigree papers for show-and-tell, along with video of her winning a ribbon at some competition. She's such a show-off. She wanted to bring her horse, but the principal wouldn't let her."

He settled Olivia at the coffee table in the living room, which was now invitation central. The cards she'd bought weeks before had balloons on them—no horses. She had to fill in the date, time, and a short message on each one, then include a parental release form from the pile on the table, and mark off the names on her list. She grumbled about having to do the grunt work for her own party, but it was good-natured grumbling.

Matthew picked up his phone and dialed Nicole's number. It was a little too early for their nightly call, but he wanted to tell her how Olivia had reacted. Nicole's call notes picked up, so he left a message telling her that the party news had gone over big. As if that outcome had ever been in doubt.

While the phone was at hand and the subject was on his mind, he fished Becca's card out of his wallet and punched in the home number she'd scrawled on the back.

"Matthew? Hi!"

"Hi. I wanted to let you know that Olivia is over the moon about the party. And especially about your lending her Harvey for her big day."

"Great."

"Now she's worried that Harvey will be offended if she isn't dressed properly."

She laughed. "Believe me, if he expected a fashion plate on his back, he would have run away from me years ago."

"I figured she was worried for nothing, but in a moment of weakness, I promised I'd buy her some riding clothes."

"And now you're wondering where the heck to get them," she said, guessing his problem.

"Right. I was going to talk to Nicole, but she's probably just as clueless as I am."

"Nicole is still in Hawaii?" Becca asked.

"Yeah."

When the line went silent, he wondered for a second if they'd been cut off.

"Look," Becca said, "I've been craving a trip to my favorite tack store. I'd be happy to take Olivia. How about this weekend?"

This was a generous offer . . . but way above and beyond the call of duty. "I can understand rounding up clients for your ex-husband, but surely you're not responsible for how they dress."

"I just like Olivia. She was nice to Walt, and she has great taste in horses. And cupcakes."

"I know she'd love to go, but I might have to check with her mom."

"You should come, too, of course," she added. "If you have time. The place is just outside of DC, so it would be the afternoon."

"Well . . ." On the one hand, he hesitated to put her to the trouble. On the other, she was handing him a golden opportunity to get an errand done with minimal hassle. And he enjoyed her company.

Maybe a little too much.

But that was silly. There had never been the slightest hint of flirtation between them. A few flashes of interest, maybe. But that was just normal. To say he couldn't go would be tantamount to admitting that men and women couldn't control their primal impulses and could therefore never be friends. Which almost made it seem vital that he not shy away from the invitation.

"I'll take you up on that offer," he said. "Thanks."

They fixed the outing for Sunday afternoon. He wondered if he should wait a day or two to tell Olivia this new development. Was there a limit to how much elation an almost-eleven-year-old could stand?

The phone rang again. He picked it up without looking, assuming Becca had remembered some conflict or other reason that Sunday would be inconvenient.

Nicole's voice brought him up short. "What's up?" she asked.

"I just called to tell you that your daughter is off-the-charts happy."

"Oh. Good. Is that all?"

"I thought you'd want to know."

She let out a breath. "When you call at a different time than usual, I always worry that something has gone wrong."

"Sorry. I didn't think of that."

"But of course I'm glad that she's happy," she said. "It's nice to hear some good news for once."

He frowned at the rug. "Things not going well?"

"That's putting it mildly. We've got a design flaw disaster . . . among other disasters."

"Like what?" He was genuinely interested, in part because Nicole seemed so stressed out. There was more than the usual high-strung tension humming over the wire.

"It doesn't matter," she said. "I'm sorry I'm not in the best of moods."

"If it helps, you don't have to worry about anything here. The cake lady is going to take Olivia shopping for riding clothes. That's going to be my birthday gift to her."

"You don't have to give Olivia anything," Nicole said.

Was she kidding? "I don't think Olivia got that memo. She's been hinting that a five-year subscription to *Horse and Rider* would make a perfect birthday gift."

"I have to talk to her about that."

"No, you don't. Of course I was going to give her something."

"You mean on top of the month of your life you've already sacrificed for her benefit?"

"It's no sacrifice. It's been fun. Dad practice. By the time you come back, I'll have morphed into Ward Cleaver."

"Oh God. That's all I need."

"Then you should come home soon."

"Believe me, if I could be airlifted out of this place tomorrow, I'd welcome rescue."

She had to be the only person in the world who would refer to Hawaii as "this place."

They talked a few more minutes, and then he handed the phone to Olivia, who was watching television while she filled out invitations. She paused the screen to talk to her mom, and as Matthew settled into a chair, he found himself staring at a screenshot of a very young Becca.

When Olivia was done with her trans-Pacific enthusing, she flopped back down at her workstation.

"What are you watching?" he asked, unnecessarily.

"It's Becca's show—*Me Minus You*. I just now found it." She pointed at the screen. "That's Becca."

"I guessed. But how . . . ?"

Olivia sent him a steady look. "Matthew, duh. It's on Netflix. And you don't have to worry that I shouldn't be watching it, because it's really stupid and tame. *Dora the Explorer* was racier than this stuff."

"I remember. Sort of."

"Was all television this dorky way back then?" She looked at the screen and shook her head. "I can't believe she did her hair like that."

Becca's hair was sticking up in an off-center ponytail—an explosive pouf of hair and bow geysering out of the side of her head.

"Don't tell Becca I said her show was dorky," Olivia pleaded. "She might not let me ride Harvey."

He felt the urge to laugh at the idea of Becca holding a grudge for something like that. In fact, if she were in the room with them, he bet she would be laughing at her old self.

"Becca wouldn't go back on a promise," he assured her.

"Well, I wouldn't want her to feel bad in any case. She probably couldn't help it that they dressed her like that. And it was forever ago, so . . ."

All the way back in the 1990s, but to Olivia that probably seemed as far into the past as the Eisenhower years.

"She has a sense of humor about herself," he said.

"I know! That's why I like her. She laughs. Mom never laughs."

"Sure she does," Matthew said.

"Rarely," Olivia said. "When I grow up, I want to be like Becca. Not all serious like Mom."

"Your mom is fun. She's also crazy intelligent, and she's working on something that could help save the planet for all our sorry selves."

"But she doesn't seem happy," Olivia said. "At least, not lately. Not that we'd *know* or anything, since she isn't here."

She punched the remote, and the show on the screen leapt back to life.

Matthew zoned out. It was hard not to. The story *was* hokey—a recently deceased father was haunting his family, and only the little girl Becca played could see him. The episode played out like a farce, with a gooey coda at the end with the little girl saying good night to her ghost dad. Olivia finished one episode and started right in on the next one.

But Matthew wasn't thinking about the story, or even Becca. He was wondering about Nicole, and how Olivia was right. She hadn't seemed happy, really happy, in ages. At least, not around him.

Why was that?

Chapter 8

Becca worked all morning Sunday, which was usually her most profitable day. The shop wasn't as crowded as Saturday, but people were apt to zoom by to make serious pastry purchases—cupcakes by the dozens for football get-togethers and church functions, or whole cakes for family dinners or to take to visit grandma. The doors stayed open until they ran out of things to sell, usually mid-afternoon.

"You sure you don't mind closing up today?" she asked Pam as she waited for Matthew to pick her up.

"Not at all. Enjoy your date."

"It's not a date," Becca corrected automatically.

Pam scooted closer. "Has he mentioned what's going on in Honolulu?"

"The subject hasn't come up."

"I'm dying to know what's going on."

So far, there had been no news from Erin except for pictures she had posted on Facebook of herself looking tanned and happy in her new bathing suit in front of the surf. Many were clearly selfies.

"If she really has triumphed over Ann Taylor, you'd think she'd want to crow about it in an e-mail," Pam said.

"Maybe she thought the pictures were all the evidence we'd need."

"She looked *too* happy, if you ask me."

"How can someone look too happy?" Becca asked.

"Come on. This is a battle for Bob—winning isn't exactly winning." Pam shook her head. "Judging from that smile, I think she's found herself a cabana boy."

"Leave the dishes when you close up. I'll take them upstairs later and wash them in the dishwasher in my apartment," Becca said, wanting to change the subject.

Easier wished than done.

"If you think Erin's marriage is so secure," Pam began, "don't you feel a little weird going out with Bob's mistress's almost-husband? Doesn't that make you a potential almost-home-wrecker?"

Where to begin? "First, we aren't one hundred percent certain that she and Bob are having a fling. If there is an affair going on between them, wouldn't Erin have hopped a plane back by now?"

"Maybe she decided to stay and stalk them."

"If she was stalking them, would she be posting pictures of herself on the beach at Waikiki?"

"I guess that would be a tip-off." Pam tapped a manicured nail against her chin. "Which brings us back to my cabana boy theory."

"Also," Becca continued, "Matthew and I aren't going out—not in the way you mean. Unless you consider taking an eleven-year-old girl to a tack shop a romantic outing."

Pam sighed in frustration.

"Sometimes I could swear that you *want* me to be having an affair with the guy," Becca said. "I don't see how that would help anybody."

"You're right. I just want . . ." Pam growled in frustration. "Oh, forget it. Who knows what I want?"

Becca had no hope of answering that question, so she steered the conversation in another direction. "I sent Walt off with cupcakes for the Baptists. If he ever comes back, tell him to take the rest of the day off."

"What do you think the odds of him coming back are?"

It had to be admitted: Walt was unreliable. First, there was the sleeping thing. And for a few days he hadn't shown up at all. When he'd turned up after his longest absence, he'd simply taken up his broom and acted as if nothing had happened. Becca had decided that if something shady was going on in his life, she didn't want to know about it. Maybe that wasn't the most self-protective attitude to take, but it did prevent her from having to do something unpleasant, like possibly fire someone, or go to the county lockup to spring her employee.

"Don't get me wrong," Pam said. "I'm happier when he's not around."

"I think you've made that clear. But I can't understand why. He's a harmless enough old guy."

Pam crossed her arms. "But he doesn't belong here—and no, I'm not being a snob. I'm saying the man doesn't serve a purpose here. In the shop. We can both sweep, mop, and walk a couple dozen cupcakes to churches, so he's not doing anything we weren't getting done perfectly fine on our own."

"But he's nice," she said.

"You mean he likes you. Lots of people like you."

Becca snorted. "You obviously haven't been on the Internet." Gecko Girl was still pitching her online snit fit. Megan's Musings was now selling T-shirts featuring a picture of Becca in her most unflattering freeze frame from *Malibu High School*. The caption read TINA THINKS YOU SHOULD GET A LIFE.

"You can't hire every hard-luck case that comes along," Pam told her.

"I'm not. I've hired *this* hard-luck case. And it's just for a little while."

"That's what you said weeks ago." When Becca didn't respond by agreeing with her to fire Walt immediately, she said, "Let me put it bluntly. I think the man's a leech. He's taking advantage of you."

"He's *working*."

"He's a mooch."

Becca didn't see it—at least, it didn't seem like malicious mooching. He was more like a piece of driftwood that had temporarily snagged on something. And that something was her.

"This isn't Tinseltown," Pam said. "You're in business. Real business. No one's going to hand you an Emmy for Best Performance of a Nice Shop Lady."

Heat burned Becca's cheeks. The steam coming out of her ears could probably have powered a locomotive or two. She was used to the occasional snide "Hollywood" comment from acquaintances or customers, but not from Pam. "I can't believe you said that."

Pam managed to look both contrite and defiant. "I'm sorry. I just don't like to see anyone taking advantage of you."

"He's *not* taking advantage of me. I only pay him for the hours he's here. Mostly." Relieved to see Matthew's vehicle through the plate-glass window, Becca snatched her purse and headed for the door with a hastily mumbled, "See you later."

Matthew and Olivia were just getting out of the car when Becca stepped out into the perfect fall day. Her mood, on the other hand, was no longer perfect—a detail Matthew appeared to pick up on. His smile faded a little when their gazes met. "Everything okay?" he asked.

She nodded.

Olivia, happily oblivious, was so excited she was practically vibrating. "You get the front seat," she informed Becca. "I'm going to sit in the back."

She had a very liberal idea of what the backseat was—it basically extended as far forward as her seat belt would allow. Most of the time, her head was poking between the two front seats.

"Guess what?" Olivia asked as soon as Matthew had navigated them onto the freeway. "We watched you on television."

"Did you? Am I still in reruns?"

"Netflix," Olivia explained.

Becca glanced over at Matthew and could have sworn his face was a shade redder than it had been a minute ago. "What did you think?"

"*You* were good," Olivia said, assuming a critic's seriousness, "but the show was kind of dumb."

"Olivia," Matthew warned.

Becca laughed. "That's okay. It *was* kind of dumb."

"Did you ever meet any big movie stars?" Olivia asked.

"Sure."

"Really? Who?"

"Hm . . ." Becca smiled, trying to decide whether to provide a tease or go straight for the big guns. "George Clooney." That usually resulted in a swoon or two.

Olivia popped a bubble in her ear. "Who?"

She also popped the bubble of Becca's ego. *Oh God.* She was officially old. "I met Elijah Wood before he was a hobbit. How's that?"

"Okay, that's kind of cool." But Olivia sat back, obviously disappointed with Becca's name dropping.

After a mile or so, Matthew asked, "Did you know there's a Trekkie convention in Alexandria this weekend? I've been telling Olivia that if we have time, we'll drop by." A quick wink told her that this was more of a threat than a possibility.

Becca swiveled toward the backseat. "You don't like *Star Trek*?"

Olivia fidgeted. "That's, like, the last thing in the universe I'd do with my weekend."

"Me too," Becca said. "So don't worry."

Matthew shifted a quizzical glance her way.

"Those conventions make my skin crawl," Becca explained. "All those poor actors in stalls in a rented hall, on view like livestock at a state fair. Selling their autographs for twenty dollars a pop." The performing-monkey aspect of it made her shudder. She'd rather die than resort to that kind of desperation.

"Don't they have *Me Minus You* conventions?" Matthew asked, arching a brow at her.

"The world isn't that hard up for activities yet, thank God. I've been approached by nostalgia stuff, but I avoid it all, including 'Whatever Happened To' articles. I've moved on. I'm a cupcake lady now, and I'm fine with that."

"I'd rather be a cupcake lady than an actress," Olivia said.

"Good for you," Becca said.

"Unless I could be a really rich and famous actress. Then I might change my mind." Another pause indicated that Olivia's brain gears were still grinding away, and then she darted her head between their seats. "Hey, I know what. Becca could come to Career Day at my school and talk about cupcakes!"

"Fun," Becca said. "When?"

"A week from Wednesday. Mom was supposed to, but she probably won't be back. Matthew said he would take her place— but I've watched Matthew work and it looks really boring."

Becca checked out his reaction. He was laughing. "Don't you think Becca's doing you enough favors already, O?"

"I don't mind," Becca said.

Olivia sank back against the backseat with a triumphant fist pump. "Yes! You'll be even better than Monica's pedigree papers."

The statement confused Becca, but she was glad that someone thought she'd be interesting. Not that she liked giving presentations, as a rule. Also, she hoped Matthew wouldn't feel slighted. "I don't want to step on any toes," she told him.

"Believe me, I will not be heartbroken."

His smile, relaxed and warm, gave her heart a strange lift. He wasn't like Cal, always working the charm . . . usually because he thought he had something to apologize for. Matthew was charming and easy to get along with. But that made sense. His being involved with someone took the flirtatious, desperate-to-please element out of their relationship.

Not that she would call theirs a relationship. Not exactly. More like a . . . friendship. She took the word for a spin in her mind. Could she be friends with Matthew and Olivia without spoiling their fragile family unit? Especially when she knew it was more fragile than Matthew probably suspected?

At the tack store, Olivia stayed close to her. "What are you buying?" she asked Becca.

"Gloves." Becca misplaced riding gloves with the same frequency that she lost regular winter gloves—as fast as she could replace them. She picked over a shelf of them. She probably could have ordered them over the Internet, but she loved coming to this place. Just the smell of new leather from the saddlery department gave her a rush. It was mecca for equine freaks.

Olivia plucked a pair of riding gloves off the shelf. "Maybe I should get some, too."

"I think you'll be okay for the party without them." She was thinking of a small item or two that might make Olivia feel like a horsewoman without breaking Matthew's bank account.

But Olivia harbored grander ideas. "If I get a whole outfit now, Mom'll have to see that it won't cost much more to send me to lessons. I'll be all ready."

Ground Control to Olivia. "It's the lessons and the barn time that rack up the big bucks, not the wardrobe."

"Yeah, but lessons are different," Olivia said. "Mom didn't mind spending money on ballet and violin lessons, and I stank at both those things. I know I'll be good at riding."

Becca shook her head. Anyone could tell by talking to Olivia that she wasn't on the violins-and-tutus track of girlhood. Why had her mother been trying to ram a square peg into a round hole? Or maybe those had been Nicole's own interests when she was younger, so she'd thought her little girl would be exactly the same. It was sad when parents tried to live their kids' lives for them.

It made her all the more thankful to have been raised by her own mother. Sure, she'd cringed as a teenager when her mom hadn't seemed "normal." Normal moms of other kids she worked with were either in show business themselves or were stay-at-home moms turned stage mothers. They didn't change the subject when you asked where their father was.

But there were things she'd always loved about their life, too. Like that feeling of camaraderie they'd had. There was nothing better than hanging out with Ronnie and watching movies they'd rented. Or sitting at the table eating her mom's yummy comfort food, when she'd felt enveloped in warmth and total love. Thank God she'd had that.

She wished she'd appreciated her mom more at the time, and hadn't pestered her so much. Especially about her dad, which usually resulted in silence. The closest she'd come to the truth was once when she'd stubbornly held her ground. Didn't she have a right to know?

"I was an idiot," Ronnie had confessed. "I got involved with someone who was bad news. But that doesn't mean you should suffer."

"But there had to be something about him you liked," Becca had insisted. "Or else why would I even be here?"

Her mother had frowned then, and revealed the only tidbit about this mysterious question mark in Becca's life. "Johnny played sax."

Becca grasped greedily at these details. A name! Johnny. It wasn't an interesting name, but it was something. "Saxophone?"

"That man played music so sweet it would bring tears to your eyes." Ronnie shook her head. "He could have been a pro, if he'd held himself together."

"But what happened?"

Her mother had turned away, as if angry about something. And then she'd left the room.

For a while, Becca had imagined Johnny the saxophonist as a sort of Kenny G who had gone to seed. It wasn't pretty. Maybe sometimes it was best to know nothing at all. After all, when you had a mom who would make any sacrifice for you, what did it matter?

"Becca?" Olivia was squinting up at her. No telling how long she'd been trying to catch her attention. "What do you think I should get?"

Becca's head cleared. Not only had she been zoning out, she'd been making a lot of assumptions about Nicole falling short as a mom. While Becca was fairly certain Nicole wasn't faithful to Matthew, she didn't know the first thing about Olivia's home life. Except that she had a missing dad, and a temporarily absentee mom.

She led Olivia across the store. One item of riding gear was a shoo-in to make a kid feel she'd "arrived" as a horsewoman, even if said kid didn't know one end of a saddle from another.

Five minutes later, Olivia was preening in front of a mirror, a black riding helmet perched on her head. She stood straighter, adjusting the ribbon chin strap, her expression so determined that she might have been Velvet before the Grand National.

Other items might have been more practical. Any decent barn with a teaching program had helmets but couldn't provide, say, riding breeches, or boots. But there was something about owning that helmet that made nuts-for-horses kids feel that they were bound for equestrian glory. She could almost hear the call to hounds sounding off in Olivia's head.

Matthew rejoined them. "Look at you!" he said approvingly. "Does it fit?"

"It feels great," Olivia said. "But I think I should get one of those instead." She pointed to a row of the non-velvet helmets that always looked more like crash helmets to Becca. Which probably showed wisdom on Olivia's part, since all helmets were technically crash helmets. "It looks more practical. Maybe once I'm hunting, I can get one of these." She took the velvet one off and put it reverently aside. "Someday," she promised herself.

Becca vowed to do her best to help that someday come to pass.

After making their purchases, they stopped at a nearby shopping center with a café that had outdoor seating. Olivia spotted an ice cream place a few doors down and asked if she could get some while Matthew and Becca basked over coffees in the late-afternoon sunlight. Soon it would be too cold to sit outside, but this was a perfect Indian summer evening.

"Thank you again for doing this," Matthew said after Olivia had scooted off. "You could probably think of better ways to spend a Sunday afternoon."

"Nope. I love going to the tack store. And having Olivia along made it more fun. She's so enthusiastic about everything."

"But I got the sense that you had other things on your mind today. You seemed preoccupied with something when we picked you up."

Remembering her spat with Pam, a little of her good mood leaked away. She didn't like to argue, especially with friends. Conflict always gave her flashbacks to her days when she was dealing with Abby Wooten, before she'd ever heard the term *frenemy*. Discord made her uneasy, and her early experience with Abby had taught her how easily friendships could evaporate.

"Shop drama," she said. "Pam doesn't like having Walt around."

He smiled. "I picked up on that."

She worried Walt had probably picked up on it, too. "She thinks I'm just keeping him on because I'm a bleeding heart."

"Are you?"

She was so accustomed to her knee-jerk denials to Pam, she hadn't really put the question to herself in a serious way. *Was* she a chump? "I guess I am, a little. We don't really need him." She clucked in disgust at herself. "Doesn't that sound awful? As if I were a tycoon thinking about laying off another lump of faceless masses. I mean, who is needed and who isn't? For that matter, who *needs* cupcakes?"

"Olivia," Matthew said.

"But you see what I'm saying?" she asked. "Maybe I am a little bit of a bleeding heart, with my one-man job program. What's so bad about that? If I wanted to be a ruthless businesswoman, I could have stayed back in LA and tried harder to fit in there. Instead, I wanted to go somewhere that seemed to work on a more human, caring scale. A place where people weren't considered expendable after a flop or two. Well, Walt has flopped at life. I just want to give him a hand."

He took a moment to consider her words. That was another thing she liked about Matthew. He really listened before responding. "Maybe it's not a matter of being heartless. Your friend is probably concerned that your store won't remain financially stable if you hire people you don't need."

"But the shop is doing fine." A moment's reflection, however, exposed the lie to herself. She had been worried about money— so much so that she'd put off getting things fixed for far too long. "Okay, to tell the truth, it's always a squeeze. The other day I passed a sign advertising a job for a pizza delivery person. I actually gave it serious consideration. It wouldn't conflict with the store's hours, and I'd have a little extra cash to make some repairs."

Matthew arched a brow at her. "So you were considering taking a part-time job so you can keep Walt employed? Does that make sense?"

"No, but . . ." He was right. It sounded insane. And if the store went under, they'd all be unemployed. Poor Pam. First the real estate market had squeezed her into catch-as-catch-can work. The last thing she needed was for her second job to be put in jeopardy through Becca's wimpy business practices.

"What should I do?" she wondered aloud.

"Do you want me to talk to Walt?"

For a moment, she actually considered taking him up on the offer. It would be like being a kid again, having an adult step in and settle all her messy problems. So tempting. So laughable. "Why would you want to do that?"

"You've helped me out. And Walt's a good guy. Olivia thinks so."

She wondered how good he'd feel about Walt if he knew the man was a felon. She thought about telling him, but wouldn't that be like putting a scarlet letter on Walt's chest? Telling Pam had seemed advisable, since they worked together, but broadcasting his history to everyone she knew wouldn't be fair. He'd paid his debt to society, and he hadn't done anything wrong since.

As far as she knew.

She frowned into her latte. Where had Walt disappeared to for those couple of days when he hadn't shown up for work? And given the fact that there were so many kids in and out of the store, shouldn't she be a little more concerned? Olivia liked and trusted him. What if Pam was right and Walt turned out to be a psycho? If anything terrible happened, she would feel responsible.

"I'll talk to him myself," she said. "I've just been a wimp."

"You don't have to be ruthless," he said. "Just honest. Tell him that you don't really need help right now. Give him notice."

She nodded as Olivia fast-walked up and stopped in front of them with three scoops of ice cream perched precariously on a sugar cone. "What are you guys talking about?"

"Nothing," they said in unison.

Because "firing Walt" was not an answer that would go over well with Olivia. So much for not being a wimp.

Their response probably would have made Olivia suspicious if she hadn't been preoccupied with a glob of Rocky Road that was leaning at a dangerous angle.

During the ride home, Becca decided that she needed to stop personalizing things and act like a grown-up. Put on her big girl cupcake store owner panties and just speak freely to the guy. *"We like you, Walt, but the store doesn't need extra help right now. It's just business."*

Unfortunately, "just business" made her think of Abe Vigoda in *The Godfather*, which caused a pang because whenever she saw that movie, even though she knew that Abe Vigoda's character had been treacherous and couldn't be allowed to get away with betrayal, she always thought, "But, *come on*, it's Abe Vigoda." Didn't anyone in this cutthroat world get spared?

Walt even had Abe Vigoda eyes.

As the miles ticked away, she purposely tried to scour the sad, resigned old man expression from her brain.

Tough cupcake panties, she reminded herself as they drove back into town. She intended to speak to Walt straightaway, before her conflict-avoiding inner coward overpowered her good sense.

Unfortunately, when Matthew dropped her off in front of her place, the store was dark and the Closed—Come Again! sign hung in the window. There would be no straight-talking to Walt today.

Matthew and Olivia thanked her for the outing and drove off.

Becca went upstairs. It had been a fun day, witnessing Olivia's enthusiasm for something she'd taken for granted for so long. But more, those hours of being part of a family outing seemed precious. She hadn't had a lot of that growing up. And Matthew had helped her sort out her own problems, which was gold. Maybe his advice, on closer scrutiny, was identical to what Pam had been telling her for weeks, but a little distance had helped her see things more objectively. And she knew Matthew wasn't prejudiced against Walt, while Pam had never liked him.

As soon as she sank onto the sofa, the two furry lumps that were Willie and Cash glommed on to her like the heat-seeking beings they were. A glass of wine and their purring lulled her into relaxation. It had been a perfect day—a little work, a drive, fun company. Matthew was good-looking, though she tried not to dwell on that. She also tried not to think too much of the way her mind replayed the things he'd said—not just because he'd given her valuable advice, but because the timbre of his voice struck a chord with her. The same way his gaze meeting hers made her breath catch sometimes.

Her attraction to Matthew might have been a positive sign, if it weren't so wrong in so many ways. After dating various hangers-on and losers in her teens and early twenties, and her impetuous marriage to Cal, she was finally attracted to a solid, responsible guy. Matthew was perfect—except that someone else before her had also decided he was perfect. Of course, the fact that this someone seemed fidelity-challenged complicated matters. Maybe that made Matthew even more appealing, because she wanted to rescue him from the other woman's clutches.

But then there was the other female in his life: Olivia. She adored Matthew. Becca didn't want to bust that up.

There was no way for this to turn out well.

A clang of metal downstairs sent her bolting straight up. Cats tumbled off her and wine splashed the couch cushions as her heart hammered against her rib cage. It was dark now. And downstairs, either pots were falling on their own, or someone had broken into her shop.

Chapter 9

Heart thumping, she grabbed the largest butcher knife from the block in her kitchen and headed toward the door. The steel blade glinted against a flash of lamplight.

Her legs stopped moving. If the intruder happened to wrestle the knife from her, then most likely the damage would be done to herself. Given that she possessed the upper body strength of a boiled turnip, this was not an unlikely scenario. The last thing she wanted was to be stabbed with a big honking knife from her own kitchen.

She backtracked, her mind sifting through all the Clue game possibilities of weaponry available to her. Gun (no), lead pipe (no), wrench (downstairs), rope (how would she defend herself with a rope?) . . . She pivoted and seized the first thing she saw that looked as if it could do bodily damage—Willie and Cash's sisal-covered wood scratching post with the rope handle.

She also grabbed her phone to call 911. But what was she going to tell the dispatcher? "I think I heard a pot fall downstairs" probably wouldn't bring the cavalry to her aid. The trouble was, she wouldn't really know how much of an emergency this was until she came face-to-face with the intruder. Then it would be a race to see if she could manage to dial her cell phone while simultaneously trying to scare off the bad guy with what was essentially her cats' nail file.

She could imagine the headlines. *Gruesome End for Child Actress: Little Tina Bludgeoned by Her Own Cat Furniture.*

At least she would go out entertaining the people.

She tiptoed down the stairs, listening carefully for any noises through the stairwell walls as she descended. Silence. She opened her front door and crept out of her doorway over to the bakery's door two steps adjacent. Peering through the window, she was surprised to see lights on. Robbers in this town had crust. She could hear noises inside, but nobody was visible. She frowned. Pam wouldn't be there at this time of day. So who . . . ?

The door was still locked. She had to use her key, and winced as the tumbler turned, making a loud *click*. As she slipped inside, someone who'd been in the back of the shop suddenly stood up.

Becca let out a yelp.

In response, Walt put up his hands as if Becca were the cops. Obviously not an unfamiliar gesture.

"What are you doing?" Even though it was just Walt, she gripped the scratching post so tightly the sisal pricked her skin. "I almost called the police."

Walt looked even more alarmed. "The cops? What for?"

She toed the door shut. "I heard a noise. It scared me half to death. I thought you were a burglar."

His face screwed up in confusion and his glance darted to the scratching post. "You intended to go up against a burglar with that piece of wood? What is that? Didn't you have a gun or a knife?"

"No, I don't own a gun, and—" She really didn't want to let him know her thought process vis-à-vis knives and what weapons she would prefer to have turned against her. *She* wasn't the person who owed anyone an explanation here. "What are you doing?"

"Come see." He beckoned her forward.

Cautiously, Becca followed him around the sales counter to

the baking area. Walt made a Vanna White gesture toward a towel laid out on the floor, covered with tools.

"I fixed your dishwasher," he said. "No more hauling dishes and pans up to your apartment at night."

She couldn't believe it. Walt could fix a dishwasher?

He grinned. "I wanted to surprise you."

"You did." She hoped the surprise wasn't that the machine was now screwed up beyond all repair.

"I meant to get it all done this afternoon after Pam closed up, but I had to go to find another part."

She stepped closer to the dishwasher. Had he really fixed it? The repairman had told her that it would cost almost the replacement value to get it running again. "You think it will work now?"

"Oh yeah," he said. "It should go for a few more years. It's a solid machine. Just needed some TLC."

If he really knew what he was doing, he'd just saved her five hundred bucks, at least. "I'll need to reimburse you."

"No, this was my gift to you. To thank you."

She shifted, remembering that just a half hour ago she'd been plotting the best way to fire him. And all the while he had been playing elf, working afterhours to do something nice for her as a surprise. "You shouldn't have gone to all this trouble."

"Maybe you shouldn't have gone to the trouble to help me, either. But you did. I'm grateful."

Something inside her shriveled. Her courage, no doubt. How could she say, "It's just business," in the face of this?

"Walt . . ." She frowned. Her mind, so desperate to avoid the subject of his long-term employment prospects at the cupcake shop, latched on to an odd yet not-insignificant detail. "How did you get in?"

"Pardon?"

"How did you get into the store? You said Pam had already locked up. Did you break in?"

He shuffled back a step. "Not exactly. I had a key made from the spare you keep taped to the bottom of the butcher-block table."

He'd found her spare key? "How did you know that?"

"Well . . . I was messing around with the table because you're always complaining it wobbles. I thought it would be an easy thing to do to level it off for you, which I did."

When had he done that? In amazement, she turned to the table and gave it a gentle shove. Solid as a rock. "It's not tippy anymore. I hadn't noticed!"

"I just glued a shiv onto the short leg," he said, shrugging modestly. "Simple."

Simple, but she hadn't bothered to do it herself. Instead, she'd been sticking a folded-up business card under it, but it never stayed in place. "Thank you."

"But in the middle of doing that," he confessed, "I saw the key taped down there. And I thought . . . well, it was an answer to a little problem I'd been having."

Oh boy. *Here it comes.* "What problem?"

"See, I don't have a place to stay right now. And I thought to myself, well, if I copied that key, I could stay in here at night, slip out in the morning, and nobody'd be the wiser. So that's what I've been doing."

It took effort to keep her voice from looping up in dismay. "You've been *living here?*" In other words, just underneath her. "For how long?"

"A week."

A week! "What happened to the Marquis?"

"I had to leave, on account of some rent I owed."

A slow throb started in her temple. "But you've been working. I mean, I thought I was paying you enough to get by."

"Oh sure. You've been great. The problem is that I've had some expenses. And so I missed my rent. The place I was at was pay-as-you-go. No lease or nothing. And it wasn't much to write home about anyway."

No, it wasn't. Just the memory of dropping him off that night made her shudder. "But better than living on the floor of the shop, surely."

"It's okay here. Lots of privacy, too. I found a sleeping bag at the Salvation Army and roll it out in the storage closet. Nobody can see from the front window."

A Salvation Army sleeping bag. She didn't want to think about that.

Was it even legal for him to stay here? The street-level part of the building was zoned for business. Plus, there was no shower. Where did he bathe?

She didn't want to think about that, either.

How could he have gotten to this point? Here she'd been, floating along thinking of herself as Lady Bountiful, rescuing him from the heartless Steves of the world, but despite her imagined largesse, he seemed to be worse off than ever.

"Walt, please don't take this the wrong way. I wouldn't have even considered it my business until you took up residence in my storage closet...." She cleared her throat. "Do you have a drug problem?"

"No." He shook his head. Vehemently. "That's all over for me. I gave up all that years ago."

That was reassuring. But usually when junkies got clean, their lives improved, right? Of course, there was more than one vice in the world. "Is it alcohol?" She'd never seen him drunk, but there had to be some problem here.

"No, I got sober, too. I went to AA for years, ever since prison. Not since I been here, of course, but that's because . . ." The sigh that came out of him spoke of a long story, the details of which he obviously wanted to spare her. "The deal with the rent is, I just got behind. You don't have to worry about it."

"But I do worry. Of course I do. You work here, and now you're fixing my appliances instead of paying to have a roof over your head."

"I just paid for parts."

"But even that had to be a hundred dollars, at least. Probably more."

"A hundred dollars doesn't get you an apartment."

The throb in her temple was becoming a full-blown headache. This was desperation on a scale she'd never faced. Never wanted to face. Yet here it was.

And she'd been about to fire him.

The awful thing was, a part of her still wanted to. Some cold, knotty recess of her grinchy heart wanted to turn her back on Walt, because he'd become the incarnation of all the bad things that could happen to a person if they weren't careful, weren't born lucky. He was the living embodiment of the depressing segment of the news that made you want to flip the channel and mutter, "It's hopeless."

But there had to be hope. In any case, turning the channel wasn't an option. Walt wasn't something abstract. He was here, and he needed her help. "Where's your money going?" she asked. "Do you have a gambling addiction?"

"No. I just have debts. It's not your lookout."

"But—"

"Rebecca, if you'll just let me stay on a few more weeks, I should be able to get back on my feet again. And I'd be so grateful."

She'd heard that song before, and he seemed to be worse off now than when she'd hired him. But what else could she do? Walt was grateful. He was kind. He was even considerate . . . for someone who disappeared for days at a time and stole keys in order to trespass on her property. There was no question that she would let him stay. Of course she would.

"Where are your things?" she asked.

"What things?"

"You must own *something*," she said.

"I did, but during the day I was storing my suitcase out in the alley. A couple of days ago, someone stole it."

"That's horrible!"

"Or maybe the garbage collectors picked it up," he added hurriedly. "I might've stowed it too close to the Dumpster."

He spoke as if to reassure her. As if he worried her faith in humanity would be shaken by a suitcase theft in her own alley. But the idea of Walt's worldly possessions being picked up by the city and hauled to a landfill didn't make her feel much better. Especially since he seemed to have kept it out there to hide it from her.

"Are there any stores still open?" Even on Sunday night, there had to be somewhere that hadn't closed yet.

He lifted his shoulders, watching her warily. "Some of them, I imagine. Why?"

"We can get you an air mattress. Or a camp bed. You could set it up in my place."

"Your apartment?" He looked almost as horrified as Pam would be at the idea of his sleeping upstairs. "If it's all the same to you, I'd rather stay here."

She was equal parts insulted and relieved.

"Okay . . . but you can bring the bed up to my place during the day. And use my shower."

He nodded. "I'd appreciate that. It won't be for long, I promise."

They drove to a big-box store and bought a folding cot, a change of clothes, some toiletries, and a handled plastic tub for him to store his things. He said that seemed more practical than a suitcase. It was certainly more economical. Becca had never realized how expensive even cheap luggage was.

The shopping spree ended up costing her about what the parts for the dishwasher had probably amounted to. And now, instead of letting Walt go and acting like a firm businesswoman as Matthew had advised, she'd taken in a lodger.

So much for cupcake panties.

Chapter 10

Matthew did his best to mentally prepare for birthday day. He got up early, jogged on Nicole's treadmill, and ate a healthy break-fast. If anything required Wheaties, it was chaperoning a dozen eleven-year-old girls.

He arrived at the stables with Olivia well before the appointed hour, but Becca was there already, arranging chairs under a big tent set up between the farmhouse and the barn. The temporary enclosure was festooned with balloons and crepe-paper swags. They had planned to put up those together, so she had obviously been there awhile. Maybe Cal had helped her, a possibility that annoyed him more than it should have. As he and Olivia walked up, Becca was swatting Cal's hand away as he reached inside a bakery box.

"I have a day of hard work ahead of me," Cal complained.

"Yeah, and speaking of hard work, shouldn't you be doing some now instead of cadging snacks?"

"Hi, Becca, hi, Cal!" Olivia said, interrupting them. She'd been to Butternut Knoll only once—she'd insisted on checking it out personally—but she already looked perfectly at home.

They wished her happy birthday, and Cal pointed to the helmet that Olivia had been wearing nonstop since it was purchased. "Nice one."

"Becca helped me pick it out when Matthew took us to the city last week."

It was impossible to miss Cal's faltering smile. Or the way he glared at Matthew. Some unresolved feelings there, Matthew guessed. Becca didn't seem to notice, though.

"What else do you need me to do, Bec?" Cal asked.

"Nothing. You're just loitering at this point. And Lulu and Crackers still need to be saddled."

"Oh!" Olivia rushed to Cal's side. "I can help you. I want to learn to put on a saddle. If you show me how, I'll do the work for you."

"You've said the magic words," Becca deadpanned.

After those two left, Matthew approached the table and peeked into the boxes. One held a very large strawberry cake with HAPPY BIRTHDAY, OLIVIA written in multicolored block letters. The other, marked GLUTEN-FREE, contained some kind of brownies.

"Can I just make a wild guess?" he asked before he could talk himself out of it. When she looked at him curiously, he continued, "The divorce was your idea."

She drew back. "What makes you say that?"

"Cal. He acts more like a guy on the verge of proposing than an ex-husband."

Her lips quirked into a wry smile. "An expert on how men act before they pop the question, are you?"

He remembered his own unsuccessful results at proposing marriage to Nicole. "Sorry. None of my business." He shook his head. "I'm not sure what my business actually is today. You've done everything. It looks great."

"Thanks—it didn't take long. Now all you have to do is hang out with whatever moms decide to show up and stay instead of doing a drop-off and run."

"That doesn't sound very arduous."

She arched a brow. "You obviously haven't been around moms much."

It didn't take long for him to realize that she had a point. The party guests all drove up in a frantic ten-minute period. Most of the parents opted to drop their daughters off and collect them later, so Matthew was busy promising to keep their children in one piece. Fingers crossed. It was a miracle that no one had gotten lost or had forgotten to bring or e-mail the permission slips required by Cal. He'd been dreading the possibility of a kid being dropped off without one and not being able to participate.

His parental reassurances were conducted to the sounds of laughter and joyous squeals behind him. Eleven-year-old girls had the tendency to greet each other as if they had been separated for months instead of days. Their joy was charming but ear-splitting.

The only party guest who wasn't greeted by squeals and laughter was Monica Minter, who arrived in a gargantuan truck pulling a horse trailer. The girl stepped out of her shiny mammoth carriage in impressive equestrian regalia—polished black riding boots up to her kneecaps, jodhpurs, a red jacket over a button-down shirt with a tie, and a black riding helmet. The kind Olivia had decided was too fancy.

The birthday girl hurried over to greet the newcomer, her expression a perfect mix of awe and envy. These only increased when a man—the Minter groom?—strode around to the back of the trailer, opened it, and led out a black gelding with a white star on his muzzle while another man, presumably Mr. Minter, caught the moment on his camera. The horse's coat shone with health and indefatigable grooming, and its long, feathery tail twitched as gracefully as a woman showing off her silky, full-bodied locks in a shampoo ad. Matthew didn't know much about horses, but when Olivia stared with parted lips at the horse and exclaimed the word, "Beautiful," he couldn't help but agree.

The Minters stayed—Mr. Minter to video every moment his

daughter was on Allegro, and Gayle Minter to sit back and watch them in satisfaction. Another mom introduced herself as Meg Jentz, but Matthew felt he already knew her. He and Meg had been e-mailing back and forth all week about allergens—animal, airborne, and food-related. Meg had concerns that she voiced to Matthew in such voluminous, gruesome detail that she made Nicole seem like the most laissez-faire parent ever.

Heretofore, he'd never understood the instant, irreversible damage that could be done by cat dander, gluten, dairy, nuts or ingestion of anything that had ever had contact with any part of a nut, or how pervasive these substances were. By the end of three e-mail volleys, he was somewhat certain that no one at the birthday party would be exposed to mollusks, but that was about all. He'd had to refer Mrs. Jentz to Becca for reassurances that her daughter would not die during the course of the birthday party. Becca had obviously made the brownies for Deirdre Jentz's benefit, although when Deirdre arrived, EpiPen dangling around her neck in a needlepoint pouch, Meg Jentz bore a carton of brown rice milk and gluten- and nut-free fruit bars. "Just in case," she said, looking doubtfully at the specially prepared brownies.

For the first thirty minutes, the girls sat in the stands next to the training ring while Cal conducted a horse basics and safety lesson. Becca was with the kids while Matthew stayed back at the tent with the two moms.

"Poor Monica," Gayle Minter said. "She must be bored out of her mind. She's known how to behave around horses since she was able to stand up."

Meg Jentz shook her head. "You can never be too safe. I just wish they had told me there were cats around. I'm sure I saw a stray darting around a few moments ago."

"That's a barn cat," Gayle said. "Cats are essential around barns. They keep the mice and rat populations down."

"Rats?" Meg's thoughts no doubt turned to bubonic plague.

"Cats or rodents—pick your poison," the other woman said gruffly.

Meg didn't look comfortable having to pick. "Isn't it danger-ous to have all these smaller animals around the horses? I mean, if they get skittish . . ."

Gayle snorted. "From the looks of the plugs in this barn, they would be too bored to notice. Not exactly spirited, these horses."

A muttered "thank God" passed Meg's lips.

Gayle's observation was accurate. Aside from Harvey and Alle-gro, most of the horses brought out for the girls looked as if their nerves had been deadened by riding circles around a training ring for years. Like Meg, Matthew found this comforting. The parents might have agreed not to hold the stables or him liable for any disasters, but he still preferred that everyone be alive at the end of the day.

"Some of the big horses make me nervous," Meg said.

"Allegro is perfectly tame. Spirited, but tame. You just have to know horses." Gayle swung on Matthew. "Do you know horses?"

"No, I just rode once or twice at camp."

"Camps!" Gayle harrumphed in disgust. "That's usually what makes people dislike riding. The sad animals at places like that have no pepper in them. They might as well put kids on saw-horses."

"Pepperless sounds good to me," Meg said.

"That's not the way to raise a competitive child."

"I don't want Deirdre to be competitive—at least, not at this. I just want her to live through it."

"Oh look—they're mounting up," Matthew said, glad for the distraction, even if it meant having to stand next to anxious Meg. The woman seemed to hold her breath for the entire half hour that her daughter circled the ring on the stable's oldest, gentlest mare. When Cal and Becca led the kids to begin the short trail ride, it was all Matthew could do to keep Meg from tagging along in her minivan. He finally persuaded her to return to the tent.

"Monica's going to have a fit if they don't allow her to jump a fence or two," Gayle said.

"Jump?" Meg's eyes widened. "Surely not."

"Hardly worth putting Allegro in the trailer for this kind of thing."

"Don't worry," Matthew assured Meg.

The panicked woman drew back. "It's easy for *you* not to worry. Olivia's not your daughter."

At that moment, his teeth could have ground granite into talcum power. Yet he couldn't deny the truth of the statement. "I'm still concerned about her. Very concerned."

"Yes, but it's not the same," Meg insisted.

And to think he'd felt sympathetic toward her. Now he wanted to shove a fruit bar up her nose.

Gayle eyed him in understanding. "Of course you're concerned. What if something happened to her while Nicole was away? That would be a mess."

"Awful," Meg agreed.

"Nothing can tip a shaky relationship like troubles with kids," Mrs. Minter said. "I actually read that. Somebody did a study. Family problems cause more stress to relationships than money."

"Maybe if a relationship is shaky . . ." He meant to add more, but the almost-pitying looks the two women were aiming his way cut him off.

He frowned. How could they know his relationship to Nicole was shaky?

These ladies couldn't know that Nicole hadn't wanted to be with him during the weekend she had come home. Or about Bob. For that matter, *he* didn't know about Bob. Bob was just an uneasiness scratching somewhere at the back of his mind. Yet, looking in the women's eyes, he began to feel he'd missed a huge clue.

Someone might point to Nicole's monthlong absence as all the proof he needed that the relationship was on the rocks, but she was only gone because of work. A business trip. Matthew didn't want her to pass up opportunity for his sake. Plus, Nicole had left Olivia in his care. If that didn't show love and trust, what would?

"You're just the babysitter," Olivia had said.

Maybe even she knew something he didn't.

The riders eventually returned, traveling in a tight line. Only when Olivia shot him a look, puffing her cheeks before a tired exhale, did Matthew see any sense of strain from the birthday girl. Other than that, everything seemed as it should be, although later he wondered if he was too distracted by his Nicole problem to have been paying attention at all.

Becca waved at him on her way to the barn. They had agreed in advance that she would help Cal deal with the horses after the ride while Matthew kept the festivities rolling beneath the tent. Lighting the candles proved to be the biggest challenge he faced that day, as a cool autumn wind blew in just about the time the kids came back. But the girls all crowded around, creating a windbreak, and he successfully performed his lighting duties. The kids sang, and Olivia had no trouble blowing out all the candles. Matthew didn't wonder what she'd wished for—Olivia's heart's desire was the world's most open secret.

The girls chattered away at volumes that made Matthew instinctively back away to a more peaceful corner of the tent. The party seemed to be on autopilot, so he could sit back and relax a little. The end was in sight. His focus remained mostly on Deirdre Jentz munching desultorily at her fruit bar as her longing gaze strayed to the others wolfing down cake.

Someone plopped down in the folding chair next to him. Matthew looked over and then did a double-take. Cal grinned at him. "How's Mr. Mom?"

Matthew smiled back. In the past month, he'd received similar ribbing from some of his more unimaginative coworkers. "Ready to do a victory dance," he said. "I'm glad everything worked out today. Thank you—I think Olivia's having a great time."

"She's a natural," Cal said with an appreciative nod in Olivia's direction. "Her and that other one."

"Monica?" Matthew guessed.

Cal laughed. "Oh sure. She's a champ." He nodded to Deirdre. "But that one was having the time of her life."

She wasn't now. Her mother was practically in her lap, monitoring every bite that crossed Deirdre's lips.

So far Cal hadn't struck Matthew as an incredibly earnest person, but he didn't seem to be someone who just said whatever he thought another person wanted to hear. "So Olivia seems like a natural around horses?"

"Oh yeah. I can tell. Some kids take to it like water bugs to a bathtub. That's Olivia."

Matthew sat up straighter. A man who compared a girl to a water bug definitely wasn't just currying favor. He wished Nicole were here. Maybe she'd understand that riding wasn't just a whim with Olivia.

"Becca said she was the same way," Cal said.

Matthew nodded, still thinking about Nicole. Maybe he could get Mr. Minter to post some of his birthday footage of the whole group so Nicole could see Olivia in action.

"Does she mention us?" Cal asked.

It took a moment for Matthew to figure out what he was talking about. "That you and she were married? Yeah, she told me that."

"No, I meant . . . has she ever given you an indication of where her mind's at now?" Cal's cheeks darkened a shade. "I only ask because it seems like you two have been spending a lot of time together."

Matthew grew uncomfortable. He didn't like gossiping. He also didn't like the look in Cal's eye, which somehow managed to be both curious and accusatory. "She's just been helping me out with the birthday stuff."

"Really? You two really aren't, you know, involved?"

Matthew's impulse to reassure Cal on this point warred with his desire to tell him to back off. He didn't know why. Becca's life might be none of Cal's business, but her relationship with her ex-husband was certainly not his own. At the same time, a voice in his head whispered, *This guy's not right for her.*

But what did he know? "We're just friends."

"But she obviously likes you." Cal's shoulders hunched. "You've got that responsible dad vibe going for you."

"But that's because of Olivia. Becca likes Olivia, and Olivia worships her. Without Olivia, I doubt I would even be on her radar."

"So you don't think she *likes* likes you?" Cal asked.

What kind of question was that? Matthew wondered if being around tweens was contagious. "No, I don't think she does. Not in the way you mean."

Saying it aloud caused a piercing sensation in his chest. Because he *liked* Becca, he realized. It wasn't just friendship, or nostalgia. He was falling for her, even while he was living in Nicole's house. The realization made him feel like a weasel.

Cal let out a breath. He seemed to be on the verge of saying something when chaos erupted. The cake table practically levitated as everyone stood at once, letting out a collective gasping cry. Matthew shot to his feet, trying to make sense of what he was seeing.

The focal point of the hubbub was Monica, who was dripping with what appeared to be a liter of soda that had spilled down her front. The liquid stained her snappy red jacket and the lap of her jodhpurs. Her mother was racing toward her with a handful of disposable napkins, but Matthew could tell that the damage was beyond napkin-dabbing. Maybe even beyond dry cleaning. Monica moaned, and then swung toward Olivia, who was standing just behind her, a defiant glare on her face.

After the initial shock, twelve girls and several adults all began speaking at once.

"Olivia did it!"

"I saw it!"

"It was an accident!"

That last exclamation was from Olivia, but her defiant expression made Matthew skeptical. He hurried toward the group.

"The cup just slipped," she told him.

One of Monica's supporters piped up, "She called Monica a snot. I heard her."

Monica burst into tears.

"I did not," Olivia shot back. Then, crossing her arms, she glowered at her nemesis and confessed, "I called her a *show-offy* snot. Which she is."

Chapter 11

After the ride, the girls had unsaddled the horses and did a quick sponge-and-brush of the horses before dashing off for cake. Becca stayed behind to make sure her equine charges for the day, Crackers, Harvey, and Lulu, got some extra TLC brushing and had their hooves cleaned before putting them in stalls, where they munched on hay as a reward for their party service. All the other hands were dealing with the rest of the Butternut Knoll horses that had been ridden that day, and Allegro was getting a full cool-down bath and grooming from the man the Minters brought along.

Becca went back to the tent, expecting to see twelve girls in the early stages of sugar coma. But by the time she reached them, mayhem had erupted. The group under the tent had split into two vocal factions—Pro-Olivia or Pro-Monica. Unfortunately for Olivia, it didn't take long to sort out the truth and for her support team to evaporate. Mr. Minter's camera had caught Olivia in the corner of one shot, tipping a cup of soda over Monica's shoulder. With malicious intent. It was as if some kind of devil had taken hold of her.

Important eleventh birthday lesson: Lies don't stand up well to instant replay.

After Olivia's guilt was determined, she was forced by Matthew to apologize to Monica and her parents. Matthew divided up the leftover cake among the guests, leaving none for Olivia, and also made her renounce her unopened presents, which seemed overly harsh to Becca. By the time the guests straggled away, Olivia was starting to look a little more sympathetic to everyone but the Minters, who packed up their Pepsi-soaked child and their thoroughbred and motored away in an understandable huff.

On her way out, Deirdre Jentz bid Olivia good-bye. "Happy birthday, Olivia. I had a fun time. I'm sorry about the presents, but you can have my leftover fruit bars." She handed Olivia a GladWare tub.

"Thanks," Olivia said, accepting the offering. Even a gift of fruit bars was better than no gift at all.

After her guests were gone, Olivia roller-coastered through the stages of guilt all over again in quick succession—denial, defiance, and finally resentful acceptance. "I didn't mean to do it," she explained to Becca and Matthew as they cleared off the table. "It just happened."

Becca held open the mouth of a garbage bag. "You *just happened* to overturn a drink on Monica?"

The girl's face reddened. "What I meant was, my wanting to do it just overwhelmed me. It was like I was somebody else watching me do it."

"That excuse gets trotted out in courts a lot," Becca said. "It's called temporary insanity, and it doesn't work well anymore because most people realized it was baloney."

"But it's true," Olivia insisted. "And Monica *was* hateful and show-offy."

"That was no reason to attack her," Matthew pointed out.

"You weren't around," Olivia said. "All during the ride she was making mean comments about Harvey."

Becca tensed. She'd been riding behind all the girls, trying to keep an eye out for a horse that might decide to bolt or throw someone, while Monica and Olivia had usually been toward the front of the line, with Cal. "What did she say about Harvey?"

"She said he looked dingy, for one thing. And that he wasn't really white, and maybe not even a thoroughbred. And that he was probably going to be made into glue soon." Olivia squinted at her. "You wouldn't sell Harvey to a glue factory, would you?"

"Of course not. That's crazy."

"That's what I told her." Nevertheless, she looked relieved.

"Then why throw a soda on her?" Matthew asked in exasperation. Monica's having insulted a horse clearly wasn't doing it for him, motive-wise.

Olivia's mouth set into a stubborn line. "Because she said something even worse. Something I can't repeat."

"Worse than insulting Harvey?" That was setting the bar high, in Becca's estimation.

"Well . . . just as bad," Olivia allowed.

"Wait." Matthew shook his head. "Try to get some perspective here, O. You just turned eleven, so you're supposed to have a pretty good grip on that old 'sticks and stones' saying by now. Remember? The one that says words can't harm you? Instead, the minute somebody uttered something you didn't like, you threw a toddler fit, ruining your own birthday party. You broke the biggest taboo of being a host—you attacked a guest. All the little rationalizations you come up with at this point don't matter. You're going to have to offer Monica and her family another formal apology, in person or *very* well written, and I'm going to have to explain this to Nicole, too."

Olivia was taking the bad news on the chin until Matthew mentioned her mother. "Tell Mom? Why?"

"For one thing, someone else will probably tell her. For another, when she gets back she might wonder why you're forbidden from watching television for two months."

Two months? Matthew was putting the *loco* in *in loco parentis*, in Becca's opinion, but Olivia didn't even blink at losing television privileges. "Okay, but *please* don't tell Mom. I couldn't explain it to her. That would be awful."

"You screwed up," he pointed out. "It's supposed to be awful."

"Yeah, but if Mom starts asking questions . . ." Olivia's face collapsed into a frown as another fear tumbled right on top of her last one. "Or if Monica ever tells her mom the truth about why it all happened and *that* got back to Mom, then it wouldn't just be me who was miserable. Lives would be ruined."

Matthew shook his head. "You're overdramatizing."

Olivia blurted out, "Monica told everybody that Becca's your girlfriend."

Becca went still. She didn't look at Matthew, but she could hear his gulp of surprise. "Why would she say that?" he asked.

"I don't know," Olivia said. "I guess she hates me. I *did* call her a birdbrain once during the trail ride, because I was so mad about what she said about Harvey." She looked over at Becca. "He's such a great horse. Thank you for letting me ride him."

"You handled him like a champ."

A flash of the old brightness lit Olivia's eyes, but then she hung her head, obviously remembering she was in the doghouse and probably wouldn't be allowed to ride again anytime soon. "When we got back for the cake and stuff, somebody asked if I was going to go to Hawaii to be with Mom. And I said, well, duh, probably not, since I have to go to school in Leesburg. And then I heard Monica whisper to Emily that Mom would probably want to take me with her when she finds out that you and Matthew are going out together."

This time Becca did look at Matthew. "Okay, now *I* want to dump soda on that kid. A whole two-liter jug, if possible."

His glance let her know that he found her response loyal but unhelpful.

She'd forgotten how catty kids could be—no better than their adult counterparts sometimes. After all, hadn't Pam and Erin been teasing her about her relationship with Matthew for weeks?

She should have suspected that others had noticed them together, too. If she understood gossip, what the kids were exchanging was probably the trickle-down version of the more intense, salacious chatter of their parents.

"It's not true, is it?" Olivia asked them.

"No!" she and Matthew answered in unison.

Becca was a little surprised by the vehemence in Matthew's tone. Of course, nothing *had* happened between them, but there had been times when she'd thought that he was a little attracted to her. Not that she wanted him to be.

The confusing thing was, she didn't want him *not* to be. What a mess.

"I didn't think so," Olivia said. "But if Mom heard people's stupid gossip . . ." She turned her most beseeching look Matthew's way. "I know I have to be punished, but please don't tell her what happened."

He considered the request. "We can just not go into details."

Olivia exhaled in relief. In the next moment, however, a new worry appeared to prey on her mind. "I guess you won't want to come to Career Day now," she said to Becca.

With the flurry of party-related preparations in the past few days, Becca had almost forgotten the promise she'd made to appear at the school's Career Day. The thought of it made her tired, but she'd be damned if she was going to let local chatter keep her from fulfilling a promise. Screw all the penny-ante Leesburg tongue wagging. Their small-town scandal trolling wouldn't make her cower. *Bring it, folks,* she thought. In this, she was no amateur. She'd been in the *National Enquirer.*

"Of course I'm going. I've been counting on it." Her bluster was undermined a bit when she asked, "What day?"

"Wednesday," Olivia said.

"I'll be there."

After Matthew and Olivia drove away, she went back to the barn to see Harvey, give him another quick brush, and let him out to pasture. She could also help Cal and his stable guy, Artie, if

they still needed a hand. She glanced at her watch. If she hurried, she could get everything finished up here and still make it
back to the shop before Pam closed. Then she would need to do
some prep and a batch of cakes for tomorrow. All she had to do
was get through Sunday. Then she could collapse on Monday,
when the shop was closed.

Cal met her at Harvey's stall. "Your people finally clear out?"
She nodded.

"I'm glad there was a little excitement there at the end," he
drawled. "I would hate to think I'd had a hand in a party that was
totally unmemorable."

She pulled a carrot out of her jeans for Harvey, who took it as
his due. Spoiled. She slipped his halter on while he was distracted by chewing. "Some memories I could do without." Like
the one of Olivia asking her and Matthew if the gossip was true.
That was not something she wanted to mention to Cal, however.
"That Monica kid made a crack about Harvey and glue factories
to Olivia."

Cal let out a hoot of surprise. "Good thing she didn't say it to
you. Instead of a spilled cold drink, there might have been a
homicide."

"Olivia was pretty hot." Becca shook her head, half in admiration. "I hope it was worth no presents, possible pariah status at
school, and two months of no TV."

He crossed his arms. "You sure seem wrapped up in their lives.
It's like they're your newest project."

What was he talking about? "I don't do projects."

"Of course you do. Your shop was your biggest project."

"That's not a project, it's a business. There's a difference. A
person needs to put business first to succeed."

"I never have," he said.

"I rest my case."

"First, you focused on bringing cupcakes to Leesburg like it
was your life's mission." He ticked off her life errors on the fingers of his right hand. "And around that same time, there was

me—although as a project, our marriage didn't outlast the cupcakes. Then you left me and it was your apartment for a while, and fixing it up. Pam says you've run out of steam on that."

"Not steam," Becca said. "Ready cash."

"And now there's Walt. Good luck fixing him."

"He's a person, not a project."

"With you, I'm beginning to think it's the same difference. And your success rate isn't very good with either."

Her jaw set in consternation. What a load of horseshit—and yet, her mind couldn't help sifting through the evidence and concluding that there was a hair of truth to what he was saying. Not that she was going to grant him the satisfaction of knowing that she was giving his crackpot mental ramblings any credence.

His gaze stayed on her.

"I don't know what you're talking about," she said. "The shop's turning a profit now."

"Yeah, but your apartment's still half-finished, your marriage busted up, and now you're involved with a guy who's as good as married."

Or as good as separated, she thought, remembering the problem of Nicole and Bob. She'd tried to keep those two out of her mind when dealing with Matthew. It hadn't seemed any of her business to inject her suspicions into Matthew's life.

But apparently letting suspicions run wild was the order of the day. "If you're worried about Matthew, don't be. Why would you think we're involved? Because I helped out with a party?"

"Emotionally involved, I mean. I know you're not having sex."

She took a step back. "How do you know that?"

"Because I asked him. At the party."

Heat crept up her neck. "What kind of insanity made you do that?" No wonder Matthew had been so adamant telling Olivia that there was nothing between them.

"I'm worried about you, Bec. And now you have an old loser leeching off you, too."

Anger bubbled up in her. "Loser! Says the guy who was born

with a silver spoon in his mouth—that he's pawned whenever he's gotten into trouble."

He flinched a little, but didn't fight back.

"I'm giving poor old Walt a chance not to get flushed down into the gutter of lost people," she said. "You call that being leeched off of?"

"I just worry it's going to end badly."

Did the whole world think she should show Walt the door? "Just because *we* didn't stay together doesn't mean I can't manage my life, or that I walk away from responsibilities."

He looked at her long and hard. "Maybe I'm jealous."

"Of Walt?" She laughed uncomfortably. "I can reassure you about that, at least."

He took a step closer. "I'm serious. The thing is, I wish you hadn't walked away from us." He put his hands around her upper arms and drew her to him.

"Cal—" Before she could get coherent words out, his lips were on hers. It took her a moment to compute. Her ex-husband was kissing her. Call her naïve, but she hadn't seen this coming. The lunge tactic seemed so unlike him.

She pushed him away and nearly stumbled into Harvey. Maybe keeping her horse on at the Knoll had been wrong. When she and Cal had separated, she hadn't wanted to completely bail out on him and the farm, and as far as divorces went, theirs hadn't been acrimonious. Also, good stables were hard to find, and Pam and Erin were here. Maybe to Cal, however, keeping her horse at Butternut Knoll came across as a mixed signal. She certainly hadn't meant to string him along—she'd assumed moving into her own apartment and the divorce decree were pretty convincing evidence that their relationship was over.

They had never discussed their breakup in any depth. Becca assumed they hadn't needed to. Now she saw that she needed to state her feelings so that he would believe that it was finished, once and for all. She took a breath. "Leaving you wasn't a mistake, Cal. It was righting a wrong. I married you because I wanted to belong to a new place, really belong, and be accepted. In a moment of weakness, I used you as a shortcut."

"I didn't mind."

"*I* minded," she said. "I minded as soon as I realized what a mistake I'd made. I didn't love you, Cal."

The blunt words struck home. "Whoa," he said.

Never one to follow directions, she kept going. "I liked you a lot, and I loved the idea of living out here. But using you that way was really no different from the guys who would date me because of some misconception that it would get them a toehold on the celebrity food chain. It was wrong. You deserved better than that. You still do."

He took a step backward and raised his hand in mock surrender. "Okay. I believe you." His tone was typical Cal, but she detected real hurt in his eyes.

His expression made her want to take back what she'd said, which seemed so awful now that she played it back in her own head. "I'm sorry," she said. "That came out harsher than I meant it to."

"Hey, no," he said. "Tough love." He arched a russet brow. "Or, in your case, tough like-you-a-lot. Say no more. Message received."

"I just don't want you to get depressed, or—"

His eyes flashed. "That's really not your business anymore." He turned and walked away.

She hurried through the rest of the chores, feeling an aching, awkward awareness of Cal and his resentment as they maneuvered around each other. She couldn't wait to get home. The minute she'd done enough to make it seem as though she wasn't fleeing, she led Harvey out of the barn and then stopped short with a groan.

The tent. She'd forgotten that it still needed to be taken down.

Cal appeared beside her and read her mind. "Don't worry about it."

"I can't just abandon you with it."

He snorted. Or maybe that was Harvey.

"I want to help," she insisted.

When he spoke, his gruff tone took her aback. "Artie and I can handle it. Go home."

He sounded desperate to get rid of her. Could she blame him? In the end, she let Harvey out, scooted to her car, and drove back to town before she could do any more damage.

Chapter 12

Becca had planned to spend part of Sunday thinking about her presentation for Olivia's school's Career Day, but life got in the way. Pam called that morning and said she was visiting her parents in Richmond. Since Pam had worked Saturday, Becca didn't mind being solo at the shop all day. She could always send Walt out if she had an errand that needed running. But working in the shop all day didn't leave her time to sit at the computer and really nail down what she was going to say to a roomful of fifth-graders.

After work, her encounter with Cal preoccupied her thoughts. Given how badly she'd communicated with him, she was beginning to think that she should avoid people entirely and embrace her inner hermit.

Monday the shop was closed, so she spent some quality time with Harvey. She hurried in and out of the barn as quickly as possible, worried she would bump into Cal, but Artie said he hadn't been around since Saturday night.

Where was he? Not that she wanted him there, but his absence made her anxious. Her cozy world felt very lonely all of a sudden. Forget being a hermit. She missed her buddy network.

Pam was still with her parents, and Erin was . . . well, who knew where. Becca had e-mailed her several times, but her efforts to reach out had so far been met with vague replies. *Everything's great! Hawaii is absolutely gorgeous!* Erin had sent her attachments—pictures of orchids, pineapples, and more selfies of herself grinning in front of umbrella drinks. Her smile was always huge. None of the pictures contained Bob, Becca couldn't help noticing. The e-mails contained no specifics, no gloating about her triumph over Nicole. No mention of when she was coming back, either.

If this went on much longer, she and Pam might have to fly out on a search-and-rescue mission. How could they be sure those Erin pictures weren't all from one afternoon? What if Bob and Nicole had done away with Erin and were sending the e-mails themselves to cover the fact that Erin had been tossed into the ocean? Or a volcano.

The thought of Nicole made Becca want to call Matthew, but now that impulse was checked, too. Knowing that a lot of people suspected them of being involved made getting together, however informally, seem illicit. They had assured Olivia that nothing lovey-dovey was going on, so it was probably best to hold the socializing to a minimum.

Letting him remain in the dark about Nicole felt a little dishonest, but according to the vague e-mails from Erin, her marriage was rock-solid again—or at least surviving in an *absolutely gorgeous* atmosphere—so maybe Matthew's own relationship could be salvaged, too.

In her restlessness, she even considered inviting Walt out to do something. But what would they have to talk about? Besides, she'd told him that he could stay in the store all day Monday if he felt like resting up. She didn't want to act like his employer/landlady intruding on his private time.

As she and Harvey wound their way around the familiar trails, she took in the fall color and ached for someone to share it with. Solitude was never what it was cracked up to be. For one of the few times since she'd left LA, she missed that city and her old network of friends. She rarely heard from them anymore, aside from glimpsing their updates on social media. Most considered her as far out of reach now in Virginia as they would have if she'd opened a cupcake store in Siberia.

Primarily, though, she missed her mom. After four years, the loss still pained her. Now that she was older, and less of a numb-skull, she appreciated her mother's character. If Ronnie Hudson had been here with a whole day to herself stretched out in front of her, she wouldn't have been whining about not having anyone to talk to. She would have gone out and "had a big time," which could mean anything from going to a Bingo hall, to a day of beauty at her favorite salon, or a shopping spree at the closest discount store. Her mother had never been one to waste time moping.

Becca, on the other hand, was in full-tilt self-pity mode, and thinking about her mom gave her the perfect idea for how to wallow a little deeper. She returned Harvey to the barn, gave him an extra-attentive session with the brush, and drove back to town, stopping at the grocery store on the way. She swooped down the aisles, grabbing items that she hadn't bought in years, and maybe never had purchased on her own. Generic cake mix. Red Jell-O. Canned icing. Frozen strawberries. She was on a mission. A mission that would make her old French pastry instructor from the culinary institute she'd dropped out of faint in horror.

Back at her apartment, she dug out her spare hand mixer and set to work making what was for her, and probably only her, the ultimate comfort food: her mom's strawberry cake.

No telling where her mother had found the recipe. Ronnie had been an ace at whipping up comfort meals. Every time they sat down to the dinner table at their house it was a little like tucking in at the local diner. Yet in all her mom's years of making layer cakes when they just needed a treat, Becca was willing to lay money that her mother had never encountered marzipan, and would have confused a ganache with something you slipped over your shoes when it rained. But every birthday, no fail, Ronnie whipped together a strawberry cake, and in Becca's mind, the taste of it—even the idea of it—had come to mean the ultimate indulgence. Because it meant her mother, and love.

Everyone assumed the Strawberry Cake Shop had been named after the strawberry cake Becca always had on offer. But the truth was, the store was named for a cake she'd never once considered putting on offer, a cake that would probably have all the great chefs who had graced the earth spinning in their graves. She was almost ashamed to admit even to herself that she loved it more than any other dessert in the world.

She worked quickly, mixing Jell-O and cake mix, cracking in the egg that was supposed to make homemakers feel as if they were preparing food with a nutrient or two in it. When the pans were in the oven, she wasted no time putting the frosting together from a prepared tub mixed with a thawed can of frozen strawberries that slid into the bowl with a satisfying *slurp*. She had only baked this cake once or twice on her own, years before, but she had seen her mother make it dozens of times. She could have prepared it in her sleep.

One of her deepest convictions—professionally, at least—was that cake layers should always cool completely before being iced. Today she made an exception, tossing the layers into the fridge to flash-cool them and then slathering on the pink frosting as soon as she could get away with it without creating a runny mess. When it was all done, the cake listed to one side, giving it the perfect imperfect look it would have had if it had come out of her mother's kitchen. She couldn't have been more pleased.

She was even tempted to stick a stray birthday candle into the top of it for old time's sake, but she decided that would be a little too pathetic. Instead, in honor of her mom, from her bookshelf she picked what had been Ronnie's favorite movie—*The Natural*, starring Robert Redford—and popped it into her DVD player. She'd sat through the film so many times with her mom, it was almost like having her there with her. Especially when she tucked into a piece of the cake, which had that unmistakable, chemically delicious strawberry flavor. The cake was just how she remembered it—sweet enough to melt tooth enamel on contact.

Halfway through the story of Roy Hobbs, the doorbell rang. Becca jumped, reached for the remote to pause the movie, then headed down to her door. When she opened it, Walt stood in front of her, hat in hand.

"Hello, Rebecca," he said, almost reluctantly. "I'd like to say a few words, if I may."

It sounded as if he intended to deliver a eulogy.

Maybe he was here to tell her that he needed to be moving along.

"Sure," she said, foregoing the usual plea for him to call her Becca. He looked so anxious, she wanted to put him at ease. "I just made a cake. You want some?"

Not waiting for his answer, she turned and led the way up. His footsteps behind her were slower, and by the time he crested the last stair, he was short of breath. He fanned himself with his hat brim and then followed her to the kitchen.

He usually came upstairs in the mornings to shower and eat his breakfast, so when he perched on a stool, one of the cats leapt into his lap as though greeting an old friend.

"Feel free to dislodge him, if you can."

"Cash and I are buds now," he said, treating the kitty to a lengthy chin scratch.

"It helps that you're sitting next to a cake. Cash is the first cat I've known with a sweet tooth."

Walt seemed interested in the cake, too. He inspected it with a slightly tilted head. "Strawberry, right? I always liked that."

She nodded and cut him off a piece, and without much encouragement, she blurted out the history of her mom and the cake. He listened patiently and attentively, but seemed relieved when she finished so he could finally take a bite.

"It's good." His voice cracked a little, and she could have sworn he loved it almost as much as she did. "Very good."

"I don't know why I'm feeling so sentimental about Mom today. I just miss her. I think she would have liked it here in

Leesburg." As the absurdity of the statement struck her, she laughed. Ronnie had run away from a small town and had never left LA voluntarily. "Well, maybe she would have liked to visit."

"She always preferred the big city?"

"Oh yeah. I guess she would have gone stir-crazy in Leesburg after a while."

"Yeah, I can see that." He shifted on the stool.

Stir-crazy probably hadn't been the best expression to choose. Not with Walt, who knew the real thing.

"And you say your Mom died . . . when?" he asked.

"It's been nearly four years ago now. I kind of fell apart after it happened. I felt so rootless, you know? Like I didn't have anyone in the world. I don't, actually. No siblings, not even any cousins that I know of. Just Harvey."

He looked unspeakably sorry for her. "No father?"

"No, I never knew my father. Never even knew who he was, I mean."

"That's not right." His Droopy Dog look intensified.

"It wasn't bad. Of course I wondered about my father when I was a kid. There were actually a few years when I obsessed about him—you know, who he was, what happened. I'd spin all sorts of scenarios in my head, of old movie stars who'd had to choose between claiming me or their careers. Or princes who had visited California briefly and deposited me there with Mom for safekeeping. But once I got older and understood the birds and bees a little better, Mom told me that my father wasn't anyone I'd want to know. I got the feeling that he was serious bad news. She'd even put "father unknown" on my birth certificate so I wouldn't ever have to deal with him. The only thing I ever found out from her about him was that his name was Johnny—not a princely name—and that he played saxophone. Oh, and that he'd taken off after she told him she was pregnant. A real gem."

Walt petted Cash absently, a glum expression on his face, and Becca felt a twinge of guilt for plunging them into such a maudlin conversation.

"Mom made up for the no-dad thing. She never married, but

she was Supermom. She did the work of ten people, but never spoiled me." Becca laughed. "Well, at least, *I* didn't think she spoiled me. I thought she was way too strict." Walt was still shaking his head and looking quasi-suicidal, so she asked, "What about you? Were your parents strict?"

"I loved my father, but he passed away when I was still in elementary school. He drove a truck and died in a road accident. It about killed my mother, too. She had nothing but struggles after that."

"Is she still alive?" Becca asked.

He looked surprised by the question. "Oh gosh, no. She died years ago. Cancer."

"That's what Mom died of. It was awful to see."

Walt looked pained. *Great job changing the subject to something happier, Becca.* She wasn't even sure why she'd decided to spill her family history to him, except that the subject had been on her mind and Walt was the first available ear she'd come across all day. Now she'd dragged him down with her. Poor guy.

"I apologize for prattling on about all this. All day I've been feeling mopey. You're probably regretting ringing my doorbell." She frowned. "Didn't you say you had something to talk to me about?"

"Nothing important." He nudged the plate away, held on to Cash, and slid off the bench. He set the cat on the floor with a parting pat. "I was going to tell you that I fixed a couple of the wobbly chairs. A few screws needed tightening, was all."

"Oh." Odd that he would make a special trip for that. Unless . . . "I should pay you."

He batted the offer away with a sweep of his hand through the air. "It was nothing to speak of." He started shuffling toward the door.

"Wait," she said. "Would you like a piece of cake for the road?" *The road* meaning the staircase down to the first floor.

He stopped and appeared to consider the offer, giving the cake a last, rheumy-eyed glance. He shook his head. "No thank you."

He rarely ate more than a few bites of anything, she'd noticed. It was worrying. "I could make you a sandwich."

"That's not necessary. I've got some snacks if I need anything. Thank you, though." He turned to leave but then stopped again. "That strawberry cake?"

She tilted her head expectantly, ready to give him the whole thing if he wanted it.

"Sweetest food I've ever eaten," he said.

Yet he wouldn't hear of taking any more.

When he was gone, she frowned to herself. It had been the first time she'd talked to Walt just for no reason at all, and she had immediately introduced the most depressing topics imaginable. No wonder the man had left as soon as he could politely excuse himself. After the life he'd led, the last thing he probably wanted to dwell on was his deceased parents. From the sound of things, his troubles had started early in life.

And she thought she had problems.

When she looked up, Cash had hopped onto the counter and was demolishing the leftover piece of cake Walt had left on his plate. She groaned at the thought of veterinary dental bills she couldn't afford and plucked him off the counter, offering him a conciliatory head butt before dropping him back onto the ground.

Pam called Tuesday morning, before Becca was fully awake, and left a message saying she wasn't going to make it to the shop that day. She'd stayed another night in Richmond—she said she had something to take care of there. Her voice sounded edgy. Strange.

Tuesday was never the busiest day at the shop—they didn't see much action until the after-school crowd streamed in. Becca liked the idea of a leisurely, low-traffic day, except when she got one. Then she worried that the world was burnt out on cupcakes. She would imagine herself declaring bankruptcy and having to sell out and move, maybe into a stall with Harvey. Apprehension over what she would do when she'd reached her last penny consumed her. And not just for herself. How would she support an aging horse? After Saturday, Cal probably wanted her to find a different place to board him. Different inevitably would mean more expensive.

By afternoon, she was in a state. Added to the usual angst about the looming worldwide cupcake surplus, there was the speech, still unplanned, that she was slated to give at Olivia's school the next day. Also, the vision of poor Erin as a cinder at the bottom of a Hawaiian volcano still plagued her thoughts. And what was up with Pam? She never stayed overnight at her parents' if she could help it. And then there was that puzzling phrase—something Pam had to take care of. . . .

Maybe Pam had gone to Richmond to see a doctor. But if that was the case, why hadn't she said something? The only answer Becca's frantic mind could come up with was that Pam was very sick, perhaps with something fatal, and hadn't wanted to worry her.

"Is something wrong?" Walt asked her. A brave question, after she'd talked his ear off the day before. He'd been quiet and more-than-usually wan all day.

"Just fretting about Pam." She stared at the slew of pumpkin spice cupcakes she'd made for Career Day. At least she'd been worrying productively. If her visual aids managed to put her audience in a sugar coma, maybe her speech wouldn't matter so much.

"I thought there was something on your mind," Walt said. "The same CD's been playing on the stereo for three straight hours."

He was right. And it was Philip Glass. No wonder she had a tension headache.

"Why don't you take a short break?" he said. "Go upstairs and relax for a half hour. Eat something healthy."

When Walt was telling her she looked bad, it was time to worry. "You don't mind manning the counter?" She'd never actually left him unsupervised during working hours for more than a few minutes, but he was competent. And it wasn't a busy day.

He shooed her out the door. "Go ahead. I've got this down cold."

She went upstairs, started to fix herself something to eat, then picked up the phone and called Pam.

No answer. Probably because she was in the middle of an emergency CT scan. Becca's brain had latched on to the doctor scenario and wouldn't let go.

She got out her address book, looked up the number for Pam's parents in Richmond, and dialed. She exhaled in relief when Pam's mom answered. If she was at home, chances were Pam wasn't dying in a hospital. "Hi, Mrs. Deutch. This is Becca Hudson, Pam's friend. Is Pam okay?"

The pause that followed was fraught with confusion. "I don't know . . . Did something happen?"

"Not that I know of," Becca said. "I was just wondering how she seemed to you."

"I don't know. How does she seem to you?"

Me and Pam's mom. The new Abbott and Costello.

"I haven't seen her since she took off a few days ago," Becca said, "but her message sounded odd. I was wondering if she looked okay to you."

"I haven't seen her." Mrs. Deutch's voice quavered with tension now. "You say she's disappeared?"

Becca tried to untangle the situation. Obviously, Pam had fibbed about visiting her parents. But where had she gone instead? And why lie?

As the seconds ticked by, Mrs. Deutch's concern escalated into a full-blown panic. "Where could she be? Why would she have sounded scared on the phone?"

"I never said scared," Becca said. "Just odd."

"What if she's been kidnapped?" Mrs. Deutch exclaimed. "I worry so much about her, especially about doing her little real estate business. I read a book recently about a poor Realtor who was kidnapped from an open house by a psychopath."

"Yeah, but that was fiction," Becca said.

"Has it been twenty-four hours? I need to call Jim."

Jim was Pam's father. "No, wait. Please. I'll find her—no need to panic. I'm sure everything's fine. Just a little misunderstanding." Becca forced herself into a perky brightness. "I'll have Pam give you a call as soon as I hear from her. Okay? How about that?"

The woman was still flaking out on the other end of the line when Becca finally begged off.

She hung up and collapsed onto her couch, whereupon she was immediately set upon by the felines. She petted them absently while she sifted through what little information she had. Pam had lied, and was now MIA. Maybe she wasn't dying, but there was evidently something going on with her.

Minutes passed before she remembered that Walt was still downstairs alone. She went back down, bracing for some new calamity, only to find Walt calmly serving customers. Everything was fine. In fact, he turned out to be quite the salesman.

"Someone came by needing a bunch of cupcakes for the high school," he explained. "Something about a party for the marching band. I sold them three dozen."

She nodded, then studied the shelves more critically. On Tuesdays, she didn't usually have full shelves. Not like she would on a Saturday morning, for instance. Yet the chocolate, vanilla, and lemon cupcakes she'd left before going upstairs were still there. "Where did you get the three dozen?"

He nodded toward the back. "From the pumpkin spice ones you baked this morning in your frenzy. I figured you'd be glad to get rid of those."

She looked back at the counter where she'd left the Career Day cupcakes. Damn. She'd have to make more. And Walt seemed so pleased with himself, she'd have to figure out a way to do it surreptitiously so that he wouldn't notice that he'd actually screwed up. Not that selling three dozen cupcakes was a screwup, exactly. At least it was a profitable mistake. But now she had an anniversary cake to prepare, as well as the cupcake redo.

She got to work, leaving Walt at the register. Just before closing time, she noticed that he looked tired. "Maybe *you* should go upstairs for a bit," she said. "You could have a nap on my sofa."

He shook his head. "I'm fine."

"There are some sandwich fixings in the fridge. You could make me one and bring it down in an hour or so." She'd never gotten around to eating the lunch that she'd interrupted so that she could make her ill-conceived call to Pam's mom. Also, Walt's being gone for an hour would give her about enough time to get the replacement cupcakes made. "It would be doing me a huge favor."

He considered this and let out a sigh as he scratched his scraggly chin. "I guess I could get cleaned up again while I'm up there. Get that out of the way."

"Good idea," she said.

When he was gone, she spent the next hour running between the register and her mixer. Was this harried feeling the first sign of a mind coming unhinged? She'd never been so glad to see business slow down at the dinner hour. She settled into the back as the new pumpkin cupcakes cooled, and began whipping up another batch of vanilla nutmeg buttercream.

With the stand mixer on high, she barely heard the bell over the door ring as Pam swept in. Becca nearly collapsed against her KitchenAid in relief . . . until she saw the annoyed look in Pam's eyes.

"Are you insane?" Pam shouted at her over the whir of the mixer.

Becca shut it off. "Where have you been?"

"I'll be happy to tell you that as soon as I find out what possessed you to tell my mom that I'd been kidnapped."

"I didn't say anything about kidnapping," Becca said. "I just called to ask where you were. Which I never would have done if I'd known you lied to me about going to Richmond in the first place."

Pam had the decency to look a little embarrassed about her fib. "I'm sorry. But I still don't know what made you call my mother, like I was a teenager or something."

"I've been going a little crazy, I think. And with Erin gone . . ."

Pam rolled her eyes. "She's coming back. Cal got an e-mail from her this afternoon."

"*Cal* got one?"

"We probably did, too," Pam said. "I just haven't checked my e-mail today."

Becca frowned as a weird possibility occurred to her. Cal had disappeared after Saturday night, about the same time as Pam. "Have you seen Cal?"

Pam's face flushed. "That's what I wanted to talk to you about before the whole Mom-calling-the-FBI thing came up."

"You could have talked to me at any time. I've been right here. Freaking out."

"I was out of town," Pam confessed. "With Cal."

That was weird. Pam and Cal were buddies, in a sniping kind of way, but they hadn't traveled together since the ill-starred Vegas trip. "Where did you go?"

"To this place in West Virginia. It was real pretty. Lots of fall color."

Some of that fall color no doubt matched the crimson in Pam's cheeks. As understanding dawned, Becca shook her head in disbelief. "This place you went to . . . it was a hotel?"

"More like a lodge."

A groan escaped Becca's lips before she could stop it. "What were *you* thinking?"

Her friend's posture went rigid. "What was *I* thinking? What were you thinking, telling Cal you'd never loved him?"

"He told you that?"

Of course he'd told her. How else would she know? Pam and Cal had spent the past two days together in a hotel room—all bets were off concerning what other intimate topics they'd covered. "I meant that to be private."

"It's still private," Pam said. "Cal's not blabbing it all over town. The poor guy was devastated."

"I just wanted him to get over me."

"Wow." Pam's expression hardened. "Can you hear how arrogant you sound? *Over you?* You two are divorced. Of course he's over you."

Evidently during their West Virginia debauch, Cal hadn't mentioned the pass he'd made that had started the whole mess. "I didn't mean to be arrogant. We just were having words, and I thought it would be useful to air our feelings."

"He said he was trying to warn you off getting together with a married man, and then you just turned mean on him."

Nice spin job, Cal.

"That's not exactly how it happened. And Matthew *is not* married. You know that as well as anyone. And anyway, we're not together."

Pam blew out a breath. "No, he's just treating you like his stand-in wife—"

Anger rose in Becca's throat. "He is not."

Pam rolled her eyes. "Asking you for help planning the little girl's birthday party? Taking you on shopping trips? Come on. It's weird."

"Only if you put some kind of crass spin on it, like everyone seems to be doing."

"He's chasing you. And you're going along with it."

Was she serious? "A few weeks ago, you and Erin were ribbing me about his interest as if it was funny. Now suddenly in your imagination and the imaginations of a lot of other people, Matthew and I are evil backstreet adulterers."

"A few weeks ago I thought it was just harmless flirtation."

"It's all perfectly innocent," Becca insisted. "If the lack of facts doesn't convince you, can't you at least take my word for it?"

Pam shrugged. "If you say so. But you certainly have no right to be judgmental about what *I'm* doing."

"I'm not trying to judge, but I saw him on Saturday, Pam. He was upset. I'm guessing that there was more than a little alcohol involved in this lost weekend." It was probably a lucky thing that West Virginia wasn't a quickie marriage destination.

"Yes, he was upset," Pam said. "And I was upset for him when he told me about the things you had said. You *never* loved him?"

She tossed her head. "It makes me wonder how much you ever liked any of us."

"That's not fair. You're my best friend here."

"That's what *I* thought. When you first moved here, it was a gas. I didn't even mind when you changed things."

Becca frowned. "Changed what things?"

"Well, like the friendship dynamics . . . and things. Cal had always been my buddy. We were close. And then you moved here and you were suddenly the shiny new car on the lot and the rest of us were old jalopies."

By "the rest of us," Becca assumed Pam was referring to herself. "Please don't say anything about test drives. I might throw up."

"Cal was infatuated with you, and you just sort of went along like it was your due. You were the TV star. What chance did the rest of us have?"

Becca leaned against the butcher-block table. Good thing Walt had fixed it, because she needed the support. Her legs noodled under her. She couldn't believe she was hearing this from Pam. Her friend. Pam was aware of all her insecurities—she certainly knew, or should have known, that the very last thing Becca felt like was some kind of privileged celebrity. That had been the whole point in moving here. It was her chance to start over.

"You make it sound as if I swanned in and ruined everyone's lives."

"Not ruined them, exactly," Pam said. "And maybe not permanently. At least Cal and I are together now."

Becca shifted mental gears to make the adjustment required to see Pam and Cal as anything more than buddies. It wasn't that hard, actually. "I swear to you, Pam. I thought you two were just friends."

"We were. And I know we've always argued—since forever—but there's also always been something more."

It seemed so obvious now. Pam and Cal had known each other for years, and it was an open secret that they cared for each other deeply despite all the sniping whenever they were within shouting distance of one another. They were the Beatrice and Benedick of Leesburg, and she'd bumbled into their lives and inadvertently busted them up. In Pam's place, she would have been furious. Yet never in all these years here had she felt resentment from Pam over what had happened with Cal. Becca thought back to the marriage chapel in Vegas, where Pam had been witness at the little ceremony. Her reaction—the silence, the weeping, the nausea—made perfect sense now. It must have been one of the hardest nights of her life.

"Why didn't you ever say anything?" Becca asked.

"What could I have said?"

Good question. Becca's head spun. "But this thing you have with Cal now . . ."

"It's not a *thing*," Pam said. "It's a relationship."

Becca had to tread carefully, but she didn't want to completely renounce her friendship right to urge caution. "Pam, Cal's sort of in a weird place, I think."

Too late, she realized it was the wrong thing to say.

"I didn't come here for advice," Pam announced in a clipped voice. "I came to give notice."

Becca blinked in confusion. "You're officially ending our friendship?"

"Notice that I can't work at the shop anymore," she explained. "The real estate market's picking up again, and I got a contract to represent a new condo development. And now I'd really like to spend more of my free time with Cal. I just won't have time for a second job anymore."

Becca swallowed. "Of course. I understand."

Pam's lips twisted. "Also, I know you'll call me a snob, but Walt makes me uncomfortable. I suspect the guy's been napping in the storage room. It smells like Irish Spring and old socks back there."

She was more observant than Becca had given her credit for. She'd been blind to a lot of things about Pam, evidently.

"I'll still fulfill my obligations for the next two weeks." Pam lifted her chin. "Except at some point I'll have to go to Richmond. For reals. Mom insists on seeing me so she'll know that there's not some maniac holding a gun to my head."

Becca mumbled more apologies—she suspected she should just issue a blanket apology to everyone for the past three years. Maybe nothing had been as idyllic as she thought.

She walked Pam to the door and flipped the shop's sign to Closed. She didn't care if it wasn't technically closing time yet. She was in no mental state to deal with the public. Really, she just wanted to go upstairs, eat leftover strawberry cake, and watch more weepy movies. She was ready for a tearjerker movie blubberfest.

The phone ringing on the counter made her jump out of her skin. She hurried to answer it, ready to bark, "Sorry, we're closed." The caller wasn't a customer, though.

"Rebecca?" a bright voice asked. "This is Renee Jablonsky."

"Who?"

"From *Celebrities in Peril—Child Star Edition?*"

Becca groaned, but her sound of dread didn't register with Renee Jablonsky. She suspected nothing would, short of a grand piano falling on the woman's head.

"I have terrific news! We've definitely snagged a Partridge, and we *just might* have a Brady on board."

"A what?"

"One of the children from *The Brady Bunch* is in negotiations to do the show. Because we haven't reached the contractual stage, I can't divulge names just yet, but I thought that might sway your decision."

"I don't really see how this pertains to me," Becca said.

"Well, I know that in our first conversation, you expressed concerns."

"No, I said I didn't want to do it."

"But that was before we had any talent lined up. I was just putting out feelers."

"Consider me felt, then. Also, not interested."

"Before you make a decision, you might want to know that we have a location scout in beautiful Alaska as we speak."

"Alaska?"

"Snowed-in cabin," the woman explained eagerly. "No sharks to worry about. And my executive producer informs me that the grizzlies are all in hibernation at the time of year we'll be filming."

"So it's just starvation and hypothermia we'd have to worry about, then."

"Exactly!" the woman chirped.

"Don't be shocked, but I'm still not interested."

"Okay, but I was saving the best for last. We just got a call from Abby Wooten's agent, too. Abby is in!"

Was she kidding? If the idea of six weeks in freezing Alaska wasn't bad enough, the prospect of spending any time in the wilderness with Abby was enough to send Becca's blood into sub-zero territory. Just the name Abby Wooten pressed all the wrong buttons today. Her friendship with Pam was suddenly shaky, and now here was the ghost of her old frenemy, taunting her.

"No," she said. "Definitely no."

"Maybe I should talk to your agent," Renee suggested. "Who represents you?"

"No one. I'm not in show business."

The woman laughed. "Okay. I'll be sure to keep you apprised of developments."

Becca hung up and banged the phone down on the counter. What was wrong with people?

She plastic-wrapped the icing in the mixer so it wouldn't crust over, and stuck everything in the fridge. She'd have to come down and finish the cupcakes after dinner. Right now, she was starving. She ducked into the storage room and turned off the light.

Pam was right. It did smell like Irish Spring and old socks.

Her lips curved down. What had happened to Walt? He'd gone upstairs for a shave and a sandwich and then disappeared. And just when he was starting to seem more reliable.

She grabbed her stuff and headed up to her apartment, mulling over her employee situation. With Pam gone, she was going to be back on her own again. Having Walt around might come in handy. Of course, that wasn't a long-term solution.

She reached the top of the stairs and called out a hello to Walt. She didn't want to stumble upon him if he'd left the bathroom door open or something like that. But he wasn't in the kitchen, or anywhere she could see.

She headed back to her bedroom and tossed her purse and keys on the bed. Too late, she realized she was tossing them straight at Walt, who was lying across the mattress on this back, his legs dangling off one side. The keys smacked him right against his ear, but he didn't move. Not a muscle.

Chapter 13

Taking advantage of a house without television, Matthew got busy finishing up a work project he'd only made dabbling progress on during the past week. For too long, his concerns had centered on party favors and place settings, permission forms, and whether Becca was going to call. Now it was all behind him, and he was glad. Even if, in the end, the party couldn't have been declared a rousing success, at least those distractions were out of his life. Mostly.

Through no fault of her own, Becca remained a distraction. She couldn't know how many times per day he was tempted to dial her number and shoot the breeze—to let her know how Olivia was, or to talk over an irritating thing that had happened with work, or just to hear her husky laugh. If she knew how much he thought of her, she would have been horrified. He wasn't too pleased about it himself.

As mortifying as it had been to have Olivia ask him point-blank if he and Becca were involved, it was even worse to remember how emphatically he'd responded in the negative.

Technically, it wasn't a lie, but to his own ears, in his own gut, the denial hadn't rung true. He liked Becca. If he were free . . .

But he wasn't free. Until a few weeks ago, he would have recoiled at the idea that he would look at anyone else. Part of him recoiled now. He wasn't a philanderer.

Olivia puttered into the kitchen, where he'd set up his computer on the table. He'd tried to use Nicole's home office, but he could never get over the feeling that he was trespassing there. She opened the fridge, leaving the door gaping while she weighed her beverage options.

"Didn't you just get a soda?" he asked.

"Am I being rationed on those, too, now?"

Her long-suffering tone might have worked on a less knowing listener. "No, but it's pretty late," he said. "I don't think it's a good thing to get sugared and caffeinated up before bedtime."

"Have you heard from Mom?" She grabbed a bottle of juice and then pulled a glass out of the cabinet.

"Not since the e-mail Sunday night."

"And you told her what happened at the party? All except the part I asked you not to mention?"

He'd clarified this several times already. "Yes."

"And she e-mailed back to say . . . ?"

"That she was surprised and dismayed. And that I'd done the right thing."

Actually, Nicole had written *"I never liked that Monica kid, or her crazy mother,"* but Olivia didn't need to hear that. Difficult enough to keep her chastened as it was.

The trouble was, Nicole hadn't written Olivia since the incident, or called. The silence seemed odd to Matthew, and it had a very unsettling effect on Olivia. Her nerves were clearly jangling in anticipation of being chewed out by her mother for her rudeness. "I wish she'd just call and yell at me and get it over with," she muttered. "Are you sure you told her the part about having to reimburse the Minters for the cost of Monica's jacket?"

His lips quirked up. "Next time your mom and I exchange e-mails, I'll cc you."

"That's okay. I'll take your word for it." She wandered back to her room. They would probably go through the same question-and-answer session several more times until Nicole called again.

He concentrated on the numbers on his computer screen. Or tried to.

When *was* Nicole going to call?

He powered down his computer, stood, and headed to his room. He changed into pajama pants and a T-shirt and went to brush his teeth. A soft rocking *thump* coming through the wall let him know that Olivia was still up, ostensibly doing homework but probably brooding. When he turned off the tap, another noise put his nerves on high alert. It sounded like the front door.

His first thought was that Olivia was going out—but why would she do that? Unless she'd decided to run away or something crazy. But she wasn't *that* upset about having her television privileges taken away. He hurried out, slinking through the hallway toward the front entrance like a commando. An unarmed commando.

Someone was coming in. He heard the door's security chain being latched.

He frowned. Why would a burglar latch the door *after* breaking in?

He rounded the corner and was met by a startled gasp. He choked in surprise.

Nicole sank against the back of a wingback chair. "My God, you scared me half to death."

"What are you doing here?" he asked.

A brittle laugh escaped her. "Coming home?"

Of course. He relaxed his home-defense stance. "But when did you get in? Why didn't you tell us? You didn't call, or message me."

"I know I should have, but I got a last-minute flight with practically no layover. And I felt so exhausted. We always meant to finish around this time, but the whole situation just . . . well, it sort of blew up."

"The project?"

She closed her eyes. "Do you mind if I just don't talk about it right now?"

She looked stressed. After a flight all the way from Hawaii, who could blame her?

"I just wish I'd known you were coming in," he said. "Olivia and I could have picked you up at the airport."

Nicole waved away the idea. "I took a cab back. The company pays for it."

"Right."

He was trying to think of something to say when Olivia charged into the room. Her eyes widened in amazement. "Mom!" She launched herself at her mother, nearly knocking her over before wrapping herself around her in a huge hug. "You're back!"

Nicole laughed patiently. "Yes, I am."

"For how long?" Olivia asked.

"For a long time, I hope."

Not wanting to trespass on their reunion, Matthew grabbed the handle of Nicole's suitcase, which was approximately the size of Ohio, and started to take it to the bedroom. Lucky it had wheels or it might have thrown his back into spasm.

"You might just as well roll that into the laundry room," Nicole called after him. "All the stuff in there needs washing or sending to the dry cleaners. I'll sort it out tomorrow."

He dutifully changed direction, and it occurred to him that, unlike Olivia, *his* first instinct hadn't been to run over to Nicole and hug her. They hadn't even exchanged their usual hello peck. Everything about Nicole's sudden arrival seemed ominous.

Or maybe you're not as glad to see her as you should be.

Back in the living room, Olivia was still strung so tight she was practically twanging with excitement. "Did you bring me any souvenirs?"

Nicole planted her hands on her hips. "What are you talking about? You just had your birthday—and botched it up in a big way, if my sources are correct." She telegraphed a wry smile in Matthew's direction.

Olivia sighed. "I know. I'm *really* sorry. I wrote the Minters a long letter telling them and mailed it off this morning. Do you want to see a copy? I saved the rough draft on my computer, even though Matthew told me I had to write it out in my own handwriting, on real stationery."

"Very Emily Post of him," Nicole said.

Matthew smiled even as disappointment rippled through him. He'd tried hard to convince Olivia to take this groveling seriously, and now Nicole seemed to be making light of the entire situation.

"Anyway," Olivia went on, "souvenirs aren't the same thing as birthday presents. You always bring me souvenirs when you go someplace new. It's like what we learned in school about animal groupings. Souvenirs and birthday presents are, like, different species. Like elephants and zebras."

Nicole relented. "Okay—brownie points for the science connection. You convinced me. Go to the laundry room and open my suitcase. Any bag that you see that looks like it has a grass skirt in it might be for you."

Olivia executed a joyous fist pump and tore out of the room.

When she had disappeared from view, Nicole narrowed her eyes at Matthew. "What's the matter?"

"Nothing." Belatedly, he went to her and brushed his lips against her cheek. "Am I glad to see you. Since the birthday party, Olivia's been treating me like I'm a prison camp commandant."

She chuckled, stepped out of her shoes and his embrace, and headed for the kitchen. "You can't make too much of dust-ups like this. Kids need to sort things out for themselves."

"I think so, too, usually, but this was pretty exceptional. She attacked someone—and it was caught on film. I had to watch it five times, twice in slow motion. Talk about excruciating."

Nicole frowned into the fridge, reminding him of Olivia half an hour earlier. "Where's the low-sugar cranberry juice?"

"There isn't any." Her crestfallen expression over the lack of juice irked him for some reason. "You're the only one who drinks it, and you haven't been around." If he'd had some warning . . .

She grabbed a diet soda, elbowed the door closed, and collapsed into a chair at the breakfast table.

A *whoop* of happiness floated down the hall as Olivia hit souvenir pay dirt.

"I was just trying to make her see that what she did was wrong," he said.

Nicole popped open her can. "Tossing a drink on a friend? I'm pretty sure she knew that was a major screwup. She apologized, didn't she?"

"Yeah . . ."

"Then why make a federal case of it?"

The question brought him up short. Had he overreacted? Maybe being the substitute parent had made him too strict. Although he'd assumed that Nicole would be on the same page. Olivia herself had been trembling at the idea of her mom's reaction.

Now Nicole was home, looking as if she couldn't have cared less about the party, and Olivia was in the doorway with a grass skirt over her jeans, tunelessly strumming a ukulele. "How do I look?"

"Great," they answered at once.

Olivia's smile faded and her glance flicked anxiously between them. "You were talking about me, weren't you?"

"We're done," Nicole said.

Olivia didn't look convinced. "Am I going to get punished more?"

Nicole laughed. "I think you can put away your hair shirt for the time being."

"What does that mean? Do I still not get to watch television for two months?"

Nicole cast a surprised look at Matthew, then turned back to her daughter. "You should get ready for bed. And please wait until tomorrow to start your career as the next Don Ho. I desperately need some z's tonight."

"Okay." Olivia rushed forward and hugged her again. "Good night, Mom. Thanks for my souvenirs."

"You're welcome. 'Night, O."

When Olivia was out of earshot, she gaped at Matthew. "Two months! You really are a hard-ass."

"If you had been there, you would have—"

"It was a birthday party, Matthew. These kids go to birthday parties all the time, and there's always drama. If I tried to get involved in every little dispute, I'd go insane. I have enough on my plate without worrying about Olivia's stuff."

She did look stressed out, which made him try to overlook the lecture. And the fact that she'd cut him off. And all the other indications that she didn't seem happy to see him.

"What happened in Hawaii?" he asked.

She peered at her soda can. "It's such a mess."

She obviously didn't want to talk about it, a sentiment he understood. Some days it was a relief to discuss messed-up work stuff, but other times talking about it seemed almost as irritating as living it all over again.

Though he'd agreed not to, he couldn't help asking, "Is it the project?"

"No—the project's fine. Or as fine as it can be at this stage. You know how it is. One step forward, two steps back. The usual insanity. But now there are all these personality conflicts. It's so good to be back." She let out a long sigh that had a hint of defiance in it. "I'm going to take the rest of the week off. Enjoy my life for once. Cook dinners and relax. You don't know what a strain it's been living out of hotels."

"I can imagine."

He worried about her. Nicole usually weathered work issues by steaming right ahead, single-minded. She wasn't one to let personal conflicts make her lose focus. They certainly never frazzled her to the point that she would take impromptu personal time off.

Olivia reappeared in the doorway, tapping the ends of her fingertips together in tension. "I just remembered that Career Day's tomorrow."

"Oh right." Nicole leaned back. "I forgot all about that. But it's no problem—I was just telling Matthew that I'm taking the rest of the week off, so I'm all yours. Just tell me what time to be there."

Olivia's gaze pleaded with Matthew for help.

He took a deep breath. "Becca's got it covered."

Nicole's brows arched. "The cake lady? I thought we agreed that you'd sub for me."

"Right," Olivia said, "but Matthew's job is so dull, so then I asked Becca if she'd come to the school instead and she said she would."

"Well." Nicole smiled. "Now she doesn't have to."

The assurance didn't calm Olivia. "Should I e-mail Becca and tell her not to come?"

"That would be a good idea," Nicole said. "Or better yet, I'll give her a call or an e-mail in the morning. Don't sweat it." She glanced at Matthew. "I'm not sure having women coming into the schools telling kids they can fritter away their lives making cupcakes is the greatest message anyway."

"She runs a business," he pointed out.

"Not exactly inspiring our students to reach for the stars, though, is it?"

Olivia's lips turned down at the corners, but she didn't say anything. She tossed another pained look at Matthew, which Nicole caught.

"What?" Nicole asked.

"Nothing," Olivia said quickly. "Only, since you've been traveling all day, maybe tomorrow going to my school will be a big hassle? You probably don't even have a speech prepared."

"I've got a million PowerPoint presentations to pull from," she said. "Believe me, it's no big deal. It's what I do."

"Yeah, but Becca might have been counting on being there," Olivia said.

Nicole chuckled. "Trust me on this. She'll be so relieved not to have to go, she'll be doing handsprings."

Olivia considered this. "Okay . . ."

When she was out of earshot, Nicole shook her head. "Someone hit that kid with the worry stick."

"When she's not acting like a feral beast, she tries hard to please. And she and Becca get along really well."

"Oh right," Nicole said. "The horse thing."

"They like each other a lot," he pointed out.

"Olivia likes everybody."

Except the people she doesn't, who get doused in soda pop.

Nicole yawned. "I think I'll hit the hay, too. And you're in your pajamas, so I guess it's too late for you to flee back to your own place."

He hadn't really thought about going back. "I can leave if you'd rather."

"No, stay. I could use a cuddle buddy tonight." She smiled at him.

It was the kind of look that would have had him streaking for the bedroom a few months ago. Now, he smiled back, wondering how he was going to survive his life just going through the motions. Or whether he should.

While Nicole was getting ready for bed, Matthew stared at the clock. It was after ten. Would Becca be in bed already? She was an early riser. Plus, knowing her, she would be angsting over her presentation tomorrow—the one she didn't have to give. He should call and explain.

He reached for his cell phone and speed-dialed her. The number rang several times before going to a message. After the beep, he took a deep breath in anticipation of a quick explanation, when Nicole came out of the bathroom in her short robe.

His thumb jabbed End Call.

"Who were you calling?" she asked.

"Nobody," he said. "Just checking messages."

What was he doing?

He couldn't account for the lie. It was almost as if he felt guilty for wanting to phone Becca, when there hadn't been anything in his mind but a friendly heads-up that she wouldn't need to be at the school in the morning. So why had his first reaction been to hang up when Nicole walked in? What did he have to feel guilty about?

Maybe for not being more ecstatic at Nicole's surprise home-coming?

He considered confessing why the phone had been in his hand and going ahead and calling her again. The message would spare Becca a night of angst. Then again, she would probably re-ceive Nicole's e-mail first thing tomorrow. If he e-mailed her, it could be construed as alerting her that Nicole was back, for per-sonal reasons. *By the way, Nicole is home again, please back off.*

Before he could make up his mind, a strange sound made him turn toward the bed. Nicole lay on her back, her arm flung over her face. The crook of her elbow hid her expression, but he knew at once why he hadn't been able to place the noise—he'd never heard it before. Nicole was crying.

Becca paced the waiting room of Emergency, drinking her third coffee of the night while she awaited word of Walt's condi-tion.

She wished she could do something for Walt instead of just standing around, but she wasn't even sure where he'd been taken. The last time she'd seen him was when the paramedics had ar-rived and loaded him on a stretcher into their ambulance, alive but still unconscious. Not wanting to get stuck without trans-portation in the middle of the night, she'd followed in her own car. But when she arrived at the hospital, Walt had already been admitted and taken back. Maybe the only benefit of losing con-sciousness was not having to wait among the sea of the nauseous, bleeding, and cranky people of the ER.

She again approached the receptionist, a woman with a helmet of black hair who sat on the other half of a Plexiglas barrier. Becca suspected she'd been hired specifically for the spectacularly im-penetrable I-don't-give-a-damn vibe she exuded. After each ner-vous newcomer had their inquiries met by her froggy stare and husky, drill-sergeant commands to sit and wait for their name to be called, it was clear a person had to be very desperate to bother her with a question.

But it was going on eleven now. Becca felt very desperate.

"Excuse me?"

The woman continued tapping on her computer for fifteen seconds before glancing up. "May I help you?" she asked, as if she'd never seen Becca before. As if Becca hadn't been wearing out the linoleum in front of her for the past two hours.

"Is there news about Walter Johnson?" Using his full name seemed strange. In her mind, he seemed like one of those one-name personalities, like Madonna or Cher. He was just Walt.

The woman looked up at her with an unblinking gaze. "Are you Mr. Johnson's next of kin?"

Becca wanted to weep. "I told you—I brought him in after finding him unconscious in my bed."

The woman's dark brows raised, but maybe in this situation having any kind of intimate relationship assumed between them would be better than nothing. Becca certainly hadn't gotten far being his unofficial landlady and part-time employer. "I just want to find out how he is, or if he needs anything. Has a doctor seen him?"

"If Mr. Johnson was unconscious when he was brought in, then he most certainly has been seen by someone."

"Then may I talk to that someone?"

"If you're not his immediate family—"

She let out a bleat of frustration. "I'm all he's got right now. If I don't check on his condition, no one will. Are patients who aren't lucky enough to have family just supposed to languish all alone in this hospital?"

Her outburst did nothing to soften the receptionist's demeanor. But she did seem to yield to the logic of Becca's argument. "Walter Johnson?" she asked, typing.

"Yes." Finally. Maybe the computer would be able to tell her whether he was still alive or not.

"And what is your name, please?"

Becca clenched her hands. If this was just going to start another argument over whether she was authorized to see Walt . . . "Becca Hudson."

"Hudson . . ." At first it looked as if the woman was reading off the screen, but then her head tilted and she gave Becca a closer inspection. "Rebecca Hudson? That kid on that show?"

Becca managed a tight smile. If she had to use her former celebrityhood to get through the swinging double doors to where there were people who could actually give her information, so be it. "That little kid, about a decade and a half later."

The woman smacked the countertop. "I thought you looked familiar. I used to watch you every week. Me and my daughter."

"It's nice of you to remember."

The woman shook her head in wonder. "You used to be so cute."

"Thanks."

"Especially when the show first started. So precious! Whenever you said 'Good night, Daddy,' I just wanted to reach into the television set and pinch those little chipmunk cheeks of yours." She leaned forward, chuckling. "Had a real crush on that dad of yours, too. What a hunk!"

"He certainly was."

"I saw that article in the paper a while back about your opening a bakery, and my daughter actually went and bought some cupcakes or something from you. Said they were delicious."

"Did she?" Becca asked. "That's terrific. I'll bring you some next time I'm headed out this way."

"Aw, bless your heart, but I've got diabetes, so one of those babies would probably kill me. But it's so sweet of you to offer." She chuckled. "Literally." She shook her head again. "Rebecca Hudson. What do you know."

Smile frozen, Becca shifted, trying not to seem too impatient.

"You should've given me your name right off the bat," the woman told her.

Really? Becca didn't want to quibble now that things were finally going her way, but that seemed a little unfair. Why should it matter that she'd been on TV? Did Mary Kate and Ashley get to saunter into any hospital room they wanted?

"You just sit tight and I'll get the doctor who saw Mr. Johnson to come talk to you," the woman said. "It won't be long."

When Becca turned back to the seating area, at least ten pairs of eyes were all focused on her. At first she expected resentment for using her celebrity to get her foot in through the ER doors. But for the next ten minutes, she signed autographs, fielded an inquiry about whether she had a problem with her parents stealing all the money she'd earned as a child, and told a few curious women what Jake Flannery was *really* like.

Happily, someone called her name and she gathered her purse and hurried to where a white-coated woman of about her own age stood, clipboard in hand, holding the door open with one comfort-soled shoe. In the next moment, Becca was led a few steps down a hallway painted a cheerful peach.

"I'm an intern here," the woman said in a hurried but not brusque tone. Her name tag read *Dr. Christine Atar*, which was evidently all the introduction the busy doctor had time for. "Mr. Johnson needs to stay in ICU overnight."

Becca let out her breath. He was alive. But Intensive Care didn't sound great. "Is he okay?"

A battalion of worry lines formed along the doctor's brow. "Well, I wouldn't say okay. We've revived him, and he's going to be given dialysis."

"Dialysis," Becca repeated.

The doctor cocked her head and regarded Becca more closely. "You know Mr. Johnson has ESRD."

"No," Becca said. "What's that?"

"Kidney disease."

"Is it—" She almost asked the doctor if it was serious, when obviously it was. The man had passed out. He needed dialysis.

Why hadn't he told her? Did he know it himself?

"He's had too many close calls," the doctor said, inadvertently answering the second question. "Tonight his blood pressure spiked to a dangerous level—"

Becca nodded. "I worried he was dead."

"Well, frankly, if he doesn't undergo dialysis more regularly, that is an outcome I would expect."

Becca tried to wrap her mind around this. "You said he's had close calls. You've seen him here before?"

"He was here"—the doctor flipped through several pages on her clipboard—"just a few weeks ago."

Becca shrank back from the news, wanting to deny its truth. Yet at the same, puzzling things that had happened suddenly made a little more sense, like his disappearing with no notice. "Is fatigue a symptom of kidney problems?"

"Oh yes."

Poor Walt. Being fired from his stupid gas station job for a problem that was beyond his control. She was willing to bet this was related to why he had lost his apartment, too. Why hadn't he said anything?

Maybe he thought she wouldn't have kept him on at the shop if she'd known of his condition. Or . . .

She remembered Monday afternoon, when he'd appeared at her apartment looking worried. Had he known then how sick he was and intended to tell her, maybe to ask for her help? And she had talked his ear off about how upset she still was over her mother's death. He probably thought any more bad news would send her over the edge, so he'd made up a pathetic excuse about wanting to tell her he'd fixed some wobbly chairs.

"I don't know why Mr. Johnson didn't go to his last appointment," Dr. Atar said.

Becca could guess. "Does he owe the hospital money?"

The doctor bit her lip. "I'm guessing the answer is yes, but that's not my bailiwick. You'll have to ask about that at the accounts office."

Becca nodded. "I will, although they might not tell me anything."

The doctor blinked, as if this were an odd question. "I don't see why they wouldn't."

Of course. No doubt they were less picky about who paid a patient's bills than they were about what visitors he received. "Can I see Walt?"

"You can see him briefly, but he's resting."

Becca went to the little cubicle-like room in the ICU, where Walt looked small and fragile lying on the hospital bed. Still, even this was a much more comfortable setup than the one in the back of the shop. A tide of shame rolled through her at the thought of him sleeping on the camp bed among the flour and sugar sacks.

His arms poking out of his hospital gown seemed bony and undernourished, as opposed to the sausage-like ankles and feet protruding over the other end of the bed. She'd never noticed the swelling. Had she been paying attention at all?

And she'd thought she was being so generous. Lady Bountiful taking the unfortunate worker to Target. Now she couldn't believe how stupid she'd been, how obtuse. How blind could she be?

Chapter 14

When the alarm sounded, Becca shot out her arm and whacked at the bedside table until she made contact with the offending clock. A direct hit sent it flying to the ground. Sprawled over the side of the bed, she squinted one eye open and saw it out of her reach, still buzzing.

The two cats remained curled up together on the foot of her bed, unperturbed. They had done their usual four-in-the-morning war dance, which was when she reset her alarm clock to go off a little later, so she could get enough sleep and not be a complete mess when she gave her presentation in front of Olivia's class.

The thought of Career Day sent her tumbling out of bed. She crawled to the clock, killed the alarm, and then straggled to her feet. What a day. She still had cupcakes to ice, and then school, and after that she needed to go to the bank to transfer money to her checking account so she would have funds available to put toward Walt's outstanding hospital bill.

She brushed her teeth, then tossed on some clothes that hopefully made her look like a relatively successful businesswoman and not just a burnout who baked. She even considered panty hose for a moment, but not even for the sake of Olivia and inspiring the businessmen and women of tomorrow would she struggle into a pair of those.

Downstairs, she found the shop in the condition she'd left it in the night before. The cellophane-covered cupcakes remained bare, ready to be iced, and the frosting was in a stainless-steel bowl in the refrigerator. She took it out and put it back on the mixer to loosen it up again. Meanwhile, she very belatedly tried to think of something to tell the kids. What was she supposed to say? She wondered if she should dwell on the work itself, or if she should mention the business side. Given that she'd made her big leap into commerce with about a fifth-grade understanding of economics, she doubted she could go too far over their heads.

A figure appeared at the shop entrance, causing her first to jump and then rush to open up. She threw the lock and pulled the door wide, allowing Erin to sweep inside. After hugging her, Becca had a hard time not staring. She was so astonished and relieved to see her. Not a cinder at the bottom of a volcano, then. Thank God.

"I was driving by and saw your shop light on," Erin said. "I'm supposed to be out getting breakfast." Her skin was bronzed to swimsuit model perfection, and Becca could swear she detected a hint of coconut oil, blue ocean, and sun behind the usual spritz of Chanel.

"I'm so glad to see you! When did you get back?"

Erin dropped her purse on the counter. Despite the ocean breeze she'd floated in on, a chill hung in the air. "Haven't you been reading your e-mail at all? We flew in yesterday."

"You and Bob?"

"Who did you think?"

Becca lifted her shoulders and then dropped them. "I wouldn't know. I haven't been checking my e-mail. There hasn't been time. I had the most awful night last night."

Erin snorted.

"First there was—" Becca had been about to explain the awful night right from the beginning, but that snort stopped her. It wasn't an interested, tell-me-all-about-it sound. It was a bitter snort. It threw her off. "But it's a long story," she said, changing direction. "What happened in Hawaii? You look great."

"I feel great, despite everything."

"Then you had a . . . successful trip?"

Erin folded her arms tightly. "Yes."

The silence put Becca on edge, as it clearly was meant to. She had no idea why. It was as if Erin were trying to make her feel guilty, but what did she have to feel guilty about?

To cover her jittering nerves, she circled around the counter and went back to her stainless-steel bowl of frosting. "And Bob is okay?"

"Bob is fine. We've decided to work on our marriage. We're going into couples counseling."

Becca swallowed back her surprise. "Great."

Bob wasn't known for his touchy-feeliness—or for having discernible feelings at all—so she had a hard time wrapping her mind around his having agreed to see a counselor. The last time they'd been at the same dinner party, he and Becca had ended up in an argument over his theory that pet owners were infantile and selfish because all animals belonged in the wild. Dogs, cats, budgies—if something didn't have a human brain, or wasn't being raised for human consumption, according to Bob it shouldn't be domesticated. She'd called him a soulless egghead, but only after he'd accused her of multiple counts of animal abuse because she had two cats in captivity.

The idea of him in marital counseling or any kind of psychotherapy was weird and vaguely unsettling, like those YouTube videos of parrots singing opera. She couldn't believe it was something he would do under normal circumstances. "How did you convince him to agree to that?" she asked.

As soon as the question escaped her lips, she wanted to call it back. Erin's face turned a hue of red that had nothing to do with her past week of soaking up rays in the South Pacific. "Bob *wants* to save our marriage. He suggested it. He was panicked when I told him I was thinking about a divorce."

"You told him that?"

"Well, of course." Her eyes flashed. "Why shouldn't I?"

"It's just . . . I thought you were going there to save your marriage, not to give him notice."

"I flew there to discover what was going on, and to see who this woman was. I guess *you* thought that was hilariously naïve of me."

Becca shook her head. "No, I didn't."

"Well, you obviously didn't think about enlightening me. Did you think I wouldn't find out that Nicole was the wife of the guy you've been seeing?"

Oh, for heaven's sake. "Matthew and I haven't been seeing each other. It's just that he has a little girl—"

Erin pounced on the word. "Exactly. The little girl is Nicole's daughter. And that guy, Matthew, is practically her father." She sent her a withering look. "How could you break up a home like that?"

Becca sputtered before finally spitting out, "I haven't done anything."

"Oh, please. The minute I started piecing it all together, Bob confirmed that Nicole had probably felt insecure because Matthew was stepping out on her, and so she started coming on to him at work. If she weren't so horrible, I could almost pity her."

The world felt tilted upside-down. *She* was the bad guy? Just seeing Erin mad at her for any reason was hard to take, like having the Easter Bunny turn vicious. "That's insane. Nicole knows exactly what Matthew and I have been doing."

"Of course—that's why she turned to Bob for a shoulder to cry on. She was so unhappy."

"But we've been doing *nothing*. A shopping trip in DC. A birthday party at the stables. She's been kept apprised of all of this. God, Erin, how could you think I would be a home wrecker?"

Erin's pointy jaw worked as doubt warred with wishful thinking in her eyes. "I don't know what to think. First I find out that you didn't even tell me you knew Nicole, and then last night poor Pam said you were giving her grief because she and Cal are an item. Bob says you're a loose cannon."

She certainly would have loved to lob a cannon at Bob. "I'm just worried Pam's going to get her heart broken over some kind of rebound fling."

"Rebound!" Erin said. "It's been a year since you signed the divorce papers."

"Maybe it was a mini-rebound. Cal's the person to ask about that. All I know is, on Saturday evening he was kissing me, and then hours later they evidently ran off together."

Erin's jaw dropped, and for a moment, her moral outrage about her own situation dissolved and she became a friend who wanted the scoop. "You guys were kissing? When?"

"At the stables, after Matthew—" All at once, she wished she'd stopped with "at the stables." Now she had to force herself to soldier on and finish with an unfortunate reminder of Erin's home-wrecker aspersions. "After Matthew and Olivia left."

Erin shook her head mournfully, as if this were further evidence of Becca's having undermined her. "I still can't believe that you knew about Nicole and you didn't tell me."

"I should have, I guess. At first I wasn't sure, and by the time I did know, it seemed too late. You were already flying off."

"And yet you kept seeing Matthew, knowing that his straying was endangering my marriage."

"I was *not* seeing him. Not romantically." She rolled her eyes. "I don't even know how I got wrapped up in all these relationships. I *thought* I was helping some people out, but now everyone seems to be putting the worst possible spin on it. There's nothing going on with Matthew and me, and I have no idea what the status of his relationship is. As far as I know, he's going to fight like a tiger to stay with Nicole."

"Really?" Erin asked, her eyes lighting up with hope. "You haven't been trying to bust them up?"

"*No.* In fact, I probably won't have any more to do with those people after . . ."

Damn.

Erin went on the alert. "After what?"

"Well, I promised to speak at Olivia's school Career Day," she confessed. "But Matthew's not going to be there—at least, I don't think he is. I'm just doing this for Olivia. That's why I was down here. I needed to ice these cupcakes to take with me."

Erin aimed a distrustful, wounded-puppy gaze at her. "Well. As I was saying, I was just driving by and I saw your light on in here and thought I would drop in. I wanted to tell you I'm back, and also that Pam and I have decided we don't want to do Not-Book-Club this month. It's been getting sort of old anyway. . . ."

I just wanted to drop in and tell you I don't want to be your friend anymore might not have been exactly what Erin was saying, but it was all Becca heard. Her heart sank.

Erin turned to leave, but then stopped and glanced back at the cupcakes. "Are those pumpkin spice?"

She nodded numbly.

"Would they make a good breakfast?" Erin asked.

Becca dropped two in a sack and handed them over.

After Erin left, Becca slathered icing over the remaining cakes, loaded them into boxes, and hurried for the door. She would be late, but there was no help for it. It wouldn't be the first time in her life she'd gotten a tardy mark at school. Also, she still didn't know what she was going to say, which caused a different anxiety to gnaw at her. It was almost like stage nerves, and she hadn't had those in a long time.

The parking lot at the elementary school was crowded, so she had to park at the back. By the time she speed-walked to the front door where a receptionist waited, her breath was puffing. "I'm here for Career Day. Guest of Olivia Parker."

The receptionist smiled encouragingly. "You brought goodies! Lucky class." She pointed to the right. "That will be Ms. Andrews's class. Do you need me to walk you over there?"

As if it was the first day of school.

Actually, being talked to like a grade schooler soothed her nerves. "No, I can handle it." Becca hurried down the corridor, transported back by the scents of pine floor cleanser and Elmer's Glue.

Each door had a narrow rectangular window along the side. When she arrived at the door with a sign that read Welcome to Ms. Andrews's Fifth Grade, she stopped, peered inside at the children sitting at their short desks, and spotted Olivia. At the same moment, Olivia glanced over and did a double-take, her eyes widening in surprise.

Becca assumed from her reaction that she'd given up on her. She took a breath, and pushed inside with her two bakery boxes propped on one hip.

It wasn't until she'd slipped into the room that she understood Olivia's alarm could have had another cause: mortification. The attention of everyone in the room swiveled from the front of the class toward the door. Becca, seeking out someone who looked like an elementary school teacher so she could apologize for being late, instead found herself staring at a woman giving a Power-Point presentation.

She froze. The woman's gaze focused on her, her eyes narrowing to slits. Projected onto a screen was a drawing depicting some kind of underwater turbine, including a dizzying number of directional arrows to explain the mechanics to the layman. The blackboard Nicole was standing in front of had some crude illustrations of waves and arrows, and scrawled words like *buoyant actuator* and *data telemetry*. Above it all was a name printed in block letters: *Nicole Parker.*

Oh crap. *What is* she *doing here?*

Becca could tell from Nicole's glare that the other woman was thinking the same thing.

"I'm so sorry," Becca mumbled.

She turned to flee, but before she could manage to scuttle out the door, another woman swooped across the room, hand outstretched, and grabbed her arm. "How wonderful—another visitor!"

Becca cringed and shot an apologetic glance to Olivia, who had sunk several inches lower in her desk chair. "I think some wires got crossed. I agreed to come as a sub, but now . . ." She nodded toward Nicole. "I can leave."

"No, no—we wouldn't hear of it." Ms. Andrews yanked Becca into the room and took the boxes from her. "And you've brought goodies! The more, the merrier—isn't that right, class?"

She spoke in such a bright voice, the answer was already a foregone conclusion. But even if the children had felt lukewarm about sitting through another presentation, the cupcake boxes sealed the deal.

"Yes!" they shouted in unison.

Using her pincer-like grip, Ms. Andrews hauled Becca across the room, right past Nicole, to a line of three adults sitting in folding chairs against the bookcase along the wall opposite the door. Becca lowered herself into the empty chair—obviously the one Nicole had been sitting in—and apologized to these people for being late. The man seated next to her, who seemed very familiar, shrugged and leaned over to whisper, "This lady at the front's just been confusing the pants off of everyone anyway. Me included."

During the remainder of Nicole's presentation—something about creating electricity from wave turbines anchored under the ocean—Becca shot surreptitious glances at Olivia and gleaned what had happened as Olivia mimicked opening a computer, typing, and then pointed from her chest and then to Becca.

Another e-mail snafu. She'd been in such a hurry to get over here this morning, she hadn't checked. Of course, given the fact that she knew there were several accusatory e-mails from Erin waiting for her, too, she now felt inclined to toss her computer into the nearest lake.

Nicole finally wrapped it up, and then the man next to Becca stood up and introduced himself as Grover's dad, Brad Neuhaus, a lawyer currently serving as a delegate in Virginia's state legislature. That's where Becca had seen him before—yard signs. She chuckled to herself, which earned an annoyed flick of the head from Nicole, who was now sitting next to her.

Throughout the short talk on the state's General Assembly and how it worked, Becca tried to imagine what she was going to say. The next person up was an orthopedic surgeon who entertained the kids with grisly stories of broken bones. By the time it was her turn, Becca decided it would be best if her audience were distracted. If their mouths were busy they might not notice her wobbly knees.

"My name's Becca, and I run the Strawberry Cake Shop here in Leesburg." She passed out little paper plates and plastic forks, and then distributed the cupcakes. This went over well, and mostly covered her faltering explanation of what owning a bakery was like.

When she was done, she was ready to scurry back to her seat, until she noticed that there wasn't one free. Then Ms. Andrews's pincers were on her arm again, and she beckoned the rest of the adults to stand in front of the teacher's desk to field questions from the students. Some of these questions sounded coached. "Did you want to be a (*fill-in-the-blank*—) when you were our age?" and "Did you have to go to a special school to get your job?" were favorites. Then, about five minutes into the interrogation, a hand shot up on the last row. Ms. Andrews said, "Yes, Isabel?"

Isabel looked straight at Becca. "Weren't you on television?"

Several kids nodded.

Becca smiled. "Yes, I was. I was on a show called *Me Minus You*."

A murmur spread among the desks. Becca caught one boy saying "I told you!" to another.

"How old were you?"

"Actually, I was about your age," Becca said. "I lived in California and acted until I was about fifteen."

"How did you get on television?"

"I auditioned after a television executive spotted me. My

mother worked as a secretary at a television studio." Becca shifted uncomfortably, especially when she saw the orthopedic surgeon glancing at his watch. Somewhere there was a waiting room full of people with agonizing bone pain, and he was stuck here listening to a baker rattle on about her defunct Hollywood career.

"Did you ever forget your lines?" another kid asked.

"Not too often. That was one thing I was really good at."

Another girl's hand shot up. "Could you sign an autograph for my mom? She said she used to watch you."

"Uh . . ." She shot a nervous glance at Ms. Andrews. "I guess so."

She scooted toward the desks to sign a piece of ruled notebook paper, and then found herself with a line.

The other visitors did not look pleased, a fact that even Ms. Andrews noticed. "Maybe we should ask some others some questions?"

A boy's hand went up. "What gets paid the most?"

The adults exchanged flummoxed looks. "I know it's not the person selling cupcakes," Becca said to them, "so I'll leave it to you guys to answer."

"Anyone else?" Ms. Andrews asked, pointing to a girl sitting near the front.

The girl looked at Becca. "When you made money when you were ten, did your parents let you keep it?"

"I had a hardworking mom, and she saved all the money for me. I received it when I graduated from high school."

"*All* of it?" the girl asked. "Was it a lot?"

Ms. Andrews waved her hands. "That's enough discussion of money. Money isn't the only reason we work, is it?"

Becca laughed, but sobered quickly when she noticed that no one else thought this was hilarious.

"Who in the class can name some other reasons we might pick a particular job?" Ms. Andrews asked.

Another hand was raised. "To make enough money to buy a house."

"Well, yes, but sometimes work has other rewards. Who can say what those would be?"

"So you can afford to go to Disney World every summer."

By the time the Q&A broke up, Becca was antsy to leave. She wanted to check on Walt, and then get back to the shop. After Ms. Andrews and the class formally thanked the visitors, Becca tried to scoot out, but Olivia caught up with her at the door. Her mother was right behind her.

"We sent you an e-mail," Olivia said. "Didn't you get it?"

Becca aimed an apologetic glance at Nicole. She truly hadn't meant to steal the woman's Career Day thunder. "No, I'm sorry. I've had a crazy twenty-four hours."

"So did Mom. She just got in last night."

"Oh God," Becca muttered in sympathy. "You just flew in from Hawaii last night?" She couldn't help wondering if this was the same flight Erin and Bob had come in on. Surely not. "And yet here you are this morning, giving slide shows. On time."

Nicole placed a hand on Olivia's shoulder. "I'm sorry you ended up coming when you didn't have to. Olivia tells me that we already owe you a big thanks for the wonderful party, and for letting her ride your horse."

"Don't mention it," Becca said, meaning it. "It was fun."

"I'm glad you came anyway, though," Olivia told her. "The cupcakes were good, and I might get extra credit for getting two people to come in."

"That's no way to thank Becca for the trouble she's taken," Nicole admonished Olivia. "Especially when she obviously had so little time to prepare."

Becca tried not to take offense, and chalked up the woman's frostiness to jet lag. "I'm a terrible public speaker."

Olivia's mouth dropped. "What are you talking about? You were the best one!"

Becca edged farther toward the door. "I really should scoot. I have to visit Walt in the hospital."

Olivia gasped. "What happened?"

"He's sick."

Olivia spun on her heel toward her mom. "Can we go visit Walt in the hospital after school today?"

"Who's Walt?"

"I told you about him," Olivia said. "He's the man I talked to outside the cupcake store that day." She lowered her voice. "When Grover was being such a jerk."

"The homeless man?"

"He's not homeless," Olivia and Becca chorused.

Nicole shook her head. "You have gymnastics this afternoon, remember?"

"Yeah, but I don't like gymnastics, and what if Walt dies?"

Becca backed out the door. "I'll tell Walt you send your best. He'll get a kick out of that."

"Okay," Olivia said, disappointed.

Becca fled to the parking lot, and then drove to the bank to make sure she was able to get money transferred from her savings to checking for today. After the bank, she stopped on the way to the hospital for some things Walt might like. During her mother's hospitalizations, Becca had always tried to arm herself for visits with something Ronnie loved. Sometimes the gestures had backfired—such as the favorite snacks her mom could no longer stomach, or the little evergreen decorated for Christmas that had brought on a raging headache. But she'd also hit a few home runs, like the little iPod loaded with all the show tunes her mother adored, the Wendy's Frosty, and the Chinese checkers game.

The trouble was, she didn't know Walt all that well. She ducked into a store and got him a comfy pillow, a detective fiction paperback and another book of crossword puzzles, a deck of cards, and some of the lotion she'd noticed had been disappearing from her bathroom since he'd started using her place to wash up.

When she arrived at the nurses' station at the ICU, she discovered that Walt had already been moved to a semi-private room. She was half-hoping that she would find him asleep so she could dump the stuff and run. She wasn't looking forward to the awkward conversation they needed to have. But when she got there, he was lying in the bed nearest the door, an IV in his arm. He looked just as frail as the night before, although he was awake and smiling.

She grinned. "You're up. You look better."

He chuckled. "I'll bet. They tell me you saved my life last night."

"Not really," she said. "I'm just glad I found you in time. Why on earth didn't you tell me you were so sick?"

"I've been doing okay lately," he said.

This was clearly a lie, since the hospital said he'd been here before. She didn't want to start an argument, though. Instead, she turned to the shopping bag she was carrying. "I brought you some things."

She pulled out the pillow first. "Mom always complained about hospital pillows not being fluffy enough, so I got you a new pillow and a case so the orderlies don't run off with it accidentally. Here's some other stuff, too." She handed him the plastic shopping bag to go through while she dealt with the pillow.

"I'm sorry the new pillowcase is sort of scratchy."

He laughed. "Scratchy is my middle name."

She remembered looking at his arms and noting how dry the skin was. Another side effect of his condition, probably.

He found the lotion bottle in the bag and slathered some on his arm, then sighed as if he'd just stepped into a hot, soapy tub. "That feels good."

She grinned. "I got you books and magazines, too. If there's anything specific you want or need, let me know. That goes for food, too. If I can grab anything while I'm out, just tell me."

"You shouldn't do that."

"I want to."

He shook his head. "I didn't want you to go to any trouble."

"What are friends for? If you'd told me earlier that you were sick, maybe I could have done something for you. I could have at least made sure you didn't skip your last dialysis treatment. That was crazy of you."

"I tried to keep up, but I couldn't."

"Then it was just the money?"

He shrugged. "Mostly."

She wondered what the other reason was that "mostly" didn't cover. But Walt seemed as closemouthed as ever when it came to important things.

"I know now what you were trying to tell me on Monday," she said.

His eyes widened. "You do?"

"About your kidney problem. I wish you'd just said something. I wouldn't have let you work so hard yesterday."

He sank back against his new pillow. "I forgot all about Monday." He smiled. "I remember that cake, though."

They chatted a little more, keeping their voices down because there was another man in the semi-private room who was recovering from hip surgery. Walt didn't have a lot of energy himself. After a quarter hour, he had a hard time keeping his eyes open. She got up to leave.

"Thank you so much, Rebecca," he said, on the verge of dozing off.

She was halfway down the hall before she remembered Olivia's message. She'd forgotten to give it to him. It wouldn't make sense to wake him up just to tell him that, though, so she continued on to the business office at the center of the hospital. She was shown into a cubicle where a woman sat with a computer and a pile of color-coded forms in a network of trays across the top of her desk.

"I'd like to help pay for Mr. Walter Johnson's outstanding bill," Becca said, helping herself to the visitor's chair at the side of the desk.

The woman nodded and took Walt's name. "And your name is?"

"Rebecca Hudson."

The woman peered at her screen. "All right. And would you like to pay that in full, or a partial payment?"

"How much would 'in full' mean?"

"That would be $12,386."

Becca had been poised to offer her bank card, but the thin

plastic slipped out of her boneless fingers and fell to the floor. She was glad for the distraction of picking it up. It probably saved the woman from seeing her goggling eyes. Twelve thousand dollars! She shook her head. "How could it be so much?"

"Well, your father has been here on two previous occasions, and he's not signed up for an insurance plan."

Becca shook her head. "He's not my father."

The woman peered quizzically at her screen. "Rebecca Hudson," she repeated, as if reading.

"That's right, but—"

"It says so here."

Maybe Walt had written her name down so the hospital would have someone local to call in case anything catastrophic happened to him.

"You mean I'm his emergency contact person?"

"No . . ." The woman swiveled the monitor toward her. "Here. You can see for yourself."

And there it was, in clear twelve-point text: *Next of Kin: Rebecca Hudson. Location: Leesburg. Relationship to Patient: Daughter.*

Chapter 15

Matthew had wanted to take the day off so he and Nicole could spend some time together to see how things really stood between them, but Nicole insisted she had a million things to do after she finished Career Day.

He'd felt very uneasy as he left her that morning. After Nicole's crying jag the night before—something she chalked up to post-travel nerves—he knew there was more going on than she was admitting. He'd even asked her if there was someone else.

Her eyes had widened in offense. "No—what? God! You don't know what it's like living in hotels, and being around work people all the time, and missing home and Olivia. Working out there was a twenty-four/seven mental drain. And now to come back and have you make accusations like that? That's *not* what I need."

Part of him understood jagged nerves. If he had to live for weeks on end in a hotel with just his boss and coworkers for company, he would have been ready for a padded cell. He couldn't blame her for wanting a little downtime, so early that morning he'd gone back to his place to work. He agreed to meet Nicole and Olivia for a very early dinner after gymnastics class, at Olivia's favorite restaurant.

An air of abandonment clung to his town house, although there wasn't a speck of dust anywhere. The cleaning service people had spent more time there recently than he had. After struggling to feel at home at Nicole's house, he now felt out of sorts in his own. The kitchen cupboards were bare . . . but they'd always been bare. His living room was all television and no living. He had to re-acclimate to things like the refrigerator's ice machine letting out rumbling belches every four hours, and the postman arriving later. The little clock in his office was so loud it seemed to be striking a warning about each passing second. He found it hard to concentrate. By dinnertime, the most productive thing he'd done was stuff the clock in a closet.

He'd hoped Nicole would be more relaxed after her day off, and she did seem to be trying. She wore jeans and a bright sweater set, and her hair was pulled back loosely with one of those doohickeys she had in four colors. But while her clothes said day-off casual, the tension in her body language was 5 P.M. workday all the way.

Olivia spotted him first and waved him over. "I ordered us a pizza, like usual," she informed him. "It should be here soon."

He squeezed her arm in greeting. "Am I that late?"

"No," Olivia said. "I'm that hungry."

He sank down onto the booth seat next to Nicole and gave her a quick kiss on the cheek. Her face appeared drawn. "How was your day?" he asked. "The home-cooked-meals plan of relaxation didn't pan out?"

"I realized that was a contradiction in terms. All the stuff in the fridge looked weird to me." She'd obviously been re-acclimating, too. "I would have had to go to the grocery store, and I just couldn't face it. I took a nap instead."

"Jet lag," he said.

"Probably." She got out her phone, checked it for messages, and then put it back.

They all lapsed into momentary silence.

"How was Career Day?" he asked.

"Fun!" Olivia replied.

"If that was fun," Nicole said, "your normal school day must be gruesome."

"Well, we got to miss math, and social studies. *That* was fun." She looked at Matthew. "And Becca was there. She said she never got Mom's e-mail."

"You should have seen her," Nicole said. "She breezed in late—"

"Right in the middle of Mom's talk," Olivia interjected.

"—and then she gave the lamest presentation. You could tell she hadn't prepared anything."

"Everybody loved her speech," Olivia said. "And the cupcakes."

Nicole took a sip of water. "Oh sure. Show up in front of a bunch of eleven-year-olds with sugary food and field questions about being a tween star? Anybody could pull that off."

The waitress came by and delivered the pizza and a large salad. When she was gone, Olivia grabbed a cheese and mushroom slice and leaned forward on both elbows. "Becca said Walt's in the hospital."

He frowned. "I'm sorry to hear that."

"Didn't you know?" Nicole asked.

"I haven't talked to Becca since the party. I haven't had any reason to." Although he'd been tempted to call her several times.

"Is this Walt person her boyfriend?"

Olivia nearly choked on her pizza. "Walt's, like, *really* old."

"That doesn't always mean anything," Nicole said. "Especially to these Hollywood types. They have May-December things going on all the time."

"I bet Walt's still in his fifties," Matthew said. "But he's hardly what you would call anyone's romantic dream."

Nicole shook her head impatiently. "I've never met him, so I can't say. I can't even figure out what he has to do with anybody, or why his name keeps coming up."

"He's really nice," Olivia said, growing agitated at her mother's tone. "I want to go see him in the hospital."

Before Nicole could raise her objections, Matthew said, "I'll call Becca and see what's going on. If he's still there, I'll visit and tell him you said hi."

Olivia didn't appear very excited by this arrangement, but she leaned back, sighing in resignation.

"You don't mind if I run over there this evening, do you?" he asked Nicole.

"God, no. I wasn't expecting you to come over to the house." She got out her phone again and this time left it on the table.

He tried to lure her gaze away from the inert screen. "Are you expecting a call?"

"Work," she said.

"Think they can't get along without you?" he asked.

He'd only meant it as a banal conversation filler, but her lip trembled. "I know they can. I guess I just didn't quite want to believe it."

Conversation limped along after that. By the end, the strain was even showing on Olivia, who passed up a cheesecake opportunity, claiming she might as well get back and tackle her homework. Matthew expected piglets were sprouting wings somewhere.

After leaving the restaurant, he had every intention of going home, doing a little more work, and then heading to the hospital around seven. Instead, as he drove, he couldn't help thinking about Becca. Walt's being sick had probably upset her, and in the middle of it all, she'd managed to end up giving a presentation at the elementary school when she didn't even need to. He kicked himself for not calling the night before.

Maybe he could make it up to her now. If Walt was in the hospital, she probably wanted to get away from the shop. He couldn't bake, but he'd begun his working life at the age of sixteen manning a fast-food counter, so he could pinch-hit at the shop if she needed help.

He cruised past the Strawberry Cake Shop, which appeared shut. It was still early evening. He parked, got out, and found a note pinned to the door. *The shop is closed for today. Please visit us again soon!*

Uneasiness gripped him. Was this because of Walt?

He sidestepped over to Becca's apartment's entrance and pressed the buzzer. A minute went by. He was on the verge of pulling out his phone when he heard footsteps clomping down a flight of stairs.

The door opened and Matthew was confronted with red, puffy eyes in a pale face. Becca's drawn expression caused his heart to plummet. Something bad had happened.

"Is it Walt?" he asked.

She shifted. "What do you know about Walt?"

"Just what Olivia told me. She said that Walt was in the hospital. Is he . . . ?"

Becca responded with an odd, exasperated *cluck*. "Walt's fine at the moment, but I'm losing my mind." She stepped aside. "Come on up, if you think you can take it."

He wasn't sure what that meant, but he went up the stairs. "I was worried when I saw the shop closed," he said. "Where's your friend . . . Pam, isn't it?"

"She's given me notice. In fact, I think all my friends have given me notice."

Matthew got to the top of the staircase and stared around the cavernous, half-finished loft. This was not what he'd expected. He'd thought Becca's apartment would be stuffed with homey furniture, tchotchkes, and maybe some more upscale decorative touches. This place seemed as half-done as his own.

He started forward to get out of Becca's way but then jumped back again when a gray cat darted inches from his feet.

Becca sidestepped around him. "Don't mind Willie. He's skittish. And blind. Probably mistook you for a fox."

He followed her to the kitchen, which felt like the only place to go. "Are you okay?"

"Not really, to be honest." She opened the fridge. "Would you like something to drink? I'm having an orange juice. But I also have tea? Beer?"

"I don't need anything, thanks," he said. "Why is Walt in the hospital?"

"He has some kind of kidney problem, which of course he never told me about. And the idiot skipped his dialysis. Last night I came up and found him passed out on my bed."

She gave him a rundown of the night before, going all the way up to the doctor telling her about Walt's grave condition. For relating such horrible news about a person she obviously cared about, her voice sounded flat, almost annoyed. And yet she had been crying.

"I'm so sorry," Matthew said. "I never guessed he was that sick."

"Oh, there are a lot of things about Walt that I never guessed." Becca flicked the freezer door shut and plopped ice into her glass. "But if there's anything that I've learned in the past day, it's that I'm more clueless than I ever dreamed. Apparently I've been trampling over everyone's happiness like a big emotional Godzilla and I didn't even know it. And now Walt . . ."

Her eyes squeezed shut, as if that would block out the pain of the words she'd left unspoken.

He stepped forward. "Whatever happens to Walt, you can't blame yourself. You've been great to him. You gave him a job. He seemed happy here."

She took a slug of juice. "Did you know that he was living downstairs in the shop?"

"Since when?"

"About a week and a half." She elaborated on Walt's eviction and their agreement that he could stay in the storage room short-term.

"See?" he said. "You've done everything you could for the guy. Whatever happens, you have nothing to feel guilty about."

"Guilty?" Her sharp laugh surprised him. "My problem now is

that I want to strangle the old faker. He told the hospital that he's my father."

Matthew gaped at her, not sure at first he'd heard right. "Wouldn't you know if he was or if he wasn't?"

"No, I never knew my dad. I didn't know who he was, or if he was alive. Then, when I went this morning to give the hospital money to cover some of what Walt owes, they informed me that I was down as his next of kin. He told them that I was his daughter." She shook her head. "Told *them*. Not me."

"Do you believe it?"

"I don't know. That's what I've been doing all day—pacing between these four walls and trying to figure it out. His full name is John Walter Johnson. My mom said my dad's name was Johnny. That's practically all she ever told me about him."

"That's not very conclusive," he said. "Given how common a name John is, it's not even much of a coincidence."

"I know." She folded her arms and shifted her weight onto one hip. "Other things seem right, though. For one thing, Mom always said he was a loser, and Walt certainly fits the bill."

"So do a lot of other people."

"But there's also the way he looks at me. And the fact that he came here at all. Which I know isn't sound logic, because a few other crazies have made the pilgrimage to this town to see Tina from *Me Minus You*. But Walt wasn't pushy. He just sort of . . ."

"Insinuated himself into your life," he finished for her. This was so strange. He liked Walt, but none of them really knew much about him. Obviously. There was always the chance that this was some kind of hoax.

Becca tilted her head. "It does seem as if he wormed his way into my life. But on the other hand, *I'm* the one who took all the initiative. Walt appeared on the bench in front of my store a few times, and I just grabbed the ball and ran with it. Suddenly I'm letting a strange man live in my building and paying his hospital bills."

"An ex-convict," he said, although he immediately felt sorry for reminding her.

She pressed her hands to her temples and let out a long breath. "I can't believe it. I'm usually cautious about every person who approaches me. And even though I knew Walt was shady, I just acted like the perfect patsy to his scheme. If it was a scheme." She bit her lip. "But if he is a faker, why would he do such a crappy job? Why not make some kind of attempt to be Repentant Prodigal Dad, rather than Anonymous Loser Dad?"

"What did he say?"

"I haven't talked to him yet," she said.

This took him aback. "Why not?"

"Because he's a really sick man in a hospital and I want nothing more than to storm into his room and yell at him. It's insane. One minute I'm debating calling the police and having the old jerk hauled in for fraud, and the next I'm wondering if he could give me information about my grandparents." She let out a strangled cry. "I don't know how to approach him. Is he Real Dad or Fake Dad? I'm not even sure it matters. He's either an incredibly terrible parent or a con artist."

Matthew understood how conflicted she must feel. He felt conflicted, and he wasn't personally involved. He was worried about Becca, but now that he saw her anger, a part of him wanted to defend Walt, too. "Maybe he had reasons. If your mother never explained . . ."

She sent him an incredulous look. "I'm almost thirty. A guy's got to have a really serious excuse to miss the first thirty years of his daughter's life, don't you think? Maybe if he'd been abducted by terrorists, or contracted amnesia for three decades."

Matthew nodded.

"He must want something," she said. "Why else would he come all this way to this town?"

"You'll never know for sure until you speak to him."

"And say what? 'Gee, Dad, where have you been all my life?' "

"Aren't you curious?"

"Yes!" Her mouth set into a grim line. "That's another reason I resent him. Grow up with a big question mark for a father and you become comfortable with mystery. I even got to fantasize that my dad could be anybody. But having some ex-junkie hunt me down and tell me *he's* my dad? I could live without that."

"Junkie?" Matthew frowned. "I didn't know."

"Oh, Walt's got quite a past. More of one than I ever dreamed, apparently. And he never tried to hide anything from me—except the most important detail."

Matthew pointed out, "Maybe he never intended for you to know."

"He came over here Monday night to talk, but I was in a weird mood and gave him such a depressing account of my life that he fled." She stopped, shaking her head at the memory. "I said all sorts of awful things about my unknown dad—basically called him a loser point-blank."

"But if you didn't know about him then . . ."

"That sort of makes it worse, doesn't it? He knows I was giving my unvarnished opinion. Not that I care. He deserves to hear the worst." Becca resumed her pacing. "Mom told me he was bad news. She must have worried this would happen. She never said it in so many words, but the thought that he would come crawling out of the woodwork at some point couldn't have been far from her mind."

"She probably worried when you were on television that your father would come begging for money. But he didn't do that."

A mirthless laugh snuffled out of her. "He didn't have to. All he had to do was show up and I started writing checks. I'm an idiot." She glanced at the leftover juice in her glass. "Some vodka in this would really hit the spot right now." She opened a cabinet behind her and grabbed a Smirnoff bottle by the neck.

Matthew darted around the island and interceded before she could make a grave beverage error. "Do you think that's a good idea?"

"It's been a great idea since vodka first met OJ."

"But a bad one since alcohol first met emotionally charged situations. Also, you're going to have to drive to the hospital. You need to talk to Walt. Putting it off won't help."

She gazed regretfully at the bottle and stashed it away again. "You're right. Probably best if I don't end up with a DWI on the way." When she turned around, they were standing much closer than before. "What made you come over here?"

"I wanted to find out about Walt. Also, Olivia told me about Career Day. I'm sorry about that. I should have called to tell you that you didn't need to go over there."

"Oh, that's okay," she said dismissively. "I'd almost forgotten the whole thing, to tell you the truth. That's the kind of day it's been."

"Olivia said you went over big with the kids, though."

"Did she?" A smile touched her lips. "That's nice. I never expected to find old television buffs in a room full of fifth-graders."

"Your appeal crosses generations."

"What did Nicole say?" she asked. "Seeing her there was something I didn't expect."

No kidding. "Her sudden appearance was a curveball to me, too. She just showed up last night. No warning."

"And she was ready with the PowerPoint presentation first thing this morning. I call that impressive." She turned her attention to her juice glass again. "And she's okay?"

It was a benign question, but Matthew couldn't forget last night's crying jag. "I'm not sure. She seemed tense. And not all that glad to see me. She kept saying it was a relief to be home, but she didn't look happy."

"I'm sure it's not about you."

"It could be," he said. "Maybe she senses a change."

Becca eyed him with interest. "You've changed?"

"I'm more . . . conflicted." He searched for a good way to express his feelings, while at the same time he was at a loss as to why he felt compelled to say anything at all. Especially to Becca. It was probably a mistake, but he plunged ahead. "I think she might be picking up on the fact that I have feelings for you. She might have even sensed it before I did."

He waited for Becca's reaction. She seemed so still, rigid. Then he realized that *was* her reaction. Heat crept up his neck as the silence in the kitchen stretched. He wished she'd say some-thing. Anything.

"Are you crazy?" she finally asked.

Anything but that. "Is that how you respond when men admit they like you?"

"You *can't* like me," she said. "Not the way you mean." She took a stiff step backward. "You can like-like me. Anything else would really mess things up."

"For whom?"

"Everybody. What about Olivia? She looks on you like a dad."

The thought brought a tightening to his throat. To think—when he first met Nicole, he worried about how her daughter would affect the relationship. Then Olivia became the relation-ship's glue. But that obviously wasn't enough. "She's fond of me, but she knows I'm not her father. I'm not sure, given her real fa-ther, that the word means much to her."

"That's all the more reason why you can't abandon her. Think how awful that would be."

"I'm not in a relationship with Olivia," he said. "And lately, I haven't been in a relationship with Nicole. She doesn't want to get married. Olivia called me the babysitter once. At the time I thought she was joking, but she might actually have hit the nail on the head."

Becca shook her head. "She loves you."

"I can't stay in a relationship with Nicole just for Olivia's sake."

"But you can't just walk away, can you?"

"I wouldn't walk away from Olivia."

"You'd have to," Becca pointed out. "And losing Olivia would be just the start. Relationships breed a whole social ecosystem. If one falls apart, you don't know what the consequences will be for any number of other people."

"Ecosystems?" He raked a hand through his hair in frustra-tion. "You make it sound as though we're endangered salaman-ders. I doubt that you were taking such a long, objective view when you left Cal."

"But I should have," she said. "I should have been taking the long view before Cal and I ever got involved. I caused more damage than I knew."

"That's hindsight. You can't always foresee every ripple."

"But you can't blunder ahead when you know it's a bad idea, either."

He couldn't believe they were arguing. Not a promising start to anything. "So you plan to live as if feelings don't enter the picture anymore? Or love?"

"We're not the only ones with feelings, though. What about—"

From the look on her face, he guessed that she realized the implications of her words at the same moment they hit him. *We're*. So she thought of them as a we, at least subconsciously. It wasn't a declaration of love. It wasn't kisses and joy. But that one simple contraction set a world of hope in motion.

Matthew reached forward to take her in his arms, but she darted just out of reach. "That would be so wrong. Don't you see?"

He released a ragged, regretful sigh. "I see that there's a lot unresolved."

"Understatement of the year." She took her glass and slugged down the remaining orange juice, gulping as if it actually did have vodka in it. "I can't think about this right now. I need to go to the hospital."

Watching her gather up her purse, remorse overtook him. She had the problem of Walt—possibly her long-lost father—to deal with, and he'd chosen this day to tell her how he felt about her. Great timing. No wonder she seemed flustered.

Belatedly, he remembered what he'd intended to say when he'd knocked on her door. "If you need any help manning the shop this week, call me," he said. "Call me for anything."

"You may live to regret those words." She headed for the stairwell as if she were a parting visitor, and even clattered down several steps before turning around and appearing again. "This is my apartment."

He moved past her and headed down the stairs. "Good luck,

and let me know how it goes." He stopped. "Would you like me to go with you to the hospital?"

"No—I think this is something I've got to do alone." Her lips pressed into a narrow line. "It'll be my first ever father-daughter chat."

Chapter 16

At the hospital, her body remained rooted in the driver's seat. She looked across the parking lot, dreading what she had to do, and what she might find out. Which would be worse—to spend the rest of her life with her paternity a big question mark, or to find out her dad really was a broken-down wreck of an ex-con?

Both life and elections needed to come with a none-of-the-above option.

Taking a deep breath, she extracted herself from the front seat and headed in. Butterflies fluttered in her stomach as her shoes squeaked down the linoleum halls. In contrast to this morning, she walked into Walt's room empty-handed.

Not that he seemed to notice, or mind. He looked up from the murder mystery she'd given him earlier and smiled. "Rebecca! You shouldn't have come all the way back out here to see me."

He was obviously feeling better, but he still seemed vulnerable. Without his hat, he looked a little bit like a bird without feathers. And nothing said *defenseless* like a person in a hospital gown.

She shut the door behind her and made her way to the visitor's chair next to the bed. She craned her head around the break in the curtain to see if his roommate was sleeping, but the bed had been stripped.

"Was your roommate discharged?"

"There was a little problem there." Walt pushed a button at the side of the bed, raising the back higher. "We were playing poker earlier, and Lester lost a little money."

She closed her eyes. "You swindled an old man recovering from hip surgery?"

"I didn't cheat," Walt said. "And he was the one who insisted on playing for stakes. Lay there bragging about how good at cards he was. He didn't know how many hours I'd put in playing poker."

Not a lot else to do in prison, she supposed. "What did he lose?"

"His Jell-O from lunch, two melba toast packets, and eighty-six dollars."

"Eighty-six dollars!"

"It was all fair and square," he said. "Man just wasn't the bluffer he thought he was."

Unlike Walt. She shifted in the chair. "I shouldn't have brought you those cards."

"Lester took it okay. It was his family who got upset. His wife and son came by, and the next thing I knew, the orderlies were moving him to a private room."

She couldn't think of a response to that. The idea that he had been sitting here all day blithely reading books and playing poker while she had spent the afternoon in a mental frenzy irritated her. So did the fact that she'd been sitting here less than five minutes and she was already distracted.

"How are things at the shop?" he asked.

"I closed it today."

"Not on account of me, I hope. I told you that you didn't need to trouble yourself about any of this."

"Stop," she said, annoyed by his don't-mind-me act. "Just stop. I saw your hospital paperwork, Walt. I read the form where you wrote down that I'm your daughter."

His face collapsed, the deep worry lines and wrinkles going slack. "A patient's records are supposed to be confidential."

"Not so confidential when you have someone down as your next of kin."

"Oh." He looked down at his hands, which were fiddling with the white hospital sheet. "I'm sorry you had to find out that way."

"How did you expect me to find out?" she asked, her voice tight. "Were you ever going to tell me?"

"I hadn't quite made up my mind."

"Did you plan to make it up ever? According to the doctor I talked to last night, you've been sick for some time."

He met her gaze. "That's why I didn't say anything, see? I didn't want you to feel obligated to me out of pity."

Pity? The word sent her shooting out of her chair. She strode restlessly to the foot of his bed. "You don't have to worry about that. I pitied you plenty right up to the moment when I found out who you were. Now I'm just mad." She narrowed her eyes on him. "If you really are my father. I'm not convinced."

He nodded. "Your mother was Rhonda Hudson. Ronnie."

"Google could've told you that."

"I met her when she was working as a waitress in LA. She hadn't been there long. She'd left Nebraska just after high school and needed the job, but she hated waitressing and said she'd never do it again. She had reddish blond hair, lighter than yours, and she loved musicals, Robert Redford, and the Lakers. For my twenty-fourth birthday, she made me a strawberry cake, just like the one you made the other day. When I bit into it, it was like she was right there in the room with us. Happiness on a plate, like she always said."

Becca swallowed. It wasn't that he knew those things, so much as the way he said them. He wasn't just reciting, he was dragging information out of his heart. Out of her heart.

"I'm sorry if you're disappointed. I can't blame you, though."

One of his eyebrows darted up ruefully. "I'm not exactly a king or a movie star."

"No, you're not." She remembered their conversation Monday. If he really was her father, her ramblings must have been painful to listen to.

Good, she thought, fighting against the swell of emotion building inside her. Maybe it was all true, what he said. If it wasn't, he was diabolical.

He scratched the top of one hand. "I was real surprised when you didn't recognize my full name when I gave it to you for your employee records. That was when I realized that Ronnie must not have told you anything about me."

"She told me your name was Johnny. And that you played the saxophone. That was the one good thing she had to say about you." She crossed her arms. "You do play, don't you?"

He nodded. "Tenor and baritone. But it's been a while. I hocked my saxes a long time ago, and they don't come cheap."

"And your name? What happened to that?"

"It was Johnny. John Walter Johnson. I was called Johnny Johnson. I never liked it much. Your mom and I joked about it. We were Ronnie and Johnny. Pretty stupid-sounding couple."

She folded her arms. "To hear Mom tell it, nothing about you two as a couple made sense."

He winced. "I guess she hated me. I never realized."

"What did you expect?" Becca's voice looped up, but she didn't care. She could mute her anger for her own sake, but for her mom's? That self-pitying wince made her blood boil. "Did you imagine she'd think back in fondness about the guy who'd left her pregnant?"

"I wouldn't have been any good for her."

"How do you know that? According to her, you never even tried."

"She was better off without me. We both knew it, and she told me that point-blank. I was using back then. She said she'd rather a kid of hers have no father at all than me. And then I ended up in jail, twice, which just showed me she'd been right."

"You're not using now, or in jail. At some point you managed to pull yourself together. At least a little bit."

"Because I had to. The second time I got sent up, they sent me to a rehab unit first before tossing me back into the regular pen. That's where I first saw you, during that second stretch." He shook his head. "I remember feeling shocked when I saw you in a magazine—Ronnie and you. I was surprised she didn't give you my last name."

Becca spluttered in indignation. "Why should she have done that? You weren't my father. You aren't now. I don't care if the blood in my veins is fifty percent you. As far as I'm concerned, you were a sperm donor. People don't name their kids after a sperm donor."

He hung his head. "I see that now. I get it. But at the time, it was like realizing I didn't exist at all, to her or to you. Or anybody, really. It upset me."

"Well, boo flippin'-hoo," she said, coming near to shouting. "You know what upset me? That I didn't know who you were, or why you'd never cared enough to even meet me. When I was little, I blamed myself. Isn't that stupid? I was a kid, but I thought your not being there was all my fault. I wondered if there was something about me that made my dad not want to know me. And you want to know the saddest, most twisted thing of all? When I got a little older, I blamed Mom. Mom, who probably went through God-knows-what with her own parents when she told them she was pregnant with me and wanted to keep me. They certainly never helped her out much."

"They didn't approve of me," he said. "Can't blame them for that."

"They never approved of me, either, and I do blame them for it. Now. But at the time I blamed Mom for not being nice, pretty, or whatever enough to keep my dad with us. Meanwhile, she was working her tail off to support us both. Later, I resented her because I didn't get as much stuff as the really rich kids at school, the ones who had dads who worked at fabulous jobs and moms who lavished them with everything they wanted. Mom lavished me with love, but that wasn't good enough. She also paid off our house and paid boarding for Harvey, who had been given to me when I was making lots of money on TV. Maybe she could have tapped in to my savings to defray the expenses for my horse, but she didn't. When I reached adulthood, I had most of the money I'd made as a kid, plus interest. That was Mom. She loved me even when I was an ungrateful, snotty teen. She was worth a hundred dads. In fact, if I'd traded her for a million of you, I'd still have been cheated."

His cheeks reddened. Once she'd blown off some steam, she wondered how she could feel so good about ripping into some guy who was so sick and defenseless.

He's defenseless because he put himself in this position.

Not that he was responsible for his health problems—as far as she knew. Abusing drugs all those years had to have contributed something. Or maybe he just had bad kidneys. Or maybe it was a combination.

But he did deserve every bad-dad accusation she could hurl at him.

He exhaled a long breath, then met her gaze as if he was almost afraid to do so. The look reminded her of when she'd met him. He'd seemed anxious then, too. Of course. There was no way for him to have known that she'd never seen so much as a photo of her father. If she'd recognized him, she might have wanted him gone immediately.

"I get your anger," he said.

"Good, because I don't think it's going anywhere."

"I only meant to say that I was hurt at first, all those years ago," he explained. "And then I looked around me. I was in prison. I'd been there before, but it had never seemed so damn real to me. I was surrounded by thieves, murderers, drug dealers. You name it. I was one of them. And then I looked at where you were. On television. In a different universe."

She tried to imagine it.

"That was the moment when I understood what I was," he said. "I was nothing. I might as well have taken my life and chucked it off a railroad bridge." He reached a shaky hand over for a glass of water. "I'm glad Ronnie kept my life hidden from you. She did the absolute right thing. I never let on to anyone who you were, either. I even tried to forget it myself."

A cynical laugh bubbled out of her. "Sounds like the one thing you were really successful at."

"But you see, I couldn't really forget. I'd see a picture of you, or once or twice on the television screen in the prison dayroom, and I'd think, *That's my daughter. If something that good is a part of me, I can't be all bad. I can't be a no-hoper like all the scum around me.* I started trying harder. I got my high school degree, and I tried to learn to talk better. I found different people on the block—not the ones I'd been hanging around with. Took a little shit for that, I can tell you."

She frowned, attempting to piece together the chronology. "When was this?"

"Oh, back in the late nineties, I guess. I got out in 2003."

"Over a decade ago?" Her blood pressure started to spike again.

"Well, yeah. I got out, and my first thought was looking up Ronnie and Rebecca. I've always thought of you as Rebecca. Didn't know you'd shortened it."

"You seem to have changed yours, too."

"That was part of me wanting to be different, I guess. When I got out, I started dressing a little different, and called myself Walt. That was my granddad's name. I took whatever work I could find. Real work."

"Where?"

"Los Angeles."

"You were in LA all that time?"

He nodded. "I went past Ronnie's house once or twice. I even saw you on the street, or thought I did. But I . . ." He shrugged. "I can't explain. In jail, my goal was to get out, go straight, and look up my family. But when I got out, it struck me how dumb that was. You weren't really my family, and even if I was clean, you were still better off without me. Like you said—having a person like me for a father was a cheat. And I figured Ronnie'd probably found somebody else anyway."

She had dated a few men, but nothing had ever come of those relationships. Becca always assumed it was because she was too busy working and being a mom. Now she wondered. She wondered about everything.

"I also didn't want you or Ronnie to think I was looking you up to mooch off you," he said.

"So why did you look me up here?"

"I can't say."

She pursed her lips. "Can't, or won't?"

"I lost my job, and . . ." He looked her in the eye. "The closest explanation I've got is that I just wanted to see you. So I could tell you I was sorry."

A band squeezed her chest, and she fought to take a deep breath. One sorry didn't make up for a lifetime. It didn't help her mom. And Matthew's warning was still in her head. He liked Walt, yet he'd counseled caution, and he probably still would. Walt had lost his job, so he'd looked her up. Maybe it was sentimentality that had brought him here, or maybe he'd thought she was rich.

"You've spun a believable story, but I still don't have real proof. Given your history, why should I believe you aren't conning me?"

He shrugged. "I guess you shouldn't. I wouldn't."

"A blood test would be proof."

"That'd be fine—though I don't know why you'd bother. But if it'd make you feel better, I'd understand."

"No offense, but nothing about this situation makes me feel better," she said. "If seeing me on a television screen helped you turn your life around, I'm glad. But part of me can't help wishing you'd left it at that. I liked my father better as a mystery, and I liked you better when you were just Walt."

He stared at the sheet again. "Maybe I should have left it alone."

She stood up. "I have to go home. I didn't get much sleep last night, and today has been surreal."

He looked drained himself.

When she'd gathered her things and was on the way out, he stopped her. "Becca?"

She turned.

"I didn't come here to be your father. I just wanted to see you again because . . ." He swallowed. "You're wrong. For a long time now, not a day goes by that I don't think of you, of what I missed."

She battled the response welling up in her with every last ounce of determination. "Every one of those days that went by you could have done something about that," she said. "Even if it was just a letter."

She received no satisfaction from his shamefaced expression. He looked beaten. Tired.

"I'll see you tomorrow," she told him.

She left him then, and purposefully didn't look back. Yet something in his tone had alarmed her. *I just wanted to see you again because* . . . What was she missing? Because . . . why?

Passing the nurses' station, she spotted the intern she'd talked to the night before. Becca had to keep herself from tackling the woman.

"Dr. Atar, can I speak to you?"

The doctor pivoted. "Oh, hi! Sure." Her clipped tone conveyed that she would be happy to answer any questions so long as they didn't take more than two minutes to answer.

"You mentioned Walt Johnson's disease last night," Becca prompted. "Something about his kidneys . . ."

Dr. Atar's gaze narrowed in concentration. "ESRD."

"Right." Becca had a feeling she should be writing this down, and fished through her purse for a pen. "And those letters stand for?"

"End stage renal disease."

"End stage," Becca repeated.

The words struck her with such force, she had to lean against the wall. "That means . . . well, 'end stage' probably means just what it sounds like? I mean . . . it's . . ."

"It's a terminal condition."

"Oh." Becca gulped. Words like *end* and *terminal* were not mysterious, scientific jargon. She had been in this situation before, with her mom and cancer. But suddenly, she found herself wanting to put her hands over her ears and deny, deny, deny. "But there are things to do, right? Like the dialysis. That makes him better, right?"

"It's a treatment, not a cure. There is no cure for renal failure."

"No cure," Becca repeated. "So that means . . ."

Dr. Atar met her gaze steadily, with that veil of distanced compassion doctors had to assume to keep from going insane. "Unless drastic measures are taken, which so far Mr. Johnson has said he does not want, then I'm afraid his life will be significantly shortened."

"How much shortened?"

The doctor looked reticent. "I'm not a renal specialist. I would hazard . . . a year? Two at the outset? But it could actually be less than that. He needs to see a nephrologist."

Becca's body turned leaden and cold. She nodded, not able to take it all in, but at the same time understanding exactly what he'd been trying to tell her. That bit he hadn't been able to say. *I just wanted to see you again . . . because I'm dying.*

Chapter 17

Somehow, she managed to wake up on time the next morning. She got up, brushed her teeth and dressed, but her mind never strayed too far from WebMD. She couldn't dislodge those dreadful words from her mind—*end stage. Terminal.* In all the resources she could find on the Internet, kidney disease was a long, and sometimes not-so-long, march toward either death or a transplant.

Was that where Walt was? How could she not have known?

She wanted to talk to Dr. Atar again. But she had too many questions for one of their corridor quickies.

Conflicting emotions warred within her. Could it really be that she'd found her father only to discover he was dying? Was the universe that perverse? If he actually was her father. That doubt, ever slimmer, still remained. Part of her wanted this to be a hoax. Maybe the old criminal had decided one way to get a new kidney was to find some fatherless person . . .

But she wasn't famous enough for that information about her to be widely known. If he wasn't her dad, how could he have found it out? When she was a kid, she certainly hadn't run around broadcasting the fact that she didn't know who her father was. And after she was grown up, nobody cared about her except in a vague "whatever happened to" way.

After struggling to get to sleep the night before, she'd bolted up at 3 A.M., shaken out of an uneasy sleep by the possibility that Walt might have been her real father's cell mate. Maybe her real father had died in prison, and Walt was an imposter trying to shake her down for money. He might have invented the whole story. He couldn't fake kidney disease, of course, but maybe that was the reason for the shakedown.

Now, in the cold light of day, she was pretty sure the cell-mate imposter idea was an old film plot she'd seen on Turner Classic Movies. And it hadn't seemed very believable even in black-and-white.

The lingering doubts resulted in emotional whiplash. Facts warred with emotions. Skepticism collided with caring. One minute she was straining her brain to think of things she could do to make Walt more comfortable. The next, searing rage would grab hold of her. Could he have hunted her down just so he could guilt a kidney from her? When she wasn't worried about how to save him, she hated him. Worse, she hated herself for hating him.

Just as she was opening her door to leave her apartment and open the shop, Cal pushed his way in, gangster-style. Becca gasped. Scurrying over the threshold with the lightning quickness of a cockroach, he looked desperate, hunted.

"Shut the door," he whispered, collapsing against the stairwell banister and heaving in nervous breaths. "Lock it."

She did as he directed, only because she was so surprised. And curious. "Who am I hiding you from? An angry husband? Interpol?"

"Pam."

"Is she armed?" When he shook his head, she started to unlock the door again.

The click of the tumbler panicked him. "Please. Help me.

I've gotten myself into a situation," he said. "Has Pam told you about us?"

"Pam? Is that why you're scrambling around so early?"

"I snuck out while she was still asleep." He ran a hand through his sleep-mussed hair. "She's hard to shake. What am I going to do?"

"Why are you asking me?"

"You got me into this mess," he said. "I was all mixed up on Saturday, and then Pam called. She came over to let me cry on her shoulder and to fix me some really lethal drinks. The next thing I knew, I found myself in West Virginia listening to Pam speculate about bridesmaids."

"You just *found yourself* there." As if he had nothing to do with it.

"You know what I mean. . . ." He heaved a breath. "I've barely had a moment alone all week. Or even when I've got one, she's calling me."

"Uh-huh." God forgive her for smiling at his misery. "Who did Pam decide on for maid of honor? Me or Erin?"

"Please! I'm begging for help."

"What do you want me to do?" Becca asked.

"You're Pam's friend. Do us both a favor and tell her what a lousy husband I was."

She twisted her lips in thought. "Pam could probably do worse."

Scowling, he thumped down on a stair. "I never knew till now how vicious you are."

She laughed. "I can't help you. I already warned Pam she was getting you on the rebound."

"That's it!" His eyes lit with excitement. "The rebound. That wouldn't be fair to her."

Becca shook her head. "She thought it was my inflated ego talking. Now she's pissed off at me. Doesn't even plan to keep working at the shop."

"Okay." She recognized the expression on his face as he pondered this roadblock, searching for a slant that could ease him out of any commitment. "I could explain that I don't want to come between good friends. . . ."

"Keep me out of it. I've got troubles enough."

He let out a long sigh of helpless exasperation. "What am I going to do? It's not as if I don't like her. But it's so weird. Have you ever woken up naked with your best friend? I mean, sure, Pam and I always liked hanging out together, but there's always been this smidgeon I've kept private from her."

"I've seen it," Becca reassured him. "It's bigger than a smidgeon."

"Hey—I'm being serious here."

"So am I. You do realize you're making a problem where there isn't one? All you've told me so far is that you're involved in a relationship with someone you like a lot. There are worse things."

He looked doubtful.

"Cal, have you ever considered that when we were in Vegas, you asked the wrong woman to marry you?"

His eyes bugged. "You think I should *marry* Pam?"

She laughed. "Not right this minute. But if you stopped panicking, you might realize you feel more than you think you do."

He actually seemed to consider the idea. And then, just as quickly, he dismissed it with a head shake and a full-body shiver, like Harvey trying to rid himself of a pesky horsefly. "She nags."

"You need nagging." She nudged his leg with her foot. "You also need to get out of my stairwell. I have to work."

"Can I stay in your apartment today?"

Coward. "No. Be a man. Go home. In fact, Pam's scheduled to work at the shop today."

"This morning?" He rolled his eyes. "She didn't tell me that, or else I would've stayed dug in where I was."

"If you're trying to dodge her instead of talking things over like a civilized person, you should probably go now, before she heads in to work."

He pushed himself to standing. He aimed a petulant scowl at

her, but then seemed to see her for the first time that morning. "What's wrong with you? You look like shit."

"Thanks."

"Are you feeling okay?"

"I haven't been sleeping very well lately. Walt's in the hospital, and he's . . . well, it's a long story."

Cal made sympathetic noises, but obviously didn't have time for long stories. He edged to the door, cracked it open, and peeked through. "You think she'll spot me?"

Pam wasn't due to arrive for another hour, actually, but Becca relished his paranoia. "Not if you hurry." She shook her head in wonder as he dashed down the sidewalk in a serpentine crouch.

Bare shelves greeted her when she opened up the shop. Welcoming the distraction of work, she turned the sound system to a classical radio station and got busy preparing batter. Within an hour she was pulling the first batch of cupcakes out of the oven and had several more pans queued up. After two hours, the shelves were beginning to look a little less like Soviet Russia.

Pam arrived, greeting her with a chilly, "Your eye makeup is a disaster," and then heading straight to the storage closet. She flicked the broom around the floor, pointedly not making eye contact or saying anything.

By the time she flipped the Open sign, the strain of silence had evidently become too much. She turned, glanced at Becca, and blurted out, "Did Cal ever act strange with you?"

"Always. Cal is strange."

Pam draped herself over the counter. "But I mean acting really weird. I'm beginning to think he has a secret life or something. He's really hard to get hold of on the phone. And then, when we're together, it's like he's always got somewhere else he needs to be."

"Hm."

Pam stiffened. "What do you mean by that?"

"Nothing." Becca shrugged. "Just hm."

Pam pushed herself away from the counter. "Obviously you're not the best person to talk to on this subject."

A couple arrived and looked over their offerings. For a moment, the tension lifted and Pam and Becca both bantered with the customers like old times. After the two finally made their big decision and walked out with chocolate frosted cupcakes with sprinkles, Becca and Pam turned to each other, smiling. Their smiles promptly disappeared, and they stepped back.

For the first time, the shop seemed too small. All these months, she and Pam had operated together without a hitch, but now suddenly they were bumping into each other like the Keystone Cops. And as the morning wore on, and her worries about Walt continued, she couldn't forget that her best friend was mere feet away, not talking to her. Until this morning, Becca had never realized that gabbing was such an important part of their routine. Yet she'd never felt that Pam's friendship was something she could take for granted. From the very beginning, she'd felt lucky to have fallen in with Pam and Erin. To be on the outs with them—with everyone—was dreary.

Several times, she drew breath to make an apology, and to tell Pam how happy she was that she and Cal were getting together. But then she would remember Cal dashing down the street. If she sensed the relationship was doomed, shouldn't she say something? She hadn't said anything to Erin, and look what had happened. Or maybe this was different. As a friend, was she supposed to put her anxiety aside and pretend that Pam and Cal's new relationship was hunky-dory? Would Pam have done that if their positions were reversed?

She opened the refrigerator and was almost relieved to see that they were out of lemons. She turned to Pam, glad for an excuse to escape the tension. "Can you hold down the fort while I run out for a moment?"

"Sure, that's why you pay me the big bucks."

For some reason, the flippant answer made Becca want to cry. "You know, if you don't want to stay, you don't have to give two weeks' notice. I'll get by. Frankly, it's breaking my heart to have you here and not be speaking."

Pam blinked. "I thought it was you. I didn't want to talk about Cal around you."

Probably the same way Becca didn't want to talk about Walt around Pam. To hear her problems trivialized or met with words about how she'd known all along that Walt wasn't to be trusted just wasn't what Becca needed right now.

"Look," she told Pam. "When I get back, we can hash it all out. I'll be your and Cal's biggest cheerleader."

Pam shifted warily. "I wouldn't want you to have to force yourself."

"It wouldn't be forced. I'm really happy for you. And all the worries I had about you both, they just seem less important now that I've got Walt on my mind."

Pam frowned. "What's happened with Walt? I noticed he hasn't been doing a very good job keeping this place swept up."

"He's in the hospital." Becca gave her a brief rundown of Walt's collapse and his kidney ailment. She didn't mention that he might be her father. She wasn't ready yet to announce that to the world.

"I'm sorry he's so sick," Pam said. "If I'd known . . ."

"I know. Me too." She threw a couple of fresh cupcakes into a bag and grabbed her purse. "I'll be back in a little bit."

In the produce aisle at the grocery store, her cell phone rang. Matthew's name came up on her screen, and it felt as if someone was tossing her a lifeline. She hit Talk.

"I was thinking about calling to see if you wanted to have coffee," she said.

"I'd love to, but I'm in DC today. But I was curious about how things went with Walt. You were supposed to call but you didn't."

No, she hadn't. Given all the strains going on in her life, she was wary of stepping into a situation with Matthew. She'd barely had time to think about what he'd said to her yesterday—about his feelings for her. It didn't help that his declaration had come after she'd assured Erin that there was nothing between them. She'd almost convinced herself, too.

These days it felt as if one wrong move could make her entire social structure collapse. She imagined herself grabbing her bags and fleeing from town altogether, the smoke of a failed marriage, frazzled friendships, one would-be romance, and a long-lost father behind her.

"Walt and I talked," she told him. "It went okay. I still don't know what to believe. Or what to do about him."

"He seemed distracted when I saw him," Matthew said.

"You visited him at the hospital? When?"

"Last night, late. We had a nice visit. And distracted or not, he still managed to win ten dollars from me at poker."

She shook her head. "He's finally figured out a moneymaking racket."

"How is he today?"

"I haven't been to the hospital yet. I was trying to get things done at the shop. The cupboards were a little bare over there. But I'm armed with cupcakes, so I might swing by after I finish here. I'm at the grocery store."

"Our old hangout," he said.

"Where my Walt angsting began."

There was a pause over the line before Matthew said, "If you have doubts about him, there are ways to clear them up. A DNA test."

"I'm considering that," Becca admitted. "But right now it feels . . . odd. I mean, he's in the hospital. He almost died without telling me. So now . . ."

"It's confusing, I know."

She sighed. "That's the understatement of the day. I know this sounds awful, but I wish I could dial my life back a month. I would tell month-ago me never to pick up strange men on the road."

"Your month-ago self should have known that already."

"Month-ago me was incredibly naïve. Present-day me just wants to flee to the hills."

"You can't do that," Matthew said. "Tell you what—come over to dinner with Olivia and me tonight."

"At Nicole's?"

There was a pause. "Uh, no. At my place. Nicole had to go out of town and just called to say she wouldn't be in until late. So Olivia's staying at a friend's after school and the parents will drop her at my place after I get home from work."

Nicole was going out of town? She'd only just come back.

All sorts of things about this scenario gave Becca pause. "I'm not sure . . ."

"Please?" he said. "Olivia gets bored at my place, but she might actually enjoy herself if you're there."

She couldn't say she wasn't tempted. It would be good to have someone to talk to about everything that had been going on. And Olivia would be there, which was a plus. Her presence would keep things on a platonic level. No matter how strong her own feelings, Becca didn't want to become more entangled in Matthew's life while his relationship with Nicole was still limping along.

"Okay."

"Great," he said. "You've given this worker drone something to look forward to after a long day."

There was nothing platonic about the anticipation in his voice, but the prospect of seeing a couple of friendly faces at the end of the day was too tempting for her to change her mind. She got the directions to his place and rang off.

She bought her lemons and drove to the hospital. When she went by Walt's room, clutching her cupcake sack, she found him asleep, his hat shading his eyes, siesta-style. She considered leaving the cupcakes by the side of his bed, but then remembered a nurse saying something about a restricted diet. Usually if there were restrictions, sugar and fat were the first casualties. She needed to find out more about that.

In the corridor, a glimpse of Dr. Atar made her think of a way to optimize her cupcake gift. "Dr. Atar?" She trotted after the woman's white lab coat.

The doctor swung around and Becca held out the bag. "I wanted to bring you something, to thank you."

"Is that something edible?" Dr. Atar asked. "Because I'm running on fumes right now."

"Cupcakes. Enjoy them."

"Lifesaver! I should offer you a free appendectomy."

"Free advice will do," Becca said. "Would this be a good time to talk to you about Walt?"

The doctor beckoned her and kept walking—double-time, like a person who didn't waste a second more than she had to with trivial things such as getting from one place to another. They stopped at a break area with vending machines at the end of a corridor. Dr. Atar put money in the coffee machine and waited for the mechanism to excrete something purporting to be a cappuccino. Becca regretted not bringing a thermos of coffee with her, too.

They settled at a Formica table and the doctor inhaled a chocolate cupcake.

"I was hoping to see you today," Dr. Atar said. "You'll be glad to know that your father will be discharged tomorrow. He won't be stuck over the weekend."

"He's not my father," Becca said. "Maybe not, at least."

The doctor sipped her coffee and seemed to weigh whether this was pertinent information for her to know. "Well, just so he has a place to go home to. He needs taken care of, and someone to pester him about sticking to his diet and going to his treatments."

Usually Becca felt confident of her abilities to pester people, but the prospect of being her newfound father's keeper made her heart sink.

"What about long term?" she asked the doctor. "You said he was at end stage. But if he keeps going to dialysis, he'll be okay, right?"

"Not indefinitely. There are patients who deteriorate, even with dialysis."

"What about transplants? I read on the Internet that those are more common now. Couldn't he just get a kidney?"

"It's not quite that simple."

"There are sixteen thousand done per year," Becca said, flaunting her Google skills.

"Yes, but there are waiting lists. It depends on eligibility and well, frankly, it depends on the patient and his support network. Your fa—Mr. Johnson—has been lax in going to dialysis. When a transplant is done, the surgical team wants to know that the patient will be willing to take the anti-rejection drugs regularly. Otherwise, it's a waste of a kidney. There are somewhere around a hundred thousand people on the donor waiting lists."

"That sounds sort of cold-blooded. One hundred thousand against the life of my father."

Dr. Atar leaned forward. "I thought you said he wasn't your father."

"He isn't, exactly." Becca shifted in the molded plastic chair. "Just technically."

The doctor chewed this over along with the last crumbs of cupcake. "It's different if there's a live donor. That cuts out the wait list issue, certainly."

"A live donor," Becca repeated. Someone like . . . herself.

She couldn't help recoiling a little. She didn't consider herself a selfish person, but life was difficult enough without hacking out body parts to give to strange men who wandered into her life. Weren't kidneys sort of essential? She wasn't even sure of her relationship to Walt. He was just this person who had happened to her, someone she now appeared to be saddled with.

"If you want, I can give you the names and numbers of the closest hospitals that are on the kidney registries," the doctor said. "They could tell you more than I can."

"Thank you."

Becca got the information and swung past Walt's room again.

He was awake. She told him that he would be getting out tomorrow, and that she had plans to take him to see kidney transplant specialists.

"I don't want that," he said.

Becca had felt ambivalent about the idea of getting involved in this process, but if anything Walt looked even more reluctant. Unfortunately, his digging in his heels made her want to slap the reins and mush him forward.

"It'll just be a preliminary thing," she said. "When I was reading on the Internet, they said you shouldn't waste time. Getting on the lists is important."

And he'd wasted enough time already.

His shoulders lifted in a fatalistic shrug. Maybe he would perk up when they sprang him from this place. Feeling optimistic in a hospital was difficult.

She was about to make her escape when a loud knock sounded at the door, followed by the entrance of a clown carrying a banjo. Clowns creeped her out even in circuses. Having one pop up out of the blue scared her out of her wits.

"Hi, folks! I'm Banjo!" His red, white, and blue painted mouth widened in a crazed grin. "Anybody in here want a song?"

Whether they wanted one or not, they were assaulted with a manic rendering of "Won't You Come Home, Bill Bailey?" that was made even more uncomfortable for Becca because the clown was staring at her as if *she* were the peculiar one. Being viewed as an oddity by a person in tricolor pancake makeup and yarn hair took her ego down a peg. She tried to smile, although she was sure the expression was coming across as a frozen grimace.

When he reached his wow finish, the clown flapped over to Walt in his oversized shoes. "How are we today?"

"That was pretty good," Walt said, ignoring the question altogether. "I always liked banjo. Know anything else?"

Becca barely hid her exasperation at his encouraging the man. What evil hospital administrator okayed the plan to let clowns with banjos loose in the wards? Was there a person alive who considered this Bozo-meets-*Hee-Haw* act therapeutic?

The clown turned to Becca. "Isn't your name Tina?" the clown asked Becca.

Oh dear Lord. Not now. "Uh, no."

Unfazed, he dropped his jaw and gave her an openmouthed, toothy smile. "Oh, I think it is! Banjo's a TV buff, and he's even eaten one of your super-scrumptious cakes! And now I'd like to sing a song especially for you!"

"That's not—"

"Does this ring any bells?"

As if to ramp up her discomfort to the umpteenth degree, the clown burst into the theme song from *Me Minus You*. Once upon a time, there had been a sweet ballad with that title, but the network had obviously decided that it wasn't cool enough, so they commissioned a new song set to a cheery pop tune, à la *Friends*. Even though the banjo couldn't capture the rock beat, nothing could disguise the earnest nineties cheesiness of the lyrics.

Since you been gone
Life's been all wrong.
The other day I thought I saw you, heard you, touched your hair.
You weren't there, but it seemed so true.
Was it just a little dream, crazy little scheme my-my-my mind played on meeeeee?
'Cause I just can't get used to me minus you
Me minus you!
Me minus you!

On the day she finally sloughed off this mortal coil, and some TV nut set a tribute video to her on YouTube, that would be the song playing. Though Becca didn't underestimate the appeal of having a tribute of any kind, she did wish she could have had a better theme song. It wasn't *The Mary Tyler Moore Show* theme. It wasn't even *That Girl*. But she supposed if she'd wanted a better song, she should have been a better actress.

The song also lacked a second chorus, so, uncomfortably, Banjo the therapy clown reprised the first verse, only with more emotion this time around. Becca shifted her gaze to Walt, hoping to transmit a visual apology for putting him through this. To her shock, his toes were tapping beneath the sheet. And when Banjo reached "my mind played on *meeeeeeee*," Walt joined for the rest of the song.

The man had been completely absent from her life. But somewhere along the way, he'd absorbed the theme song of that stupid show. It couldn't have been anything a guy like him would want to watch. And yet, it appeared he had.

For her.

Chapter 18

He hadn't realized how much he looked forward to seeing Becca until he answered his doorbell that night and she was there.

"You wouldn't believe the day I've had," she said as he ushered her inside. "Crazy friends, doctors, clowns."

"Real clowns?"

"*Singing* clowns." She handed him a bottle of wine. "This is the only antidote for singing clowns that I could think of. Sounds like we both need it."

"No one was singing where I was, at least." No one ever sang at the Office of Management and Budget. Which probably was a blessing.

He led her back to the kitchen, but she stopped in the living room, doing a slow 360. "I think I know why you need the wine. Your house was burglarized."

"I just moved in six months ago," he said, dismayed to hear his voice echoing around the bare walls.

"Six months? And you haven't bought a chair yet?"

"I have a couch. Why would I need a chair?"

She put her hands on her hips. "That sounds pathetic, even for a guy."

"The reason I don't have extra furniture is that I spend so much time at Nicole's."

Mentioning her name caused a subtle atmospheric disturbance. Becca broke her gaze from his and all at once seemed very interested in his television. "At least you sprang for a TV stand."

"Of course. I'm not an animal." He took in her smile and beckoned her with a tilt of his head. "The kitchen isn't quite so man cave–like. There are chairs."

They were folding chairs, but Becca didn't comment on them. She was too busy checking out his cooking stuff—what very little there was. "I'm sorry," she said. "Some people go to other people's houses and snoop through medicine cabinets or bookshelves. Me, I have to check out kitchen gadgets."

"You'll have a short snooping session here. I have a can opener, a corkscrew, and a blender."

"I'll take the corkscrew."

She opened the bottle of wine, but didn't seem too concerned about letting it rest before pouring out two glasses.

"Not too much for me," he said, starting to get out stuff for the salad. He had already emptied a bag of greens into a bowl in a feeble effort to camouflage what a lazy chef he was. "I'm driving Olivia home later."

She looked around, noticing Olivia's absence for the first time. "Where is she?"

"She called a while ago to say she was going out to eat with her friend and the friend's parents. Olivia loves restaurants. Plus, I think she's had it with my cooking." He gestured to the stove, where an empty jar of pasta sauce gave a hint about the meal to come. "I have a limited repertoire, especially for things that don't involve either a grill or a microwave."

"I love pasta." Becca recorked the bottle. "I guess I shouldn't drink too much either. I have to go home and figure out where

I'm going to put Walt. I can't spring a man from the hospital and have him sleep on a cot in my storage closet."

"True." He hadn't considered this before.

"And you've seen my apartment—there's no privacy. So I'm going to have to rig something up. I shouldn't have discarded all my screens. You don't happen to have any spare walls lying around, do you?"

"You don't really have a setup for two people," he observed.

"I know, but what can I do? I'm responsible for him. I felt that way before, but now on top of everything else, he's my maybe-dad, so I really can't turn him loose in Leesburg."

Matthew chopped a carrot. "He could stay here."

Becca's eyes widened. "*Here?* Are you crazy?"

"No crazier than you. At least my place has a second bedroom. Or a room, period."

"Yeah, but this is Walt we're talking about. He's my headache, not yours."

"I don't see it as a headache. Just a favor for a friend who's down on his luck."

"Friend?"

"Okay, an acquaintance."

Becca looked doubtful. "Sure, he's a nice enough old guy . . . although I'm not entirely convinced he's not a con artist."

"You still doubt he's your father?" He watched her face and saw the strain of uncertainty fighting with a strong hunch. "That's another reason it would be good for him to stay here," he continued. "I don't have any skin in the game, so to speak. If you're worried that he's trying to play on your sympathies, that won't be so much of an issue if he's not underfoot all the time."

"No, all my sympathy would be for you, because he'd be under *your* feet."

He shook his head. "I'm not around that much. Although now that Nicole's back, I . . ."

As soon as he started to say the words, he didn't know how to finish. Now that Nicole was back, the future seemed more uncertain than ever. He'd spoken reflexively, because so much of his life in Leesburg had been wrapped up in Nicole and Olivia. But now that she was back and he was no longer responsible for Olivia, there didn't seem to be anything holding them together.

Becca watched him intently. "Nicole had to take off on another business trip already?"

"A short business jaunt, she said."

She sipped her wine. "Don't take this the wrong way, but I think your head's a little screwed up right now. A few days ago you were telling me that you and Nicole were basically through."

"We are, but it's complicated. There's been practically no time for us to talk things out."

"Uh-huh."

He hated how he sounded. "The relationship is on its last legs, but Nicole's seemed so stressed out lately, I haven't wanted to add to it by having *the conversation*. And Olivia's being around complicates things."

Becca didn't say anything for a long while, and his discomfort grew.

"I'm not a cheater," he said. "I invited you here as a friend. Which I hope you are, and will be, no matter what happens." The more he spoke, the more he wanted to tell himself to shut up. Everything was coming out all wrong.

"I will be," she agreed. "And I believe you're not a cheater. But I still worry that I'm blundering into something at the worst possible moment." She tilted her head. "Did Nicole say where she was going?"

"Baltimore. She's supposed to be back tonight."

Becca absorbed this information. "That's another reason I couldn't pawn Walt off on you right now. You've got your own problems."

From her worried expression, he began to wonder if "going to Baltimore" was a new euphemism for unsavory activity.

"I don't really see any connection. And as for Walt being in the way, whether I'm here or not doesn't matter. During my month at Nicole's with Olivia, I got used to having someone around all the time. This place feels so empty by comparison."

She laughed. "This place *is* empty."

"Right—there's plenty of room. Another person around wouldn't bother me. I swear."

"Let me think about it," she said. "They're releasing him tomorrow."

"Tomorrow would be fine."

Her gaze met his. "I still don't think you know what you're letting yourself in for, but I appreciate the offer."

"I suppose I should ask Walt if he has any preference," he said. "We've been discussing him as if he were a minor."

"His instinct seems to be to dig in his heels and do nothing. When I mentioned going to the transplant doctors, he immediately dismissed the idea."

"That was your first reaction, too, as I recall. You worried Walt had come all this way to wheedle a kidney out of you. Now you're hauling him off to the transplant center."

"Just to get facts," she said. "I certainly don't plan on going under the knife myself. But he could get on a donor list, and it sounds as if he needs to get on one soon."

"But the decision is Walt's," Matthew pointed out.

"Of course." She looked at the collection of veggies next to the cutting board. "I've been sitting here rehashing my problems while letting you do all the work."

"It's not really work." But he stepped aside and let her chop cucumbers and tomatoes while he finished the pasta. He told her about his day in DC, sitting in on a meeting with his crazy boss, who cracked Brazil nuts during everyone's presentations.

While they ate, Matthew asked about her visit with Walt, and she went into more detail about her conversation with Walt and the therapy clown. Matthew could just imagine her face when Banjo had started singing.

She seemed amused now, though. "And to think, I came to Leesburg with the belief that I could escape my past. Now I'm having it sung to me in public places."

"You talk as if you were involved in some kind of nefarious activity back in Los Angeles."

"Some of the critics certainly thought so," she said.

He leaned forward. "Why would you want to escape your past? You lived an experience that a lot of people dream about."

"But they dream of the good parts," she said. "Going to awards ceremonies in limos, flying first class, and being paid a lot. They don't think about the stab of rejection when you can't find work and you realize that everyone sees you as a product with an expired shelf life. Or friends turning their backs on you because your ratings are in the toilet. I guess becoming a TV trivia question is a kind of immortality, so that's not bad, but along with that comes being confused with all the child stars who ended up suicides, druggies, or generally screwed-up people. I've had someone come up to me in the mall and tell me that she'd heard I'd OD'd. Turns out she was confusing me with the actress who played Buffy in *Family Affair*."

"Your shows were a quarter of a century apart," Matthew said.

"To some people it's all a blur. Everybody gets mixed up about something. I can never remember my conquistadors. Did Vasco da Gama discover the Aztec Empire or the Cape of Good Hope? Maybe that mall lady could have told me, but she definitely had her pigtailed TV kids confused."

They were doing dishes when Olivia was dropped off. Matthew let her in and noticed she wasn't quite her ebullient self. She didn't even seem all that glad to see Becca. In fact, she barely made eye contact with her, staring around the kitchen instead, like a detective looking for clues.

"Did you have fun?" Matthew asked her.

Olivia shrugged. "It was Deirdre and her mom." As if that explained everything.

"Oh right," Becca said. "The fruit bar girl."

"It's not her fault that she can't eat stuff," Olivia said.

Conversation flagged, which surprised Matthew. Usually Olivia lit up like a sparkler when Becca was around, but not tonight.

After Becca left, Olivia flopped onto the couch and shot an accusing glare at him. "I thought you and Becca were just friends."

"We are."

"How come you two are hanging out without Mom?" she asked. "You were drinking wine, even. Isn't that what people do on dates?"

"On dates, or when they happen to feel like drinking a glass of wine," he said. "Olivia, if there's something bothering you—"

"It doesn't matter," she said, cutting him off. "I know adults are liars. I just don't understand why you can't be honest about it."

Despite the pretzel logic, the words made sense in an emotional way, and they hit their mark. Looking at Olivia, he was ashamed. He'd known for weeks that his relationship with Nicole was fizzling. He'd just been too much of a coward to do anything about it. Plus, Olivia made breaking up with Nicole infinitely harder. They'd bonded. He didn't feel like a real parent, but he couldn't imagine just bowing out of her life. But that was what he was going to have to do, wasn't it?

It was nearly ten o'clock when Nicole called. "I'm so sorry," she said in a flustered voice. "How are things?"

"Fine," he said.

"Well, they're not fine here."

"You're still working this late?"

The question was met with a frosty pause. "Yes. This late. Do you think you could take O over to my house and stay with her one more night? I'll be back in the morning."

"Of course. It's no problem," he lied, not relishing driving over to Nicole's.

He passed the phone to Olivia. While she was saying good night to her mom, he packed an overnight bag. *One more night*, Nicole had said.

As if she didn't intend for there to be other nights, either.

"I'm sorry you have to babysit me again," Olivia said, sulking a little against the passenger-side window on the way back to her house.

"I'm not."

"You don't seem happy," she said.

"Neither do you. What's wrong?"

He glanced over and caught her biting her lip. "Nothing's

been right since Mom got back," she said. "First she was sort of frantic, and then she spent a day crying. And then she just decided to go back to work, even though she'd said she was going to take a week off and we'd have all sorts of time together. She's barely even asked about the birthday party."

"Your mom loves her work. She's lucky that way."

"She loves her work more than me," Olivia grumbled.

"Not true."

They waited through a traffic light before Olivia said in a rush, "Sometimes I wish you and Becca were my parents."

"O, that doesn't make sense."

"Maybe not, but I'm almost a hundred percent sure I'd be happier if you were."

"I'll take that as a compliment," he said as they pulled into Nicole's driveway. "Also as evidence that the grass is always greener on the other side of the fence."

"But I've been on your side of the fence," she pointed out. "You weren't going to let me watch television till Christmas, remember? And that's still better than a mom who's either not here or crying all the time."

That night, he resolved to settle things once and for all with Nicole. Part of the reason he'd been a coward was Olivia, but Olivia had just given him a pretty clear lesson in kids-are-not-fools. Dragging things out this way wasn't fair to her, or anyone.

No matter where Becca moved it, the screen could only do so much. It could block the view of her bed from the kitchen, or it could block the bed from the couch in the living room area. But no amount of angling could provide privacy from both vantages.

She'd have to go to a store in the morning and buy another screen, or else the apartment would never work for two people. Or maybe she should find a handyman to build a wall. Walt was handy himself. But it probably wasn't reasonable to ask a man a few days out of ICU to renovate her loft. The goal was to keep him *out* of the hospital.

What Walt needed was his own place. Of course, that would be a lot more expensive than an Ikea screen.

She sighed and scurried over to her computer, where she had been checking her bank balance earlier. Unfortunately, none of the figures had magically changed in the past hour. She wasn't destitute, but she didn't have money to burn. What once had been a financial cushion was now yoga-mat thin. And to think, last month she'd been lamenting not being able to get her cats' teeth cleaned. Now she had a terminally ill maybe-dad on her hands.

And if he wasn't her dad? What if she ended up draining all her savings and Sheetrocking her apartment for some old guy who wasn't even related to her?

A loud buzz made her jump.

She trundled downstairs and shouted through the door. "Who is it? I'm wielding a pickax."

"You don't own a pickax." A voice barely recognizable as Erin's penetrated the oaken barrier. "Open up."

Becca threw the lock and swung the door open. Erin, red-eyed, practically trembled on the small stoop. Two large suitcases and various totes and carry-alls were planted on the bricks next to her. "Can I stay with you for a few days? I brought groceries."

Becca swallowed. *Where am I going to put everybody?* But this was Erin. Yesterday she'd feared Erin was giving up on their friendship. There was no thought of turning her away now. "Of course."

Erin grabbed half the bags, and Becca loaded herself down with the rest, kicked the door shut, and followed her friend upstairs.

In the kitchen, Erin made straight for a half-full bottle of wine on the counter.

Becca put the heaviest suitcase down and unhooked some tote bags from her shoulders. "That's really heavy." She nudged the suitcase with her toe. "What's in there?"

"Several days' worth of clothes and my grandmother's silver

service. It's a hundred and twelve pieces." Erin twisted toward the shelf where the wineglasses were kept. "I think this calls for a drink. Do you want a glass?"

Becca bit her lip. If Erin had fled her house with the family silver, the situation was going to take more than a simple chat over a glass of wine to sort out. They needed a powwow. "Better get down three glasses," she said, reaching for her phone. "I think this calls for an emergency meeting of the Not-Book-Club."

A half hour later, Pam had joined them, and she was adamant that Erin shouldn't leave her house. "Your house should be your fortress. Do not cede ground. Make Bob move."

"He'll have to leave anyway. I'm going to sell it."

Becca could tell Pam's commonsense instincts and concern for her friend were at war with the prospect of a hefty Realtor commission. For years, Erin's house had been her pride and joy. She cared for the place with the over-the-top nurturing that some people reserved for French poodles or orchids.

"I hate the place," Erin said. "I thought I'd be happy there. I thought I'd raise a family. Instead, I've spent too long rattling around in it by myself, feeling depressed."

Becca still had a hard time grasping the situation. "A few days ago you were telling me that you and Bob were going to live happily ever after. What happened to couples counseling?"

Erin toppled over on the couch as if someone had yelled "Timber!" over her. "We were supposed to go, but Bob couldn't make it. I went to one session by myself and talked about my marriage for over an hour. I was expecting the therapist to tell me that I needed to bring Bob back so we could talk through everything as a couple."

"She didn't want you to come back?" Pam asked.

"Oh yes. She said I should come back. But to deal with Bob, she suggested a private investigator and a lawyer."

"A marriage counselor told you to hire a detective?" Becca asked.

"At least she didn't suggest a hit man," Pam said.

"She said she had a cousin who used to be on the police force, so when Bob told me he had to go to Baltimore for a business meeting, I called the cousin and had him followed."

Baltimore. Becca had a sinking feeling. Her hunch about Nicole had been correct.

"Noah said Bob never went to Baltimore," Erin said.

Pam's brows rose. "Your detective's name is Noah?"

It seemed odd to Becca, too. Most investigators she knew of had names like Mike. Then again, the detectives she knew were also fictional.

Erin nodded. "Noah said Bob and Nicole headed straight to DC and checked into the St. Regis. Neither of them had luggage."

Pam arched a brow at Becca. "Maybe you should give Noah's name to Matthew."

"I can just e-mail him the report," Erin said listlessly.

"Is that ethical, to have a therapist and a detective working in tandem?" Becca asked.

"I don't give a damn about ethics anymore," Erin said. "This is war."

Her emotions seemed to be at war, too. Becca was glad Erin wasn't home alone. "I don't understand. You said you were happy in Hawaii."

"I was, sort of. Hawaii's a paradise. I was hanging out on beautiful beaches, sipping fruity drinks, and sightseeing. It's hard to be miserable while you're swimming with dolphins. Of course, I noticed Bob was sending me out sightseeing while he worked. But as far as I could tell, everything was okay. I caught Nicole glaring at me a few times across the hotel restaurant, but other than that, I had no proof of anything going on. And Bob said Nicole was just going through some problems in her personal life." She ducked her head apologetically at Becca. "After a few days of sun and surf, I convinced myself it must have something to do with you and Matthew.

"But then one day after a snorkeling trip Bob had arranged for me, when I got back to the room I found an earring on the carpet of the hotel room. A really boring gold hoop that was just that Nicole woman all over. Really—she has no style. So I gave Bob an ultimatum: Nicole or me. He swore he didn't love her, that she was just clingy and pushy, and probably worshiped him a little because he was more brilliant than she was. So, long story short, he agreed to counseling and a fresh start."

"But before the fresh start could begin," Pam said, "he was already up to his old tricks."

"Well, fine." Erin glared at her wineglass. "He's welcome to Nicole and her kid. He always said we should put off children as long as possible. Now he'll have a teenager."

"She's just eleven," Becca said. What did Olivia do to deserve Bob? She would be heartbroken to have Matthew elbowed out of her life.

"I've changed all the locks on my house," Erin continued, "and Noah gave me the name of a mover who came over tonight. Cost me a bundle, but I threw all of Bob's stuff into a pod, and the mover is hauling it over to Nicole's house under cover of darkness."

"Then why leave your house?" Pam asked.

"I don't want Bob to know where I am. I don't want to talk to him. For a few days, I want him to think of me as an evil phantom who may or may not be watching his every move. Tonight I had a bottle of champagne delivered to the lovebirds' hotel room, compliments of me." She looked at Becca. "You sure you don't mind if I stay awhile?"

"Not at all." She would have to think of some alternative for Walt. Matthew's offer jumped to mind . . . but Matthew had problems of his own now. Bigger than he knew.

Erin grabbed her hand. "I'm so sorry for screeching at you the other day. I don't have any excuse except that I must have been in thrall to the gods of displaced anger." Her gaze took in both Becca and Pam. "I know you guys have been in a tough spot."

"Not as tough as you were," Pam said.

"We didn't want to interfere if there really was a chance that you could salvage your marriage," Becca added.

"Nope. Unsalvageable." Erin took a gulp of wine, swallowed, and then smiled with the forced brightness of a morning anchor-woman. "And you know what? I'm perfectly okay now. I'm free. For the past year or so I've been thinking there was something wrong with me. That *I* was the problem. Now I feel as free as a kid on spring break."

"Please don't become a Girl Gone Wild," Pam said.

"Who knows? Maybe I'll finally figure out what to do with my-self." Erin leaned over to Becca. "Anyway, I mean it. I hope this frees up your guy now. Maybe you and he can get together."

"I'm not sure starting up a new relationship will be high on his to-do list." Also, the man would be on the rebound, which never seemed like a good time to catch anyone. But she'd learned not to bring up the word *rebound* around Pam. "First I have to figure out what I'm going to do about Walt."

Erin recoiled. "That old vagrant? You two aren't . . . ?"

Becca nearly choked on her Malbec. "No!" Erin had obviously put the most creepy spin on her words. She just didn't know how creepy.

"Walt's in the hospital," Pam explained.

Becca took a deep breath. "Also, there's a very good chance that Walt is my father."

Two blowfish gapes stared back at her.

"No way," Pam said.

"I thought you didn't know your father."

"I do now. Or at least it looks that way." She brought them up to speed on her conversations with Walt.

"Oh God." Pam shook her head. "What a shock. And there I was hassling you about Cal while you had this horror going on. I mean, I'm sure you dreamed about your long-lost father showing up, probably as Warren Buffett or somebody like that. Not an ex-con with flaky skin."

"It's not a horror," Becca said, "except . . ." She was stunned to feel her throat closing up. ". . . he's really sick. He has terminal kidney disease. It looks as if he might not have all that long to live. I mean, sure, he's not a dream dad and part of me feels furious, but if he is actually my father, there's no time even to stay angry with him."

Tears stood in her eyes, blurring her friends' faces. Two hands reached out, one squeezing her arm, the other her leg just above her knee.

Erin straightened. "He needs a new kidney."

"Right—a transplant," Pam said. "Like *Steel Magnolias*."

Erin glared at Pam. "Not a good example."

"Oh right," Pam muttered.

"I have no intention of being a donor," Becca said. "There are other ways, but I'm sort of overwhelmed at having to figure this all out."

"My grandfather practically built the transplant center in this county," Erin said. "I'll make calls tomorrow to see if there's anyone we can get you in to see right away. You and Walt."

"You can do that?" Becca asked.

"I can try." Erin frowned. "Unless you'd rather I try to pull some strings at Johns Hopkins?"

"The nearby hospital would be great," Becca assured her, feeling so much gratitude she worried she might fall apart. "Thank you!"

Pam put her glass in her hand, picked up the bottle, and topped off everyone. "Let's drink to your maybe-dad, even if he's Walt, not Warren."

"And new beginnings," Erin said.

During everything that had happened this week, the worst part had been not having these two women to turn to. Having them back again was gold. Becca smiled, feeling as if she could manage whatever the future was going to toss her way now.

"To Not-Book-Club," she said.

The clinking of their glasses was the brightest sound she'd heard all day.

Chapter 19

When Matthew woke up, he began mentally practicing the words. *We need to talk. This isn't working. It's not you, it's ... both of us.*

No matter how many times he muttered the words at the mirror in Nicole's bathroom, he couldn't make them sound less dickish to his own ears. Was there any way to break up with someone without sounding like an asshole? Part of the problem was that he and Nicole never talked about their relationship. So of course when he forced himself to say things like "growing apart" it was bound to sound awkward, like trying to get around a foreign country with a phonetic phrase book. He wasn't fluent in Breakup.

He tried to think what his answer would be if she asked if there was someone else. Was there? Becca might count as a someone else—to him. He wasn't sure Becca would agree. They weren't involved, unless you gave the term its most prudish, sinning-in-one's-heart spin. Probably it would be better to leave Becca out of it altogether.

He and Olivia hurried out of the house in their usual rush to make it to school on time. Stepping onto the porch, they both stopped short. A storage pod sat in the driveway where Nicole's car was usually parked.

"What's *that?*" Olivia shouted.

"It's something people store their belongings in when they're moving, or renovating a house."

"What's it doing here?"

Good question. "Maybe it's a mistake."

But it looked ominous. Was Nicole planning on moving without telling him? Why else would someone have deposited a storage pod in her driveway in the middle of the night?

As if she'd absorbed his uneasiness, Olivia was somber as he dropped her off at school. She opened a door and took a deep breath. "Good-bye, Matthew."

He tried to laugh. "You sound like I'm dropping you off forever. At the School of Doom."

"You know what I mean," she said.

He did know. But how did she?

He gave her a quick hug and she darted out of the car, disappearing into the stream of kids heading toward the front door of the building.

Depression seeped into his bones as he pulled into traffic, and intensified when he realized he'd left his laptop at home. In his hurry to get to Nicole's last night, he'd forgotten it. He U-turned and drove back to his place, dashed inside, and grabbed the computer bag. He made a quick sweep of the town house to double-check that everything was locked and turned off, and was speeding out the door when he nearly mowed down Nicole. He stopped mid-step, inches from her.

"You're not working from home today?" Nicole asked him.

"No."

"Well, do you have a minute?" Without waiting for an answer, she swept past him into the house.

Too puzzled to question whether he did have time, he followed her. "When did you get back?"

"Just now," she said. "I tried to catch you at my house, but you'd already left."

"Did you see the pod?" he asked.

Nicole blinked. "The what?" As if she could have missed it. Her tone made him realize that she knew exactly what the pod was doing there. She just hadn't decided what to say about it.

"Is it yours?" he asked.

"Of course not."

"How did it get there in the middle of the night?"

"Well, *I* didn't put it there," she said.

They stared at each other a moment. Now that they were face-to-face, all the phrases he'd been practicing in front of the mirror fled his brain. He was too confused. Why was she here? Her appearance puzzled him, too. She wore jeans and a wrinkled shirt—not her usual office attire, even on Friday. And wrinkles were never Nicole's style. Her hair hung loose, almost as if she hadn't bothered combing it before jumping in the car and getting on the road this morning.

Of course, she must have left early if she drove all the way from Baltimore this morning. It was still just after eight. What was going on?

Flustered, Nicole homed in on the coffeemaker. She lifted the stainless-steel carafe and deflated a little to discover it empty. "Oh, that's right. You were at my place this morning."

He frowned. It was hard to say what he needed to say when she seemed so fidgety and distracted.

She inhaled as if preparing to plunge into icy waters. "Well, never mind," she said in her matter-of-fact voice. "I really should just get straight to the point."

So there was a point to this visit. Maybe *he* needed coffee.

"The deal is," she continued, "this isn't working. You and me. I hate to do this—and I really can't think of a way to say it without sounding like a complete bitch—but I think we should call it quits."

The blunt statement rocked him on his heels. *She* was dumping *him*? He was supposed to be breaking it off with her.

"Quits." That wording hadn't occurred to him. If it had, he probably would have dismissed it for sounding too curt and heartless. But it did get the point across.

"I'm sorry," she said. "I know this comes as a shock, but I've felt things haven't been right between us for a long time."

He'd dreamed once that he'd stepped onto a stage in a school play after studying the wrong part. He had the same disoriented feeling now. "Is there someone else?"

"No." She walked back from the statement almost immediately. "Well, sort of."

"Maybe that's why things haven't been right."

"It's complicated," she said, as if that explained cheating, no matter how "sort of" it was. Of course, he'd had his own sort-of relationship. The big glass house he was living in kept him silent.

"Look, I know you're angry—"

"I'm not," he assured her.

"You have every right to be."

Definitely someone else, he thought. "I'm worried about Olivia," he said.

Nicole shook her head. "She'll be fine. I've had other boyfriends she's felt close to. She's adaptable."

"Maybe not as much as you think. Did you ever once stop and think that it might not be good to drag a man into her life if you weren't serious?"

"I *was* serious," she said. "I didn't see this happening. It just did."

"Like how whatever happened last night just did?"

Tears stood in Nicole's eyes. "I've had a very rough week, okay? I realize this is coming out of the blue for you, but you don't know what it's been like for me."

"Not out of the blue," he said. "I knew something was out of whack. I thought it was me."

She pressed her hand against the bridge of her nose—a gesture she made when she was trying to gather focus. When she removed it, she was more clear-eyed. "I guess we handled this just right, then. It's a good thing we didn't let our lives get too mixed up."

Was she insane?

"You've got your place, I've got mine," she said.

Places seemed the least of their worries. "There's Olivia," he reminded her. "She's been upset. I think she saw this coming."

"I'll have to do something for her."

"Spending time with her is what she craves from you more than anything."

Nicole's mouth twisted up on one side. "So after a month, you're an Olivia expert."

He let the comment pass. Arguing would get them nowhere, and the more Nicole talked, the more he wanted to crack the empty coffee carafe over her head. Besides, he should be glad to reap the benefits of dissolving a non-functional relationship without the downside of having to be the jerk who initiated it.

"When your father walks out of your life when you're five, you get used to loss," Nicole observed.

Matthew wasn't so sure. He thought of Becca, who'd never known her father and had carried that void around with her all these years.

Nicole squared her shoulders. "Anyway, there's nothing I can do about it. I can't stay in a relationship to please Olivia."

No. He'd said the same thing to Becca earlier. But he wouldn't be surprised if, looking back, those weeks taking care of Olivia didn't turn out to be his fondest take-away from his relationship to Nicole.

She construed his silence as criticism. "I refuse to feel guilty about this. It wasn't as if *we* were married." She fidgeted with the paper towel holder on the counter.

"I'm guessing someone involved is?"

She lifted her chin. "This is why I never wanted us to get married. Marriage makes everything harder. It's a disaster."

Olivia's gloomy expression in the car came back to him. "And you think this isn't one?"

* * *

He called in sick, even going so far as to fake a stuffy nose over the phone for his boss. He couldn't face going to the office and engaging in mindless banter about the World Series or whatever the water cooler topic of the day was going to be.

That morning he rattled around his empty town house, trying to make sense of the new reality of his life. He'd known a split was coming. He wasn't even particularly devastated. But the fact was he'd followed Nicole to Leesburg, and now he felt as if his life had been blown off course. What was he doing here, and where should he go next?

Becca was never far from his thoughts. Days ago, he'd been dreaming of their having a relationship, but ironically, that seemed more impractical now that he was free. He certainly couldn't knock on her door now and announce, "Great news! Nicole dumped me!" The idea of jumping straight into a new relationship right after dissolving another one struck him as all wrong. Which could have been what Becca herself had been hinting at. It was awful timing.

And how much of his attraction to Becca had simply been about his relationship to Nicole being in meltdown? Maybe his brain had been subconsciously reaching for something homey, familiar. After all, Becca was a face from his youth. A vestige from that faraway time when life seemed simpler. Back when he was twelve.

Also, she was from another world. She'd met George Clooney, for Pete's sake.

By noon he was mentally making plans to close up the town house and move back to DC. Maybe he could sublet the place till the end of his lease. His commute would be saner again. He would be unfettered from another person and her problems.

The thought of Olivia gave him a pang. She'd never felt like a fetter.

He started making lists. First, he would have to look for a place near DC. A one-bedroom bachelor pad. Pacing around his sixteen hundred empty square feet here, he couldn't imagine why he'd rented a house so big.

When his phone rang, he had the crazy idea that it might be Nicole—that she'd changed her mind, or decided she'd spoken too hastily. Marching to the table to grab the phone, he steeled himself. If she'd had a change of heart, she was in for a shock.

Becca's number appeared on the little screen. He hesitated, then pressed Talk.

"Are you at work?" she asked. "Is this a bad time?"

"Actually, I called in sick today. I'm at home."

"Do you need anything? Orange juice?"

"No, it's . . ." He stopped, and then confessed, "I'm malingering."

"Mind if I come over for a minute? I wanted to talk to you."

"I'm not sure that's a good idea. . . ."

"I have some pick-me-up cupcakes. This day calls for them. Also, I wanted to talk to you about Walt."

The name jostled his own crisis out of his brain momentarily. For the past few hours, he'd forgotten other people had problems, too. Ones much tougher than his. "Okay, when do you—"

"Now?"

He swallowed. He couldn't even remember if he'd shaved yet. This morning, when he'd woken up at Nicole's, felt like a million years ago. But he couldn't think of a way to put Becca off that didn't involve explaining that his life had been shaken up. "Okay."

"Great. Give me fifteen minutes."

In less than that, she was standing in his living room, handing him a box of rum raisin cupcakes. She peered intently into his eyes. "Are you sure you're not really sick?"

"Just tired."

"Have you eaten anything today? Anything real?"

"Coffee."

She turned him around and frog-marched him into the kitchen. "Please tell me you've got some eggs or something in here." She opened his fridge and inspected its paltry contents.

She proceeded to make him a sandwich. While she worked, he spilled his news about Nicole. Becca listened, occasionally shaking her head in sympathy. He watched her expressions carefully, on the lookout for encouraging signs. But no. If she was harboring hopes that they would get together, she was hiding them very well.

She pushed the plate across the counter to him. "I'm so sorry. I know how awful it must be for you. Even if you and Nicole were having problems."

"It's Olivia who I'm most worried about. Being cut out of her life is the most brutal part."

There was no disguising the depression that settled over her. It matched his own. "She adores you."

This was why people in the middle of a breakup needed to hide away from the world. They did nothing but spread woe.

"How is she supposed to make sense of this? It's hard enough for me. But adults are used to breaking up with people and never seeing them again," he said.

Becca leaned against the counter, smiling wryly. "Unfortunately, I'm *not* used to that. This is a tough town for escaping your romantic past."

"That's why I'm thinking about moving back to DC."

She straightened, alarmed. "Right away?"

"When I find a place. I only moved to Leesburg to be near Nicole and Olivia."

"Oh." She shifted. "I know this is going to sound awfully self-centered coming at this time, but I was wondering if you still had any room for Walt. Just short-term."

He smiled. "Only you would consider it selfish to ask for a favor for someone else."

"Well, he's not your responsibility."

"He doesn't have to be yours, either," he pointed out.

"Yes, he does. If he's my dad, I can't just let the hospital release him onto the streets. Even if he's not, I still feel some responsibility for him, since he was staying at my place when he collapsed. Anyway, my friend Erin's helping me get him an appointment at the transplant center near here. Maybe there's hope for him."

The name Erin jarred Matthew. *"I ran into Erin the other day,"*

Dave had said, weeks and weeks ago. *"Bob cheats on her like crazy. . . ."* It couldn't just be a coincidence, could it? "You know Erin?" He searched for a last name. *"Bob's* Erin?"

Becca's gaze didn't quite meet his. "Actually, yeah. She's a good friend. She's staying at my apartment for a few days."

Right. It was all becoming clear now. He shifted. "You probably knew when you called. . . ."

She ducked her head. "I knew. I'm sorry. I should have said something, but I didn't think it was my place."

He frowned. So that was how she'd been so quick with the tea and sympathy. He'd been telling her old news. "If Erin's your friend, I'm guessing you've known about this for some time."

She appeared to weigh her words. "I suspected, but I wasn't sure. Erin said she was trying to save her marriage."

"But you knew that I was having doubts about Nicole. You never thought of giving me a heads-up?"

"I didn't want to get involved in anyone's breakup," she said. "And I worried it would come off as self-serving."

He stilled. "Why?"

"Well, because . . ." She turned away, flustered. "I never liked Bob, and I can't say I think much of Nicole, but I didn't want to dance on the grave of anyone's relationship."

He didn't think that was what she'd originally meant to say, but he let it go. He tamped down the spike of anger he felt at being kept in the dark, too. Becca was right. In her place, he might have played it just as close to the vest. It was hard to fault someone for being too discreet, even if the discretion had come at his expense.

"I see what you mean about this being a hard town to hide in." It sounded as if he'd been the last to know about his own breakup.

"Erin's upset at the moment, so I'm putting her up," she said. "That's why there's no room at the inn for Walt."

"He can stay here." It actually seemed fitting that he would offer his place as a solution to her overcrowding situation, so Erin could be looked after by friends. A show of solidarity between the victims of the Nicole-Bob shakeup.

"Are you sure?" Becca asked. "I can pay you rent for Walt."

"That's crazy," he said. "I have an extra room. It's just got a fold-out futon couch, though. Not much else."

"Walt's used to minimalism. In fact . . ." She swallowed. "Before you take him in, there's something you need to know. Walt's spent a pretty big chunk of his life in prison."

Matthew frowned, trying to make the mental adjustment this news required. Becca had told him he'd kicked a drug habit, but not that he was a criminal. "That nice old guy?"

"That nice old guy used to be a heroin addict and an armed robber. He's been clean and arrest-free for over a decade, but I wouldn't blame you for deciding that you don't want a person with his past installed in your spare room. In fact, now that I'm saying it aloud, I feel as if I'm being unfair, putting you in this position."

Matthew tried to square the words *armed robber* with that withered, harmless-looking man in the porkpie hat. It was like hearing that Captain Kangaroo had been an evil pirate. "When did you find this out?"

"He told me the first day I met him."

"Before you knew he was your father?"

"Before I knew anything about him at all. One thing about Walt, he's not pretending to be something he's not." Her brows knit. "If you don't count pretending to be just a guy when he was my dad. *If* he is my dad. That's the other thing. There's still a chance he might be a huge fraud—in which case, all bets are off."

No matter what lurked in the man's past, he couldn't see Walt suddenly turning criminal again now. If he'd wanted to, the guy could have robbed Becca's shop weeks ago. "I don't have much here worth stealing."

Hope shone in her eyes. "You'd still consider it, then?"

"I don't know how much longer I'll be here, but . . ." He took a breath. "Sure. Okay."

She practically pirouetted across the kitchen to hug him. "Thank you! If he needs anything, just let me know. I can bring towels, sheets—anything."

That simple, all-too-short hug made his day. It was harder to focus after it was over. "I'm not sure how comfortable he'll be here. That futon is a remnant of my post-college days."

"That'll seem luxurious to Walt. I had him sleeping on a cot we bought in the camping supplies department of Target." She met his gaze. "I meant what I said about paying you."

"And I meant what I said about his being welcome here."

"But if you're moving . . ."

He looked at her, again trying to detect any hint of how she felt about his leaving. And not just how it would affect the availability of an extra room for Walt.

And to think, just an hour ago, he'd been contemplating being alone and unfettered. He'd been ready to shut himself off, but no sooner had he cracked the door open to Becca than it started filling up again. His brain told him to tread carefully, but when he looked into Becca's bright eyes, caution evaporated.

In the afternoon, Becca packed all Walt's belongings into his Rubbermaid tub and went to pick him up. He was up, dressed, and ready to go, but as per hospital rules, she had to wheel him to the front of the hospital and have him wait while she drove the Subaru around to collect him.

"Feels good to be free," he said, watching the autumnal world out the passenger side window. "But I'd prefer it if you'd just take me back to the shop."

He'd been resistant to living at Matthew's, but she thought she'd convinced him it was the best solution. "You can't live in the storeroom anymore, and I told you that Erin's at my place."

"But how am I going to get to the cake shop to do my work? If Matthew has to drive me, that'll be a big hassle for him."

"You don't have to work now. Just concentrate on feeling better."

"I feel as fine as I'm ever going to," he insisted. "But I've got to have something to do, and some way to make money."

"No, you don't. At least, not right now. Just relax for a few days."

He tapped his hands against his knees. "Relax," he repeated. "You mean do nothing. I already spent too much of my life doing nothing. Eight years."

"Hopefully Matthew's place will be a little better than jail."

"I don't mean to complain," he said. "I just don't want to be a burden to anybody."

"Matthew's glad to have you, and his spare room is sitting empty right now. You're not a burden."

"If I could just find a place like I had before . . ."

Remembering his old flophouse on Ferber Road, she shuddered. "Give this a few days. I'm trying to get you an appointment to see a transplant surgeon. They should be getting back to me soon."

"That sounds like a lot of trouble for nothing."

It was all she could do not to smack her forehead against the steering wheel. "Your life isn't nothing."

He muttered something under his breath, then remained silent the rest of the way to Matthew's house. Once there, he insisted on hauling in his own tub of belongings. When he deposited it in the spare room, he wiped his forehead and stared around the four walls. "This place is about as bare as a jail cell," he said to Matthew. "How long have you lived here?"

"Six months."

"Looks like you're ready to make a quick getaway."

As Walt explored the town house, checking things out, Becca and Matthew trailed after him to watch his reactions as they might if they'd brought a new cat home. Walt spent the longest time inspecting the kitchen, testing chairs for tippiness and seeing if there were any loose drawer pulls.

"Nothing for you to fix here," she said.

He picked up Matthew's wand blender and squinted at it.

"That's a mixer," she piped up.

"For making smoothies," Matthew said.

"A smoothie's a—"

Walt barked out a laugh and set the utensil down. "I know what a smoothie is. I wasn't born yesterday. Or sprung yesterday."

Sometimes she suspected he liked to mention his jail time just to mess with their heads.

The town house boasted a postage-stamp backyard, and Matthew had placed a few pieces of lawn furniture out there.

"You've got more stuff outside than in," Walt observed, going out to take a look. He settled into a plastic chaise longue, zipped his jacket up to his chin, and closed his eyes. Becca and Matthew watched him nodding off from the other side of the sliding glass door.

"It feels like I'm dropping a kid off at camp," she said. "Thank you for doing this. I promise it won't be forever. And if there are any problems—"

"There won't be," he assured her.

"But if there are, just call me. I'll figure something out, even if I have to boot Erin back to her own house." She drew back. "Come to think of it, maybe I should have just moved Walt over there. That would have given Bob a shock."

Matthew winced a little, and she immediately regretted having that name slip out. Matthew and Nicole's breakup was making for fraught conversations all over town. Their boring little burg had suddenly become a hotbed of interrelated gossip, like a soap opera. It felt as if *All My Children* was alive and well and living in Leesburg.

Matthew took her hand. "Don't worry about it," he said, as if he'd guessed her thoughts.

She glanced down at their linked hands and tried not to think about how right they looked together, or about all the neurons a simple touch of skin against skin could set off inside a body.

"You've heard of the rebound, haven't you?" she asked him.

"No, never," he joked.

"Starting something one day after a relationship ends would definitely qualify."

He took her hesitance with good grace. "Nice to be schooled in impulse control by a woman who picks up ex-convicts at gas stations."

She tugged her hand back and crossed her arms, laughing. "Sometimes I think I exist solely to be a cautionary tale to others."

" 'Don't Let This Happen to You—The Life of Rebecca Hudson,' " he said.

She tried to be serious again. "Honestly. I hope that you don't think that by taking in Walt . . ."

He waggled his brows. "Now that your maybe-dad's installed in my spare room, I'm on the inside track."

"I mean it," she said. "I'm really grateful . . ."

He shook his head. "Would you stop? I know. You've thanked me a hundred times. And believe me, there's no quid pro quo. I'm glad to help out."

Since she wasn't allowed to voice her gratitude anymore, she smiled it, and they turned and looked out the window at Walt, still snoozing away in the puny shade of a recently planted maple. The trouble wasn't the quid pro quo that didn't exist in Matthew's thoughts. It was that her heart felt full, and indebted.

Chapter 20

Matthew told himself that he just wanted to beat the afternoon rush hour. He *was not* hurrying home from work early because a guy who'd spent eight years in a California penitentiary was staying in his town house.

Completely unrelated.

He gripped the steering wheel and cursed the speed limit.

His assurances to Becca about being glad to help out hadn't been a lie. Not when he'd given them. He was glad to take Walt in. He'd met the news of the man's shady—okay, criminal—past with bravado. *Nothing to steal in the house anyway.* The weekend had passed without incident. But all day as he'd been sitting at his desk, he'd thought of little things, and some not-so-little. Like his home office and computer. Walt didn't strike him as tech savvy enough to be a cybercriminal. A guy who looked puzzled by a wand blender wasn't likely to crack his encryption software. But there was always the old-fashioned pawnshop. The computer itself was worth something. And some of his older files and documents were sitting in an unlocked file cabinet. A gold mine for an identity thief.

Even if the man was clean as a whistle, who knew what his friends were? Telling Walt that he couldn't have visitors had never occurred to him. In fact, he'd urged him repeatedly to make himself at home. Mostly because he'd found Walt *too* polite. The night before, while Matthew was doing work research online, Walt had checked to make sure the sound of the television wouldn't bother Matthew. Then he'd turned on the closed captions and muted the volume. Later, he'd knocked on the door to ask Matthew if it was okay if he took some ice from the freezer.

It had been hard to hide his exasperation. "Help yourself." Seriously. Did he really believe he needed permission to take ice cubes?

Matthew just hoped his "help yourself" didn't result in Walt's helping himself to his belongings and hitting the road.

When he pulled into the town house's driveway, right away something seemed wrong. The place looked odd. Different. It took him a moment to figure it out—the windows were open. Even on perfect days, Matthew generally kept the AC on and the shades pulled. Now, although there was a fall chill in the air, the town house windows were wide open. Jazz music drifted out on the late afternoon breeze. Odder still, a blue bicycle leaned against the front stoop.

His first thought was to wonder where Walt had found a bike. On closer inspection, he realized that he knew that bicycle.

Inside the house, the music grew louder, and there was also laughter. Familiar laughter. He followed the sound to the kitchen, where Olivia was sitting cross-legged on a chair at the kitchen table, a fistful of cards in her hand. When she spotted him, she grinned ear to ear. "Hi, Matthew! Walt's telling me about somebody called Sonny Rollins and teaching me to play poker."

Matthew bit back a sigh as he dropped his briefcase. He hadn't foreseen this scenario. He looked at Walt, who smiled affably and gave him a quick shrug, as if to say, *What was I supposed to do?*

"Did you bicycle all the way over here?" Matthew asked her.

Olivia blew a bubble. "Just from the Y. I'm supposed to be

over there again after school. But it's awful there, so I came here to find you."

"I'm back to working full days in Washington."

"I forgot," Olivia said. "But Walt was here, so it all worked out."

The bravado in her delivery couldn't hide the anxiety in her expression. He would have given anything to be able to tell her to come and hang out here whenever she wanted, but they both knew that would never fly.

"I have to take you back now," he said.

Her mouth trembled before settling into a scowl. "Why?"

"First, because you said yourself that you're supposed to be at the Y. Do you think they won't notice that you're missing? They'll call your mom."

"She won't care."

"Are you kidding? She'll be panicked." The next part was more delicate. "And you have to know that she doesn't want you hanging around here. Around me."

"Or me, probably," Walt added.

Anger flared in her eyes. "Why not? A month ago she left me with you. And she doesn't even know Walt."

"Hon, I'm guessing she wouldn't want to," Walt said.

That was an understatement.

Olivia crossed her arms. "I don't care what she wants. Who is Mom to judge?" she asked Matthew. "She left you for Bob, and believe me, that is *not* an upgrade."

It was hard not to laugh, or to love her more for her loyalty. "Thanks," Matthew said.

"I mean it," she said. "At first I thought everything went crazy because Mom had heard about you and Becca hanging out together. Then I got home from school and Bob was there. Like, living in my house. Mom said he had to stay because he'd been locked out of his own place. *Locked out.* How does that happen to a grown man?"

Walt shook his head. "I can think of several ways."

"Well, one way is that Bob's an idiot," Olivia said. "Although not to hear him tell it. According to him, he's a genius. The first conversation I had with him was all about the colleges he'd been to and the degrees he had. Then he asked me where I wanted to go to college, and I told him I didn't know, but wherever it was, I wouldn't spend the rest of my life bragging about it. Then I got sent to my room."

Matthew sat down. "I'm sorry about all this, O. I worried that you would think I didn't care about you, or that I wouldn't miss our hanging out together."

"What else was I supposed to think?" Her eyes flashed in accusation. "You didn't even call."

"The truth is, I didn't want to have to say good-bye. I suck at those."

Tears stood in her eyes. "Mom can't pick my friends. You're still my friend, aren't you?"

"Of course. Always. But—"

"I don't tell her that she can't see Bob," she said. "Although *that* would make sense."

"The difference is," Matthew said, "she's your mom. She's doing what she thinks is right for her. For both of you."

Olivia snorted.

"And you know she wouldn't want you over here when she's paid for the afterschool program at the Y, so I need to take you back."

"It's not fair," she said.

"No, it's not," he agreed. "I wish I could say this is the worst case of life-is-not-fair you'll ever come up against."

Walt clucked his tongue. "Life is a rough ride."

It took some doing, but Matthew finally convinced Olivia to load her bike into his SUV. On the way to the Y on Fairfax Street, they had to pass downtown.

"Cupcakes!" Olivia's cry nearly gave him a heart attack.

"We don't have time," Matthew said.

"Mom doesn't pick me up until six fifteen," she argued. "Just one cupcake. Please? Please-please-please-please-please—?"

He had a hunch the *pleases* would have gone on for several more blocks or maybe even infinity if he hadn't hooked the vehicle into a free space on the street. Olivia's requests had always been hard to resist, and now that she needed cheering up, he was more susceptible to them than ever.

A puzzled expression pulled at Becca's brow as he and Olivia walked through the shop's door.

He sent her a shrug and a barely perceptible shake of the head as if to say *No, I'm not back together with Nicole.*

As if that were in any doubt.

Becca smiled at Olivia. "Hey. What can I get you?"

"I want a job," Olivia announced in a bullhorn voice.

Becca sputtered in surprise, and heads bobbed their way. It looked like old home week in the cupcake store. Pam was behind the counter, and Cal was leaning against the coffee station reading *The Loudoun Times-Mirror.* What was he doing there? Another woman was parked at one of the small round tables with a laptop. A capacious handbag, a jacket, scarf, and a few shopping bags took up all available space around her. Either she was also a good friend of Becca's or the cake shop was now taking boarders.

Matthew suspected he knew who she was, but his mind backed away from putting a name to that forlorn-elf face.

"You said you would hire me, once," Olivia told Becca.

"When you were older, she said," Matthew reminded her.

Olivia bobbed on her heels. "I'm older now. A month older. But it feels like years."

Becca's mouth turned down at the corners. "I've had a month like that myself."

"Will you give me a job?"

"I'd love to," Becca said, "but I can't. Child labor's illegal. Also, it wouldn't be much fun for you."

"It would be better than the Y," Olivia said. "I hate it over there. First they make us do kids' Zumba, and then they make us study. It's like jail."

"Zumba study hall." Pam shook her head in commiseration.

The woman at the table nodded, adding, "Much worse than regular jail."

Becca glared at them to let them know they were being unhelpful, and then Cal looked up from his paper. "Any study hall always seemed like jail to me."

At the sound of his voice, Olivia gasped and pivoted. When she'd made her beeline for Becca, she'd walked right past him. "Cal!" She zipped over to him. "Would *you* give me a job?"

Cal's expression as Olivia buttonholed him was classic deer-in-headlights. "I . . . uh . . ."

Matthew tried to tug Olivia back toward the door, but she shrugged him off and stood her ground. "I could do a lot of chores out there. I'd clean stalls or whatever. Even ride horses, if they need exercise. You wouldn't even have to pay me."

Cal's pained expression searched out Becca and then Matthew for help.

"You have to be realistic," Matthew told Olivia. "How would you even get to the stables after school?"

"My bike."

"It's miles out there," he reminded her.

"And it's going to be winter soon," Cal added.

Taking pity on Cal, Becca wrapped up a strawberry cupcake for Olivia and set it on the counter. "Here—this is on the house. I promise, the moment I can hire you, I will."

Olivia's face was scarlet as she glared at them all. "Everyone is so selfish—nobody wants to help even when I'm willing to work like a slave for them!" She turned on her heel, then stopped, pivoted, and snatched the cupcake bag from the counter. "Thanks," she said. "I'm sorry for whining, but Walt's right. Life really is a rough ride."

She stomped out.

Matthew backed apologetically toward the door, too. "I'm sorry," he told Becca, including the others in the sweep of his gaze. "I had no idea she was going to ambush you."

"I understand." Becca tilted her head. "Is everything okay otherwise?"

He lifted his shoulders. "So far."

"Tell Walt I'm picking him up tomorrow morning at ten," she said.

He nodded and then hurried out the door, hoping he could get Olivia back to the Y before Nicole discovered her daughter had gone AWOL.

As the thought occurred to him, his phone rang. He looked at the screen and groaned. Nothing to do but face the music. He hit Talk. "Nicole, don't worry. She's fine." He took a deep breath, and let the blast of maternal anxiety, relief, and anger wash over him.

This would teach him to leave the office early.

When the bell over the door tinkled Matthew and Olivia's departure, Becca and the others exchanged glances. The tornado of anguish that had just blown through left them all slightly stunned.

"What was that all about?" Pam asked.

"I think it was about the effect of adult craziness on kids." Becca's heart felt bludgeoned. "I didn't know what to say to her."

"So that was Olivia." Erin sagged in her chair. "More collateral damage."

How she could still be sitting down after being installed at the table for hours was beyond Becca's comprehension. Erin's moment of feeling triumphant and free had surrendered to a weekend of moping and fear for her future. As if a woman with several million dollars had anything to be afraid of. She was on her fifteenth cup of coffee of the day, and almost as many cupcakes. Between caffeine, sugar, and manic-depression, it was amazing that her body hadn't shorted out.

"She really put me on the spot," Cal said.

Erin sighed. "Poor kid."

Pam clucked her tongue thoughtfully. "Shame about those child labor laws. I bet Olivia would make a good worker. If the world could just find a way to harness the excess energy of middle schoolers . . ."

"Maybe I should start up an afterschool apprentice program," Becca mused. "Have kids come over and do my work for me. Kids like to make cakes."

"Kids like to *eat* cakes," Cal said.

Pam nixed the idea. "If children get the unbearable urge to

work in a kitchen, I'm guessing their moms would prefer to be the beneficiaries."

"True." Becca sighed. "Oh well. It was a nice dream for the ten seconds it lasted."

Over in her corner, Erin stirred out of her funk. "When I was a kid, I did sort of have an afternoon job at a stable."

The three of them gaped at her in amazement.

"You did?" Becca asked.

"Yeah. The family chauffeur would pick me up after school and take me to the stable, where I rode and took care of horses. Light chores—just what Olivia was talking about, actually. It was slave labor, but it was fun. Also, one of my uncles owned the stables, so it was free for me, but other kids actually paid. I think there was even a little bus or van that went by a few of the public schools to pick up kids. Their parents would collect them on the way home after work. Lots of stables do that, I think."

Becca was going to say something, but she was distracted by Cal letting out a wince. "Ow!" he yelped at Pam.

Standing next to him, she had his arm in an anaconda-like squeeze. "We could have an afterschool program at Butternut Knoll."

"We?" Cal blinked.

From the feverish look in Pam's eyes, her brain had bolted out the gate. "It would be perfect. There are always a few kids who ride after school, and you're great with the weekend classes. All you have to do is give them thirty minutes of instruction, then let them ride a little, then do a few chores. They'd pay you."

"Yeah, but . . ." He frowned. "Thirty minutes of instruction every day?"

She gave him a light whack on the arm. "Thirty minutes is nothing. This is a good idea. It would bring money in, and it might actually save you work."

Saving work seemed to appeal to him, at least. "It's an interesting idea. Definitely worth looking into."

Erin brightened. "And I came up with it. Amazing! Maybe I have a bright future as a business thinker-upper. Is that a job?"

Pam circled around to Erin's table and practically lifted her up by the armpits. "No, but right now you have a bright immediate future as a cupcake saleslady." She propelled Erin over to the counter and transferred her Strawberry Cake Shop apron to her.

Becca watched the exchange in bemused silence. Looked like she was getting a new employee.

"I'm sorry," Pam told her. "I'm giving notice again. Cal needs me."

"I do?" Cal asked, startled. "You mean, right now?"

"We need to get out to the stables and start planning this out." Pam prodded him toward the door. "Also, we have to stop by Home Depot and grab some things. We could build a few more storage shelves for the kids to put their stuff."

"Shelves?" Dawning panic showed in Cal's eyes. "Shouldn't we let the idea sit awhile? Allow it to brew a little?"

"Why wait? We could be making cash and rescuing Olivia from Zumba study hall."

"Olivia," Cal muttered. "That kid has a lot to answer for."

After Pam had pushed Cal out of the shop, Becca shifted her attention to Erin, who was studying the cash register cautiously, as if it were a rare, exotic, and possibly dangerous beast. "Is something wrong?"

"No." Erin gave one of the buttons a tentative poke. "I've just never been on this side of one of these before."

"Now you can see how the other half lives." Becca laughed and turned to get back to bake-work. It didn't occur to her until much, much later that Erin hadn't seemed amused at all.

Chapter 21

Becca assumed that when she brought Walt in for his appointment, the doctors would look at his medical history, take a blood sample, and then sign him up ASAP for the National Kidney Registry she'd read about on the Internet. After all, the man was obviously sick.

Instead, the appointment turned into an afternoon-long ordeal. The expected blood draw, during which the technician drained Walt with vampire-like thoroughness, was followed by X-rays and a stress test. While he was being shuttled between departments, Becca set up later appointments for a colonoscopy and vaccines, and received information on getting Walt on an insurance plan. And she waited. Sometimes she was waiting with Walt, sometimes alone. She probably had enough time to finally finish *Ulysses*, but she opted for an Angry Birds marathon on her phone. Together, she and Walt were counseled by a nutritionist on the importance of sticking with a low-salt, low-protein diet. Then another doctor read Walt the riot act about keeping up with dialysis treatments.

By the time they sat down with an actual transplant surgeon, Walt looked as exhausted as Becca felt. Dr. Laverents, an earnest, soft-spoken man about Walt's age, informed Becca that they would have to wait for test results to get on the registry, and that in the meantime she should probably see about also signing Walt up with another transplant center in a neighboring region.

Her entire life, she'd never given much thought to how transplants worked, or the ratio of how many organs were needed to those that were available. The shortage was eye-opening, and discouraging. Donors were in short supply, so there was a protocol for who received organs, with children understandably receiving priority. The thought of a child having to endure what Walt was going through depressed Becca so much that she nearly missed the point of the good doctor's talk.

The upshot, Dr. Laverents said, was that most patients who needed transplants had to wait. Sometimes a long time.

"How long?" she asked.

"Sometimes years."

Becca had read about long waits on the Internet, but she'd also heard some cases were resolved right away. For some reason, she'd expected the medical professionals to take one look at Walt and shoot him to the top of the list. Turned out, Walt was not a special case. Or an unusual one.

Dr. Laverents went on to explain a formula to guesstimate how long the wait would be at any transplant center. The calculations included taking the number of people on a center's registered recipient waiting list and factoring in the number of transplants the center performed, minus the rate of "attrition."

Becca repeated that last word, which heretofore she'd only associated with World History class and World War I trench warfare. "What do you mean by attrition?"

The doctor steepled his hands. "Attrition takes into account all the reasons people drop off the lists. Some receive living donor transplants, or transplants at a different center. Or they develop a condition that makes them ineligible for the operation."

"Or they die," Walt guessed.

From the shadow that crossed Dr. Laverents's face, Becca guessed this was the reality the kindly man had been tap-dancing around. "Some people do die waiting," he confirmed. "We try our hardest not to let that happen."

Becca left the meeting shaken. *Don't panic.* In the car, she assured Walt, "We'll get you on several lists. Don't worry."

"I'm not worried. It's an ordeal, though."

"No, it's not." Not when she considered the alternative.

"Plus, I don't have insurance," he said. "I did have some back in LA, but I lost it when I was laid off my last job. Then I never went through the hassle of signing up again. . . ."

She glanced back at the pile of folders she'd accumulated throughout the course of the day. "I'm going to look into that. That woman in Administration mentioned several websites I needed to go to, including the government one . . ." She'd talked to so many people, and received so much advice and literature. It was daunting.

"And they put you through all those tests at every new place, the man said," Walt went on. "It's not pleasant."

She gripped the steering wheel so tightly her hands were going numb. "It's another day of tests versus your life," she pointed out, trying not to sound too irritated. She reminded herself how much she dreaded just getting her annual flu shot. The tests he'd undergone today were just the tip of the iceberg.

"Seems to me all those organs should go to those little kids and young people. Give them a chance."

"They do. The doctor explained that they take age and physical condition into consideration."

He was silent for a moment. "I don't want to cause you any more trouble."

"It's no trouble," she said, her vocal cords straining with the effort it took not to shout.

She was happy to drop him off at the town house, and Walt looked ready to get away from her, too. He climbed out of the car and shambled toward Matthew's front door. Guilt for feeling annoyed with him filled her. Poor guy had been poked and inspected all day, and then had been told he'd have to do it all over again somewhere else. And that it might all come to nothing. He could die.

The strange thing was, *she* seemed more upset by that last news than he was. Instead, he kept dwelling on the inconvenience. Was she going to have to drag him the whole way through the process? What if she wasn't successful? He might die waiting, and he was her only living relation.

If he actually was her father. What if he wasn't?

That last thought made her wince. She should have insisted on a paternity test the first time the subject had come up. Now asking for one would seem like saying that she didn't want to bother with any of this if he wasn't a blood relation. But she had been concerned about Walt before the father issue had come up, so it wasn't as if she'd just drop him if they didn't share the same genes.

She drove back downtown, brooding. Poor Walt. He seemed depressed, restless. The problem was he had nothing to do. Rattling around in Matthew's town house and watching TV all the time couldn't be fun. She needed to connect him to something he loved—something that would give him a little hope. Which would be easier if she knew him better.

At the shop, the Closed sign was on the door. Her dashboard clock read 4:25. And it was Thursday—still plenty of people out and about. Why would Erin have closed up already?

She hurried inside the shop to assure herself that the place had suffered no obvious calamity. At first glance, nothing appeared amiss. The water heater hadn't broken, there was no fire damage, and the shelves were picked clean.

She eyed the empty glass, impressed. Just that morning, those shelves had been crammed full of goodies. Erin must have sold out—on her first solo day, too. Maybe her friend had found her true calling.

She took the stairs two at a time, ready to congratulate Erin on a job fantastically done. When she reached the upstairs landing, though, the apartment was nearly dark. And quiet. Her body went clammy. The silence reminded her of the night she'd found Walt passed out on her bed.

Squinting across the long room, she spotted the outline of a slumped form on the couch. She rushed over and snapped on a floor lamp.

Jack-in-the-box fast, Erin bolted up to sitting. Becca hopped back in surprise, nearly stepping on the cats twining around her legs. She'd been ready to perform CPR, but Erin looked fine—except for her bloodshot eyes and the mascara streaming down her cheeks.

Becca's stomach clenched. In the last day or so, Erin had seemed a little better, but now she'd boomeranged back to despair. "What's wrong?"

Erin put her fist to her mouth, then brought it down and gulped in a breath. "Today I failed at everything."

Becca sagged onto the cushion next to her, relieved that there wasn't a life-and-death crisis underway. "You scared me. I thought something horrible had happened."

"It did," Erin said. "I realized how useless my life is."

Becca bit back a groan. After her day at the transplant center, she wasn't sure she was up for a poor-little-rich-girl discussion. "Your life has not been useless. That's absurd."

"See? Even you don't take my problems seriously."

"I'm sorry. I just spent a day in a building full of people fighting for their lives. They all would have traded anything to be twenty-nine and in good health."

Erin clutched a throw pillow and sank back. "I knew you wouldn't understand. You don't know what it's like. You had a whole career begin and end by the time you were fifteen."

"Thanks for the reminder."

"I mean, that's a *good* thing. You had to change direction. You learned to navigate life's choppy waters. But how do you learn how to navigate when you've just been coasting for twenty-nine years?"

Becca started to understand the crux of the problem. Better yet, she saw that there might be something here that she could fix. "First of all, don't compare yourself to anyone else, least of all me. It's not as if I *did* anything to get a career when I was a little kid. At the time, people would pat me on the head and tell me that I was a little go-getter, and of course I believed them. But it was a lie. The truth was I happened to be in the right place at the right time. I had a look some producer thought would work. I could recite lines—but not particularly better than any number of little kids could have done."

Erin blinked at her. "So?"

"So I was lucky, just like you were lucky to be born with a big bank account behind you. Stop beating yourself up. You aren't the only fortunate person in the world." She couldn't believe she was consoling someone for being rich. Especially when she was about to spend her evening figuring out how to get her maybe-dad on public assistance. "Everybody reaches a point when they have to reboot."

"But what am I going to do?" Another tear splashed across the mascara-streaked plains of Erin's cheek. "I always screw every-thing up."

"Will you stop belittling yourself? You didn't screw up your marriage. Bob did. And what you're going to do is pick yourself up just like you've been doing. You can always work at the store until you hatch a better plan."

Wrong thing to say, apparently. Sure, it wasn't the greatest job offer, but Becca didn't expect her friend to fall over in despair at the prospect, which is what happened.

"You don't know what happened today," Erin said.

Oh God. "What happened? I thought you did great. You sold out."

"No, I didn't." Her voice was barely intelligible because she'd face-planted a pillow. "I gave everything away."

A few seconds ticked by before Becca's brain processed the muffled words. "You gave everything away . . . as in, for free?"

Erin nodded, then lifted her head up a bit. Testing to see if it was safe to show her face.

"All the cupcakes?" Becca asked, numb. "Cakes, brownies . . ."

"Everything."

Becca swallowed. Only Herculean restraint kept her from yelling. "Why would you do that?"

"I don't know." Erin's voice keened with tension. "I mean, I *do* know why. The cash register jammed or something, and I couldn't get it to work. And I didn't know what to do. There were all these people there, waiting to buy stuff. I couldn't just send them away."

"So you just *gave* everything away?" Was she crazy?

"Well, yeah. And to be honest, it felt great," Erin confessed. "Like a big party. Everybody looked so happy."

"I'll bet." Now it was Becca's turn to collapse. She sank against the couch cushions, doing some mental accounting. Which was not her strong suit.

"They gave a lot of money to the tip jar," Erin said.

"We don't have a tip jar."

"I put a coffee cup out. We made sixty-three dollars. People are really generous when things are free. That's kind of nice to think about, isn't it?"

Becca grunted. Even with the tip cup, the day would be about a three-hundred-and-fifty-dollar net loss. Crap. "Why didn't you call me?"

"You were at the hospital. What could you do?"

"Well, for starters, I probably could have told you *how to fix the cash register.*"

Erin winced. "Also, I just felt so stupid. I mean, even teenagers working at McDonald's could have handled the situation better. So I just . . . snapped, I guess."

Becca began to feel as mad at herself as at Erin. What was the first thing they taught in management class at the business course she'd dropped out of? *A manager takes responsibility.* Erin had just started, and Becca had been so distracted lately she hadn't been paying attention to whether she was catching on to everything or not. She'd been assuming Erin was Pam. She never should have left her in charge of the store. Now she wanted to strangle Erin. And herself.

Erin shook her head. "I knew you would be mad."

"No . . ." Her gravelly rasp of a voice wasn't fooling anybody.

"I'll pay for it all, of course," Erin promised. "Whatever you think is right. I was going to just leave you a thousand dollars and run away, but I decided that would be childish."

More childish than giving away a storeful of baked goods?

"What were you going to do after you left the cash?" Becca said.

"I don't know." Erin shrugged. "Run away to Mexico?"

Only Erin would think that running away to Mexico was something she should do after *giving* someone money.

Becca stood and held a hand out to Erin, who blinked at it suspiciously.

"You don't need to buy your way out of a blunder, or move to Mexico." Becca pried her friend off the couch and dragged her toward the staircase.

"Where are we going?"

"Downstairs. I'll show you the problem with the cash register. It's old—I bought it used—and it sticks sometimes. I should have warned you about it."

In the shop, Becca went over the things she should have the moment after Pam had slapped her apron on Erin. Cupcake Store 101. After walking her through several mock sales and teaching her exactly how to whack the temperamental cash register back to life when it jammed, she had her help make batter and bake and frost several cakes.

Three hours later, Erin looked tired and floury, but less inclined to flee the country. Becca finished with a quiz, drill sergeant–style. "What's your batter's enemy?"

"Lumps," Erin replied.

"How much frosting is too much?"

"There's no such thing as too much frosting."

They were making progress.

Like a coach, Becca sent her upstairs for a shower and a good night's sleep while she finished cleaning up the shop. She didn't feel a bit tired herself. Baking had given her a second wind—it had also provided an escape valve for all her broodiness about Walt and the other tens of thousands of people waiting on kidney transplant lists. But those people weren't easy to dislodge from her thoughts, and now that she was alone again, they settled right back in.

So many people, so much need. So many struggles that made her own previous concerns about the fortunes of the cake shop seem minor by comparison. For days, she'd tried to convince herself that Walt and his problems weren't really her lookout. She'd told herself she'd do a few things for him—like getting him on the transplant list—just so she could clear her conscience, and then her life would continue as before.

Attrition. She wished she could banish that word from her brain. Unfortunately, it had burrowed in deep.

Matthew's phone rang while he and Walt were watching sports news. He reached into his pocket, saw who it was, and hit Talk.

"Are you feeling as claustrophobic as I am?" Becca asked.

He laughed in acknowledgment. It was true. Having another person living in your house didn't seem like a big deal . . . until there was another person living in your house. He liked Walt, but two guys rattling around the town house all evening didn't make for a lot of privacy. Walt probably felt the pinch, too, although he would never complain.

"Would you like to go for a drink?" she asked.

"Right now?" He looked at his watch. Just after nine.

A chuckle came over the line. "I know. It would be like we're adults or something. Crazy idea. I've had a crazy day, which might explain it."

"Any place in particular?" he asked.

She named a bar in a shopping center equidistant from their two places.

"See you in ten," he said.

When Matthew hung up, Walt spoke without glancing away from the television. "Something wrong with Rebecca?"

"How did you know it was her?"

"Because you were laughing. You always seem happiest when you're with her."

He did?

"I'm glad she's got someone to talk to," Walt said.

Matthew stood. "I told her I'd meet her for a drink." He hesitated a moment, then asked, "Would you like to come along?" He was pretty sure Becca wouldn't want Walt there, but he couldn't see walking out without at least making the offer.

Walt glanced over at him. "On your date?"

"It's not a date."

The other man smiled, then looked back at the television. "Thanks, but I can't drink anyway. You two have fun."

Becca was already sipping something in a corner booth when he arrived. "You must have really needed that."

"It's ginger ale," she said. "I have to get up for work early tomorrow. Cupcaking requires a clear head."

Matthew ordered a beer. "I just work for the government."

"Walt driving you to drink?"

"No, no. We get along okay. He's been giving me lessons around the kitchen. Did you know he was a short-order cook after they let him out of prison? Man makes a mean Spanish omelet."

"There's a lot about him I don't know," she said, her lips turning down again.

"We sometimes get in each other's way, but it's been nice having him around, actually. He saw how upset I was that day with Olivia."

"What did he say to you?"

"Nothing. We just played cards for a while."

She smacked her fingers against the edge of the table. "Men are amazing. You have a huge problem and don't even talk about it."

"Talking doesn't always help things."

"But losing money to Walt did?"

"I didn't lose any money," he said.

She rolled her eyes. "A miracle."

"I lost my Saturday morning," he clarified. "The stakes were that I would take him garage saling."

"What for?"

Matthew tilted his head. "I'm not sure. He said he needed a few things. But he might just want to get out. The town house isn't really convenient to buses. I think he feels isolated. But I would have taken him even if I hadn't lost."

Becca dug through her purse. "If he needs something, I have money."

He held up his hand, palm out. "No need for that. I don't think he wants anything expensive. A shirt, maybe."

She pushed a wad of cash across the table. "I never paid him for the last days of work he did. Give him this for me."

He took the money. "All right—if he earned it, that might be okay. I don't think he likes charity."

"He doesn't," she agreed. "That's part of the problem. Whenever anyone mentioned insurance and other assistance today, I could see Walt tuning out. I had to explain that *not* signing up for aid means that he absolutely will default on his financial obligations down the road and end up in the ER. If I ever wondered where my lack of money sense came from . . ."

It was the first time he'd heard her speak of Walt as anything but her maybe-dad. "You've done okay."

Shaking her head, she confessed, "I'm at the end of my *Me*

Minus You money. I sank it all into schools I eventually dropped out of, moving, my building, and the startup costs of my business. And now it looks like I'm going to toss what's left at a guy who might or might not be my father."

He could feel his brow pulling into a frown. "Walt's never asked for anything, has he?"

"Oh no. He doesn't want to be any trouble. The problem is, I can't get him out of my mind. My whole life, I wondered who my father was. I spent my adolescence playing opposite a fictional ghost dad. Part of the reason I did a good job was because I wanted to be that kid. Even though the character's dad was a ghost, I would have traded places with her. And now here he is—my ghost dad in the flesh. And rather than be any trouble, he's decided he'd rather just fade away or something. I'm not going to let him fade away on me."

"What can you do?"

"I've thought about it all day. I can give him a kidney."

Matthew gaped in surprise at her about-face on this issue. "Are you sure you want to do that?"

"He could die if I don't. The doctors are already looking at him like he's a goner. They don't say so in so many words, but I can tell. When Dr. Laverents was telling me about the waiting lists today, it started to sink in. The numbers are stacked against him. An old ex-heroin addict and ex-thief isn't going to be at the top of anyone's list. He needs a live donor, someone who knows him and wants to help. Who would that be besides me?"

He kept his gaze on her. "Still, shouldn't you think a little more before you do anything radical?"

"There's not much time to deliberate. You live with Walt. You can see how he is. And what's so radical about saving your father's life?"

"If he is your father," he said. "You're the one who keeps saying he might not be."

She gnawed on her lower lip for a moment, reminding him of

Olivia struggling over her math homework. "I guess I should find that out."

"DNA testing," he said. "In two weeks you would know one way or another."

Her shoulders lifted. "I know I should, but the whole idea of paternity testing keeps shutting down my brain. It makes sense that I should find out for certain. Yet at the same time, it feels sort of weird to say, 'I'll give you my kidney as long as you're the louse who abandoned my mom and never contacted us until you were dying.' I almost felt more generous toward him when he was just plain Walt." She frowned. "Although I don't know if I felt offer-him-body-parts generous . . ."

She would make light of anything, but *generosity* seemed inadequate when it came to talk about giving a part of one's body to someone.

"The strange thing is, the old Walt I *felt like* rescuing, and the new Walt I feel obligated to. But why? Because he's family? He never did one damn thing for me. Never."

Matthew nodded, letting her vent. He couldn't imagine going through anything like this. It was hard to think of anything to say that could help her. All he could do was listen.

"I keep wondering what my mom was thinking. I get that she thought Walt wouldn't be a good father, but didn't she ever think this day would arrive? She knew he was *out there*. Committing crimes, and then behind bars, but still out there in the world."

"She probably thought that after a quarter century had gone by, it was a non-issue."

"Can family ever be a non-issue?" She met his gaze, then sank back against the booth. "This must all seem insane to you."

"I think it would be really hard to experience what you have. I admire the way you're handling it. I have a hard time wrapping my mind around how disorienting it must be for you."

"You've never had any long-lost parents show up on your doorstep?"

His lips crooked into a smile. "My family's so normal they squeak. I'm from Indiana—it's all marching bands and harvest festivals. My mom and dad were the town's Sweet Corn King and Queen their senior year."

They talked until they had sipped down the dregs of their drinks, and when Matthew walked Becca out to her car, they were still yakking. Despite the chill in the air, it seemed a perfect night. All at once, more than anything he wished they were in some romantic city where they could stroll through a lamp-lit park, instead of huddled by a Subaru under the buzzing fluorescent lights of a sprawling, near-empty parking lot.

When she reached for her door handle, he did, too. The weird valet-parking-attendant move startled him as much as it did her at first, but when their hands touched, he understood where the impulse had come from. He held her hand, and then gently drew her to him.

The moment their lips touched, he knew this hadn't been an insane rebound impulse. She fitted against him perfectly, and he wanted to pull her closer, let his hands roam over the curves that had taken up so much room in his imagination lately. His pulse picked up, and it was all he could do not to suggest driving to some secluded spot, like teenagers.

Becca pulled back. "What are we doing?"

"What I've wanted to do for weeks," he murmured against her lips. There. He'd admitted it.

"This is crazy." Disappointment pierced him, until she added, "Neither of us even has an apartment to call his own."

"I was just thinking about our current privacy shortage. Does Leesburg have a lover's lane?"

She laughed. "I'm not sure I'm spry enough for that anymore. Plus, I have to get up and make a wedding cake tomorrow. Big day."

"When's the wedding?"

"Day after tomorrow. I have to deliver the cake Saturday morning. You've got Saturday morning plans, too."

His mind was a blank. "I do?"

"You're hitting the garage sales with Walt."

A wisp of her bangs was being lifted in the breeze, and he couldn't resist the impulse to comb it back into place. "What are you doing after the cake delivery?"

"Working." She added, a bit mysteriously, "And there's something I need to do for Walt. I want to get him a gift . . . and maybe fill in another piece of the puzzle of who Walt Johnson really is."

Chapter 22

Only her determination to be the very best friend possible to Pam made Becca push Nicole Parker's doorbell. This was not an encounter she relished having, nor was she the best person she could think of for the job. She was fairly competent at selling cupcakes. But as a spokesperson for the newly formed Butternut Knoll Afterschool Equestrian Program? The jury was still out.

She pressed her shoulders back, clutching the folder of flyers Pam had given her under her arm. She didn't know why she needed an entire sheaf of the things, since she'd only been given the task of talking to one person. When Pam had approached her this morning, Becca had tried to point out that she might not be the best candidate to put the appeal to Nicole.

"I'm sort of seeing Matthew," she'd admitted to Pam, hoping she wasn't blushing. The kiss in the parking lot hadn't been far from her mind since it happened, and the thoughts were usually accompanied by a crazy schoolgirl flush.

"Everybody's known that for weeks," Pam said, dismissing the argument.

"But now it's kind of true."

"It was always kind of true," Pam insisted, before her eyes bulged in a double-take. "Why? What happened?"

"He kissed me."

"That must have been some kiss. You look like a strawberry that's sprouted hair."

Yup, she could feel the heat in her cheeks. "It was."

"But that's great!" At first, Becca thought Pam was congratulating her on the relationship, but it turned out she meant it was great for Butternut Knoll. "Think about it. Nicole will probably be relieved that Matthew's found somebody else. It's better than having an ex who's heartbroken and bitter, right?"

"Maybe . . ."

"And you have a closer personal connection to Olivia, so that might mean something to Nicole. She'll be more inclined to send Olivia to the Knoll on your recommendation."

Becca had been about to inform her that one thing she knew about Nicole was that the woman was set against her daughter taking up horseback riding, but at that point, Erin had come in, and they'd dropped the subject. Pam had hung a flyer in the window and set a stack by the cash register. On parting, she pressed the folder containing the leftovers into Becca's hands and said pointedly, "These are for you to give anyone you know personally who might be interested." Upon parting, she mouthed, *"Please."*

So for Pam and Cal's sake, here she stood. She'd had to deliver the wedding cake, so she was already out and about. And since she had her own personal errand she intended to run, she decided she should get Pam's task over with. She didn't know what she'd do if Bob answered the door. Or Olivia, for that matter. It didn't seem fair to discuss the program around Olivia, especially if her mom didn't go for the idea. Which was a distinct possibility. She didn't want to break anyone's heart.

But she was in luck—if having Nicole herself pull open the door could be called luck. The woman trained a cool up-and-down stare on Becca. "This is odd," she declared by way of greeting.

It was almost a relief to have the pressure of sunny politeness taken off her shoulders. "I need to talk to you," Becca said.

"About Matthew?" Nicole asked. "That's all over."

"It's about Olivia," Becca said. "Matthew doesn't even know I'm here."

Obviously curious, Nicole stepped back to usher her in.

"Is Olivia . . . ?" Becca darted a tentative glance around.

Nicole shook her head before she could finish the sentence. "She had a sleepover at a friend's house. She's not back yet."

For some reason, Becca expected to be taken back to the kitchen. Instead, Nicole steered her the few steps to the living room and nodded toward a wing chair before settling herself in a matching one just opposite.

"What's this about?" she said, not offering a drink, or even a smile.

Becca suddenly sympathized with the door-to-door salesmen of yesteryear. In fact, she suspected she'd have better luck selling Nicole miracle elixirs or encyclopedias than getting her to send her daughter to Butternut Knoll every day.

She took a flyer out of Pam's folder and handed it across to Nicole. At the cupcake shop, she'd thought the flyer looked professional. It had been printed on glossy paper, but now that she was presenting it to someone, she noticed that there were more pictures than actual information. The program itself was laid out in simple bullet-point fashion, promising personal growth and achievement through:

- *Daily riding lessons*
- *The basics of horse handling, including safety*
- *Grooming and basic stable management techniques*
- *Equipment handling and care*

  (Transportation from school included in fee!!)

Watching Nicole flick her glance over it, Becca wondered if she shouldn't have come right out and said, *"I'm drumming up business for this program my ex-husband and friend just cobbled together."* Instead, she reached for phrasing that would be more persuasive. "The program is in its infancy, but I thought Olivia would—"

"Yes."

Becca blinked, confused. "Yes . . . ?"

"Yes, she'd love to do it," Nicole said. "Yes, I'm interested. Should I write you a check?"

Becca had to think about that. She'd rung the doorbell expecting a hard sell. She'd spent the car ride over imagining arguments and counter-arguments, and was prepared to wheedle and cajole. One thing she hadn't been prepared for was instant capitulation. "A check would be fine." She swallowed. "You can make it out to Cal McGinty."

Nicole stood. "I'll be right back."

Becca remained in her chair, stunned by her own success. While Nicole was gone, she peered around the room in curiosity. She'd always assumed brainy people had messy houses—that their thoughts went into important problems, not into dusting and tidying. But just as her neat blond hair and business-casual appearance cried out local news anchorwoman instead of scientist, Nicole's home screamed anal-retentive homemaker, not absentee parent. So much perfection would have been depressing, except for the small detail of Nicole's dumping Matthew. How could anyone be that stupid? There was serious disorder in that brain somewhere if she thought she'd be happier yoked for life to Bob.

When Nicole returned, she had her checkbook and was already uncapping a fountain pen. "The rates on this flyer are listed by the month. Should I pay one month in advance?"

"That would be fine," Becca said, winging it. It had never occurred to her to ask Pam how to proceed if she was actually successful.

"Maybe I can convince Olivia's friend Deirdre's mom to sign her up," Nicole said. "It would be nice if Olivia had another pal with her."

Deirdre? *Good luck with that.* From what Becca had seen, Deirdre's mom was nervous about letting her kid breathe on her own. Although . . . Becca wondered if she should try her luck on Deirdre's mom herself. This seemed to be her lucky day for persuasion.

Or maybe she was overestimating her own powers. Looking a gift horse (so to speak) in the mouth was foolish, but when she reached out to take Nicole's proffered check, she couldn't help asking, "What changed your mind? I was afraid you'd be dead-set against Olivia riding every day."

Nicole leaned back in her chair. At first she looked as if she was going to tell Becca to mind her own beeswax, but then she let out a long breath. "I just want her to be happy."

The memory of Olivia's plaintive voice in the cupcake shop, begging for a job, came back to her. "She'll definitely be happy."

"I was never going to let her ride," Nicole admitted. "Maybe it's irrational, but to me all this equestrian stuff is just marginally safer than letting her swim with sharks every afternoon. I never thought the day would dawn when I'd agree to something like this. But then, I was just thinking of Olivia as my daughter. I was forgetting that she also has to be her own person."

Becca nodded.

"I think riding is a foolhardy way to spend free time," Nicole said. "But I'm not infallible, as Olivia's pointed out to me a million times in the past weeks."

"I'm sure she'll be as safe and careful as she can be," Becca answered. "I was going to offer to let her ride my horse, Harvey, during the week. He's big, but he's gentle. He's an old man now, and hasn't thrown anyone in over a decade."

"That's nice of you. Thank you. Olivia will be over the moon." Nicole shook her head. "You know, when you first hold your baby in your arms, you tell yourself you'll make any sacrifice so that they'll be happy. I never realized that the real sacrifice would be my own peace of mind." She stood up—a not-so-subtle indication that the conversation had reached its natural close. "But that's family, I guess. You'll do anything for them."

Becca got to her feet. "I discovered the same thing myself recently."

Once her encounter with Nicole was concluded, Becca got back in her car and unfolded the address she'd written down earlier. When she'd looked up the music store online, she'd been surprised that it was less than a mile from where she lived. How had she never noticed it? But nothing about Gibney's Music was memorable. It stood next to an older shopping center, and its squat, stucco façade and faded sign seemed unremarkable by design. The interior wasn't much better. The gray carpet beneath her feet was worn through almost to the backing in places, and the whole store had a mildewed, metallic odor, like the inside of an old trombone case.

The man who came out from a workroom in the back at the sound of the doorbell also looked in need of updating. He had flyaway Einstein hair, and Mork from Ork suspenders stretching over an impressive gut. His green T-shirt decorated with a treble clef declared the wearer to be NOTHING BUT TREBLE.

Becca smiled at him in greeting and then looked over at the wall where a surprising number of instruments were displayed on holders. As a businesswoman, she was impressed by the variety, as well as by the fact that the man stayed in business at all. How many clarinets and flugelhorns could a person sell in a town the size of Leesburg?

"I'm looking for a saxophone," she said.

"For a student?" he asked.

"No—the man knows how to play really well. Someone told me he could have been a professional."

The folds of the man's face gathered together. "We don't rent professional instruments."

"Then what do pros do?"

"They buy."

She stepped forward and looked at the price on a medium

sized–looking saxophone. *$6,998.00.* She gasped. No wonder Walt had hocked his and never replaced them.

"I can't afford that."

"We rent student instruments by the week or month. There's a two-week minimum."

"Okay. Could you rent me the best saxophone you have for two weeks?"

"Sure. What does he play?"

Hadn't they already covered this? "Saxophone."

"There are different kinds."

Right. Damn. She stared up at the wall again. Walt had even mentioned what he played, but she couldn't remember.

Seeing her confusion, the man prompted, "Soprano . . . alto . . . tenor . . . baritone . . ."

Tenor—that was it. She frowned. Or was it baritone. Or both.

"What would be cheaper? Tenor or baritone?"

"Tenor." His eyes lit up. "Tell you what. I can rent you this old model I fixed up. I was going to put it on eBay, but I wouldn't mind keeping it around for a while. It's an old Buescher Top Hat and Cane. A classic!"

She couldn't bring herself to tell the man he might have been speaking Swahili to her. Besides, he was already rushing to the back to retrieve it.

Fifteen minutes later, she schlepped the sax in its tattered wood case across the Strawberry Cake Store's threshold. She'd been gone longer than anticipated, and she half-expected Erin to have run away to South America. Instead, all was calm. A modest line trailed away from the counter, and Erin looked perfectly in control of the situation. Progress.

Erin glanced down at the case as Becca dragged it back to the storeroom. "Are you going on a trip?"

"It's a gift for Walt. And a test, sort of." Less conclusive than a DNA test, but she was curious to see how he'd respond.

Erin shook her head. "You're making even less sense than usual. Maybe you should have a cupcake."

What Becca craved was caffeine, but first she helped out at the counter and caught up with serving the customers. As soon as they were alone again, Erin cornered her by the coffee station. "So how was it?"

Becca thought about the music store. "Being in that musty place made me glad I run a cake shop."

"It was musty?" Erin jumped on the detail with surprising glee. "Good. Bob has allergies."

Bob? Becca spent a split second connecting the dots. Somehow Erin had found out that she'd gone to talk to Nicole. "The *music store* was musty. Nicole's house wasn't. That woman's neat as a pin."

Erin frowned. "Did you see Bob?"

"How did you know I was over there?"

"Pam called to find out how your 'mission' had gone. It took me approximately thirty seconds to pump the specifics out of her."

Of course. "Bob wasn't there," she told Erin. Or if he was, he'd been hiding in a closet or something.

"What did she say about him?"

"I was just there to talk about Olivia. Bob's name didn't even come up."

Erin folded her arms. "And what about the after-school thing? Did she tell you to take a hike?"

"No, she wrote Cal a check."

Erin glowered at Becca's handbag, stowed below the register. "I can't believe Pam and Cal would take that creature's money."

"Erin . . ."

"I can't help it," Erin declared. "I resent her."

"But it's for Olivia's sake. You said yourself that she was collateral damage in the whole affair, just like you."

"I know. I shouldn't feel so petty. I feel like my soul is shriveling."

Becca sipped her coffee, trying to understand.

Erin's lips turned down. "I keep waking up at two in the morning, in a swivet, completely pissed off at myself. I'll think, 'I married him. I actually vowed to spend my life with that asshole, till death. What went wrong?'" She laughed grudgingly. "As if anything could have gone right. If you're to the point that you think someone's an ass, it's best you get away from him, right?"

"You're better off without him."

"Yeah, but for some reason, knowing that doesn't make it any easier right now." She wiped crumbs off the counter next to the register. "I feel like one of those jilted Victorian ladies. Maybe I should renounce the world, move back into my place, and let it crumble around me. I could wear the same dress for the next fifty years."

Said the woman whose closets bulged with clothes, some of which probably had the price tags still attached.

The bell over the door tinkled, and they both swiveled smiles in that direction. Walt and Matthew came in. Matthew looked directly into Becca's eyes, and suddenly she was back in that parking lot again. Heaven help her. There were so many reasons not to start a relationship with anyone right now. On the other side of the scale, though, stood Matthew. Those eyes and that mood-lifting smile tipped everything in his favor.

Walt approached her eagerly, an old shopping bag in his hands. "Me and Matthew hit an estate sale," he said. "I found this."

He produced a pink and lavender backpack. On the front grinned the cast of *Me Minus You,* including Becca at her tween zenith of awkward—ponytailed head tilted, hand on her jutting hip. She'd only seen one of these before, in the box of *Me Minus You* memorabilia she'd discovered in her mom's closet after Ronnie's funeral. Her mother had packed away mugs, magazines, a school binder, and the backpack. Why, Becca never knew. Was it supposed to be a time capsule, a keepsake for future generations? In her grief, Becca had dropped it all off at the local Salvation Army. She couldn't think why anyone would ever care about any of this stuff.

"Wow," she said, staring at the thing. "Is that what you went shopping for?"

"Nah, I needed shirts," Walt said. "But then I saw this and I knew I wanted it more."

"How much does one of these go for?" she asked.

"I paid ten bucks, but it was in a box full of kids' books. We dropped those off at the library."

She recoiled. Ten dollars! "Did you try to talk them down?"

Walt looked almost offended. "Why would I do that? It'll be worth way more than that after you sign it for me."

She shook her head. It would be worth exactly fifty cents, she imagined. "Walt, what a waste of money."

"I don't think so." He held it up, admiring it again. "It makes me proud."

Proud? The sight of herself in her off-the-shoulder T-shirt and her spastic ponytail made her cringe with embarrassment. It was exactly what she'd been fleeing from for the past decade or more. *I did that, and I didn't even make a success of it.* Maybe she understood Erin's desire to hide herself away, after all. Her psyche had been living in its own crumbling house.

"Sign it for me?" Walt asked, handing her a Magic Marker and the backpack.

A glob of something blocked Becca's throat, and she swallowed several times, trying to get past it. Here was a man who had battled demons she couldn't begin to imagine. He barely had any money to his name to last him who-knew-how-long, and he'd spent ten bucks on a beat-up polyester backpack of a long-cancelled sitcom. Why would someone do that?

She shook her head as she signed her name, not wanting to put a word to the answer. The look in his eyes as he stared at her signature on that hideous, cheesy backpack told her all she needed to know. He even looped it over his shoulder and struck a jaunty pose for everybody.

"Stylish!" Erin said. "Becca bought something this morning, too." She nodded toward the case.

Everyone stared at the handled box blankly, except for Walt, who knew what it was at once. He went straight for it, entranced. Flipping the case open, he gasped. "A Top Hat and Cane," he said reverently, even though the sax didn't look like much to Becca. Its age showed in its worn lacquer, which was dark, scratched up, and pitted in places.

"I rented it. I thought you might enjoy having something to keep you occupied during the day."

"Oh yes, I would." He smiled at Becca, and then, in an instant, she was pulled into a big bear hug. "Thank you."

Tears prickled her eyes and she pulled away. *First hug from my father,* she thought, *and I'm falling to pieces.* Part of the reason she got the thing was to see if he even played at all. He'd barely mentioned saxophones since she'd met him.

He looked almost as choked up as she felt. Maybe he was that glad to have a sax again.

"Play something," Matthew said.

Walt ran his hands over the pearled keys and then lifted a diffident glance. "Oh, I don't know . . . after all these years, I should work up some chops before I inflict a song on you folks." He closed up the case, latched it, and looked over at Becca again. "But I sure do thank you."

She nodded, feeling that lump again, and was glad for the distraction of a newly arrived customer. When Walt and Matthew left, loading the sax into Matthew's car, along with the purple backpack, she knew exactly what she needed to do next. She got out her phone and punched in the number for the transplant clinic.

Chapter 23

On her second visit to the transplant center, Becca arrived prepared. The tote bag she carried with her bulged with a day's worth of food and waiting room activities. She'd brought a book, a magazine, an extra magazine, lunch, and a bottle of juice to sip after the blood draw, in case she got woozy. She'd also packed a sweater, because the last time the hospital thermostat had been set to tooth chattering.

Her first stop of the day was a simple finger prick to determine blood type. No big deal—for anyone who wasn't a wimp at the sight of blood—but she dug out the juice, just in case. This was just the first step of a long medical journey, and she needed to adjust to having people poking needles into her.

She'd barely taken two swigs of vitality-restoring apple-grape juice when the nurse came back in and informed her that she needed to see Dr. Laverents.

Quick action. She liked it.

The surgeon waited patiently as she settled herself into a chair and steadied her overloaded tote bag at her feet.

"I'm sorry, but it looks like you're not a match," he announced.

The words came so unexpectedly, Becca couldn't quite comprehend them at first.

"Your blood type is not compatible with Mr. Johnson's. You're AB. Mr. Johnson is type O." He launched into an impromptu review of the requirements for blood donors and recipients, and even produced a chart of blood-type matching to make it all clearer.

The letters on the grid blurred in front of her. "How can we be incompatible? He's my father."

Unless he really wasn't?

Dr. Laverents settled back in his chair. "Unfortunately, family members don't always share the same blood type. If they did, it would simplify our work here quite a bit, and make it much easier to find donors."

"But . . ." Becca didn't know what else there was to say. She'd geared herself up to be a hero—to save Walt's life. Now that door was shut. "There's nothing else I can do?"

The surgeon threaded his fingers together and looked on her with understanding. "You can make sure Mr. Johnson keeps as healthy as possible for as long as possible. He still needs to have his diagnostics tended to and kept updated, right down to a clean bill of health from a dentist. These things are important."

"Of course, but . . ."

She was just taking up the doctor's time, for no reason except that she was in shock. It hadn't been easy to decide to give up a part of herself, but to decide and then be told that she couldn't be a donor made her want to thrash around on the floor and weep, or chain herself to Dr. Laverents's desk. But this man couldn't change her blood type.

She stood up, and so did he. "I'm sorry." The man's eyes brimmed with compassion, which helped. "I know this must be a disappointment."

He knew it because he'd probably been through this hundreds

of times. She guessed this man saw more tragedy in a week than she would in a lifetime.

She thanked him and headed for the door. Before reaching it, she stopped. "Does not sharing a blood type make it more likely that two people aren't related?"

"It's impossible to tell from blood type alone," he answered. "Family testing involves comparing DNA. That's not exactly my line."

"Mine, either." A time machine would have been invaluable to her at this moment. She could travel back in time and pay more attention in biology class. "Thank you."

Outside, in her car, she sat frozen, too keyed up with frustration to go back to the shop yet. What was she going to do now? She dug her lunch out of the tote bag and ate it there in the parking lot. As she chewed her sandwich, her thoughts replayed all the strange events of the past month and a half. What had become of her calm, slightly boring life? Walt had just appeared. She still didn't know who he was, really—but she'd been willing to give the man a kidney, even without a DNA test. Now that she couldn't, her emotions were going haywire.

Maybe he wasn't her father after all.

Not for the first time, anger at her mother surged through her. If only her mother had told her more. If she'd been too embarrassed to admit in person that she'd had sex with a heroin-addicted thief—understandable—couldn't she at least have left a posthumous note? *By the way, if a strange guy with a criminal record shows up wearing a funny hat, that's your dad.* How hard would that have been?

Then she felt another wave of anger for blaming her mom. Maybe Ronnie hadn't told her about Walt because he wasn't really her father at all. The guy might just be pulling off the con of a lifetime. He could have found out about Ronnie from someone else. Or maybe he could have dated Ronnie, but still not be her father. Just because he knew about strawberry cake and quoted her mom, she'd been ready to do anything for him. But

Ronnie had probably made that cake for lots of people, and mentioned happiness on a plate to others, too.

She wadded up the napkin she had packed with her lunch and tossed it and the Tupperware container into the passenger seat. Purposefully, she turned the key in the ignition.

If Walt was nothing but an old faker, she was going to find out once and for all, before the next months of her life went down a rabbit hole of Medicaid bureaucrats, colonoscopy appointments, and God knows what else. All for the sake of some old con artist with sad eyes.

And now that she thought about it, what about his eyes? They were nothing like her own. She glanced in the rearview mirror. Nothing in her face reminded her of Walt. When people found long-lost relatives in books and movies, they were supposed to look alike. You were just supposed to know. Like in *The Natural.* The kid at the end looks *just like* Robert Redford. But she couldn't name one trait she shared with Walt. Not one.

The only thing she'd known about her father was that his name was Johnny and that he played the saxophone. But Walt went by Walt—for whatever bogus reason—and when she'd given him a saxophone, he hadn't even taken it out of the case. She'd been too dizzy with sentimentality at that moment to notice that this reputed near-pro musician hadn't blown one single note, and had muttered instead about "his chops." His chops. How emotionally screwed up had she been not to have registered how lame that sounded?

She'd wanted to believe in Walt so badly, she'd been ready to fall for anything.

Her skepticism returned with a fury. Her heart hammered against her chest and her hands began thumping angrily against the steering wheel. When she thought about how she'd dragged Matthew into this crazy situation, she broke out into a sweat. He had been urging caution from the start.

By the time she pulled into Matthew's driveway, she was so angry at herself and at Walt, she was ready to toss the man out on his ear without listening to another bogus explanation. She wanted to be free of this man. To have her life back. To not feel vulnerable and hopeless and raw.

She leapt out of the Subaru, barking her knee against the door as she slammed it shut. She bent over in pain, and that's when she heard it: the rich, plaintive wailing of a saxophone.

Walt hadn't had to work long to get his chops back, apparently, because the melodious tones of the old Top Hat and Cane projected loud and clear. Becca didn't really know the first things about saxophones, or jazz. Or music, period. She didn't have to. The song she heard was delivered with such skill, such feeling, it was as if the player were blessing the very air around her, displacing silence with full, robust sound.

She knew the melody. Knew it almost as if each note were stenciled on her heart. "Till There Was You."

Anger left her so quickly, its absence left her boneless. Forgetting her scraped knee, she sagged against the Subaru. She couldn't move, couldn't do anything but listen, and remember. Her mom hadn't been a *Music Man* freak, or a Shirley Jones groupie. It wasn't The Beatles who had made her love this song. It had been Walt.

"The way that man could play would bring tears to your eyes."

It was so true. That sound soared right to her heart. She was crying now.

She didn't know how long she stood there before Walt noticed the car in the driveway and came out, but suddenly she was leaning against him, sobbing.

"What's wrong?" he asked. "What happened?"

"That was . . ." She could barely gulp out words. ". . . Mom's favorite song."

"Mine, too. I used to play it for her." He swallowed. "I know this is hard to believe, because I wasn't any kind of a match for Ronnie. She was a diamond—everything I wasn't. But I loved her. I loved her so much it still hurts."

That, Becca guessed, was what they had in common.

* * *

In the town house, he made her some coffee. "The real deal," he said, "with caffeine. Just because I can't have it doesn't mean you can't enjoy it."

"Thank you." She felt silly now for having such a breakdown, and for not making her own coffee. She was perfectly okay.

"You know who played that song best?" he asked. "Sonny Rollins. I'll lend you a CD of his. That's sweet music."

She cupped her hands around the mug to warm them.

He studied her. "It wasn't just the song that upset you, was it?"

She shook her head. "I was at the hospital. I'd decided to be your donor. But I didn't even make it past the blood-type test. We're not a match."

He frowned, and took his time answering. "I wish you hadn't gone through all that."

"All that?" Wasn't he listening? "I wasn't there thirty minutes."

"I don't want you to be the donor. That wouldn't be right."

"Why not?"

"It's not the way things should work. What if you have children of your own one day? What if one of them needed a kidney—and there'd you'd be stuck with just one."

"That's a lot of ifs and hypothetical kids. Meanwhile, you need one now. No ifs about it."

"You should hang on to all the body parts you can," he insisted.

She raked a hand through her hair. God, he was frustrating. "The point is, I *can't* donate, no matter how much I want to. It's impossible. And I started to think, well, maybe since our blood doesn't match . . ."

He nodded. "I get it."

"I'm so sorry. I kept having doubts."

His eyebrows arched. "And you think that song proves anything?"

"Not just the song. Everything. I believe you."

He thought this over for a moment. "We should do one of

those tests. That would make sense, I guess. But it doesn't really matter whether you believe me or not. I got nothing to offer you, and I'm not looking for anything. In fact, I've accepted too much of your hospitality already."

"No, you haven't. I stuck you in a storage room!" She still cringed at the memory. "My own father."

He shook his head. "You've got this nice guy interested in you, and here I am, in the way."

"Forget that. You're probably keeping us from being really stupid and jumping the gun."

"You *should* jump," he said. "While you're young. Look, I'm nobody to say how to live your life, but Matthew's a good one. Seriously. Great-paying job. Clean cut. I've been keeping my eyes open. I can spot a hinky type a mile off."

That wasn't hard to believe. "I've already rushed into one marriage, which didn't work out so well. Next time, I want it to last more than six months."

He scratched his stubbly chin. "Okay, but I still think you'd be better off without me in the way."

"You're not in the way." How many times did she have to say it? "And we'll get you on the lists and find a donor for you. Don't worry."

"I do worry. For one thing, there's the money."

"Once I get the insurance situation sorted out—"

"I still owe money. And there are always more costs," he said. "Co-pays. Unexpected stuff. Dental. Plus my living expenses. I'm nearly flat, and you are, too."

She drew back. "No, I'm not."

He tilted a skeptical glance at her. "You didn't even have the money to fix your dishwasher."

"I was just economizing," she assured him.

He contemplated his hands for a moment before meeting her gaze again. "I appreciate all you've done, I really do, but I've got to make my own way, and—"

"Forget it," she said. "We'll figure out the money thing. We will. And you'll be able to work again. *And* we'll find you a donor kidney, or . . ." Her words trailed off as the thought refused to find a way to complete itself.

He smiled ruefully. "Or die trying?"

That evening, Becca tapped her pencil eraser against her chin and gave her Quicken window the evil eye. Where had all the money gone? And where was there room to economize? She never thought of herself as a penny-pincher, but there were no lavish expenditures for her to cut out to offset the growing Walt bill.

Except one. By far, her biggest personal expense was Harvey. His upkeep, even boarding him at the relatively no-frills Butternut Knoll, averaged her nearly five hundred dollars per month. That was huge. The outlay might go up as he aged, too, if he developed a chronic health problem. There was no question that her finances would make a lot more sense if she didn't have Harvey.

The only catch was, she would just as soon saw off her own arm as give him up.

"What you need is an accountant," Erin said, circling behind her. "You should use my guy, Brad. He saves me oodles in taxes."

"I'm guessing Brad charges oodles, too."

"I've never paid much attention," Erin said. "But he's worth his weight in gold."

Becca shot her an amused glance, and wound up doing a double-take. Erin's black wool jersey dress fit her like a second skin. "Where are you going?"

"Noah's picking me up."

"Noah, the detective?"

She nodded. "We're meeting with Marv, my lawyer."

Becca frowned. "I thought Marv was Bob's lawyer."

"He was, but he was mine before we married, so I'm declaring custody of him." She stepped into a pair of four-inch pumps. "There's a lot to go over."

Acute support-staff envy struck Becca. Erin always seemed to attract a fleet of men to ease her over life's bumps. Having a trust fund probably didn't hurt, but Erin was also the kind of person people wanted to help—like a fledgling that had fallen out of the nest. Some dowdy chicks flopped around on the ground and were left for the feral cats. But Erin was the sweet downy chick that made people line shoe boxes in cotton and call the Audubon Society.

"Noah and I are hoping that Marv will green-light my going back to the house."

"I'm sure he will."

Erin put a manicured hand on her shoulder. "But whether he does or doesn't, I'm going to pay you for my time here."

"Shut up."

"And I want to keep working at the cake shop," Erin continued. "I really like it there."

"Of course." In a short time, Erin had become very popular with customers. Free Cake Day probably had something to do with that. She wasn't a bad baker, either. "I hope you do, but—"

The doorbell rang, and Erin clattered down the stairs to let Noah in.

Becca stood up and smoothed back her hair, ready to greet the gentleman caller. Before they came back up, however, her phone rang. It was Matthew.

"Thank God you picked up," he said.

The urgency in his voice sent a chill through her. "What's wrong?"

"When I got home from work tonight, I found a note from Walt on the kitchen table."

Her heart beat double-time. Erin reappeared and, seeing her on the phone and noting her worried expression, tiptoed to retrieve her coat and purse. A lanky young man with floppy brown hair and a beaky nose trailed after her, smiling shyly at Becca. At any other time, she would have thought he was adorable, but now it was all she could do to concentrate on what Matthew was telling her.

"The note says, 'Thank you very much for letting me stay. Here's five dollars. Please return the saxophone to Rebecca. The

Sonny Rollins CD is for her, too. She'll know why. Your friend, Walt Johnson.' I looked in his room. His plastic tub is gone."

"Oh no." She had to remind herself to breathe.

Erin flicked a concerned glance her way. Becca met her gaze, frozen.

"Have you seen him?" Matthew asked.

"Not since this afternoon. Hold on." She snagged Noah's coat sleeve as he edged toward the door. "You're a detective, right?"

Noah's eyes went owl-wide, but he nodded.

"I have a job for you."

It took some doing, but Noah untangled the mystery of Walt's whereabouts faster than her own frantic brain could have. Checking all the local bus stations, he discovered that Walt had bought a ticket that would connect him to the Greyhound line in Frederick, Maryland. Becca, with Matthew, jumped in the Subaru and drove hell-for-leather for Frederick. She couldn't believe Walt was just going to leave her, going to get on a bus and head out without so much as a good-bye.

"I hope we're not too late," she said.

Matthew sent an anxious glance in the direction of the speedometer. "I'm hoping a cop doesn't get you in his radar."

When she streaked into the bus station, she found Walt in the waiting room, sunk low in a chair, his legs pushed out straight in front of him and propped up on his plastic tub. He clutched his *Me Minus You* purple backpack and appeared asleep. She rushed toward him but stopped short of waking him. She was almost afraid to use her voice—unsure whether it would come out as a shriek or a wail.

Some sixth sense must have alerted him to her presence. His eyes opened, and he pushed himself up straighter. "Rebecca. You shouldn't have come all this way."

"Were you just going to leave?" she asked, her voice shaking with the effort not to yell. "Just slink off in the middle of the night?"

He looked behind her, where Matthew stood. "I left a note. I didn't want to trouble you."

That word. "Walt, you're nothing *but* trouble! We had to get a detective to help us find you. And what if we'd been thirty minutes later?"

"Bus doesn't leave for another hour," he said.

She took deep breaths in and out to control her anger. At herself as well as at him. Had she not made herself clear this afternoon? "Where are you going?"

"Back to LA."

"Why?"

He shrugged. "It's what I know."

"Do you have friends there? Anyone to take care of you?"

His chin dipped toward his chest. "I'll be okay."

"No, you won't." She kicked his tub in frustration. "You'll die, and you don't even care. You're just going to give up, without a thought about how it will affect me or anybody else."

"You're wrong," he said. "I might not be worth much, but selfish?" He shook his head. "Not so. I gave up Ronnie because I was no good. Because I knew she and you were better off without me. Was I wrong? I don't think so. Look at you—at what you became. You've got so much. I couldn't be prouder."

"But I don't have any family."

"You'll make your own."

"But *you're* my family. Right now. You're all I have."

"If you think that, you're not paying attention. Family is people who love you. You've got that in spades. My being here will only screw everything up."

"You'll only screw it up if you leave now," she argued. "What's gotten into you? I thought you'd changed, that you were going to try to make things right. Or else what was the point in finding me at all?"

"I *have* changed. And I'm glad I got this opportunity to see you. When I came to Virginia, it was sort of a last-ditch thing. I'd lost my job, and those LA doctors weren't giving me too long. So I figured, well, bucket-list time. What's the last thing you'd like to do here on earth? *Find Rebecca*, I thought. That's all I meant to do—find you. I didn't want to disrupt your life like this. I met you, which is more than I hoped for. And all I really wanted."

"In that case, you could have left weeks ago."

He drummed his fingers restlessly on the backpack. "I meant to. I was going to work at that gas station till I had enough to get back to LA. But then you took me in, and I fell sick, and it got harder and harder to leave."

"But it's not hard to now?"

"Hardest thing I've done in a long time," he said, and his voice sounded so ragged that she could believe him. "You're a good person. Caring. You make me think maybe my life hasn't all been a big waste. But I don't want to take anything more from you than you've already given. That wouldn't be right. Knowing you a little has been enough for me."

She would not let him do this. "It's not enough for *me*. I'm not letting you on that bus. I don't care if I have to block the door with my body. You're not giving up."

"I don't want to take a part of anyone's life," he said. "I had my chance. I didn't do so hot, but I'm satisfied. Now that I've seen you, I am. If there are lives to save, let it be for the little kids and the young people with big futures. The people who haven't screwed up yet."

"No." Becca threw herself into the seat next to him. "A month ago you could have made that choice, but now it's too late. You found me. I have a father now, when I assumed I didn't have any blood relation left who I would ever know. I have questions about the past that only you can answer—about grandparents and great-grandparents and you. And Mom. Okay, you messed up your life. You ran out on us, for whatever reason, and you've been the crappiest father imaginable. But now that you're here, in my life, you've got one responsibility. Just one. To stay. I didn't ask you to come find me, but you did. And I'm not going to let you leave. Or give up. You might not be selfish, but I am. I won't let you go."

"It would be for the best."

"No, it wouldn't. Because I would live the rest of my life feeling I should have saved you."

Walt's gaze met hers. "You might not be able to save me anyway."

"Maybe not, but I'm going to do everything in my power. Everything."

He thumbed the ridiculous knapsack, and she could feel his resistance fading. "What about money? I can't work steady. I'm a drain on you."

"Don't worry about that. I have it all figured out."

There weren't many options. Harvey flashed before her eyes—her beautiful horse, her dream, that last bit of her youth. How else could she either reduce expenses or make more money? Maybe Olivia would take him, or . . .

Her heart hurt.

Suddenly, she knew what she had to do. *Bite the bullet, Becca.*

He arched a brow. "You're not thinking of doing anything crooked, are you?"

She smiled sadly. Actually, she almost wished she did have the nerve to rob a bank. It seemed more palatable than what she actually had in mind, which was going to be painful. Very painful.

She looked up at Matthew, who was still standing by. His eyes telegraphed his concern.

"Just leave it to me," she said.

Celebrities in Peril!: Child Star Edition
Transcript of Contestant Interview
REBECCA HUDSON

IN INTERVIEW ROOM: SNOWY ALASKA EXT. PHOTO w/ SHOW LOGO IN BACKGROUND.
Rebecca, dressed in jeans and cable sweater, smiles at camera a little self-consciously.

INTERVIEWER:
Why are you participating in *Celebrities in Peril!*?

REBECCA:
Why?

Laughs self-consciously, then shakes her head. Looks at the interviewer more thoughtfully.

I'm doing this for my dad, actually. Growing up, I never knew my father. He and my mom split up before I was born, and then he went through some really tough times. He was addicted to drugs, did some bad things, and actually served time in prison.

QUICK CUT TO BLACK-AND-WHITE MUG SHOT OVER (BLURRED) PRISON RECORD. A BUREAUCRATIC STAMP HITS THE RECORD AND LEAVES THE WORDS 8 YEARS IN RED BLOCK LETTERS.

REBECCA:
After he got out, he didn't feel he could look me up. He didn't want to come off as a dad mooching off his celebrity daughter, you know? Which is ridiculous, because that's so not who he is.

CUT TO FILM OF THE FATHER, in new clothes and funny hat, playing saxophone. MUSIC CONTINUES.

REBECCA:
A few years ago, I moved to Leesburg, Virginia, and opened my shop.

EXT. OF THE STRAWBERRY CAKE SHOP, then quick cut to INT. OF THE SHOP, Rebecca with cupcakes, serving customers.

REBECCA:
That's when Walt finally found me. And then I discovered he

has a terminal kidney disease and needs a transplant. Since my mom died, Walt is all the family I have. So we're praying we'll find a donor. In the meantime, I'm doing the show to raise funds to cover medical costs. Whatever happens, I'm so grateful I've got this chance to help my father get a second chance.

MUSIC SWELLS. CUT TO BECCA HUGGING HER DAD. FADE OUT.

Celebrities in Peril!: Child Star Edition
Transcript of Contestant Interview
ABBY WOOTEN

IN INTERVIEW ROOM: SNOWY ALASKA EXT. PHOTO w/ SHOW LOGO IN BACKGROUND.

INTERVIEWER:
Why are you participating in *Celebrities in Peril!*?

ABBY:
She is dressed in coat with fur hoodie, and looks directly at the camera.

I'm in it to win it.

Chapter 24

Somewhere in Alaska . . .

"If anyone expects me to butcher a moose, they've got another think coming," Abby said, stomping her feet. Her elaborate boots looked like something NASA might have fabricated for a voyage to an icy planet. Their shiny nylon-and-leather construction gave off more glare than the snow beneath them. "I warned them I was vegetarian in my very first interview."

Becca, exhausted from the effort of pick axing through the ice to set their fishing line, couldn't bring herself to worry much about the next cabin challenge, as the tasks were called on the show. This one was tough enough. "Do you think we're trying to catch tofu out here?"

Abby's nose wrinkled—it was about the only part of her not covered by protective gear. "Okay, I'm a pescatarian or whatever. At least fish aren't cute, with sad little eyes. And it's not like they bleed disgustingly when you cut them open." When Becca turned away, she added, "They don't, do they? I mean, not like a moose would, right?"

"Not quite like a moose."

Abby looked relieved, and vindicated.

So far no one had breathed a word about killing moose, but Abby was particularly concerned about the possibility. Borrowing trouble was one of her favorite pastimes. Becca was happy just to arrive at the end of the day not dead of frostbite or as a wolf pack's dinner. The future? She would slaughter that moose when she came to it, so to speak.

Abby edged as close as she deemed safe to the edge of the ice hole and peered down. "Do you think we're going to catch anything?"

That *we* would have made Becca laugh if she hadn't been so tired. Becca had been the one to pitch their little shelter—a tent—on the ice, and hack their way through to the water. Abby had done a lot of directing, and worrying, and had frequently mugged adorably for the benefit of the videographer who wisely remained huddled just inside the tent flap.

"Because it looks like the other team is already beating us," Abby said, pointing at the tent a hundred yards away, where two fish were hanging on a pole, taunting them.

"Damn." The fish were clearly biting better for the *Cosby–Full House* duo.

They were the only two teams out today because the rest of the group had been assigned the task of coming up with a fix for the cabin chimney, which had been billowing smoke into their shelter since they had erected it at the beginning. Putting their prefab shelter together had been Cabin Challenge #1, and the endeavor had nearly resulted in a mass former child star extinction. The sprawling hut—with parts pre-painted to look like a weathered, rustic log cabin—had come with Ikea-like instructions and diagrams. Unfortunately, the resulting structure proved just as frustrating to assemble, and even less durable. The first night, an interior wall had collapsed on one bunk bed, and asphyxiation had been a constant worry.

Becca had to hand it to Renee Jablonsky. The woman couldn't have thought up a scenario better suited to bring out tensions than trapping them all in a snowbound, smoky cabin. Even though they were one stand of trees away from modernly equipped trailers with emergency generators, where the director and his crew lived, the isolation and simulated hardships nevertheless played on all their emotions and insecurities. One inmate was soon discovered to have smuggled several quarts of vodka in her hiking pack. (*"How do you think they survive in Siberia?"*) Vodka Girl had also been the first person Renee, sporting a dramatic scarlet parka with a faux fur hood, had dismissed in their weekly bonfire ritual, which always ended with the banished person handing his or her torch back to Renee.

Lately, Becca had started to dream of being the chosen torch surrenderer. Money be damned. How could she screw up enough to earn a plane ride out of this wilderness? The trouble was, screwing up had consequences in terms of survival or at least comfort, so in the heat of the challenge it was hard to give up entirely.

Maybe this grudging survival instinct was what had caused Abby to glom on to her. Abby had talked tough in the beginning, but from the moment the plane had dropped them off in this forsaken place, she'd wandered around in near-nervous breakdown mode. She had claimed the bunk over Becca's, though, and basically stuck to her like glue, as if they'd never stopped being besties.

"*We?*" Becca asked her now.

Abby yanked off her snow goggles and blinked her watery blue-green eyes. The years had not altered the heart-shaped face, jutting chin, or the round eyes that had made her such a memorable screen presence. Given their history, Becca had assumed that Abby would be her adversary. Yet this morning, for instance, Abby had volunteered to ice-fish with Becca instead of working with the cabin-repair crew, even though it would mean stuffing herself into unflattering long underwear to keep from freezing her butt off.

"I think we should form an alliance," Abby said in a low voice—as if no one could hear them. As if there wasn't a digital videographer two feet away.

They had been instructed to act as if no one was watching them. But telling a group of people who had been weaned on sound sets to ignore cameras was like ordering lions to ignore lame baby gazelles.

"Wrong show," Becca said. Alliances wouldn't really get them anywhere, because the cabin mates didn't get to choose who stayed and who would be eliminated. The decision was all Renee's. She monitored the footage assembled by the directors and did her own calculations of who would attract ratings. So far, the people who had been axed were either dangerously substance-dependent or, worse, dull.

"But it would help," Abby argued. "If we made ourselves an inseparable pair, maybe the audience wouldn't want to see us broken up. Who wants to see best friends torn apart?"

"We're not best friends," Becca said. "We haven't even spoken for over a decade."

"But we're old friends reunited. At least that's something."

"Something what?"

Abby leaned in. "Some angle for the audience to pick up on, stupid. Let's face it. *Me Minus You* never had the ratings most of these other shows had. I mean, *Little House*! Come on, is that fair? She spent her whole childhood in the top ten, and in a goddamned cabin, too. No one's going to want to see *her* get the ax. Ditto the Partridge guy, even though he's old, crazy, and likely to get us all killed."

That was the truth.

"You and me, Becca, we're sitting ducks. We have to be wily."

It was all clear now. "I wondered why you were suddenly my best pal. I thought maybe you felt insecure and were gravitating toward the familiar. I knew it couldn't be because you liked me."

Abby's eyes flew open dramatically. "Of course I like you. We grew up together."

"Wrong. We went through adolescence together. Frankly, I'm beginning to wonder if you ever grew up at all. I certainly don't trust you any more than I did then."

"How can you say that?"

"Because you dumped me when I no longer was getting work. You think I didn't realize that?"

"What could I do? I was busy, and I heard you were in some public school. I had my own problems." She shot an almost-imperceptible sidewise glance toward the camera. "Most ordinary people don't understand how difficult growing up on television can be. So many trade-offs . . ."

Becca bit her lip. She needed to leave rising to the bait to the poor fish under the ice. All this discussion was doing was giving Abby what she wanted—conflict footage that would make them more dramatically interesting to viewers and less likely to be selected by the red parka of doom at the next bonfire.

Ignoring Abby, she checked the line. Still nothing.

Abby groaned in frustration and started stamping again. "Oh, who cares? We're going to freeze to death out here before this stupid show airs, anyway."

"You should have worn more layers." Becca was sporting multiple pairs of Polartec long underwear. They kept her warm, and she also hoped they would pose an extra challenge to any predator wanting to make a snack of her.

Abby clucked. "I don't want to be photographed with Michelin Man ass, thank you very much."

Becca glared at her.

"*What?*" Abby asked, all innocence. "What's the matter with you? Christ, in the old days you at least had a sense of humor."

"You mean I didn't mind when you insulted me?"

"Is this about the heifer thing? Honestly, how was I supposed to know that would catch on?"

Despite the cold, heat suffused Becca's face. "*You* said that?"

Abby shrugged. "You chunked out. It was funny."

Becca bit her lip. *Don't push her head under the icy water while the camera is rolling.*

"Oh, look at the frowny face," Abby sneered. "God, you were always so sensitive. No wonder you couldn't hack it and had to go hide yourself away in some Podunk town."

"That Podunk town is a very nice place."

Abby laughed. "I'm sure it is, if you can't make the grade anywhere else."

Anywhere else? "You're saying that there's your little patch of Southern California, and then everywhere else."

"You know what I mean," Abby said. "You felt like a failure, so you decided to go be a big fish in a miniscule pond."

Becca sputtered. "Abby, I run a cupcake store. That's not a big fish activity. My customers are bigger fish than I'll ever be. They work interesting jobs that solve other people's problems. They actually help people—some even rescue or heal people. What we're doing here is ridiculous. It doesn't make either of us better or more worthy. Or bigger."

Abby shook her head. "Then why are you here? Why are you grandstanding in front of Mr. and Mrs. John Q. Public? You're just trying to make me look bad, I'll bet."

Becca released a frustrated huff and stood up. She couldn't take it anymore. Maybe she could beg Renee to release her from her contract. Or she could do some crazy thing—would killing Abby be crazy enough?—and hand in her torch. She'd even weep for the cameras, if that's what was required. She looked over at the videographer, hoping he would get a good angle of her holding Abby's head under the icy water till the bubbles stopped.

To her astonishment, the camera guy wasn't even shooting them. Maybe he hadn't been for a few minutes. While she and Abby had been sniping at each other, he had directed his camera up the hill, where the cabin was. Smoke billowed out of the chimney—unfortunately, it was also pouring out the front door and the windows. Becca could see flames, too, and former child stars running in circles, tossing snow at their burning cabin.

The videographer shook his head and muttered, "I wonder how that happened."

Becca and Abby, momentarily forgetting their spat, exchanged knowing looks and blurted out the most obvious answer, almost in unison.

"Danny."

The Morning Show!
Transcript of Segment 3: Real Peril in Alaska

PAULA (host):
CUT TO VIDEO OF A CABIN BURNING AGAINST A SNOWY MOUNTAIN LANDSCAPE.

The Morning Show has received dramatic footage of the conflagration on a reality star show set that resulted in the hospitalization of several former child stars and crew members who were on the scene. One star, still unidentified, remains in the hospital this morning for observation. The entire cast of *Celebrities in Peril!: Child Star Edition* was evacuated to Anchorage for a short hiatus. We're lucky to be joined by two of those cast members, whom some of you may remember from the nineties sitcom *Me Minus You*. Rebecca Hudson and Abby Wooten have joined us via satellite from our affiliate in Anchorage, where it is very early. Good morning, ladies!

REBECCA:
Hello.

ABBY:
Good morning, Paula! (*waves*) Hi, America!

PAULA:
First—how great to see the two of you together again. A lot of us remember your rivalry on *Me Minus You*, so it's great to see you reunited. And yet, what a traumatizing experience for you both. Can you speak to us about all the emotions you must have felt as you were watching that cabin go up in flames?

ABBY:
It *was* traumatizing, Paula. I feel fortunate to have survived the

ordeal, and I'm so grateful to the brave crew and all the emergency workers who helped us survive it.

REBECCA:
Abby and I were ice-fishing when it happened. Not really close, actually.

ABBY:
But naturally, we rushed to help the moment we saw the smoke. Fortunately, everyone was out by the time we arrived on the scene. Then we did everything in our power to save the structure itself.

REBECCA:
But they wouldn't let us near the fire, because of liability issues.

PAULA:
Of course! Well, I'm certain you're both glad for a little break.

ABBY:
We are, and I personally am so grateful to C.I.P. for providing trauma counselors. The producers of the show have been wonderful, especially Renee Jablonsky, whom I like to call our fearless leader. She's absolutely amazing!

REBECCA:
Yes. And you wouldn't believe how luxurious it feels to have a hotel room to myself now.

PAULA:
(*laughs*) I'll bet! Your producers have told us, Rebecca, of the very moving story of your sick father, who is waiting for a kidney transplant. We want to play a little bit of the interview the two of you did for our audience.

EXCERPT OF INTERVIEW OF REBECCA HUDSON DE-
SCRIBING FINDING HER FATHER AGAIN.

We thought it would be nice to let you say hello to him, and all
the folks at the Strawberry Cake Shop, in Leesburg, Virginia.
Look at your monitor.

SCREEN SPLITS. BECCA LEANS FORWARD TO LOOK
AT PROVIDED MONITOR. ON OTHER SIDE, A BIG
CROWD AT THE BAKERY. AFTER A PAUSE, THE
CROWD WAVES AND WHOOPS.

REBECCA:

Oh my God!

WALTER JOHNSON, REBECCA'S FATHER:

Hi there! You doing okay?

REBECCA:

Of course. Is that Erin and Pam with you? And Olivia!

CAMERA PANS, STOPS ON SEVERAL FACES
SHOUTING HELLO TO HER.

REBECCA:

How's business?

WALTER:

We're doing good. Don't worry. Just worry about staying alive up
there, away from bears or what-have-you.

REBECCA:

I'm trying my best. You take care of yourself, too.

PAULA:

How fantastic that we could provide a little reunion here on the

show for you. And those cupcakes look delicious! We should
have booked you for a cooking segment.

REBECCA:

It so happens my schedule freed up this week. . . .

PAULA:

(*laughs*) Right now, we have to go to a commercial. When we
come back, easy holiday decoration ideas . . . made completely
from gourds! We'll talk to—

ABBY:

Paula?

PAULA:

Yes?

ABBY:

I'd be delighted to come back, too. Anytime.

PAULA:

Oh. (*Uncomfortable chuckle*) Of course. (*To camera*) I'll be back
with holiday gourds right after this message.

Becca sank against the backseat of the hired town car, relieved
to be heading back to the hotel. "Thank God that's over." She
hoped that their television appearance took care of any *Celebrities
in Peril!* obligations for the day.

Abby flicked her an annoyed glance. "I can't believe you. Did
you arrange in advance to hog that interview?"

Becca smiled at the memory. "You mean the thing with the
hookup to my shop? That was a total surprise." It had been such
a treat to see everyone. Although she wished Matthew had been
there. She hadn't spotted him in the crowd.

"Right." Abby's voice dripped with skepticism. "You had *no idea*."

"I didn't."

Abby crossed her arms. Becca could see where she was coming from. It was bad enough to have to awaken before the crack of dawn and get dressed and made up to do that stupid morning show, but then to be ignored probably rankled her.

"Where did this long-lost sick dad come from?" Abby asked.

She made it sound as if Becca had invented him as a publicity stunt. Which was something Becca could imagine Abby actually doing. "Renee must have told them about him. You know how she is. They taped me talking about Walt for my show intro."

Abby's eyes bulged. "So that's why you didn't want to form an alliance. You're already working the sick-dad sympathy angle." She slid down the seat in a pout. "There's no way I can win."

"Honestly, Abby, what does it matter? It's only a goofy reality show."

"You just don't get it, do you?"

Becca had no idea what *it* referred to. "I'm not sure."

"Of course you don't." Abby practically twitched in disdain. "It was always smooth sailing for you. Your very first show was a hit, and that was it. You never had to claw your way up doing cereal commercials and playing tiny parts or not getting called back after auditions. You had it easy, and then when the going got just a little tough, what did you do? You quit."

"I didn't quit right away. I wasn't getting any work, though. If it weren't for you, I probably wouldn't have scrounged up that one good guest spot on *Malibu High School*."

"If it weren't for me?" Abby snorted. "Hardly."

Becca drew back. "What do you mean?"

"I mean, that's *not* the way it happened. I had nothing to do with your getting that role. They just gave it to you because the director thought it would be like a rematch or something—only with you playing a bitch to my mean girl this time. It pissed me off that they even put you on the show."

"Pissed you off?"

"Well, yeah. The mean girl was what *I* did well. I at least had that going for me. I'd played second banana to your Little-Miss-Perfect Tina all those years, and now here you came to steal my thunder. That's why I begged them to have you and not Mallory die in the car wreck."

"*You* told them to write me out?"

Abby sniffed. "I told my agent working around you was causing me psychological stress. I was one of the original cast, and at that point I was just a junior on the show. I had a year to go on my contract."

Becca frowned. She'd known she and Abby hadn't been best friends anymore at that point, but she never would have guessed that Abby was actively working behind the scenes to have her fired.

"I can't believe you did that. I thought it was me. That I was no good."

Abby rolled her eyes. "You are so naïve. What does good or bad matter? It's persistence that counts, and strategizing. Just like now. To hold on, you have to think of some way to make the producers want to keep you." She tapped her fingers against the armrest. "I guess I should thank my lucky stars that we're going to be one cast member down thanks to smoke inhalation. That gives me another week, at least."

Becca could barely follow the woman's rambling monologue. *Abby got me fired.* All these years, she'd felt as if she'd failed, been rejected. Instead, she'd been sabotaged.

The car pulled up to the hotel entrance to drop them off. Abby reached for the door handle. "I'm warning you, Becca. If you're not going to work with me, the gloves are going to come off."

Looking into that heart-shaped face from her youth, Becca felt ice in her veins. She hoped her expression didn't give her own feelings away. Gloves off? Ha. Her own gloves were already off, and the brass knuckles were being slipped on. "I understand."

Abby opened her door, and frigid air blew in. Becca didn't move.

"Aren't you getting out?" Abby asked.

Becca shook her head. "Not just yet. I have a little errand to run." She leaned forward and asked the driver, "Is that okay?"

"Fine by me," he said. "Your producer hired me for the day."

Abby's eyes narrowed in suspicion. "Where are you going? It's not even eight in the morning yet."

"I know. If anyone asks for me, tell them I'll only be gone an hour, tops."

Abby was still frozen in mid-exit, her face contorted in mistrust.

Becca smiled. "Do you mind? You're letting in the cold."

Abby finally got out and closed the door. Becca asked the driver, "Could you take me to the nearest grocery store?"

If the way to survival was strategy, she was going to start plotting now. She had one simple goal: to outlast Abby.

Chapter 25

The new location the company had scouted was farther up the mountain, and though professional workmen had done most of the heavy preparation before "the talent" joined in with their hammers, screwdrivers, and laughable muscle power, by the time they had erected Prefab Rustic Shelter #2, they were all pooped. Also, for a few harrowing minutes it had looked as if they might lose a Walton to cardiac arrest.

To guard against high winds, this cabin was secured to the rocky earth beneath it using guy wires. All that was keeping them from being blown off the mountain were a few metal ropes that had been hammered into place by bedraggled former child stars. This wasn't a comforting thought.

Abby seemed to be having a hard time holding it together since they returned from Anchorage, Becca had noticed. One minute she'd been a gung-ho Bob the Builder, and then she'd stubbed her toe on a support beam and started to unravel. Now she was back to worrying about moose. "If the next challenge is a moose hunt, I'm going to lodge a protest with PETA." It was as if she expected the producers to insert a laugh track every time she said *moose*.

The strange thing was, Abby had snuck back exercise equipment—arm weights and a jump rope—from their Anchorage hiatus. When she wasn't whining about her sore toe, she was simulating Rocky's training montage. In thirty-second bursts, she would pump iron with the intensity of a person determined to bring a moose down with her bare hands.

No one joined in the moose speculation, so Abby retreated to the corner and frantically jumped rope for fifteen seconds. The rhythmic thwacking sound of the plastic rope was getting on everyone's nerves.

This, Becca decided, would be the perfect time to bring out her own secret weapon. "Anyone want to help me make a cake?" she asked.

Heads lifted in interest as Becca produced a contraband box of cake mix.

"We aren't supposed to bring food!" Abby shouted across the cabin. "You're cheating!"

Becca blinked. "Is it any worse than the energy bars you've smuggled in with you?"

Abby stared daggers at her. Becca felt a little bad for snitching on the energy bars. But she'd known Abby would want to grandstand against the cake experiment before the cameras. And, as Abby herself had said, the gloves were off.

"Preparing it in the Dutch oven over the fire will be a challenge, but by the time Renee views the tapes of what we're doing, we'll have already devoured it. I'll take all the blame."

Within seconds, a crowd gathered around Becca, while Abby executed another furious jump rope blast on the other side of the cabin.

While in Anchorage, Becca had studied YouTube videos about campfire cooking, but given her lack of hands-on experience, the primitive cast-iron tools she had to work with, and the open fire, Becca worried the strawberry cake gambit would be a disaster. To her surprise, within an hour and a half she'd managed to produce an almost-presentable cake. She saved the last of the frozen strawberries she'd hidden and mixed them into the frosting she'd sneaked in.

"This is the kind of cake my mom used to make on my birthday," she told the group as they beheld the finished product. "Just like it's always happy hour somewhere, it must be someone's birthday somewhere, right?"

They decided that instead of "Happy Birthday," they should sing everyone's theme songs. One by one, starting with the earliest, they belted out a song corresponding with everyone's signature show. Instrumentals were tricky, but attempts were made to harmonize.

Poor Abby, who had been doing her best to boycott the cake event, couldn't bring herself to sit out the songfest. It was too showbiz for her to resist. She even plastered on a big grin and put a stiff arm around Becca's shoulder when the group got around to "Me Minus You." For once, Becca smiled and sang the inane lyrics lustily and loud. She owed that show a debt, especially now. As she looked around at the goofy grins on everyone's faces, she felt almost guilty for the years she'd cringed at the tune, at the aggressive fans, at the weird nostalgia. The show had been her bread and butter, had allowed her to avoid the worst struggles many faced. Despite it all, it had given her a great life—something her mom could have told her all along.

"What was the theme song to *Malibu High School*, Abby?"

Abby, thrilled to be at the center of things at last, lit up as if surprised. "Oh, you remember it."

The cabin mates exchanged questioning glances. Nobody remembered.

Awkwardly, Abby ended up performing the instrumental theme song on her own, two choruses, with jazz-hand enthusiasm winding up to a manic finale. Everyone clapped when she was done, but only after a pause that Becca was willing to bet would feel like an eternity when it aired on television.

She smiled at Abby, whose razzle-dazzle quickly deflated. "Sure you won't have a piece of cake?" Becca asked her.

The supply plane flew in the latest news from home the next morning, but it was late, so there wasn't much time to open mail before the next cabin challenge was revealed. Becca got a letter from Matthew, and she rushed to her bunk to skim it. As much as she hated being away from Matthew, she loved getting letters. It seemed so much more intimate to read his cramped scrawl rather than the usual Times New Roman font in an e-mail.

Dear Becca,

I'm so glad I got to talk to you on the phone while you were in Anchorage. The imposed silence was killing me. As much as I enjoy the excuse to write you old-fashioned letters, I can't help imagining all sorts of nightmarish wilderness scenarios. I know you're worried about wolves, but I'm more concerned with avalanches and blizzards.

She was with him on the avalanches. Probably best if she didn't tell him about the guy wires bolting their cabin down to the mountain.

I spend a lot of my free time these days hanging out at the cake shop. Even though you're not there, the scents of butter and sugar always make me think of you. And Walt is there, usually camped at a table playing cards or chess with whoever will give him a game. (Don't worry—no stakes!) Olivia came by the other day. Guess what? Nicole wants to buy her a horse. But get this: she's waiting till you get back, so you can advise them. Olivia is so excited, and she's giving you all the credit for her good fortune.

Speaking of fortunes . . . Since your appearance on The Morning Show, *the Strawberry Cake Shop has been booming. Erin is holding down the fort like a champ. Walt mans the register when needed, and occasionally blows a tune now for the crowd. He's enjoying local celebrity status. Regulars say the cupcakes aren't as good as when you're here, though.*

The best news is that Walt might have found a donor. Don't get your hopes up too high just yet, but keep your fingers crossed.

There was more, but Becca got tugged away from her bunk by a crew member who'd been sent to fetch her. In front of the fireplace, everyone was gathered in a circle, and Renee revealed the next challenge to them: a scavenger hunt. This time, there would be no teams. Each contestant would be on his own.

On his own with a videographer.

To make the moment of hearing their next task more dramatic, Renee always ended her directions with the question, "Are you up to the challenge?"

Usually, Becca had difficulty working up the proper solemnity and camera-ready determination. But not this time. *Am I ready?* Olivia was getting a horse, the store was doing well, Matthew was waiting for her, and Walt might have a donor. The wind was at her back, and she was ready for anything.

"I am up to the challenge," she declared.

After everyone had made their vow of readiness, the game was on. Becca turned and found herself almost bumping into Abby. Abby had received a care package in the mail, and now she opened her jacket to reveal what it was—one of the TINA THINKS YOU SHOULD GET A LIFE T-shirts that Gecko Girl had been selling on Megan's Musings. Becca looked at herself in her awkward teen phase, making a sour face. Her gaze lifted to Abby, who was smirking at her. "Like it?" Abby vogued for the three nearest videographers.

Becca laughed, much to the other woman's consternation. Abby's triumphant smile melted.

"I love it!" Becca said. "Maybe I'll sell those in my shop when I get back."

She gave Abby a quick, dismissive pat on the shoulder and went to collect her snowshoes.

During other challenges, Becca hadn't particularly cared if she didn't pound the most nails in while erecting the shelter, or that she captured fewer fish than the other team, or whether or not her team won the sled relay. It had helped that there was usually someone else melting down during each event—a former child star falling off a rafter after od'ing on "vitamins," or throwing a hissy fit, or burning down Cabin #1.

But during those events, she had been in a group, or at least a pair. She hadn't felt pressure on herself, because others were proving themselves less competent and more ill-behaved than she was. And she also hadn't wanted to win so much.

During the scavenger hunt, however, it was just her tromping around on snowshoes with a retrieval list and a bored videographer. They had a GPS to keep them from getting hopelessly screwed up, direction-wise, but Becca still felt anxious. Abby's determination to best her preyed on her mind. Out in the white wilderness, buried beneath layers of gear and goggles so that her own heartbeat felt amplified in her hood, each sound registered as a threat. Every crunch was potentially Abby snowshoeing up behind her. The whistle of wind through evergreen was Abby's victory whoop. A raptor's screech was Abby saying, "I begged them to have you and not Mallory die in the car wreck."

I'm becoming as demented as she is.

Mindful of the camera tracking her, she tried to keep a lid on the crazy. To stay on task. She had to locate a lot of unsavory things—including a live bug, a bone, and a feather. The sub-zero temps didn't make scavenging easy. She tried to keep her cursing and groans of disgust to a minimum as she hunted, but it was difficult. For the bone, she was going to snap one off a little squirrel or chipmunk who had been mostly devoured. But her bulky, insulated gloves made her so clumsy, she finally ended up stuffing the entire grisly little carcass into a Ziploc baggie.

It was the last item. "Let's head back," she said.

The videographer nodded. He was probably regretting not going to law school.

It felt as if she had been stumbling around in the snow forever, so she was surprised to learn she was the first person to return. Maybe her Abby paranoia had helped. She got a high-five from the director and crew and retired to a fireside chair with some cocoa.

As the others straggled in, Becca watched for Abby. Daylight started to wane and there was still no sign of her. Finally, security formed a rescue party and set out with dogs, sleds, and high-powered searchlights. Several of the contestants made distressed noises about Abby's welfare, as well as a wisecrack or two about ravening moose herds. Then they all settled down to a game of Monopoly.

They were still playing when Abby was half-dragged through the door, weeping and shivering beneath her polar gear. The players reluctantly pushed their game table away from the fireplace to give Abby maximum warmth. As she pulled off her frosted glasses, she gawked at the table in outrage. "I was out there, maybe dying, maybe being devoured by who knows what, and you guys were playing a board game?"

"They wouldn't let us join the search party," Becca explained. "Something about insurance risk."

"Besides, there were only two sleds," someone else said.

Abby's jaw dropped. "If it had been one of you—Becca, for instance—*nothing* would have kept me from going out to look. Nothing."

The rest of the contestants exchanged glances. Some looked abashed, while others just seemed impatient to get back to the game. Meanwhile, Becca noticed that the director and his crew were reviewing footage in a monitor in anticipation of the night's big bonfire. Abby's videographer was gesticulating at the tiny screen, and looked pissed.

Abby glanced over, too, and her moral indignation morphed into growing hysteria. "I could have died out there! They sent me out without a GPS. It's a miracle I found my way back at all."

"You didn't," Becca pointed out. "They had to go find you."

"I was only a mile or so away."

A mile in this wilderness was like thirty miles of normal terrain. It was amazing that she hadn't suffered some kind of injury. Most of the cabin mates admitted that it would suck if Abby got kicked off the show because they forgot to put a GPS in her treasure hunt kit.

At the bonfire ceremony, the contestants all gathered around a fire blazing in a clearing to await Renee's dramatic arrival in her scarlet Inuit-style gear. They stood holding their torches, which stank of the lighter fluid the tips had been soaking in all day, to make them less likely to punk out on camera. Because of the smell, Becca always felt slightly woozy at the bonfires.

"You all have shown resourcefulness and resilience during this trying week," Renee intoned solemnly. "Every one of you is a winner. Has-beens? I'd call you better-than-evers!"

Then came the demerits. Becca got a slap on the wrist for the cake. Abby, who had been tearful since the ceremony started, smirked at her across the blaze.

"Abby, will you please step forward?"

A hush fell over them, broken only by the crackling flames and Abby's snuffling. Everybody knew this meant the end of her, and as she trembled forward, it was clear Abby knew, too.

"It's not fair," she mumbled, tearing up like a contestant from *America's Next Top Model*.

Becca had expected Renee to bring up Abby's sniping and unpleasant personality traits, and she did enumerate a few of those. But then she played video montage of Abby growing ever-more hysterical throughout the treasure hunt as she was unable to find anything. The footage culminated in a shot of Abby "dropping" her GPS device and kicking snow over it. Evidently getting lost and blaming not having a GPS had been her ruse to both camouflage her incompetence and put her at the center of attention.

While Abby broke down in sobs, Renee scolded her mercilessly for wasting resources on an unnecessary rescue. Then she stepped forward, gloved hands extended, and asked Abby to surrender her torch. Abby wept inconsolably, then tossed her torch into the snow. "I hate you!" she yelled at Renee. She turned to the others. "I hate you all!"

She fled inside.

Becca couldn't help a swell of admiration. Love her or hate her, Abby always made for lively television.

On the televised show, after the loser's torch was passed back, the camera would then cut to that person getting on a plane and being flown off the mountain. But the real reality was more awkward. Night flying was more dangerous, so the plane carrying the axed cast member would not leave until the following morning.

They all spent a last tense night with Abby, who did not recover from her loss with good grace. She hunched on her bunk, weeping noisily and honking into a tissue all through dinner, refusing to eat anything except her contraband energy bars, the wrappers of which she rustled extra-noisily.

Becca tried to ignore her as everyone else did. But everyone didn't have to sleep in the bunk directly underneath Abby. She told herself she should be happy—she'd achieved her goal of outlasting Abby on the show. The bad news, of course, was that her own win was a Pyrrhic victory, since she now had to spend at least another week in Alaska.

When she awoke the next morning, Becca shivered out of bed and got dressed as soon as possible. She always tried to be up before the others, before taping commenced and the stupid cabin tasks would begin. She shoved her feet into snow boots, layered on sweaters and coat, scarf and hat, and headed outside, tensing against the cold. As always, the air was so chilly it seemed to freeze her lungs at first. She went to the edge of the hill, taking in the spectacular view of the valley below. The whole world had been dusted by fresh snow, and in the perfect stillness of the morning light, the landscape was bathed in a burnished glow. Sometimes, early in the morning like this, she could catch sight of wildlife—glimpses of caribou, wolves, and foxes, and those hearty birds who stuck around for the winters.

This morning, unfortunately, the only other being out with her was Abby, who had followed her. When Becca identified her under her puffy white coat, she groaned. So much for tranquility.

Abby tromped right up to her. "I'm never going to forgive you for this," she declared.

"For what?"

"For undermining me. Don't deny it."

"You underestimate yourself," Becca said. "You're your own worst enemy, not me."

Abby planted gloved hands on her hips. "I could have won this if it hadn't been for you. Your antagonism wreaked havoc on my nerves."

Becca laughed. "You can stop now. The cameras aren't rolling."

"Good." Abby crunched closer. "Then they won't see this."

Becca caught sight of Abby's outstretched arm and stepped back in time to avoid the push. Unfortunately, the step back did just as much damage as a shove would have. She stumbled backward and then slid, wheeling her arms in a hopeless bid to restore her balance. The fall, when it came, registered at first as a brief shock of being airborne, her heart in her throat. Landing knocked the air out of her, and she couldn't say how long she lay there before the agony hit her. She opened her eyes to Abby directly above, peering down at her over the drop-off.

"Becca?" Abby asked, her voice quavering as if she hadn't quite thought through the consequences of shoving someone off a mountain.

Becca groaned. "Get help."

Abby nodded in panic. "Okay, but you realize I didn't touch you, right? I mean, I really didn't."

Becca tried to answer, but hissed in a breath instead. She did a quick check to see if all her parts were in working order. Everything moved, except her leg, which was twisted in a weird way and hurt too damn much to be paralyzed. "Just get help," she bit out. She was wolf bait out here.

"Because I should tell you right now, suing me would be really pointless," Abby shouted down at her. "I'm all tapped out. My condo's double-mortgaged."

"Go!"

Abby nodded, and in the next instant the hurried crunch of retreating footsteps reached Becca's ears. She closed her eyes again and heard Abby screaming. "Help! Becca fell off the mountain!"

Technically true—leaving out the detail that she'd fallen to avoid being pushed. However, falling off the mountain would be her ticket home, which would be nice. As long as she wasn't maimed for life. Her only regret was that she wouldn't be there to witness Abby's walk of shame to the airplane, and then see her flown out of her life forever. At least it would be caught on tape. For Becca, it would be must-see TV.

So many lawyers filled Becca's hospital room, it was difficult to breathe. Tort anxiety filled the air.

"We will pay you for the run of the show, although of course you won't get the winner's bonus," Renee explained to her. The producer was flanked by three—count 'em—three attorneys.

Being paid for shows she wasn't going to appear on was good. Especially since they were covering medical costs and a generous cash settlement. But she was curious. "What's the final challenge?"

"A cross-country sled dog race," Renee said.

Putting her former cabin mates behind a team of huskies seemed like a dicey proposition. Especially for the canines. "I hope those dogs know what they're doing."

"Our technical advisors tell us it's foolproof," Renee said.

Of course. What could go wrong?

Becca thought about her situation a little more. "Won't my departure cause a problem? You'll be one week short, material-wise."

"Oh no. Your fall is enough for almost an entire episode. We got some very dramatic footage of the rescue helicopter. And of course, Abby cried a lot, which is good." She frowned. "It means we'll have to delay showing her being flown out, but your fall will make a great cliff-hanger. We kept Abby on an extra day to stage a reenactment. With editing, it shouldn't look too cheesy."

Becca wouldn't have thought cheesiness would be an obstacle.

She spent an hour signing releases, nondisclosure agreements, and forms outlining the show's promise to cover hospital and other medical bills incurred from her accident. She hoped she wouldn't have to draw too much on the latter. The doctors she'd spoken to so far had said her fractured leg would mend as good as new.

Finally, everyone cleared out, and she sank back against her pillows. She was slightly annoyed to see one last person left standing at the door. Then she recognized him. "Matthew!" As fast as she could, she hit the button to raise the back of her bed.

She held out her arms, but he didn't need much coaxing. They kissed, and she had to resist the urge to yank him down on the bed with her. The spirit was willing, but her leg might not appreciate it.

"I brought you some things." He produced a Strawberry Cake Shop box. Becca groaned in happiness to see it. Suddenly, the prospect of going home and living her life again felt real. "Erin's been experimenting with caramel-sea salt frosting," he said. "She wants to know what you think."

Her immediate thought was that it looked delish.

"And Walt downloaded some music onto your iPod. He wanted me to bring it to you."

"How is he?"

Matthew's brow scrunched. "He didn't feel up to the trip. That's why you have me instead."

"You'll do," she said. "In your letter you said they'd found a donor for Walt. What's going on with that?"

"That's what I wanted to talk to you about." Matthew pulled his chair closer to the bed. "I'm the donor."

The blood drained out of Becca's face, leaving her light-headed. She sank back again. "I don't like this."

"Why?" he asked. "We've been doing all sorts of antigen and antibody tests. I'm a perfect match."

"It doesn't matter," she insisted. "This is wrong."

"It's no more wrong than you donating, or some other close friend or relative."

"But you're not close. You only know him because of me."

"And doesn't that mean something? The father of the woman I love?"

That word, *love*, would have made her melt . . . had this been any other moment. They had been together for months, although the crazy show had put an unwelcome hold on their budding relationship. It was too soon to talk about everlasting devotion and giving up kidneys for each other's relatives, wasn't it? "Relationships can fall apart. Even love can fall apart," she said. "Look at you and Nicole."

He shook his head emphatically. "Not the same. Nicole and I weren't right for each other."

"But you thought you were."

"I was wrong, and I should have known it from the beginning. Or at least from the moment she said she didn't want to marry me."

"What if we never get married?" she countered.

"Do you want to?"

"Well, yeah, but—" She broke off, stunned at what she was saying. A mad smile tugged at her lips. She hadn't hesitated at all. And now that the words were out there, she didn't want to retract them. "Yeah."

He grinned back at her. "If I'd known you'd be so easy, I would have come armed with a diamond ring, not just cupcakes and your own iPod."

She laughed. "Not so sure about that—I *really like* cupcakes." She tried to be serious again. "This is all going way too fast. And you don't have to give my father a kidney for me to say yes. The timing feels wrong to me."

"I know. Believe me, I've seen a whole battery of counselors at the transplant center. I'm not attaching any strings to the donation. What I'm doing, I'm doing for Walt. He's become my friend." He shook his head. "I know more about jazz, poker, and incarceration now than I ever could have imagined."

He was half-joking, but she nodded in understanding. Walt had taught her a few things, too. The past months had taken both her and Matthew in directions they could never have expected. The most amazing thing was that their separate paths had crossed and re-crossed, and now their futures were bound up together.

"The important thing right now is to get you home," Matthew said.

"You don't know how good that sounds. Or how far away home has seemed for all these weeks." But when she bit into Erin's cupcake, and looked into Matthew's eyes, home was suddenly right there with her.

Epilogue

March

"The doctor says I might be able to go home in another week," Walt said. "Can you believe it?"

Matthew gave him a high-five. "I'm being sprung tomorrow."

It was almost over. At least for Matthew. Though his spare kidney was already hard at work inside Walt, apparently the transplant recipient had a lot more danger signs to watch for than the donor, because of possible infections or organ rejection.

Matthew turned to Becca, whose hand he was holding. She'd been accompanying him on his walks around the hospital since the first day after surgery, when he'd been surprised to be rousted out of bed by the nurses.

"What do you think?" he asked her. "Would now be too early to set a date?"

They had avoided talking about getting married until the ordeal was over. He hadn't wanted there to be any misplaced feeling of obligation on her part. But now he was impatient for the rest of their lives to get started.

She smiled at him. "What is it about hospitals that makes you so matrimonially minded?"

He pressed his lips to her temple. "The sweet scent of rubbing alcohol. It does something to me."

Walt smiled at them. "You two are finally getting married?"

"Didn't you know?" Becca asked. "Matthew's reason for giving you a kidney was to keep you alive so you could walk me down the aisle."

Walt beamed. "I'd be delighted."

A duo of nurses came in and clustered around Walt. "We need to take your vitals and change your IV, Mr. Johnson."

"Okay," he said amiably.

"I'll be back this evening," Becca promised him.

Walt flicked an anxious glance at Matthew. "Walt and I are watching TV tonight," Matthew informed her.

One of the nurses laughed. "Thursday night—we can't miss *Celebrities in Peril!*." She winked at Becca. "That Abby! She's such a witch. I can't wait till someone sticks her on a plane and flies her off."

Becca laughed. "Okay. I'll come by and we can all watch together. Is that okay?"

Walt nodded. "Sure, but no spoilers."

"Don't worry—I'm legally forbidden from blabbing," she told him. "Call me at the shop if you need anything. I'm going to be there this afternoon."

"Don't worry about me. I'm getting four-star service."

Out in the hallway, Matthew said, "Your dad is the ideal patient."

"Right. Because he doesn't want to be any trouble."

They strolled the unit until they came to an atrium at the end of the hallway. Sunlight beamed through high windows. "I was thinking," Matthew said, "that maybe Walt can stay on at your place, and we can find a house in Leesburg, closer to your shop." Since coming back from Alaska, Becca had been living at the town house. Her healing leg made her apartment stairs difficult to maneuver. She'd been off the crutches for months now, but the truth was, they liked living together. Besides, Walt was enjoying the apartment above the shop. If she moved back into it, they would have to figure out where to put him.

"A house," she repeated.

"Hopefully with a little more charm than the town house."

"Pam will be so excited," Becca said. "She loves helping people house-hunt. And Erin could help me fix up a new place."

"There," Matthew said. "If it would make Pam and Erin happy, we should definitely start looking right away." He was only half-joking, actually. He liked Erin and Pam—and since Cal was so nice, not to mention laid-back, Matthew was even getting used to the idea of hanging out with his future wife's ex-husband.

"Is this really going to work out?" Becca shook her head in wonder. "It all felt so insurmountable when we started. There was Alaska and two operations to get through. And before that, you were still with Nicole. I can't believe no one's going to come pull the plug on all our happiness."

"It's not television. You don't have to face cancellation."

She laughed. "Or turn in my torch?"

He squeezed her hand. He didn't care if they were in a hospital. When he was with her, there was nowhere else he'd rather be. "As far as I'm concerned, you can consider it an eternal flame."

"Becca!"

As she was getting out of her car in front of the Strawberry Cake Shop, Becca saw Olivia running toward her. She skidded to a stop inches from Becca.

"I thought I'd missed you," she said, panting. "I wanted to give you this." She held out a framed eight-by-ten picture of herself sitting atop Ripples, the sweet pinto gelding they'd found at a Maryland farm in February. Ripples now lived at Butternut Knoll, where Olivia was a regular.

"Great picture," Becca said. "I'll put it in a place of honor on the cake shop wall."

Olivia seemed pleased, but then her expression sobered. "Is Walt okay? And Matthew?"

Becca squeezed her shoulder. "They're both doing good. Matthew's going to be out tomorrow. Maybe when he gets a little better, we can get started on our secret project."

Their secret project was to turn Matthew into a horseman. So far he had resisted the equine dark side, but they had high hopes for the summer.

Olivia cut a glance down the street, to an idling SUV. "Mom's waiting for me," she said. "I've got to go. I'll see you at Butternut Knoll!"

Becca waved her off and went inside. The cake shop was crowded. Customers new and old had flocked to the store since the show started airing. On the way to the register, Becca signed two Strawberry Cake Shop bags, and one TINA THINKS YOU SHOULD GET A LIFE tee. People loved the shirts, and seemed to consider them a hilarious homage to her television career. Apparently there really was no bad publicity.

Even Gecko Girl had reached out to her since *Celebrities in Peril!* had begun, and told her that she was rooting for her. Time and T-shirt sales had softened her feelings toward Becca's earlier snub.

A publisher had approached Becca about writing a book about her experiences, especially having Walt find her. Eight months ago, the idea of penning a celeb autobiography would have made her howl with laughter, but writing about Walt and the transplant experience actually appealed to her, so she was mulling over the offer. It helped that Erin had become such a great assistant at the shop. If business stayed robust after the madness of the *Celebrities in Peril!* broadcast was over, they might even be able to open a second shop in another town.

But that was jumping ahead. Right now she was just happy to have lots of customers, and to see Pam and Erin both there. Becca hurried over to take Pam's place. "Thank you so much for helping. You don't have to, you know."

"I was just in the neighborhood. I've already done the kid pickup."

Pam was in charge of Butternut Knoll's afterschool shuttle. Becca suspected Pam was actually in charge of everything, but Cal hadn't realized it yet.

"How are the sickos?" Pam asked.

"Better every day. The doctors say—" Becca did a double-take, noting the way Pam was jutting out her left arm, the hand poised artfully. A diamond winked from the third finger. Becca yelped in surprise, then hurried closer to inspect the ring. "Congratulations! When did all this happen?"

Pam posed the hand like a professional model, milking the moment. "Cal gave it to me this morning. There was a ring box next to the toaster."

Becca clucked. "That sounds like something he'd do."

"Right," Pam said. "And I was ready to stomp out because he woke me up to tell me he was hungry and would I make him some breakfast."

"The engagement was nearly toast," Erin said. Everyone in hearing distance, even customers, groaned.

Becca admired Pam's ring some more. "It's gorgeous."

"They're thinking of a July fourth weekend wedding," Erin said.

Pam nodded. "Cal wants a wedding at Butternut Knoll, with fireworks." Her brow wrinkled. "In fact, I think the fireworks might be the biggest attraction for him."

Becca laughed. "I doubt that."

Pam looked from Becca and Erin and back again. "There's going to have to be another quirk, besides the fireworks. Two maids of honor."

Becca and Erin grinned. "And your maids of honor will also be doing the cake," Becca told her.

"I was counting on it," Pam said.

Becca had to help Erin tend to customers, but she asked Pam to come back later so the three of them could toast the engagement. This called for an extra-special Not-Book-Club. They agreed to meet up at Becca's after Becca got back from visiting Walt and Matthew in the hospital.

Erin nodded to the photo of Olivia and Ripples. "Cute! New picture for the wall?"

"I need to find a good spot for it," Becca said.

Becca looked at the picture again, and felt as if Olivia's huge smile had taken up residence in her heart. She hadn't wanted to steal Pam's thunder by telling everyone that she and Matthew were going to be tying the knot themselves soon, and that her father would be giving her away. One engagement at a time was plenty. Besides, there was something delicious about holding in all this happiness, all this hope.

The moment reminded her of standing over one of those strawberry cakes her mother used to make for her birthday. Hovering over those blazing candles each year, breath held, head full of wishes, all things had seemed possible. And even if every wish didn't come true, there was always the cake itself. As long as there was cake, life was good.

Acknowledgments

While I was writing this book, my sister Suzanne Bass was invaluable to me. Not only did she answer my horse questions, she was also the one who introduced me to Leesburg, Virginia. Though I hope I captured a little of the town's charm, most of the specific places mentioned in the story are made up and any mistakes that might have slipped in concerning the area are entirely my own.

As usual, I owe a heap of gratitude to Annelise Robey and the rest of the crew at the Jane Rotrosen Agency, and also to my editor, John Scognamiglio, and all the great people at Kensington Publishing. Working with wonderful people is one of life's joys.

Thanks to Joe, for his patience, proofreading, and incredible cooking.

Finally, a special shout-out to my mom, Patsy Bass, for all the birthday cakes. I haven't tasted the strawberry cake mentioned in the book for over thirty years, but I still dream about it.

LIFE IS SWEET

Elizabeth Bass

About This Guide

The suggested questions are included
to enhance your group's reading of
Elizabeth Bass's *Life Is Sweet*.

Discussion Questions

1. Becca is a former television child star and she carries a lot of emotional baggage from her experience in Hollywood. Do you think she is overly sensitive when it comes to fans and nostalgia? Is she right to be wary of the public?

2. Were there any child actors you particularly liked? Do you enjoy "Whatever Happened To?" stories?

3. Before the book begins, Becca has tossed a dart at a map, moved across the country, and started a bakery. Have you ever dreamed of uprooting your life and opening your own business? If so, where would you go, and what kind of business do you dream of starting?

4. Becca impetuously helps a stranger by offering him a job. Do you think she was right to do this?

5. Did you have an inkling of Walt's true identity? What would you do if a long-lost relative arrived on your doorstep?

6. Did you sympathize with Walt's motive to find his daughter? Since he had been absent from his daughter's life, do you think he should have left her alone, or do you believe he has a chance to redeem himself as a father even at this late date?

7. Becca feels friction with her friends at various points during the book. Do you feel that they behave fairly with each other? Should Becca and Pam have mentioned Nicole to Erin?

8. Thoughts of her old frenemy Abby Wooten haunt Becca. Do you think this affects how she interacts with her current friends? Do you think Becca behaves badly when she meets Abby again?

9. Organ donation is an issue in the book. Have you ever considered becoming an organ donor? Do you think Matthew does the right thing in the story?

10. The disintegration of Nicole and Matthew's relationship is central to the story, and it's complicated by the fact Olivia likes Matthew so much. What did you think of Matthew and Olivia's friendship? Did Nicole make a mistake in allowing her daughter to develop a bond with her boyfriend when she knew that she didn't want to marry Matthew?

11. Do you watch reality shows? Which are your favorites? Would you ever want to be a contestant on one?

12. Becca discusses her love of her mother's strawberry cake, and the powerful sense-memory it evokes in her. Is there any comfort food that can bring back a specific person or time in your life?

GREAT BOOKS,
GREAT SAVINGS!

When You Visit Our Website:
www.kensingtonbooks.com
You Can Save Money Off The Retail Price
Of Any Book You Purchase!

- **All Your Favorite Kensington Authors**
- **New Releases & Timeless Classics**
- **Overnight Shipping Available**
- **eBooks Available For Many Titles**
- **All Major Credit Cards Accepted**

Visit Us Today To Start Saving!
www.kensingtonbooks.com

All Orders Are Subject To Availability.
Shipping and Handling Charges Apply.
Offers and Prices Subject To Change Without Notice.